Touch Me

Touch Me

SUSAN LYONS

APHRODISIA

KENSINGTON BOOKS

http://www.kensingtonbooks.com

APHRODISIA BOOKS are published by

Kensington Publishing Corp.
850 Third Avenue
New York, NY 10022

ISBN-13: 978-0-7582-1702-8
ISBN-10: 0-7582-1702-1

First Kensington Trade Paperback Printing: September 2007

10 9 8 7 6 5 4 3 2 1

Printed in the United States of America

1

Ann Montgomery struggled to extricate herself from the driver's seat of her Miata. The cute convertible was built for jeans and sandals, not a business skirt, panty hose, and pumps. For a woman who'd speed down twisty country roads, and have hot, body-contorting sex in the passenger seat, not drive the same two miles back and forth to the office seven days a week.

She patted the shiny red paint and whispered, "Poor baby, you deserve a more fun owner than me." Pain stabbed through her jaw. *Aagh. How can I chat with my friends, not to mention eat dinner, when I can barely open my freaking mouth?* She ground her teeth.

"Ouch! Damn!" Oh yeah, right. Tooth-grinding was part of the reason her jaw hurt so much. At the age of twenty-eight, she truly was a physical mess.

For some reason, admitting it actually lifted her spirits.

"You all right, miss? Want valet service?" A cute young guy, couldn't be more than twenty, rushed up, reaching for her keys.

"I'm fine, and yes, please." She allowed herself the pleasure of watching him slide his long legs into the driver's seat. He intercepted her gaze and sent her a wink and a flashing grin.

No doubt he flirted with every sex-starved older woman whose car he parked, yet she couldn't help smiling. *Oh, yeah, hottie, you could give me a little special service!*

If she even remembered how to have sex. It had been so long since she'd played with anything phallic that wasn't battery operated.

Shaking her head, she walked toward Il Giardino, this week's Awesome Foursome dinner spot. Their evenings of outdoor dining were coming to an end now that it was September. Tonight, though, the weather was perfect for the wonderful enclosed patio that made you feel like you were in Italy.

Not that Ann had ever been to Italy, much less even taken a week off in the four years since she'd joined Smythe Levinson LLP, one of the biggest law firms in Vancouver. Places like Il Giardino were as close as she'd ever get to a holiday if she kept working the way she had been. Which she had to, to continue building the career she'd always wanted.

Set a measurable goal; determine the steps required to reach it; and invest all your energy in achieving that goal.

Yes, Mother, you've been telling me that since—oh, probably since I was a fetus.

Did everyone else's mother pop into their brain periodically, like hers did? Meredith Montgomery was always dressed in a navy pin-striped suit and ivory silk shirt. Always sitting erect, legs crossed. Always criticizing or giving direction. Usually both.

How does this dinner fit your career plan? You're sidetracking, wasting energy.

I'm not, Mother. My friends give me perspective, keep me in touch with the real world. Those things are important. She was perfectly aware she was arguing a case. And, because she knew it wouldn't impress the mother-judge, she left out one of the most important factors. Being with her friends was fun.

And sometimes, girls just wanna have fun! She was entitled to one evening of fun a week.

To hell with her aches and pains, and the mother-voice; she was set to enjoy every moment of this lovely September evening with her three best—make that "only"—friends.

"I'm meeting friends," she told the hostess, then made her way through the dim restaurant. The door to the sunlit patio beckoned. She paused before stepping through.

The overblown flowers of late summer cascaded from hanging baskets and planters, the light of a setting sun sparkled off wineglasses, the air was full of the chattery hum of animated conversation and the mingled scents of flowers and garlic. Best of all, she saw Suzanne, Jenny, and Rina at a table in the corner. They hadn't noticed her yet, which was a good thing, because a sudden rush of moisture flooded her eyes. She was so lucky to have these women in her life.

Ann blinked away the tears and hurried over to them, smiling as they looked up.

Suzanne Brennan lifted a wine bottle from a cooler and poured a glass. Her red-gold hair cascaded in waves over a turquoise blouse, catching fire in this light.

Ann hung her suit jacket on the back of her chair and sat down, and Suze handed her the glass. "Bet you could use this. You're running late."

Ann took it gratefully and sipped, wishing she could open her mouth wider for a long, cool swallow. The wine was fresh and tingly. "Pinot Grigio? Oh, that's good. Sorry I'm late. Had to go to the dentist."

"Look Ma, no cavities?" Jenny Yuen teased, flipping raven wings of hair back to reveal pink flamingo earrings that matched her short-sleeved top.

"No cavities. But I wish there had been."

"What?" Rina Goldberg's brow wrinkled. Summer had darkened her olive skin and tonight she looked like a gypsy with her wild dark curls, chocolate eyes, crystal-and-bead ear-rings, and filmy white blouse.

God, I'm so drab compared to these women. What on earth do they see in me? "My jaws have been aching," she told them. *Not only drab, but dull.* The other three had exciting things—like men—going on in their lives. Still, she needed the sympa-thy she knew they'd give.

"You mentioned that last week," Suzanne said, looking con-cerned. "It didn't get better?"

"Worse." Ann reached into her navy leather purse and pulled out the familiar bottle of over-the-counter Tylenol with codeine. Then, encountering a crackly drugstore bag, she brought it out, ripped it open, and took out the bottle of muscle relaxants. "It's lucky we're eating Italian tonight because risotto's all I'm up to chewing."

"What did your dentist say?" Rina asked.

"There's nothing wrong with my teeth. It's stress."

"Stress?" Suzanne raised her eyebrows.

"Well, if anyone's stressed, it's you, Annie," Jenny said.

Annie. No one else in the world had ever called her Annie. But that was Jen for you, and it made Ann feel like one of the girls.

"That groove in your forehead's becoming permanent," Jen went on.

Now I need freaking Botox, on top of muscle relaxants and painkillers. "It's not just me," Ann said defensively. "My den-tist says it happens to lots of women in their twenties with busy careers. We're not dealing very well with stress."

"Sex," Jenny said promptly.

Ann sent her a mock scowl. "Easy for you to say, now that you're hooked up with your Mr. February firefighter."

"Vibrators still work," Rina said.

"You and Al *still* aren't having sex?" Jenny asked Rina. Then she waved a hand, "No, wait, it's still Ann's turn." She rested her elbows on the table and leaned toward Ann. "So you're saying nothing more's happened with that lawyer from Toronto who turned out to be married?"

"Of course it hasn't," Suzanne said.

Easy for you to say! Ann wanted to roll her eyes. Suzanne had such a black-and-white view of life: the guy's married, so don't fall for him. Yeah, right. Maybe if he'd said he was married when they first met . . .

Still, she did have values. "No, nothing's happened, and it won't. He's still at my office, we're still working together and we've agreed that's all it can ever be." Despite the fact that one little glance from David across the mahogany table in the firm's library got her so hot and bothered she wanted to fling herself across the damned table and scream, "To hell with values!"

She moaned with pain. Damn, she'd been grinding her teeth again.

"Go on about the dentist," Rina said. "What are you supposed to do?"

"Eat soft food. Don't open my mouth too wide, and—"

Jenny's hoot of laughter interrupted her. "Just as well you *don't* have a guy in your life."

"What? Oh." Ann had been celibate so long it took her a moment to figure out what Jenny meant, and then she couldn't help but laugh even though that hurt, too. "It gets better," she said slyly. "If I want to eat something *big*, I have to cut it up into small bites."

"So, if you do find a man, he has to have a tiny dick," Jenny said. "Or else . . ." She held up her knife and fork and made cutting motions, and Rina said, "Which is exactly what David deserves, for not telling you up front he was married."

"I told you, he was trying to focus on work, not the problems with his marriage. When the firm asked him to help with the Charter of Rights case here, he saw it as an opportunity to, you know, leave his personal issues behind. Then he met me, we worked well together, got along. He wanted to believe it was harmless."

"If it was, he'd have had no reason to hide the fact he was married," Suzanne said.

"I suppose," Ann said. "But haven't you heard of willful blindness? I'm sure we've all been guilty of it a time or two." She sighed. "I'll get over him, but it's hard to do when we're still working together. And I really don't need yet another stress."

"Not with your poor jaw," Rina said. She glanced up as a striking dark-haired waitress topped off their wine, murmured, "Thanks," then turned back to Ann. "So, as long as David's here, you'll still have that stress. D'you really think watching how you eat will fix your jaw?"

"Oh, there's more. Heat, don't yawn too widely. Massage inside and outside. Wear a mouth guard at night." Ann gave a wry chuckle. "Yeah, not a problem. I don't think my vibrator's going to protest too much." She paused. "Note to self: Buy batteries. And I—"

The other three were staring at her. "Damn. Did I say that out loud?"

They all nodded. "That's the second time," Suzanne said. "You did it a few weeks ago."

Rina frowned at Suzanne, then turned to Ann. "What else were you going to say?"

Humor the crazy lady? Ann decided to let it go. "My dentist prescribed muscle relaxants." She picked up the bottle. "In fact, I think I'll take one now. Along with a couple of my old faithfuls."

"Wait a minute." Rina put a hand on hers. "Pills and alcohol? And you're driving?"

"I always take the codeine pills. They don't make me sleepy, just help my headaches."

Jenny raised an eyebrow. "They don't make you sleepy because you belt back enough caffeine to wake a corpse."

"And you've developed a tolerance to the painkillers," Suzanne said. "The muscle relaxants are new. And they're prescription, so they're strong."

Don't gang up on me! Can't you see, I just want the freaking pain to go away? Still, she could see the sense in what her friends were saying. Besides, they were making her sound like a drug addict. She wasn't; she just had a more demanding life and sometimes her body needed a little help to make it through the long, challenging days. She washed a couple of her regular pills down with wine then put the new bottle back in her purse. "Okay, I'll take these at bedtime."

"Sounds good," Rina said. "But all the same, the pills treat symptoms. If the cause of the problem is stress, and the stress isn't going away . . ."

"Yeah," Ann said gloomily. "I'm supposed to do relaxation stuff, learn how to deal better with stress." She picked up her wineglass and scowled at it. "But I don't have time."

A laugh spluttered out of Suzanne, then she cut it off. "Sorry."

Ann grinned reluctantly. "I know. You're right. I thought I had my life under control, but my jaw's telling me I'm a screwup."

"Those killer headaches have been trying to tell you for a while," Jenny said.

Rina nodded. "How many painkillers have you taken today?"

I'm supposed to keep count?

When she didn't answer, Suzanne asked, "Did the dentist suggest anything for relaxation?"

Ann snorted. "Spend less time working."

The other three exchanged glances but didn't say a word.

How many times had the Foursome had this conversation, with Ann's friends telling her she worked too hard?

"But," Ann said, "you know my career plan calls for work, work, and more work."

She was getting three sets of "you're crazy" vibes coming her way.

They're not ambitious. They're content to settle. Her mother's tone was scornful.

Yeah, but I love them just the same. There's room in the world for nonachievers too.

Her mother shook her head briskly. *I have no patience for people like that.*

We've been here before, Mother, and we disagree. They're important to me.

"Ann?" Suzanne said.

"Sorry. So, the second suggestion was yoga." She gave an exaggerated eye-roll to lighten the atmosphere. "Been there, done that, it didn't work. As you well know."

Grins, all around the table. That was how they'd met. Signed up for a yoga class, suffered their way through it, bitched together in the changing room afterward, then went out for coffee and bonded. Ditched yoga in favor of food and chat.

"You could try again," Rina said. "I've been thinking about it."

Ann stared at her. Rina was a devout nonexerciser. She was pretty much a noneater too—on a perennial diet, disparaging her voluptuous curves as fat. Things must be getting serious with Al, if Rina was thinking about exercise.

"Or come pole dancing with Suze and me," Jen said, pulling on a rose-colored cardigan. "It definitely de-stresses you."

Ann shook her head. Despite her friends' spirited defense of pole dancing, it still sounded demeaning to women. Like playing stripper. Besides, she was so uncoordinated, she'd embarrass the hell out of herself, trying to strut and twirl, to act sexy and seductive.

"The next suggestion was meditation," Ann said drily. "Can't you just see me sitting for half an hour a day going 'om'?"

Three heads shook vigorously. "You are *so* not the New Age type," Jenny commented.

The sun was almost gone, the air cooling despite the patio heaters. Ann draped her jacket over her shoulders. "Then there's physiotherapy or massage."

Jenny snapped her fingers. "Yes, massage! And spa stuff like seaweed wraps and facials."

"Hmm." Ann's first reaction was to say she didn't have time, but obviously she was going to have to *make* time, with her body falling apart like this. Not a good state of affairs for an associate who hoped to make partner sooner rather than later.

Crap, she hoped her mother didn't find out what a mess she was. Meredith was a feminist through and through. She believed women were strong and could—and should—be superachievers. Weakness wasn't tolerated. *Thank God that voice in my head doesn't report back to the real woman in Toronto.*

"There's this awesome place I heard about," Jenny went on, brown eyes sparkling. "Pure Indulgence. I want to research it for a story." A freelance journalist, Jenny wrote articles on human-interest topics. That's how she'd met Scott, her hot new boyfriend: doing a story on a firefighter calendar competition, which he'd won, hands down. And shirt off.

"Tell me more," Ann said, tempted and trying to ignore the mother-voice that said, *A complete waste of time and money.*

"It costs a lot," Jenny warned. "But everyone says it's worth every penny."

Ann had to grin at how neatly Jen had answered the criticism Ann hadn't even spoken.

"They have all kinds of massage," Jenny went on, "as well as all the other spa-type stuff. And the best thing is, the masseurs are all eye candy. Imagine getting a sensuous massage from a Greek god."

Pure Indulgence definitely sounded appealing.

"Might take your mind off David," Rina said.

That would be an excellent thing. Her painkiller intake had upped since she'd learned her attractive colleague was married.

"You spend so much time at your desk," Suzanne said. "It's really hard on your body. I'm sure massage would help."

Okay, her friends made some excellent points. *Note to self: Check website for Pure Indulgence.*

Quickly she glanced around. No one was staring. Good, she'd kept that one to herself.

The dark-haired waitress paused beside their table. "Ladies, I didn't want to interrupt your conversation. Any questions about the menu? Are you ready to order?"

"I am," Ann said. "I'm starving." When had she last eaten, anyhow? "Risotto, please."

"Tonight we're offering wild mushroom, asparagus, or seafood risotto."

"Seafood."

Rina, the dieter, ordered a salmon carpaccio appetizer as her whole dinner, and Suzanne went for sea bass with rice and sea asparagus. Jenny—who at one hundred pounds could outeat all of them and not gain an ounce—chose grilled New York steak with roasted potatoes.

They ordered another bottle of Pinot Grigio, then Ann said, "Enough about my pathetic life. Rina, how's it going with Al?" Rina, a musician who played the clarinet in an orchestra and taught both clarinet and piano, had recently started dating the uncle of one of her students.

Her friend gave a gentle smile. "It's progressing. But slowly." Rina shot a glance at Jenny. "Before you ask again, no, no sex yet. But I'm sure *you* have something to contribute on the topic of sex."

Jenny grinned smugly. "Catwalk fantasy."

Jenny's and Scott's sex life was governed by the Fantasy Rules, which allowed them to act out each other's sexual fantasies.

"Catwalk?" Suzanne asked. "Like, in modeling?"

Jenny nodded vigorously, black hair rippling like that of an actress in a shampoo commercial. "I'm this haughty fashion model, up on the catwalk. Scott's a guy in the audience. Our eyes meet, there's an immediate connection. I strut my stuff, pretend to ignore him, but he's watching me with this hungry look, and it's making me hot."

Ann tried to imagine being so confident of her own attractiveness that she'd pretend to strut along a catwalk. But then, confidence wasn't Jenny's problem. Her issues had to do with the conflict between her traditional Chinese family's wishes and her own modern Western ones.

In the beginning, Ann had figured the fantasies were a way of keeping Scott from getting too close, from knowing the true Jenny. Jen had also insisted their relationship remain a secret. But recently she'd begun opening herself to Scott. She'd even told her folks she was dating a white man, knowing full well how much they'd disapprove. Scott's German family wasn't any more thrilled about him dating an Asian woman.

Ann was about to ask how things were going with the families, but the meals arrived and then Rina turned the subject to Suzanne. "How are you and Jaxon doing, now that you're back at university and don't have so much time to get together?" Suze was at UBC studying to be a vet, and her African American boyfriend practiced law in San Francisco.

Suzanne sighed. "I miss him like crazy. I haven't seen him in two weeks."

"Two whole weeks," Ann teased gently.

"You're still doing phone sex and e-mail sex, right?" Jenny asked, making significant inroads on the steak while Ann nibbled the delicious risotto.

"And we're *talking*, too," Suzanne said drily. "But the more we talk, the more I want to be with him."

Jenny was nodding, which made Ann smile. Jen had been such a commitment-phobe until the sexy firefighter wormed his way into her heart.

Ann leaned back in her chair. The painkillers had taken care of her headache, but her shoulders and jaw still hurt, and the cooling air didn't help. She slipped her arms into the sleeves of her jacket and raised the collar. Summer really was over. But what a summer it had been. Suze and Jen had quite possibly found the loves of their lives. Even Rina was dating seriously.

And as for me? Nutbar had to go and fall for a married man.

Melancholy threatened to descend on her tired shoulders, but she shrugged it off. A new season was starting, and what better time than autumn to burn the old leaves and turn over a new one? She'd get over that stupid infatuation, deal with her stress issues and—anything was possible—maybe find a real guy to replace her battery-operated boyfriend.

Pure Indulgence lived up to its name. Ann felt out of place in her business clothes as she walked into the plush spa Thursday afternoon. Yes, the suit was a Jacqueline Conoir, but it was black and had tailored lines, whereas everything in here was delicate and feminine. Furniture in rattan and wicker with upholstery in shades of peach and mauve. Glass-topped tables displaying exquisite orchids. Huge watercolors of flowers, done in a lush, sensual style.

No music, but instead birdsong. It sounded like a summer morning in the country. At least she guessed that was what it sounded like. Being a city girl, she didn't have much—make that any—experience with country mornings. No doubt it was supposed to be relaxing, but it was too twittery for her nerves.

She stepped up to the reception desk, where a blonde with a peaches-and-cream complexion—no doubt she'd been hired to match the decor—smiled at her.

Wait a minute, where was the male eye candy Jenny had promised? Oh well, Ann was here for her health, not her libido.

"Ann Montgomery," she said. "I have an appointment."

"Ann, hello," the blonde said warmly. "I'm Kristi. Welcome to Pure Indulgence." She handed over a clipboard. "Would you mind filling out this form? And can I get you something to drink? Maybe a sparkling mineral water?"

Gag. Will she kick me out if I ask for pure caffeine? "Do you have coffee?"

Another bright smile. "Of course. Chocolate almond, vanilla hazelnut, Costa Rican, or Kona? Or espresso, cappuccino, or a latte?"

Wow. The spa advertised that it customized its service to each individual, and she'd figured that was marketing hype. But now she could believe it.

She needed high-test, not designer stuff. "Kona, please. Strong and black."

"I'll be right back."

Ann sat in a rattan chair with mauve cushions and began to fill in the form. Oh good, Kristi was back, handing her a mug.

Excellent coffee. As Ann sipped, careful not to open her sore jaw too wide, she felt caffeine surge through her veins like a transfusion of energy.

She continued with the form. Medical history. No, she'd never had any of the three dozen illnesses. Efficiently she worked her way through a list of symptoms.

Now she was supposed to describe her reason for coming to Pure Indulgence. *Stress,* she wrote. *Aching jaw, neck, shoulders.*

Headaches. She felt all those aches now, below the superficial buzz from the coffee. Damn, she really was a wreck. And it was her own stupid fault for ignoring the warning signs, for being so focused on her work and her idiotic infatuation with David that she neglected her health.

A new leaf, she reminded herself. *I'll make time for two or three back massages. I'm young and healthy; I'll be in shape in no time.*

She signed the form with a flourish, then looked up. "Kristi? I'm finished."

"Great. I'll take you in now."

Ann got up, juggling the clipboard, her purse, and the coffee mug—because there was no way she was letting go of her caffeine.

Kristi rose gracefully and joined her. "Just to confirm, you said you only needed a couple of sessions, right?"

"Absolutely."

The other woman, who had a graceful, hip-swaying walk, led her down a hall. "Perfect. I'm giving you to Adonis. He won't be here more than another month or two, but that should do you just fine." She tapped on a door marked "Consultations."

Okay, you lost me back at Adonis. Good God, does this place make their masseurs use the names of Greek gods? Jenny must have known, when she'd made that comment about Ann getting her massage from a gorgeous Greek god.

Ann was grinning when she opened the door and stepped through.

The smile froze, and so did all forward motion. *Oh. My. God.* If ever a man deserved the name Adonis, it was the one who rose from behind the desk across the room.

Clad in a sand-colored T-shirt and matching cotton pants, he almost looked naked because the clothing so closely matched his skin color. The body revealed by the clingy tee was—oh, yeah!—sculpted. For the first time, she really understood the meaning of that word. With his clothes off, this guy would look like a sculpture of a Greek god.

She tore her gaze from his body and focused on his face. Strong planes, sensual mouth, wide chocolate-brown eyes, and hair that was too long, too tousled for a law office. Hair streaked in shades of blond and brown, framing his handsome face perfectly. Hair that made her itch to run her fingers through it.

He came out from behind the desk, smiling. Oh, damn, his smile tipped up to the right and ended in a dimple. Her heart stuttered.

He was young, maybe younger than she was, and her taste normally ran to mature men. But she had to admit this guy was seriously hot.

"Ann?"

"Y-yes." Oh God, her voice was stuttering, too. This was ridiculous; she could present cases in court and remain perfectly poised. She took a deep breath and walked toward him. "Kristi said your name is . . . Adonis?" Despite her best efforts, she couldn't keep the amusement from her voice.

His smile widened, the dimple deepened, his eyes sparkled. The man had one killer smile. "Adonis Stefanakis."

"Stefanakis?"

He nodded. "Yeah, my dad's Greek." His voice was low pitched and resonant. "Adonis is my real name, but if it makes you feel weird, call me Don."

"Don." She tried it out. Nope, didn't suit him. "I'll stick with Adonis."

"You'll get used to it."

But would she ever get used to looking at a man who was this stunning?

"Okay, that's settled," he said. "Ann and Adonis."

She could just imagine Jenny wrinkling her nose, saying, "Cheesy! Ann and Adonis, sitting in a tree, k-i-s-s . . ."

He held out his hand. Long-fingered, elegant, but strong looking.

Time to get real. That k-i-s-s part sure isn't going to happen. Here she was, a plain woman with a plain name, and he was a Greek god with a name to fit. She put her mug on the desk. "Nice to meet you." She grasped his hand firmly, started a business-like handshake.

He slowed her, controlling her hand with his firm, warm grip. Holding her hand, more than shaking it. And it felt good. Too damned good, and not like business at all.

Something surged through her veins again, and this time it wasn't caffeine. It carried way more punch. And the punch was heading straight for her sex. Suddenly she felt hot, damp, needy.

So needy, she shivered with it. Hurriedly she pulled her hand from Adonis's grip, scared to look at him for fear he'd read her thoughts. Could she *be* any more pathetic? Though he must be used to it, with female clients.

He cleared his throat and she glanced up to see him gesture to a chair. "Have a seat."

Too plush, too comfy. It was hard to sit up straight, keep her knees together, make sure her skirt didn't ride up. Adonis had crossed back to the desk and was leaning against it, one butt-cheek hitched up on it. The cotton of his pants pulled across his firm thigh and her gaze drifted higher as she wondered if his package was of godlike proportions.

She jerked her gaze away, which made her neck crack. "Ouch." When she focused on his face, she found he was studying her.

She held up the clipboard, making a barrier between them. "You'll want this."

"Not yet."

Adonis smiled at the woman perched so nervously on the edge of the chair. Pretty. Not in a knock-your-eyes-out way but in an even better one. The kind that snuck up on you, and grew stronger the more you looked at her.

If there was one thing Adonis knew and appreciated, it was women. His mom had run the household, his three older sisters had bossed and pampered him, and he'd dated way more than his fair share of sexy women.

He was a connoisseur of lovely ladies, and this one ranked high. Slim but curvy. Classy bone structure. Skin the color of a milky latte with cinnamon freckles sprinkled across the top. Short, elegant hair, tawny with a thousand shades of brown. Hazel eyes with flecks of gold and mossy green; big, beautiful eyes with dark fringes of lash. One of those huge, wide, mobile mouths like Julia Roberts had. The kind that makes a guy think of . . . Oh shit, his cock was stirring at the thought of that mouth wrapped around it.

Just as it had earlier, when energy—sexual energy—had flowed between their linked hands. Without knowing a thing about each other, their bodies had made an instant connection. Not something that often happened to him. And here, in a therapeutic setting, it was wrong.

She frowned. "Don't you want to know why I'm here?"

Sensible woman. She was doing her best to deny that inappropriate connection. He had to, too. He went behind the desk to hide his growing hard-on. "You've already told me."

"I did not." She scowled, her jaw tightened, he could see she was grinding her teeth. "You're thinking of someone else."

Not likely, when she was in the room. Something about her called out to him. Partly it was sexual, but part was recognizing her pain, wanting to help her. Wanting to see her when she was relaxed and laughing.

Wanting to see her expression when she climaxed.

Inside his boxers, his cock rose up his belly. He took a couple of deep breaths and tried to focus on his job. "You don't need to tell me in words. Your body's plenty communicative."

Including the flush of sexual heat on her cheeks. Focusing on his job, he said, "You frown enough that you're getting vertical grooves in your forehead, and the tightness around your eyes says you have a headache. True?"

She narrowed her eyes and the groove deepened. "True," she said warily.

"Your shoulders are high and tight, hunched forward. Too much time at a desk, and you're carrying a lot of tension. No wonder you get headaches."

"My jaw's sore, too." She said it almost reluctantly, like it was a sin to be in pain.

"You grind your teeth. You did it a minute ago."

"A minute . . . ? Oh." A glint of humor sparked in her eyes. "I do it when I'm frustrated."

He smiled, enjoying the way her face lightened. "Anything else? Besides back, neck, headaches, jaw?"

One corner of that lush mouth lifted. "Is there anything left?"

Oh, yeah. Breasts. Full enough to curve her tailored suit jacket. And legs. Long, killer legs. Just right to wrap around a guy.

And now he had a full-blown woody.

Ann was a client. Damn. Usually he had no trouble keeping things professional, even though clients often came on to him. Which she sure wasn't doing. She'd been nothing but business-like herself, despite the flush that telegraphed her awareness of him.

Why did he respond to this woman, when he knew he shouldn't?

He realized he was staring at her, and she was staring back, eyes wide and shiny. Another sign that she felt this powerful attraction, too.

Suddenly she jerked her head down, which must have hurt, to stare at the clipboard.

"What do you do, anyhow?" he asked. "To get so stressed?"

"Lawyer." Her shoulders squared, like she was telling herself to get a grip. "So, what do we do next?" Her cheeks flushed brighter and she waved the clipboard. "I mean, you'll want to see this, right? Do you have any more questions? Do I see Kristi to make an appointment?"

Those long legs shifted, like she wanted to spring to her feet and dash away. Or, maybe, spring to her feet and wrap her legs around him and climb his body?

Adonis stifled a groan. Oh, man, was he hurting. His cock cried out for touch. Relief. He cleared his throat. "Appointment? Didn't you already book a massage for today?"

"Oh, yeah, right. Of course." She was off balance, too.

"Great." Shit, not great at all. Maybe he should get someone else to do it. Because all he could think of was doing her. It'd be torture to touch her when he had to stay professional, when what he really wanted was to savor every inch of her body and make love with her for hours.

If he was right—and he knew he was—that she felt the attraction too, maybe she'd be uncomfortable having him do the massage. "You're ready to go ahead?" he asked. "If you'd rather change to another day, or a different therapist, that's okay. You need to feel comfortable with the person who's doing, uh, your massage."

Her eyes narrowed and he sensed she was having an internal debate. Then her head lifted, jaw firm. "I scheduled a massage, I need it, I'm sure you're competent. What happens next?"

"You need to take your clothes off."

"What?" She stared up, wide-eyed again.

His turn to glance away. He messed with some papers on the desk, trying to ignore the demanding ache in his groin. "Kristi will take you to a massage room and tell you what to do." Normally he'd do it himself, but no way. Not with a woody tenting his fly.

"Uh, okay." She sounded as flustered as he was. He figured that wasn't her normal state.

She rose quickly, awkwardly, knocking a hip against the arm of her chair. A woman, he thought, who worked too hard and wasn't in touch with her body. Did that carry through to her sensuality, her sexuality?

Not his business. He was here to help her heal her body, not explore her sexuality.

And, if he was going to get through this massage, there was something he needed to take care of first. His own throbbing sex.

She paused in the doorway. "So, I'll see you in the massage room?"

He nodded. "I'll be along when you've had a chance to get comfortable."

More like, when he'd had a chance to get comfortable.

When he was making love with a woman, he knew all the tantric techniques for slowing down, preventing ejaculation, moving sexual energy away from his genitals. But right now, he didn't give a damn about all that crap. He wanted relief, hard and fast.

The moment she closed the door, he got up to lock it. He grabbed a hand towel and a bottle of unscented massage oil and retreated back behind the desk. A squirt of oil into one hand, then he lowered his clothing. His cock sprang into his hand and he gripped it hard. Man, he was ready to burst, and he'd only just met the woman. He began to pump, using long, firm strokes.

Ann. A classy name for a classy lady.

Glancing over to the chair she'd sat in, he imagined her rising, stripping off her jacket, walking toward him with her naked breasts all pert and bouncy. Kneeling down on the carpet by his chair, smiling up with that sexy mouth, then bending to take him between her lips.

Running her tongue around him, drawing him in. Firm, wet. Licking and sucking.

Man, that felt good.

But even better, he wanted to be between those long legs. Feel them wrap around him as he thrust hard and fast into her tight, hot, silky depths. The slip and slide of flesh against flesh, the pressure building, growing, climbing until . . .

He exploded in climax.

2

Ann lay faceup on a massage table, naked under a mauve sheet that covered her from breasts to toes. Kristi had told her she could keep her panties on, but, due to her fondness for teddies, Ann hadn't been wearing any. Ill-prepared. Totally unlike her, and she hated it.

Note to self: If I continue with massage, buy panties. Big, safe granny panties!

A layer of protection—symbolic as much as real—between her celibate-too-long body and the fantasy-inspiring hands of Adonis Stefanakis.

And never, but never, book a full-body massage.

She was *not* having fun. Ann was, as the other members of the Awesome Foursome often reminded her, a control freak. She wasn't comfortable—except with them—unless she was in control of the situation. She could handle a subordinate position, like being a student or junior lawyer, because it was a learning situation *she* had chosen. She was in control of her education and would decide what she learned from her teacher.

This silly attraction to a Greek god was way out of her comfort zone.

But I chose massage. I am in control. Adonis is in my life solely to serve my needs.

Serve her needs? She groaned. Her normally incisive brain had been taken over by lustful fantasies.

She should have rebooked with another therapist. But that would have been an admission, to herself at least, that she couldn't handle the situation. Not good.

Why had he made that offer, anyway? Had her attraction been so obvious? She'd just bet he had tons of women clients come on to him. No way would she be one. She could handle this.

Damn it, massage is supposed to be relaxing. *I have to stop stressing.* The small room was soothing with the pale peach walls, dim lighting, and watercolors of flowers, but she was so keyed up that when the door opened she almost screamed and leaped off the table.

Which would have been a big mistake, given her state of undress.

Was it her imagination, or did Adonis seem less than composed himself? He held a clipboard in front of him almost as if he was using it the way she had, as a barrier between them. Was he afraid she was going to toss aside the sheet and jump him?

He moved around behind her, where she couldn't see him, and said, "I've read your info form. No medical conditions, eh?"

Damned if she'd twist her sore neck to see him, so she spoke to the ceiling. "No."

"You haven't had any x-rays of your neck or shoulders?"

She'd already filled out this information, but the lawyer in her knew he needed to ask these questions, as a protection against a client suing the spa. "No. Just my jaw."

"Okay, we'll take it easy the first time, and see how you feel."

Tense. Really tense. And why was she reading a double entendre into what he'd said?

"I'm going to start with a physical assessment," the voice from behind her said, sounding more at ease. Getting into his professional rhythm, she figured, after whatever had thrown him off balance. Maybe the aura of pure lust rising from her skin?

Well, he'd had the professionalism to ignore it, so she would too. "Assessment?"

"I need to make sure I don't feel anything problematic that might require you to get x-rays or see a doctor."

"Makes sense. What do I do?"

"Just lie there and relax. Let me know if anything hurts when I touch you."

"Okay. You want me to roll over?" He'd need to examine her back, right?

"Not yet." Then his hands were on her shoulders, from behind. Warm, firm but gentle. There was nothing in his touch to make her jump, yet she did.

He paused. "Okay?"

"Yeah. Sorry. It's just—" *That I'm not used to being touched.*

"Breathe deeply and slowly. Focus on your breathing."

She obeyed, and both her desire and her nervousness abated.

As he ran his hands over her shoulders, probed delicately with his fingertips, she reflected that she couldn't remember ever being touched like this. Professionally, with no ulterior motive. Not like her lovers, who'd focused on breasts and genitals, seeking to arouse themselves as well as her. Not like the Foursome, who hugged affectionately, patted hands and arms. Not like her mother, who touched only when necessary.

Touch. Simple human touch. Amazing how good it could feel. It helped that Adonis was behind her. Unable to see his face, she could almost forget that the person touching her was one of the sexiest guys she'd ever seen.

"Ouch." Pain broke through her drifting thoughts. She realized his hands had moved from her shoulders down to the muscles above the top curve of her breasts. Why on earth would those muscles hurt? Then his fingers moved into the center, to her breastbone, and even that hurt. "That's bone. How can it be sore?"

"Muscles attach there. And the muscles hurt for a couple of reasons. They're a place people carry stress, and it's an effect of hunching forward. You work at a desk?"

Ann nodded. "Desk, computer, law books."

"Always leaning forward. Everything tightens, shortens." His hands were stroking now, slow and deft. "Ever do any exercises for the rhomboids—the muscles down your back? Or break up the desk work with stretches?"

She huffed. "Don't you know the answer, or has my body stopped communicating?"

His hands paused, resting near where the top of the sheet covered her breasts. And, suddenly, she was again aware of him as a man. A sexy, desirable man whose clever fingers were only inches from her naked breasts.

Her nipples chose that moment to communicate, by leaping to attention. Damn! That sheet was way too thin.

"Yeah," he said. "I know the answer."

And what was the question again? Do you turn me on? Well, duh. Her nipples were screaming that particular fact.

"Don't have time for exercise, right?" he asked.

Exercise. Oh, yeah, that had been his question. "Uh, no."

"I need you to roll over so I can check your back."

And just how was she going to roll over under the sheet, without flashing the guy? On the other hand, she definitely didn't want his assistance with that flimsy sheet.

"I'll put some music on," he said. "Anything special you like for relaxing?"

Music. Like touch, it was pretty much absent from her life, except what happened to be on the car radio when she made the short drive to and from work. She'd have loved to be able to suggest something—to keep that tiny bit of control—but nothing came to mind. "Whatever you recommend. Just not that twittery birdsong that was playing in the reception area."

He chuckled softly.

When she heard the soft clatter of disk cases, she grabbed the sheet and, trying to hold it securely, scuttled over onto her stomach. As she craned around to make sure the sheet covered her butt, her neck gave another twinge. "I can't even turn over without hurting," she complained, scowling at Adonis's back.

"Sorry," he said, sounding guilty. "I'd have offered to help but—" He turned and their gazes met.

Oh wow, was this what Jenny and Suzanne meant when they talked about sparks? His gaze drifted down her body and every inch of naked skin—even those under the sheet—warmed as if he'd touched it.

"But?" He'd have been tempted to peek?

"I wasn't sure you'd be comfortable. You seem kind of nervous. It being your first time."

Damn. Knowing her cheeks were heating, Ann hurriedly buried her face in the face rest with its hole for her eyes, nose, and mouth. Sparks? No, hallucinations. Clearly he wasn't interested, sexually, in a plain, boring woman like her.

Great. Another new symptom. Hallucinations. Hmm, could they be a side effect of the muscle relaxants?

"I've been taking muscle relaxants," she said, speaking to the floor. "They help, but I'm wondering about possible side effects."

"Such as?"

Thinking a hottie masseur wants to screw me senseless?

"Nothing in particular. Just wondering if there's anything I should watch out for." *Like temporary insanity?*

"Drowsiness, loss of focus, clumsiness."

"I'm always clumsy anyhow," she admitted ruefully. "I'm one of those Klutzes-R-Us people who bangs into doors, desk corners. My hips are always black-and-blue."

He cleared his throat. "Be careful about driving if you're sleepy or dizzy."

"I drink enough caffeine; drowsiness isn't a problem. Anything else?"

"Muscle relaxants can upset your stomach."

"Not so far. I eat like a horse. Whenever I can find time to eat."

He sighed. "Ann, you need regular meals. Good, natural food, a balanced diet. Cut down on the caffeine, get a good night's sleep, more exercise. All those things help with stress. At least you don't smoke."

"How do you know?" This was weird, talking at the floor while Adonis, somewhere behind her, flipped through CDs.

"I'd have smelled it on you."

Smelled it? *So, what* does *he smell? Stale coffee breath?*

Why should she care? She was a client. A pathetic, horny, workaholic client whose only love interest was a married man and . . . Wait a minute. Since she'd first laid eyes on Adonis, she hadn't thought of David. She smiled. And now that she was, she had to admit that while the lawyer was attractive, he didn't have the same charisma, the sexy physicality of Adonis.

All right! Maybe her aching jaw hadn't been cured yet, but she had a new man to fantasize about, and she'd just bet she was going to have one hell of an orgasm when she climbed into bed tonight with her vibrator.

Music began to play. She hadn't known what to expect, but this was a surprise. It was a flute, piercing yet round and full, mellow yet haunting. Slow music that drifted into the air, making her think of whale song and eagles flying. Outdoorsy, which she wasn't, and yet this music spoke to something deep inside her. "Who is that?"

"R. Carlos Nakai."

Never heard of him. "Nice."

Not enough to relax her, though, because she felt so vulnerable and exposed, lying facedown like this. "Tell me what you're going to do, so I'm prepared."

"I'll start with your shoulders and work down your back." His voice came from over her left shoulder.

She braced herself for his touch.

He gave a half sigh, half chuckle. "Relax. Listen to the music, sink into it."

She tried, but her skin was supersensitive. Especially as he edged the sheet lower and worked from her shoulders down her spine, doing his assessment vertebra by vertebra, to the hollow at the base. His touch wasn't sexual but a part of her wished it was, imagined it was. The fantasy was enough to bring a flood of moisture between her thighs. Damn, the sheet was going to be damp when she got up. This was too embarrassing.

Adonis's hands stroked, circled, probed gently. So big, so firm, so deft, they made her feel more feminine than she'd felt in a long time. Feminine, aware, sensual. Sexual, as she lay with her back exposed to him, all the way down to where the sheet draped her buttocks.

"I don't feel any injuries," he said, pulling the sheet back up to her shoulders. "You're right; it's stress, tiredness, muscle strain."

Right. *Diagnostic* touch, not sexual. "Can you help me?" She tried to sound businesslike.

"I can make you feel better."

She'd just bet he could. Maybe better than she'd ever felt before.

Except, what she had in mind wasn't on his agenda for today.

Jesus, get a grip! On my sanity, not his cock.

She *believed* in the bounds of professional relationships. Damn, she must have been spending too much time with the Foursome. Suzanne, with all her talk of hot sex with Jaxon. Jenny, describing her and Scott's crazy sexual fantasies.

Massage fantasy? Yeah, that's what she was doing. Jenny would die laughing.

No, Jenny'd take that massage fantasy idea to Scott, and enact it. *Damn it, it's* my *fantasy. If anyone gets to do it, it should be me.*

"All right," Adonis said, "I'll start the massage. You can choose what oil you want. Close your eyes."

Yeah, like that was going to happen. She wasn't that trusting. But she squinted her eyes partway shut as he said, "I'll give you three oils to smell, and you'll know which scent is right."

"Bring them on." Peeking through her eyelashes she saw his hand appear below the face rest, holding a frosted glass bottle. The air filled with a flowery, exotic scent. "That's pretty. Makes me think of the tropics." And of a bubble bath, preferably with a sexy partner.

"I'm taking it away. Breathe deeply a couple of times, then I'll give you the second."

This one was quite different. Sharp, almost astringent, but pleasant. Invigorating. "I like that, too." She could use some at work, whenever her energy flagged. Another good thing about this one: it didn't make her think of sex.

"A couple more deep breaths, then the final choice."

This one combined flowers and herbs, and made her imagine an Italian garden. "That's my favorite. What is it?"

"Lavender, chamomile, and geranium. It's a blend that's especially good for stress, headaches, muscle aches."

She had the feeling he'd known all along which she'd choose. "Well, I have headaches and muscle aches, so why did you even bother giving me options?" She hated being manipulated.

"Your body knows what it needs. I thought we should let it tell us."

A subtle put-down, but he was right. "You mean, before my jaw gets so sore I can't eat?"

He laughed. "Yeah, that'd be good."

Or so sore I couldn't open it and suck on your cock, even if you wanted me to?

"I'll warm it in my hands," he said.

"What?" she yelped. He was going to warm his cock?

"Uh, the oil? Warm the oil?"

Jesus, she truly was pathetic. "Sure, good."

"I'll start with your shoulders, then down your back. Then I'll have you turn over and I'll massage your face. I can do jaw massage from inside your mouth, too. Not everyone's comfortable with it, though."

His fingers invading her mouth? Nope. Way too much. "I don't think so. I'm doing that myself. My dentist gave me instructions."

His hands settled on her shoulders and he began to stroke, smoothing in the oil, warming her skin. "I'll take it easy, since this is our first time. We'll see how you feel afterward. Whether I can go deeper, next time."

Oh yeah, I can take it. Go deep. Really, really deep.

"Relax," he said softly.

Easy for him to say. A strange man was touching her body, the context wasn't sexual except in her freaking fantasies, and she was vulnerable under those big hands. How could she possibly relax?

"Where did you study massage?" she asked. Talking made

her feel more in control. Besides, if she reassured herself about his qualifications, maybe she'd be more comfortable.

"Here in BC. We have some of the best training in the world. And tough exams."

"You're certified?" The website had said all the massage therapists were, but it never hurt to check your facts.

He laughed. "Yeah, I actually passed those exams. I'm registered with the College of Massage Therapists."

So the Greek god had brains, too. "It's a comprehensive program?"

"Anatomy, physiology, assessment, massage techniques. And I've picked up a variety of different methods in other countries." He was still stroking, in a circular motion on each shoulder, but putting more weight into it.

She could almost feel her muscles stretching. "You travel around, learning massage?"

He chuckled. "Not exactly. I like to travel. When the weather starts to get cold here, I head for the sunshine. And because of my training, I can usually get a job in a spa."

His looks wouldn't hurt, either.

"I've been to Belize and India. Last winter it was Thailand. I learned about Thai bodywork."

"What's that?"

"It's more participatory. You and the therapist work through stretches and exercises."

"Sounds like yoga." She shuddered. "I don't like yoga."

"How come?"

"Too slow. I got impatient."

A chuckle. "Yeah, I can see how that'd happen. But Ann, there's a time for slow. Every life needs balance."

Great. She'd come for a massage and was getting lectures on her diet and lifestyle. Still, given how much pain she was in, maybe he had a point.

Yes, fine, she'd have a massage when she got sore. And one dinner with the Foursome each week. She could do balance. Just not yoga.

"Tight spot here," he said, and Ann felt his thumb begin to dig in. One thumb, stroking, circling, and pressing, then the other following it.

It hurt, and she automatically tensed.

"Breathe deep and long," he said. "Breathe into my hands, breathe through the pain, let the tension go."

She tried it and found the pain was manageable.

"Keep breathing. Focus on your breath. Listen to the music, take in the scent of the oil."

"Try to relax?"

He laughed softly, but his hands kept moving. "Don't try. That takes too much work. Just breathe, listen, smell. Let yourself drift. Some people go to sleep."

With his hands on them? How old were these "people"? Or maybe they were guys. Straight guys.

Still, as Adonis worked up her neck, the warm scented oil, the rhythmic touch, the haunting music began to create a certain magic. Ann found herself sinking into the table, her thoughts for once not on legal files. She couldn't even keep track of what was going through her mind. When she tried to catch on to the last thought, it had already slipped away.

She breathed deeply, felt her back rise and fall under his hands and tried not to tense when he pulled the sheet lower and dug deep to work out the knots.

Her headache was gone. How cool was that?

When he reached her lower back, she became all too conscious of her nudity again.

His hands grasped her waist, then moved in, stroking, stretching, kneading.

He looked at nearly naked women every hour of the day. But for her, this was a new experience, exhilarating and a little scary. His hands so easily spanned her waist, those long, deft fingers were so close to her naked butt yet didn't stray beneath the sheet. Tonight, when she was in bed with her vibrator and her fantasy, she knew exactly where those hands would be going.

Even though Adonis's touch wasn't sexual, her back had absorbed more male contact in the last twenty or thirty minutes than in all the years before. How strange, that no date or lover had ever given her even a shoulder massage. But then, she held people at a distance. Didn't welcome intimacy. Just, sometimes, sex. When she was in the mood.

Like now. With the man who, as he stroked away her pain, made her body tingle with sexual awareness and need.

How weird. Normally, for her to be in the mood for sex, it took lots of wine, lots of conversation with an intellectually stimulating guy like David. She needed a mental connection, plus something to break down her inhibitions.

She didn't trust a man with her body.

Is that true? It was a *ding!* moment. Her brain had tossed the thought out of nowhere, and she had to stop and examine it.

She'd never thought of it that way before. Sure, she'd had some hot sex, but only when *she* set the rules. Damn, she was just as bad as Suze and Jenny, with their rules to have sex by.

But here she was now, letting Adonis range freely over her back. And enjoying every second, to the point that her pussy was throbbing and wet.

Of course, she *was* in control. She had chosen to have a massage and she was paying for it. There was a contract. It was a different kind of trust than in an intimate relationship.

Though her physical reaction was definitely intimate. Sexual.

Well, duh. Music and scented air, a hot guy with great hands. Herself naked and horny. What woman wouldn't be thinking about sex?

Especially when those wonderful hands were working the hollow at the base of her spine, just above her buttocks. She couldn't help squirming.

His hands froze and she heard him suck in a breath.

She froze, and he took up where he'd left off, making deep, smoothing motions with both thumbs upward through the hollow above her backside.

Why hadn't she told him her butt ached, too? The idea of a whole-body massage was getting more and more appealing.

Ann held back a nervous giggle. While she was at it, she could definitely tell him her pussy hurt, because that was pure truth. She was swollen, achy, hungry for a touch from those long, strong, beautifully shaped fingers.

Not to mention something else she was sure was long, strong, and beautifully shaped.

"Are we almost done?" Her voice came out choky. "Is it time to roll over?"

And reveal nipples that were so tightly beaded they'd poke holes through the sheet. *Note to self: Tape down my nipples before the next massage!*

"I'll change the CD." Was she imagining things, or did his voice sound uneven, too? "Unless you want help with the sheet?" he added.

"No! I'll manage fine." She stretched back to reach for the sheet. Yeah, her muscles were moving more fluidly, and with less pain. Adonis knew his job.

"I, uh, need to get another CD from the other room," he said.

He'd been flipping through a dozen or more CDs earlier. Why did he need to leave and find another? Or did he just want to give her privacy?

She'd been struggling to turn over while still keeping her grip on the sheet and now, klutz that she was, overbalanced. Her hip started to slide off the table. "Oh, crap!"

He was there in a flash, grabbing her by the shoulders and steadying her as she kept her death grip on the sheet.

She glanced down. Yes, her breasts were still covered. Then, as Adonis let go of her shoulders, her gaze focused on him. More precisely, on the monster erection that tented his pants.

"Oh!" A hot, heavy wave of arousal surged through her. She squeezed her thighs tight against the ache, the pulse between them.

She couldn't tear her gaze away from his fly, and he couldn't seem to move, either.

She recovered first. Pretending something didn't exist never solved a problem. So she said, "It's okay. I guess, uh, it happens sometimes, when you're massaging a woman." Especially a woman who was squirming around and oozing lust from every pore.

And of course it was unprofessional to let her see his reaction. Even if, in her case, she was more flattered than offended.

No, she was just plain horny enough to scream.

Adonis could have died of shame, but for the glitter in Ann's eyes, the flush on her cheeks, the tremble in her hands as they clenched the bunched-up sheet. She was turned on, too.

And, yeah, that did sometimes happen during a massage. For the client, but not for him. He'd learned how to think about a client's body as compared to a lover's body, even when he was doing a full-body massage. So why the *hell* couldn't he do it with Ann?

Because he wanted her. As a lover. So strongly that even after masturbating, after using all the tantric techniques he could remember, he'd got erect again. Just from massaging her back.

This was crazy. She wasn't his type. She was uptight and mistreated her body by not exercising, not eating properly. But then, there were those eyes and lips. A self-deprecating humor that called out to him. Amazing chemistry between them.

She was out of his league. Classy, a lawyer, four years older, as he'd seen on her chart. Yet, she was turned on, too.

No, even if she was willing, he couldn't have sex with her here and now. It would violate ethical standards, not to mention his own values.

He had to apologize. Find her another therapist or finish the massage if she was willing. He loved making people feel better, and he wanted to do that for her. After, he'd talk to her about changing their relationship from professional to personal.

While he'd been standing there, silent and obviously horny, she hadn't moved, either. Except to shift her gaze—seemingly reluctantly—from his groin to his face.

He took a couple of steps backward. "I'm sorry. It shouldn't have happened and I shouldn't have let you see. It's unprofessional. And you're wrong, this has never happened to me before. It's you. It's because I'm touching *you*."

She sucked in a breath. "Me?"

"There's something . . ." He shrugged. "Yeah, I'm attracted to you. But I'd never take advantage of this situation."

"G-good," she said, sounding uncertain. "So, uh, what happens next?"

She could report him and he'd lose his job. Maybe his license to practice the profession he loved. She held the power, and all because he hadn't been able to control his reaction to her.

He took a deep breath. "I could finish the massage. Or I could get someone else, if you prefer."

"Can you finish? When you're . . . you know?"

Busting out of his pants? Yeah, even if it killed him. "I'm good at self-control." Or at least he had been, before Ann.

She let out her breath slowly. "Control is good. And professionalism."

"Lie back, breathe, see if you can relax again. I'm sorry, now you're tense again." He sighed. How could she ever relax and trust him now? "Look, if you'd rather quit, I'll make sure you get a refund."

"N-no. I'll stay. My head's feeling a lot better. The massage has really helped." Slowly she eased back until she was flat on the table. As she loosened her hold on the sheet, one edge of the cotton slipped down, uncovering her left breast almost down to the areola.

Adonis barely suppressed a groan. He should find some subtle way of readjusting the sheet. But he didn't. He went behind her, poured more oil into his palms, and wished he could touch his cock. Three, four seconds, that's all it would take. Instead, he laid his hands gently on Ann's shoulders, repeating the initial soothing, warming strokes he'd started with on her back.

"That feels so good," she said.

She sure had some knotted muscles but he had to be careful. If he dug in too deeply, she'd feel bruised tomorrow. It was a fine balance, figuring out how deep to go.

Deep. Yeah, he wanted to be embedded deep inside her, between those long, shapely legs.

He kneaded her chest muscles and she sighed and shifted position. The sheet slid another couple of inches, baring her nipple. A coral nipple, beaded tight.

His mouth filled with saliva at the thought of sucking on that nipple. His cock pressed against the headrest of the table. If he'd been naked, her silky hair would have drifted across it.

He stretched forward to work out the tightness in her pecs, his fingers so close to that bare nipple. Her skin was flower-petal soft and her breasts lifted as her breathing quickened.

She raised her head and started at the sight of her nipple. But she didn't pull up the sheet. "Do you do full-body massage?" The question came out as a breathy whisper.

3

It was like a punch to his gut, robbing him of air. Adonis sucked in a breath. "Yes."

"I want one." She reached up, and with a flick of her wrist, the sheet had fallen to her waist, baring her torso.

Two lovely breasts, nipples pink and peaked, clear in the message they were sending. *Touch us.*

Full-body massage, for a therapist, was supposed to be about healing. Not sensuality. Not eroticism, which was what she clearly wanted.

He had to respect a woman who knew what she wanted and asked for it, even if her request put him in an untenable position. There were places in town that offered erotic massage, but he couldn't bear the thought of another man's hands on her body.

"Ann, we don't do that kind of massage here."

She didn't pretend not to understand. "But I want it. Why can't you?"

"Professional ethics," he said softly.

"Damn! That's not fair. Please, Adonis?"

He gazed into her desperate eyes. A stronger man could have resisted her, but he wasn't that guy. Knowing he was crossing a boundary, he stroked both hands down over her breasts.

If he'd had any notion he could keep the massage purely therapeutic, it died a speedy death when Ann moaned, arched her back, and thrust her breasts into his hands.

He massaged, stroked, caressed, teased her nipples between his fingers.

Her head moved from side to side. No wincing, she was feeling no pain now. Except the ache of building arousal. He could read it in the way her body tightened, her breasts heaved, her hips squirmed.

And as her arousal built, so did his.

He took a deep breath, focused on his breathing. Tried to relax every muscle, to disperse sexual energy away from his rigid cock. Damn it, he refused to let himself climax.

As for Ann, though . . . Her lower body was twisting under the sheet and she was breathing in short, gasping pants. She wanted to come.

"Adonis?" Her hazel eyes were open, imploring him. "Full body?"

The sheet still covered her hips. He'd be crossing another boundary if he flicked it away. But hadn't he already committed himself, the moment her breasts had thrust into his hands in clear invitation, and he'd accepted?

She didn't know a thing about dispersing sexual energy and avoiding orgasm, and this wasn't the time to teach her. All he knew right now was that a man couldn't leave a woman aching and unsatisfied. For him, that was an even stronger value than his professional ethics.

"Adonis!" Now her tone was demanding, her eyes fierce with need. She grabbed the sheet and yanked it away.

My God, she was naked!

No cotton bikinis, no boy-briefs, no tap pants, not even a

thong. Just Ann. Curvy hips, flat abdomen, pretty curls of tawny hair against creamy skin. Slim thighs that opened as she twisted on the massage table. And between them, slick, pouty lips, a deeper rose than her nipples.

His cock surged and he tried again to focus on his breathing. This was about Ann. His own needs were irrelevant. He couldn't have sex with her, but he could continue to massage. Sensually. Giving her what she needed.

He lifted his hands from her breasts and moved from behind her.

She turned her head, gaze going straight to his fly. "I want you," she whispered. "Take your pants off."

He squeezed his eyes shut against temptation, then opened them again. "Can't. I've broken almost every rule in the book, but I won't break that one."

Her eyes narrowed. "Damn it, I need you."

What was he thinking, doing something like this at Pure Indulgence? Had he gone crazy? Or just crazy for the beautiful woman on the table, whose overstressed body was craving relief? "I know. And I'll massage you, if you want."

"I need more than massage," she snapped.

"I'll give you what you need."

Her eyes narrowed again as she figured out what he meant, then they widened, gleaming wickedly. "You'll give me what I need with massage. With those talented hands. All those *techniques* you've learned. Oh yeah, I'll vote for more massage."

He'd made a promise and she'd accepted his offer. There was no going back.

Gently he caressed her abdomen, threaded his fingers through her pubic hair. Her knees bent and separated in clear invitation.

He stroked her outer lips, sliding his fingers up and down against their slickness.

She moaned, "Oh, yes," and squeezed her eyes shut.

He moved to her inner lips, taking his time, enjoying her heat, her little whimpers of pleasure, the way her hips twisted.

His fingers moved faster, gliding across her swollen flesh, then he curved two fingers and eased them into her. She clenched around him and he could feel her reaching, close but not quite there, wanting it so badly. Wanting it now, tired of waiting, afraid she'd slide off that edge if she didn't come now. Tense, the woman was so tense, and impatient.

Adonis was tense too, despite all his efforts to stay calm. If he didn't watch out, if he prolonged this any more, he was going to come with her.

The thumb of his other hand found her pearly bud and caressed it lightly. He heard her gasp and wished he was kissing her. Wished he could swallow every moan, capture the sound of her climax in his mouth.

Instead he thrust his fingers deep inside her, found her G-spot, and stroked it as he caressed her clit again and again. Her body arched and he felt all her internal muscles contract.

Then she was coming, throbbing against his fingers, her pussy thrusting hard into his hand.

Ann gave herself up to the waves of sensation, then as the spasms died down, let out a sigh of pure satisfaction. What an amazing orgasm!

Gradually she came back to earth, and when she did she lurched upright. "Oh my God! I can't believe I did that!"

"Don't be, uh . . . I mean, uh . . ."

She stared at Adonis for a second. Saw the flush on his cheeks, felt her entire body turn lobster red. Was she insane? She'd let—no, pretty much demanded—that her massage therapist touch her intimately, and bring her to climax. And she was sitting in front of him stark naked.

"Give me the sheet," she demanded, clamping one arm over her breasts as she reached out a hand.

Silently, Adonis complied, then moved a couple of steps away. "Are you all right?"

Her fascinated gaze sought his groin. Jesus, he was hard. Still hard, so hard, the bulge in his pants didn't leave much doubt about the size of his attributes. Her pussy throbbed in response. Damn, she wanted him. Still, again, even after that wrenching climax.

I've gone mad! And I'm still freaking naked! "I'm fine," she said grimly. Could she *be* any more embarrassed? Hurriedly she grabbed the sheet from him and wrapped herself in it toga-style. This stranger had seen her naked, vulnerable, needy. She'd begged him to make her come, and he had. He'd watched as she writhed, moaned, and made a fool of herself.

This was so out of character for her. Yes, she liked sex, believed it was a physical need that deserved satisfying, but normally it took her a while to loosen up and get into it. Of course, today the scented-oil massage had done the loosening. Those strong, deft, seductive hands . . .

Damn it, Adonis had manipulated her. He'd been totally in control of her body, it was his fault she'd acted this way. Yes, he'd manipulated her—

To climax. A stunning, world-class climax. Because she'd made it very clear that's what she needed.

A man who took care of a woman. Much as she wanted to shift the blame, it was hard to be mad at the guy. And from the size of that erection, he was suffering.

Her fault. She believed sex should be mutual. A good lover brought her partner to orgasm, too.

Damn it, she could be a good lover! She knew men who'd attest to that fact. But Adonis hadn't given her the opportunity. He'd rejected her when she'd offered intercourse.

"I don't know what to say." His uncertain tone matched his words. "I was unprofessional. But I didn't want you to . . ."

To go unsatisfied, when she was so obviously desperate?

Summoning an ounce of pride, she squared her shoulders. "It's not your fault. I didn't give you much choice."

The right corner of his mouth lifted in a tentative half smile. "Gotta respect a woman who knows what she wants."

He was so damned cute. And he didn't seem to be laughing at her. Smiling, yes, but she sensed it was *with* her. Relaxing a little, she said wryly, "Knows what she wants, and takes it?" Something she'd never been uninhibited enough to do before.

"Oh, yeah." He'd stopped smiling and his eyes gleamed with desire. His cock was still hard. Damned if the man wasn't still turned on. By her.

Oh my God, I'm actually hot! Not pathetic. I did something outrageously sexy, and got a Greek god aroused.

"There's a problem, though," she said.

"Yeah, I know." Now he looked glum.

"The problem," she said, dropping her gaze deliberately to his crotch, "is that you refused to give me what I really wanted." What was she doing? Honestly trying to understand why he'd gone so far, but no farther? Or was she flirting? Teasing him?

Don't speak without thinking first, Ann. It can get you into trouble.

"Go away, Mother," she muttered under her breath.

"What?" Adonis frowned. "Did you say you wanted me to go away?"

"No, I was just . . ." *Talking to my mother in Toronto, while you and I are in the middle of discussing sex.* He'd know for sure she was crazy. "Adonis, why did you go so far, but draw the line on actually—" Damn, she wasn't usually one to mince words. "Having intercourse?"

His flush deepened. "I already violated so many professional ethics." Those beautiful chocolate eyes were troubled.

Yes, he had. But so had she, because a business contract went two ways. A client shouldn't try to seduce her therapist. "I'm not going to file a complaint." She tried a tentative smile. "I definitely have no complaints."

His eyes warmed, he smiled, the dimple flashed. God, he was adorable. She could eat him up. With her tongue. If he'd give her half a chance.

"Thanks," he told her. "I appreciate that. I mean, about not reporting me."

"You don't appreciate the compliment on your performance?" Okay, now she was flirting. What had happened to her usual common sense?

Quickly she went on. "Sorry, this isn't the real me. I don't know what's happened to me this afternoon. It must be the muscle relaxants. I haven't been myself since—" She broke off. No, she'd started taking the prescription two days ago, and the fantasies and eroticism had only started when she saw Adonis.

He shook his head slowly. His grin had become cocky and knowing. "It's not the meds."

She tilted her chin. "How can you be sure?"

The grin widened. "Because I'm not on them."

The words sank into her brain. Despite what he said, and the undeniably *hard* evidence under the fly of his pants, she still had trouble believing he found her desirable. A plain Jane like her wasn't in his league. "You feel, uh, something too?"

"Oh, yeah. And believe me, I've never violated professional ethics before."

"It must be the massage, though," she said uncertainly. "I'm not used to being touched that way." Yet she suspected that, if someone else massaged her, she'd feel awkward and tense, not wanton. "And you're not used to someone responding the way I did, so I guess it's natural you'd—." She broke off because he was shaking his head.

"It's us. We both felt it the moment we shook hands."

She studied his face. He seemed to mean it. "You felt that, too?"

"And started to get turned on. Why d'you think I hid behind that desk?"

"Really?" Now there was a mind-blowing idea. He'd been aroused, just touching her hand? She wouldn't believe him, except all the facts fit. All that *hard* evidence, that still showed no sign of wilting. But still, she was Ann and he was Adonis. "It doesn't make sense."

"Lust is supposed to make sense?"

Put that way... "No, but why would we lust after each other when we barely know each other?" Okay, it was obvious why any woman whose genitals hadn't shriveled up and disappeared would lust after this Greek god, but what she really meant was, why would he feel that way about her?

He took a step toward her. "Does the reason matter?"

She resisted leaning toward him, or away. Of course reasons mattered. She was a lawyer. Logical, analytical.

A naked lawyer who'd done something utterly irrational. And wanted to do it again.

It wasn't just the throb in her pussy speaking. Her female pride said, this time she wanted to satisfy his needs, too. Now, before her old self returned, inhibitions and all.

"You're still hard." She aimed for a sexy purr. "I could take care of that for you."

His mouth curved. "You have no idea how tempting that is. But no, not now."

"The massage is over." And so, technically, was his excuse of professional ethics. Why would a guy with a hard-on like that be so willing to turn down her offer?

He reached out as if he was going to touch her shoulder, then pulled back his hand. "This is my job, Ann. I could break the rules to give you pleasure, but not out of selfishness."

"So, this is it? I get an orgasm and you get blue balls?"

"For now. But I'd like to see you again. Personally, privately. If you make that offer again, when we're alone, believe me, I'll take you up on it."

An invitation from a true hottie. Wow, he really did find her sexy.

But what kind of invitation? Didn't sound like he was talking about a movie and drinks. After all, it wasn't like the two of them had anything in common, except mutual lust. No, he was accepting her offer to take care of his hard-on. "For sex," she said, to make sure their minds were *ad idem*—as one. It was a fundamental requirement for a contract: a meeting of the minds.

"For hours and hours of sensual touching and tasting and, yeah, sex."

Cute, how he wanted to pretty it up, like she was some romantic *girl*, but the bottom line was, they were both talking about sex. The charge in the air between them confirmed it. She was very aware of her nakedness under the thin sheet, of her tight nipples and swollen sex. Not to mention Adonis's own swollen sex under his cotton pants.

"And that's not a violation of your professional ethics?" she asked, wanting to be sure of her facts. "If I'm your client?" As a lawyer, she wouldn't have sex with a client, in or out of the office, though there'd been a couple of times she'd been tempted.

"You ask a lot of questions," he said softly. "Trying to back out?"

"No!" she said quickly. *Are we really going to do this? Or am I all talk, no action?* "I just want to be sure we know what we're doing. That you won't get in trouble."

The dimple flashed. "Why am I thinking, that hooking up with you is bound to be trouble?"

Hooking up. He really did mean this. Sex. The two of them. Together. She swallowed. She'd never done anything like this.

The men she had sex with were ones she'd known a while, at least had dinner with. They'd had long conversations, respected each other's minds.

Why pretty it up with long conversation? I don't have time for that anyhow. Sex, plain and simple. And hot. Monkey sex. With a Greek god. What could be better? Already she could imagine that hard cock sliding between her slick lips, following the path his fingers had taken earlier. Yes, this was exactly what she needed in her life. Not much more time and commitment than with her vibrator, but *way* more sexually satisfying.

"I want you to switch to another massage therapist," he said, breaking into her train of thought.

"What? You mean, like, fire you? But, wouldn't that seem as if I wasn't"—she blushed—"satisfied with your services? I could tell Kristi I want to see how I feel, before I decide if I continue with massage." *Good God, I'm actually going to do this.*

"Sure." He shifted his legs, like he was trying to get comfortable. His erection hadn't subsided as they'd been talking. Probably because he, like she, had been imagining sex together.

"If I fire you now, can we have sex right away?" she asked, half teasing, half hopeful.

A rueful chuckle. "I wish."

"That's a no." If she dropped the sheet, would he change his mind? No, he was right. This wasn't the right time or place. It would be cruel of her to tease him any longer.

But how totally cool that I have this sexual power!

"Sorry," he said. "But I promise, if you give me a chance I'll make it up to you."

The man was certainly confident of his sexual prowess. Best guess, he had a right to be.

If she accepted his offer, she could have sex with Adonis. Not just in her fantasies, but in real life. She was absolutely sure the Greek god's cock would feel a hundred times better than her vibrator. The question was, would she be able to recapture this afternoon's wanton woman, or would she return to being the old, uptight Ann?

"I know you're not into exercise or yoga," he said, a teasing note in his voice now, "but long, slow lovemaking and orgasm is a great way of relieving stress."

Did he think she had *no* life? "I have orgasms," she said defensively. So, okay, for too many months to count, her orgasmic life had been strictly solo, but she sure as hell wasn't telling him that.

"You'll have better ones with me."

Monday at six on the dot, Ann drove down Robson Street, where the meters were "no parking" between three and six. Smug over her timing, she swung the Miata into a spot right across from Tropika. Jenny'd recommended the Malaysian restaurant after going with Scott.

A light September drizzle misted the air, but not enough to warrant an umbrella as she plugged the meter. What a difference a week made, she thought as she flicked drops out of her hair and took the stairs to the second floor.

Last week it had been sunny, this week the weather was gray and damp, but Ann felt ten times—make that twenty times—better than last Monday. Almost giddy with excitement.

My turn, my turn, my turn! About time I get to be the one with the sexy story.

She paused in the restaurant doorway, approving the high-ceilinged room with minimalist Asian decor, as she looked for her friends. Despite being on time for once, she was the last to arrive. The other three sat at a window table, each with a glass of beer.

Jenny looked up and waved, her long-sleeved sweater another sign of autumn approaching. Ann hurried across the room to join the group.

"Hi, Ann," Suzanne said. "You're looking better. How's your jaw?"

Ann opened her mouth—carefully and not too wide. "Much improved. My dentist gave me a sheet with all sorts of instructions. Like, even how to yawn, if you can believe it."

"I remember the part about not opening your mouth too wide." Jenny opened her own mouth in a big, suggestive O. "Guess that hasn't been a problem?"

Wait until Little Miss Fantasy Rules heard about Adonis. "Not yet. But—" She broke off as a waiter in black pants and an embroidered Asian-style jacket appeared beside her.

His tray held a glass and an unopened bottle of beer. "The ladies ordered for you."

"Perfect." Her head ached and, out of habit, she pulled out her painkillers. Then she tossed the bottle back in her purse. The pain wasn't that bad. The massage had helped, and she'd been doing stretches from a handout Adonis had given her. Maybe beer would do the trick.

"Are you taking the muscle relaxants?" Rina murmured, as the waiter poured Ann's beer.

Ann turned to her, thinking she looked like an Italian painting, with her black hair, Mediterranean coloring, and garnet-red top. "I did for a few days, but I've stopped. Don't need them anymore." She couldn't help smiling.

The waiter placed the glass in front of her and she said, "Thanks."

"That's great," Suzanne said. "Your dentist's instructions must be really good."

"Excellent instructions, and I'm obeying them to the letter." Ann's smile widened. "Doing stretches too. And I went for a massage."

Jenny leaned forward, black hair swinging, brown eyes sparkling. "At Pure Indulgence?"

When Ann nodded, she demanded, "Well? Tell all. Eye candy, like I said?"

"Everything was just as you predicted. Serious eye candy. The therapist was gorgeous."

"Drop-dead gorgeous?" Suzanne asked, just as Jenny said, "Pussy-soaking gorgeous?"

Ann chuckled. She envied Jen and her ability to come out with whatever the hell was on her mind, no matter how outrageous. "Greek-god gorgeous." She took a sip of beer, enjoying the slightly bitter taste. "Like a sculpture of a perfect man. With streaky, dirty-blond hair, brown eyes, strong features. And guess what, his name's Adonis."

"Oh, gimme a break!" Jenny said. "That's just too cheesy."

"Honestly, it's his real name. His father's Greek."

"He sounds so hot," Rina said. "Was he really good?" She giggled. "I mean, at massage?"

Over their time together the Foursome had had some utterly frank conversations, especially about sex. These were the only three people in the world she'd ever dare tell this story to, and she'd been looking forward to it. Building anticipation, she sipped her beer then put the glass down. "I fired him."

"What?" Rina said, as Suzanne said, "Oh no, what happened?"

Jenny's voice was louder than both of theirs put together. "You're *certifiable*, Annie!"

Ann picked up her glass and drank some more beer, making them wait. She was a litigator; she knew everything there was to know about timing a presentation. Then, trying to keep her face straight, she said, "What happened? Well, he did an assessment and confirmed there was no physiological damage, just aches caused by stress. He massaged my back—oh, and offered me a choice of three scented oils."

"Nice," Rina said appreciatively. "So, what went wrong?"

"Wasn't he good with his hands?" Jenny asked.

"He was *excellent* with his hands. The massage felt great. A bit painful, when he worked out some knots."

Three puzzled, impatient faces stared at her, and she had a hell of a time holding back her smile. "He finished my back. Then he had me turn over and he massaged the front of my shoulders. Then he worked his way down, gave me an orgasm and—"

"What?" three voices screeched.

Ann let the smile burst out. "That's why I fired him."

"Now I know you're insane," Jenny said.

"He made me do it," Ann said.

"He made you *come* and you *fired* him?" Jenny tended to be loud, and tonight her comment seemed to ring through the restaurant.

Ann, you and your friends are embarrassing yourselves in public.

"Sshh," Ann said to both her mother and Jenny. "What I meant was, afterward he made me fire him. So he wouldn't be violating professional ethics."

Suzanne frowned. "A little late for that, if he had sex with you at the spa."

"Define sex," Ann said, realizing her headache had gone and she felt amazing. She sipped her beer contentedly.

Suzanne rolled her eyes. "Oh, please. The only person in the world who can't define sex is Bill Clinton. So I take it, you didn't actually have intercourse. But all the same—"

"Yeah," Jenny broke in, "if he went down on you, you had sex."

"He didn't."

"Then how . . . ?" Rina frowned in puzzlement.

"With his incredible fingers. He massaged me. In all the right places, in all the right ways."

All three of them gaped at her, wearing expressions ranging from stunned to envious. "Oh, man," Jenny sighed reverently. "Pure indulgence, for sure."

Ann gave a satisfied grin. It might not top Suzanne's and Jenny's recent sex stories, but her adventure with Adonis definitely measured up.

"Fingers can be very, very good," Rina said slowly, dreamily.

"You're thinking about that piano player at music school?" Suzanne asked.

Ann remembered how Rina had talked about the best sex in her life. With a pianist who'd made her come with his magical fingers. Three times. Atop a grand piano in a recital room.

The details of a story like that tended to stick with you.

"Giancarlo had the *best* fingers," Rina said.

"I'd put Adonis up against him," Ann teased.

"How're Al's fingers?" Jenny asked Rina.

"Al?" It seemed to take Rina a moment to remember the man she was dating. "Oh, they're fine. I mean, they're normal guy fingers."

"But does he know what to do with them?" Jenny asked. "So many men don't have a clue how to use their fingers." She glanced around the table. "I'm talking pre-Scott, right? For a tough-guy firefighter, the man's pretty good with his hands."

"So's Jaxon," Suzanne said. She winked at Ann. "For a *lawyer*." She turned to Rina. "And Al?"

Rina flushed. "He does okay with my breasts. That's as far as we've got."

Ann remembered Adonis's fingers on her own breasts, and her nipples tightened. Then she remembered how she'd refused to let him stop there, had bared her body and invited his intimate touch. She could feel her cheeks color. Rina'd been dating Al for a couple of months now, and they hadn't gone as far as Ann had with a complete stranger, within an hour of meeting.

"Hey, Annie?" It was Jen.

"What?"

"Don't be embarrassed for being a wild woman."

"A wild woman?" Ann chuckled. "Okay, I'll accept that label and wear it proudly."

"Let's get back to hands," Suzanne said. "Tell us about Adonis's. Let us live vicariously."

Ann didn't have to be asked twice. "I know he's been trained to use his hands, but it's more than that. They're beautiful. Strong, long-fingered. The kind of hands you look at and think, maybe he plays the piano or guitar. And when he went from professional to, uh, intimate with the massage, it was like . . ." Her body shivered deliciously at the memory.

She turned to Rina, as a thought struck her. "Like he really was a musician playing an instrument. One he was very familiar with, that he loved playing."

There was a hush, then Jenny said, "Wow. Super wow."

Ann nodded, and noticed Rina was nodding too, a faraway gleam in her eyes. Romanticizing things, as always. For God's sake, it was just an orgasm.

Suzanne said, "All right, it sounds really sexy, but the fact is, he was breaking the rules. Ann, that's not a good thing."

"No, but you weren't there. The thing is—" She broke off, flushing. "I pretty much begged him. He was turned on, too," she hurried to say, "it wasn't just me. But he wanted to draw a line and I didn't let him. I told him to massage me all over, and to, uh, make me come."

"Go, wild woman," Jenny said approvingly.

Suzanne's lips twitched. "Yeah, the guy wouldn't have been much of a gentleman to refuse a lady in need."

"And I was *so* in need by that point."

"It was special, wasn't it?" Rina asked, looking concerned. "I mean, it's not like he does this with other clients?"

"He said he doesn't. I believe him." *I trust this man's hands, and his word, more than most men I've known for months, even years. How weird is that?*

Ann, don't be a fool. Her mother was scowling. *You can never trust a man.*

Jenny tapped Ann's arm, calling her back. "Okay, then what? He made beautiful music and you sang a big O. And?"

"He had this huge erection but he wouldn't let me do anything about it. It was frustrating, but I respect that he has ethics."

The others nodded. "Unlike David," Suzanne said, "who couldn't be bothered mentioning he was married."

"This is *not* about David." Jenny looked past Ann, waved a hand and mouthed, "Not yet."

"Waiter," she explained. "And no, we're not ordering yet. I want to hear the rest of this. Come on, Ann, tell us about firing him."

"He wants to see me. If we're not therapist and client, then he doesn't have to worry about ethics. So, I fired him, then we made plans." Ann paused, deliberately. "For sex. Sex by any definition—in other words, intercourse."

"You've already hooked up and had *sex*?" Jenny screeched. "Without telling us?"

"Would I do that?" Ann said drily. "And shut up, okay? You don't have to share my sex life with everyone in the restaurant." Thank heavens she was facing the window, not the other diners. "No, we haven't gotten together yet."

"Why not?" Suzanne asked. "I mean, how can you stand waiting?"

"Anticipation?" The truth was, every day's wait made her more anxious. What if, when they saw each other again, that amazing chemistry was gone? She sighed. "Adonis already had plans for the weekend. He and a couple of friends went to Long Beach for a few days. Camping, kayaking, rugged outdoor guy stuff like that."

And I've always gone for the intellectual type. But what a cool contrast—the sensitive, sensual hands and that macho out-doorsy image.

"A few days? Is he on holiday?" Suzanne asked.

"He only works part-time. Three or four days a week." Definitely not ambitious, but why should she care? It wasn't like she was dating the man, just having sex with him. "Anyhow, he gets back tonight, but of course I was booked."

"Glad to know you have your priorities straight," Jenny said. "Despite the lure of sex."

No man ever got in the way of the Foursome's get-togethers.

"And tomorrow night he has a family thing, so we're on for Wednesday," Ann told them. In the meantime, he'd been giving her plenty of orgasms *in absentia*. She could hold off another couple of nights on experiencing the real thing.

Or was she secretly relieved she didn't have to test out that chemistry?

"Anticipation does whet the appetite," Jenny said.

And fuel her anxiety.

"What's wrong?" Suzanne asked. "That frown line's back in your forehead."

"Nerves," Ann confessed quietly. "It's been a while since I've done this. And never with such a gorgeous guy, who has so much sexual confidence. D'you know, he's traveled to India and Thailand? God knows what techniques he's picked up."

"Kama Sutra," Jenny said. When Ann winced she said, "It doesn't have to be intimidating. You could buy a book, study up. You like doing research."

"I don't have time to research *sex*. I shouldn't have to research it."

"Then don't," Suzanne said. "Relax and go with the flow. It's not about performance, it's about having fun."

4

"Everything's about performance," Ann said.

"Why do I get the feeling your mother just entered the room?" Rina asked.

"I thought I knew all about sex," Ann said softly. "I've had a few lovers, done lots of things. Now, I wonder if I'm going to seem naïve and inexperienced."

"You could play young virgin and pretend he's this older, sophisticated, experienced guy," Jenny suggested. "You have a thing for older guys anyhow."

There went Jenny with her fantasies again. "I'm not into being the weak partner in a relationship, even if it's only role play," Ann said. "That's a turnoff for me." She scowled at Jenny. "And just for your information, Adonis is *not* an older guy. I think he's younger than I am."

"Then the relationship's doomed," Jenny joked.

"It's definitely not a *relationship*."

"Just sex with a boy toy," Jenny said slyly. "You cougar, you."

This time she did make Ann smile, and they were all chuckling when the waiter came up. "Are you ready to order *now*?"

"Oops." Suzanne rolled her eyes.

Ann realized they'd been talking for an hour. "Yes, please." All she'd eaten today was a stale doughnut in the coffee room.

"Trust me to order?" Jenny asked. "Scott and I had the most fantastic meal here."

The others, who'd just picked up their menus, put them down again. They all knew each other's tastes. Jenny ordered a meal to share: soup, pad thai, chicken with yellow curry, beef with ginger and veggies.

Then Suzanne asked Ann, "So you have a date with Adonis on Wednesday?"

"Not exactly a date." She didn't have time to date, and with Adonis her priority was clear. "He's coming over to my place for sex."

"Booty call," Jen teased.

"Your place?" Rina asked. "You trust him that much?"

Hmm. Yes, inviting the man into her home—into her body!— meant she believed he was trustworthy. Pretty strange. She wasn't as adamant as her mother about not trusting men, but normally it took her a while. All the same, her instincts were supported by logic. "He's a registered massage therapist and I know where he works."

"And he's not married?" Suzanne asked. "You did check?"

"After David? You bet I asked. He said, 'Good God, no!' like it was the last conceivable thing he'd do."

"Does that bother you?" Suzanne asked.

"Why would it? He's just a . . ." She glanced at Jen, grinned, and finished. "Booty call."

"Wild woman," Jen said approvingly.

"Exactly." Ann grinned at her. "And it's not like I'm thinking about marriage, either."

Suzanne leaned forward. "We've talked about marriage and kids lots of times. You all tease me about my *Leave It To Beaver* notion of home and family. I know Jen and Rina want marriage and kids one day. Right?"

Two dark heads nodded.

Suzanne turned back to Ann. "But you're always quiet."

"I don't view marriage the way you three do," Ann said. "For you, it's about love and support, sharing lives, building a family together."

Rina nodded. "And communication and common values. Finding a way to live that's good for both of you, and your kids."

"And your parents' marriage wasn't like that?" Ann asked cautiously. Rina had said a thing or two to suggest her folks—both now deceased—had had their problems.

"It wasn't horrible." Rina paused as their waiter brought a big bowl of soup and four smaller bowls. "But my mom was a traditional Jew. She'd been raised in a Jewish community with religious rituals, and that's how she wanted to live. With Dad in the Air Force, we lived on bases, moved around. There wasn't a Jewish community to connect to, often not a synagogue nearby. Mom couldn't live the way she wanted to."

"Wasn't your Dad Jewish, too?" Jenny asked, ladling soup for all of them.

"Sure. Mom wouldn't have married outside the faith. But Dad wasn't into the rituals. And they didn't communicate and resolve their problems." She turned to Jenny. "If you and Scott are serious about each other, you have to talk about this kind of thing."

"I know." Jenny grimaced. "With us, it's not religious issues, it's family ones. Especially with my crazy old-country family." She tasted the soup and moaned. "God, this is yummy. It's *tom kah gai*. Chicken with coconut milk, mushrooms, lemongrass, lime leaves, galangal root."

Ann took a cautious sip of the broth. "Chili pepper too. Hot, but great. So tell us, Jenny, how *is* it going with your family, now they know you're dating a white guy?" She spooned up more soup, then reached for her beer to cool her mouth.

"Aagh." Jenny put down her soup spoon. "Everyone's doing a we're-so-disappointed-in-you guilt trip, and giving me the same old reasons why it's a *really bad thing* to date non-Chinese. Much less a man who fights fires rather than working in a nice safe office."

"This is exactly what you were afraid of, isn't it?" Ann said. "That's why you were keeping Scott a secret. So, is it as horrible as you'd expected?"

Jenny wrinkled her nose. "Yes, but no. They're doing all the same stuff they did with my brother when he was engaged to a white girl, but I'm not as susceptible to it."

"How come?" Rina asked.

"Anthony's the oldest kid, only son. There was even more pressure on him." Her eyes narrowed. "I don't mean to dis my family, but they're wrong about this and I'm not letting them rule my life. They think they'll wear me down, but it's not going to happen."

"Good for you," Rina said. "That takes guts, Jen."

"I'll say," Ann said. "It's hard to stand up to your parents." The few times she'd tried it with her mother, it had been like preparing a case to argue in the Supreme Court of Canada. Unsurprisingly, she always lost.

Suzanne, who had a wonderful relationship with her parents, had kept quiet through the conversation. Now she said, "How's Cat doing?"

Jenny's fourteen-year-old sister had been involved in a car accident a couple of weeks ago. She'd suffered a broken arm and cracked ribs.

Jenny gave a rueful smile. "Healing fine. But man, the brat's a real pain in the ass. Can't believe I was so worried about her."

"At least she's a live pain," Ann said, as Rina protested, "You adore your sister." Suzanne came in with, "Of course you were worried."

They all laughed, then Ann said, "And things are still good with you and Scott?"

"We're fighting," Jenny said, not sounding upset.

"Over what?" Ann asked.

"You know I said I'd got the assignment to cover the shoot for the firefighter calendar photos? He doesn't want me doing it."

"Poor baby feels threatened," Ann said. "Tell him it's a pity his male ego is so fragile that he's scared he won't measure up to the competition."

"Good one!" Jenny pointed a finger at Ann. "I'm *so* using that. And, on the subject of articles, check the *Province* on Friday for my story on the importance of learning lifesaving techniques. And the *Georgia Straight* on Thursday for my pole-dance piece. Complete with a photo of Suzie Q." She ladled the rest of the soup into their bowls.

"Congratulations, Jen," Ann said.

"Thanks. And, by the way, don't think I didn't notice."

"Uh, notice what?"

"You jammed out on sharing your feelings about marriage."

"Oh." Ann hadn't done it intentionally. Must be a subconscious avoidance mechanism. She sighed. "In one word, conflicted."

She sipped beer as she reflected. "My mother always said a woman needs a man like a fish needs a bicycle. Yet I can see that the romantic ideal of marriage is appealing. And"—she raised a hand in Suzanne's direction—"I'll say it before you do. Some marriages can be wonderful, like your parents' is. But, seriously, can you see me in that picture? My career's my top priority. Why would I trade a fascinating job for grocery shopping and diapers?"

Jenny rolled her eyes. "Join the modern age. You can work and still have kids. Maybe not be a workaholic though."

"I don't want a mediocre career. Mediocrity is the curse of today's society. People aren't willing to put in the hard work to be the best they can be."

"Sounds like your mom talking again," Suzanne commented.

"She's right about this," Ann said, trying not to sound defensive.

"Well, she built a brilliant career *and* raised a brilliant daughter," Rina pointed out.

"And that's without having a husband," Jenny said. "If your dad had been there, he would have—or damn well should have—shared the work." She shoved aside her empty soup bowl. "Who the hell said the woman has to do all the chores? Look at Scott. He's a great cook, his apartment's neater than my bedroom. Firefighters are so well trained."

"You're right," Ann said. "The people in a relationship *should* share the workload. That's how my mother raised me, it's how things ran in our household. We shared the chores, with me doing whatever I was capable of at my age."

"Just the two of you?" Suzanne asked. "Never any man around?"

Ann shook her head. "Mother was pretty much anti men. She went to university during the early days of feminism, and she bought in."

"Feminism doesn't say you have to hate men," Suzanne said.

"She interpreted it as saying men are the oppressor. The enemy."

Jenny was frowning. "Yeah, but the bra-burner obviously boinked at least one guy."

Ann shrugged. "I don't know the story. She refused to talk about my father. Other than to say he was an asshole." Ann was still curious and resentful that her mother wouldn't tell her the big secret. On the other hand, if her biological father was a serial killer, would she want to know?

Rina frowned. "Even if he ran out on her, did she really let one bad experience sour her against all men? That's pretty immature."

Ann gave a surprised laugh. "God, I'd love to see you say that to her face." How could anyone call her mother—one of the leading intellectual property lawyers in the world—"immature"?

"You don't buy into her interpretation of feminism, though," Rina said. "You've had lovers."

"Older guys," Jenny said quietly.

"Believe me, I am *not* looking to have sex with a father-substitute," Ann said. "Yuck!" She toyed with her beer glass. "No, I like men, but I do stay in control of the relationship." And if she was looking for a father—authority—figure, that wouldn't be the case, would it? Unless subconsciously she wanted to control the father who'd abandoned her . . .

Maybe I need to go and get my head shrunk!

"Ultimately, though," Suzanne said, "you have to open your heart and trust if you're ever going to think about marriage."

When Adonis had massaged her, Ann had thought about how she normally didn't trust a man with her body. Hearts were even more fragile. Could she ever trust a man with hers?

Why should she? Look at David. She'd started to let herself feel attracted, then he'd told her he was married.

The only person you can ever trust is yourself.

Thanks, Mother.

And what Suzanne said was right, too. How could you marry if you didn't open up and trust? So, what all this came down to was, marriage worked for some people and not for others. Would she ever trade control for trust? Not likely.

She realized Jenny and Rina were looking reflective, too, and a little troubled. Ann got the feeling trust came easier to Suze than to the rest of them.

They sat back as a busboy cleared the empty soup bowls and a waiter slid several platters onto their table.

Ann sipped the last drops of beer. Interesting how none of them had used the word "love." Which came first, trust or love? "I need another beer," she told the waiter, and her friends ordered another round, too.

Why was she even thinking about marriage? The only two men in her life were a married lawyer and a . . . booty call, as Jenny referred to Adonis.

"Ann?" She looked up to see Rina studying her. "I thought you were starving."

She saw the others had already started serving themselves, and promptly caught up. "This looks great, Jen."

"What are you going to wear on Wednesday?" Suzanne asked Ann.

She swallowed a mouthful of yellow curry. "I was thinking a teddy and a silk robe. Maybe black lace or semi-sheer? Or should it be something more girlie?" She turned to Jenny. "No, not pink. That's your color, not mine."

Her friend forked up some pad thai. "Black's perfect for you. Sexy, classy."

"Sexy is good, but do I want to go for classy?"

"You don't have a choice," Rina said, her eyes warm with affection. "That's how you look."

Suzanne nodded. "Yeah. You could tart yourself up like a bimbo and you'd still look classy. So milk it for all it's worth. Go with semi-sheer black. You'll knock him off his feet."

Oh sure, like *that* was going to happen. But she loved her girlfriends' support. She tucked eagerly into the meal, glad everything was bite-size and tender. Her jaw barely twinged.

"About your apartment, though," Suzanne said. "I don't mean to offend you, but it could use some work."

"What's wrong with it?" Her one-bedroom condo served her purposes well. She was only there to sleep, or work into the small hours of the morning, anyhow. "I have nice furniture. When I bought the condo two years ago, my real estate agent recommended a place in Yaletown. It was great; I stopped in one day after work and got everything I needed."

"Seriously?" Suzanne asked. "In one trip?"

"I don't have time to shop. It's a waste of billable hours."

They looked at her like she'd grown another head.

"It's not true every woman in the world was born with the shopping gene," she defended herself.

"You buy lingerie," Suzanne pointed out.

"Okay, I have the lingerie-shopping gene. But not the shoe one, the clothes one, or the furniture one."

Rina, nibbling on a piece of broccoli, said, "I *love* shopping for stuff for my house."

"Sure, because you're a nester," Ann said. After a childhood of constant moving, no wonder Rina was so fond of her North Van bungalow. "And of course you want a nice home, you're there so much." Rina taught music out of her house. "But I'm never home."

"You'll be home Wednesday night," Suzanne said. "Maybe you could get a few things to warm the place up? To express your personality?"

"Damn." Now they'd got her feeling insecure about her home.

"Take some time off work and go shopping," Suzanne said.

"And if you want one-stop," Rina chimed in, "go to a place like Pier 1 or Chintz & Company. They have a great collection of stuff from all over the world. Wander through and pick up anything that strikes your fancy."

That almost sounded like fun. Maybe she could figure out how to be spontaneous.

But what would she do once she got the goodies home? She let out a soft moan. "Fine, but how would I know where to put things? I don't have any sense of design."

"Ooh," Rina said, eyes sparkling. "Bet I could find you some help."

Suzanne and Jenny nodded enthusiastically. "Tomorrow night at your place," Jenny said.

Ann laughed. "A home makeover? You three are the best."

"We know it," Jenny said smugly. "But, shit, girl, you're gonna have sex with a Greek god. Gotta make sure the scene's set right."

Adonis was yawning as he walked up the stairs to his second-floor apartment in a renovated old home in Kitsilano. It had been a great few days camping at Long Beach with his two oldest buds, Jagdeep Singh and Mike Brandick. A total guy outdoors thing. Kayaking, windsurfing, then winding down the day drinking beer around a campfire.

The drive back, taking turns at the wheel, was long but comfortable in Jag's Lexus GX 470. Man, talk about a luxury SUV.

Nice to have rich friends, he thought as he unlocked his door. He wasn't jealous, though. Material goods tied you down. To a job, to a city.

Not like him, who had this comfy one-bedroom rental place that came fully furnished. Nice elderly couple downstairs as his landlords, no requirement for a lease.

He'd been here, what was it? Six months? Since he'd come back from Thailand. He dropped his duffel on the floor by the bed. Tomorrow he'd unpack. All he wanted now was to crash and get a good night's sleep.

Ann Montgomery had been costing him sleep. Even after long days of fresh air and strenuous exercise at Long Beach, when he'd rolled into his sleeping bag his mind had come back to her. As his body reminded him, they had unfinished business.

Wednesday night. Her place. An evening of lovemaking.

He slipped a hand inside his old jeans and freed his growing erection, then bent down to remove his bathroom kit from his duffel.

As he walked to the bathroom, he glanced around his bedroom. It was okay, but basic. Good thing Ann had picked her place for Wednesday. Classy lawyer like her, she was probably into *decor*. Women did stuff like that, even the ones who didn't earn much. With what Ann must make, he'd bet her place was the opposite of his.

He started to brush his teeth. Okay, they didn't have much in common. Didn't matter. They had what counted. Instant chemistry. Be fun to see where that took them. He had a month or two before he'd escape the cold and head somewhere sunny for the winter. Belize, maybe. Good diving there.

On his way to bed, he glanced at the photo of his parents on the dresser. His mom was like him; loved the sun, hated winter. You'd think his dad would be that way, too, living on Crete until he met the Canadian hippie who persuaded him to return home with her.

But Dad was all about duty and practicality. A man built a business and a family, and stuck with them.

Adonis would get another lecture when he took off this winter. He'd be disappointing his father again. But that was an old story. It had been that way ever since he was a kid. The last child, the only son after three daughters, he'd been saddled with a load of paternal expectations. And hadn't met even one of them. Crap. Thinking about his dad was always a downer.

Better to think about Ann. Now there was a woman who needed to learn how to lay back and relax. And he was just the guy to teach her.

Adonis rarely got nervous, but that's how he felt Wednesday night as he approached Ann's address. She lived in False Creek, among a collection of upscale town houses and condo buildings.

He'd walked the couple of miles from his place. He didn't own a car, had no reason to.

Her building was a three-story with red brick and cream-colored plaster. Flowers cascaded from balcony planter boxes. A Porsche Boxster drove past. It belonged here. Did he?

He pressed her number. "It's me, Adonis."

When she buzzed him in, he pulled the door open. What should he expect? Last week, there'd been so much heat between the two of them, it had almost scorched him. That's when they'd made this date for sex.

But now, it was days later. Would the heat still be there?

He took the stairs to the third floor and arrived out of breath—not from the climb but from nervous anticipation. At his first tap, the door swung open and . . . "Oh, man!"

She was dressed for sex.

Her figure was showcased by a silky black wrap that gaped at the neck and reached only to the middle of her shapely thighs. The plunging neckline revealed cleavage and the top of her breasts covered in something black and almost sheer. Sheer enough to call attention to, rather than hide, what lay beneath.

Her neck was long and elegant, and there was a flush on her perfect cheekbones. She reached up to pull the neckline of her robe together, and her hand trembled. Her hair was tousled—either deliberately, to look sexy, or because she'd run her fingers through it.

Was she nervous, too, or just ready to rumble? Hard to tell. The only thing he did know was, he was very, very hot for her. "You look incredible," he told her as his cock began to swell.

Her eyes were so bright they almost glittered, but he couldn't read her expression. Was she disappointed, seeing him? Should he have worn something fancier than jeans and a white T-shirt? He didn't own much else. One suit, for family events. But, even though Ann was a lawyer, he sure as hell wasn't into wearing a suit and tie on a date.

"You look, uh, good, too," she responded, her gaze scanning him up and down, settling around his middle. Tracking his growing erection.

She'd let go her grip on the robe and was breathing rapidly, chest rising and falling above that tantalizing neckline. Her shoulders were high and tight, though.

He was usually so good at reading body language, but tonight he couldn't tell what she wanted. He'd like to believe she was aroused, but maybe she was just nervous, off balance. Perhaps having second thoughts.

He had no doubts what he wanted. To kiss her and begin the slow, delicious process of exploring her body with a lover's touch.

She shoved the door open wider and he went through quickly, kicking off his sandals, then walked into the living room and glanced around.

The woman had interested him from the moment he laid eyes on her. Her striking face, beautifully tailored suit, the pain that made her vulnerable, the clipboard she'd used as a defense. He'd sensed she was a complex person.

This room revealed even more about her. The basic furniture was dark wood, simple and almost stark in line, probably expensive. But scattered almost at random there were a few bright, intriguing, personal touches. Vividly striped cushions on the couch, a tapestry that looked Thai hanging on a wall, a couple of balsa-wood giraffes by the gas fireplace.

In a dark corner, a brass bowl with a tangle of bright red poppies that had to be artificial, given the lack of light. But then, on a table closer to the balcony windows, a tall orchid plant with dozens of sunny yellow blossoms. The balcony door was open a crack and the fireplace was burning. So were about a dozen candles, scattered around the room.

The place was an intriguing combination of formal and personal. "Nice. It suits you."

"It does?" She sounded almost surprised.

He stuffed a fist in his pocket to try and mask his growing woody, and turned to face her. She'd closed the front door but was standing near it. "Sure," he said. "Classy, unpredictable. Some fun, warm touches." He glanced toward the balcony door. "Got a view of the water?"

She shook her head, flashed a quick smile. "When I make partner."

Upwardly mobile, like his oldest sister, Andromeda. Andie was a research biologist at the university. He respected that kind of ambition, even if it wasn't his thing. "And when you make partner, you'll have more time off work, to enjoy the view?"

She blinked, seemingly taken aback. "Uh, I'm not sure. Not necessarily."

Then what was the point? It would be rude to ask, so he didn't.

Which left them both standing there, staring at each other. She was clearly stressed, from the tight way she held herself, and he had no clue what she wanted from him.

He glanced past her and noticed the sleek black cat curled up on a chair in the corner. "Hey, you have a cat."

She chuckled, sounding more relaxed. "His name's Tyger. Go say hello." She smirked. "Unless you're allergic."

He wasn't, and he *was* an animal lover. But as he approached the cat, he felt foolish. It was a stuffed animal. All the same, he gave it a stroke before he turned. "Okay, you got me."

"Isn't he a beauty? A friend of mine, a vet student, gave him to me. She says every apartment needs a cat, and she knows I'm not home enough to look after a real one."

Nice to know Ann had friends, that she wasn't a complete workaholic.

He handed her the plastic bag with the bottle of wine he'd bought. The guy at the wine shop had recommended the Australian Shiraz Cabernet. "How's the neck and jaw doing?"

"Coming along, thanks. The stretches help." She opened the bag. "Oh, I love Australian reds." Another smile flashed, then was gone. "Let's open it. I could use something to, uh . . ."

"Relax?" He gave a soft chuckle. "Yeah. Me, too. Hey, feel like a massage?" It probably wouldn't do anything for his own peace of mind, given his last experience with her, but it might help her unwind.

She shook her head. "Thanks, but that's not why you're here." She flushed. "I mean, this isn't, uh . . ." She broke off. "Let's have some wine."

He followed her into the kitchen where she wielded a fancy corkscrew with expertise, rather than handing the bottle to him to open.

When she reached up to take wineglasses from a cupboard, the short robe slid high up the backs of her legs. His mouth went dry and his cock grew harder. "Jesus, Ann."

"What?" Startled, she turned, backing up against the counter, fingers releasing so the glasses started to tumble.

He grabbed for them, caught them before they hit the floor. Straightening, he was right in front of her. Their bodies almost touched.

"Adonis." His name came out on a sigh, almost a whimper. A needy whimper.

Carefully he reached past her, one arm on either side of her body, and shoved the glasses to the back of the counter. Then he rested his hands on the edge of the counter, trapping her between his arms. Her cheeks were still flushed and so were her neck and chest.

He gazed into her eyes, thinking he could spend hours counting the sparkly flecks that dotted her warm hazel irises.

"Oh," she sighed, and her lush mouth captured his attention.

"I've never kissed you," he said. He'd been thinking about that ever since she'd left the spa last week. How could they have been so intimate, yet never kissed? Kissing was one of his favorite things. And she had the most kissable mouth he'd ever seen.

How could he have let her get away without kissing her?

It wasn't going to happen twice.

He leaned forward and tilted his head down to hers. She moved toward him, expression wary yet eager. What a great moment, seeing her face come closer, catching all the glints of gold and green in those pretty eyes. Then focusing in on that full mouth.

He touched his lips to hers in a gentle, barely-there caress, not letting any part of their bodies come into contact except their mouths.

She gave a quick, surprised inhalation that parted her lips a little. Then her breath sighed out. He closed his eyes for a moment and inhaled a blend of aromas more tantalizing than any of the spa's massage oils. Mint on her breath, peach from her skin, coconut from her hair, and under it all the musk of aroused woman.

No, not aroused woman. Nothing that generic. The delicate heat of Ann. He recognized it from last week.

He kissed his way softly across her bottom lip then started on the top one. Oh, man, this kiss had been worth waiting for. Her lips were full, firm, the skin so soft he wanted to lick it. So he did, in little flicks of his tongue. Then he licked the crease between her lips, letting her peppermint breath sigh into his own mouth.

This woman got to him. They hadn't even French-kissed yet, and his body was so hungry for her. If he'd been a few years younger, he would've wanted to rip her clothes off. But now he knew how great it could be to savor the sensations, draw them out, make the lovemaking last as long as he possibly could.

Oh, yeah, he had a woody. But it could wait. This was too damned good to rush.

Seemed Ann had different ideas. She reached out to wrap her arms around him and pull him closer so the fly of his jeans rubbed her belly. Then she opened her mouth and boldly thrust her tongue between his lips.

He groaned at her sweet invasion. Then he eased back and put his hands on her shoulders. "Hey, slow down."

Her eyes narrowed and that frown line appeared in her forehead. "What? Why?"

"Because sex is better if it's slower."

She studied him a moment longer, then twisted out of his grip and turned to face the counter. "We forgot about the wine."

He didn't give a shit about the wine, all he wanted was to kiss her some more. But it seemed they were on different wavelengths.

5

Ann tried to steady her breathing enough so she could pick up the wine bottle and pour. What was going on with this guy? His erection told her he wanted her, but just like last Thursday, he was pulling back. Last week he'd cited professional ethics and she'd understood. But now? They'd booked an appointment for sex, but he hadn't touched her when he walked in. Then, when things finally heated up, he cooled them down.

He wants to go slower? No man in his right mind wants to go slower.

Damn. When he'd come in she'd been uncertain, turned on but too embarrassed to be bold. It had been such a relief when he'd taken the initiative and kissed her. But now, here she was all wound up, and he'd pulled back.

Wasn't she sexy enough for him?

She turned back and handed Adonis a glass, darting a glance down to verify the erection she'd felt. Yup, a raging hard-on. *It* seemed to think she was sexy enough.

"You want to slow down?" she said. "Fine, let's sit down, drink some wine, have a chat."

"Uh, okay." He took it from her with a baffled expression.

Well, good, that makes two of us who don't know what the hell's going on here.

If nothing else, she'd got him off balance. It was kind of a fun feeling.

Hot monkey sex would be more fun.

Yes, but she was with a guy who didn't show any signs of delivering it.

The only way to deal with a problem is to confront it.

Yeah, thanks Mother. And would you butt out of my freaking sex life?

Still, her mother was right. So, when Ann and Adonis were seated side by side on the couch, she said, "Okay, what's with this *slow* thing? You're aroused, I'm aroused, why should we go slow?"

"Do you know anything about tantric sex?"

Damn, a pop quiz—and no one told me which lesson to study.

"Tantric sex?" *Was that Asian?* "No, I don't."

"It's slow and sensuous, you can ride peaks and valleys for hours. Gaze into each other's eyes until you lose track of everything else. Connect your breathing and your sexual energy."

What a load of crap! "Oh?" she said, trying to sound polite.

"Whatever sex you've had, it's nothing compared to tantric."

She could barely stop from rolling her eyes. He was just a macho know-it-all, albeit one who was into some New Age touchy-feely stuff. Why was it every man in the world figured he knew how to make a woman come? In truth, most of them were hopeless. The woman had to control the situation if she wanted satisfaction. At least that's how it worked for Ann.

Even at Pure Indulgence. It had been his hands that made her come, but she'd been in charge. Under the influence of meds, scented oil, a Greek god's massage, perhaps, but still in control of the situation.

She lifted her glass. The first taste of wine was so good, she took a healthy slug.

For her, orgasm didn't come easily. She had to be in the right mood, the angle and pressure had to be perfect, the guy couldn't have bad breath or make weird sounds.

She'd been in the right mood tonight, when she started to kiss Adonis. Didn't the idiot know that? Why had he gone and spoiled it?

Because he wanted to be in charge.

Men always have to be in charge. It goes along with having a penis.

Yeah, Mother, you're probably right about this guy.

Ann was halfway tempted to boot him out the door. But if she did, she'd have to confess to her friends.

They'd be sympathetic. But Jen would tease, Rina'd say she should have let Adonis use his magic fingers, Suze would boast that Jaxon never spoiled the mood. And then there was one indisputable fact: she'd never seen Adonis's package, and she was curious. Very, very curious.

The bottom line was, she'd been revved up and ready to go, and she could easily be horny again. Especially with a guy who looked like a Greek god. But only if she had control.

She realized she'd been sipping wine as she analyzed the situation. Now her glass was empty, so she refilled it. Adonis had barely touched his own wine.

"What's wrong?" he asked, his expression concerned. "Did I do something wrong?"

She sighed. "Adonis, I'm sure tantric sex is great." Again she suppressed an eye-roll. "And slow kisses can be great. But this time, if you're, uh, still into it, can we do it my way?"

"Your way?" He looked wary.

Oh great, he thinks I'm going to handcuff him and bring out a whip!

She choked back a giggle as he said, "What's your way?"

"Don't worry, nothing weird. I want—" She broke off. "Look, I only have two hours and we've already wasted twenty minutes."

"Two hours?" He shook his head. "You're going somewhere after this?"

"No, but I have to work."

Head tilted to one side, he studied her. "You managed to clear your schedule for two hours of sex. With me."

Booty call. Jen's teasing voice echoed in her head.

Ann dragged a hand through her hair. "I'm sorry, that sounds insulting. Damn, this is going all wrong! Last week we were so hot for each other, I thought we'd pick up where we left off. Wild, fast sex. I'd been imagining it for days. I was all keyed up."

He was watching her like he couldn't figure her out.

She hurried on. "When you came in, I was nervous, not sure things would work out. Then you kissed me, and wow, it was great, I was really hot. But now I've lost the mood." She gave her head an impatient shake. "*We've* lost the mood. I probably killed the damned mood. This was a mistake. I should've known it would never work." She took a gulp of wine.

Adonis sipped some wine, still studying her. Then he began to smile and that sexy dimple flashed. "Okay, I see where you were coming from. And I'm going on record that scheduling sex is nuts. But, if you gotta do it, next time mark down at least six hours."

Six hours? You want to have sex with me for six hours?

"So, we have a choice," he went on. "Write the whole thing off as a mistake." The dimple winked again. "But that'd be a waste of an hour and forty—no, thirty-five—minutes."

The man really was irresistible. Her lips twitched. "I hate to waste time."

"Yeah, I got that. So, let's get on with it." He leaned forward. "What puts you in the mood, Ann?" His voice was soft, seductive.

"Wine helps." She gave him a wry grin and lifted her glass. Her biggest problem was performance anxiety. Worrying about being the perfect lover got her so stressed it was hard to feel sexy. A self-defeating cycle, she knew, but alcohol helped.

Still, how could she not be anxious with Adonis? Look at him, sprawled on her couch—firm thighs and impressive package curving his worn jeans, muscles shifting and flexing under his T-shirt, tanned forearms, and beautiful hands—he made her whole body throb with desire. Definitely out of her league.

And yet . . . He *was* here with her, and he did want to have sex with her. So it was time to get over her insecurities, take control, and get with the program.

What would most get them both back in a sexy mood? She closed her eyes for a moment, a picture formed behind her lids, and she began to smile. "I want your clothes off," she said, eyes still shut. Ever since she'd met him, she'd wanted to see him naked.

"I want to see your body," she went on, rushing to get the words out before she chickened out. It was one thing to be in control, and quite another to express sexual need. That's where her inhibitions really came into play. Maybe she needed more wine. No, she could do this.

"I want to touch you, watch you respond to me. I want to make you hard, and I want to have sex with you." She finished in a rush, then dared to ease her eyes open.

His smile was sexy and knowing. "Gee, I dunno. Sounds like a lot of self-sacrifice on my part."

His comment, his smile, relaxed her enough to chuckle. "I'm guessing you'll survive."

"I'm guessing I will." He gave her a smoldering look that

sent heat racing through her, all the way to her pussy, which, she realized, was already wet.

"Okay, Ann, consider me your slave." His voice was husky. "Tell me what to do."

Slave? Her own personal sex slave? When Jenny had told the Foursome that she and Scott were enacting each other's fantasies, the first fantasy that had come to Ann's mind was a sex slave. And now Adonis was offering her what she'd dreamed of. She squeezed her legs together against the throbbing pulse of need between them.

She knew just the right setting for her slave. Thanks to a little help from her friends. "Let's take the wine and some candles into the bedroom."

He rose, all grace and power. "Your wish is my command."

Oh yeah, she could definitely get into this.

She stood too, nowhere near as smoothly. "Bring the wine." As she turned to walk away, she let the robe slide off one shoulder—a hint of things to come—then flicked it back up. She gathered a few candles from the mantle and headed for her bedroom, knowing he'd follow.

The cherry-colored wooden bedroom set had been purchased during her original one-stop shopping. Tonight she'd put gold-colored sheets on the bed. They matched the silky spread and throw pillows she'd picked up at Pier 1, in rich shades of ruby, gold, and moss green. The scarlet bowl and brass elephant on her dresser came from Pier 1, too. But the perfect touch had been provided by mischievous Jen, who'd presented her with a set of Kama Sutra pictures for her wall.

Despite the desk in the corner, the bedroom looked sexy, kind of Asian. A little decadent. Not like the room of a workaholic lawyer, which it had looked like up until last night.

Very aware of Adonis, so large and male, leaning against the doorframe watching her, she set the candles on the dresser.

Turning to her miniature entertainment unit, she slipped in the CD Rina had bought for her. Diana Krall's *Love Scenes*. Trust Rina to pick something romantic, but then Krall probably didn't have a CD called *Sex Scenes*. They'd listened to the music last night while decorating her apartment, and she had to admit the gentle jazz, the drifty voice, were plenty sexy and seductive.

Okay, the scene was set. Now she just needed to unveil the centerpiece. She turned to face Adonis.

When she loosened the tie of her robe so the sides parted, revealing her semi-sheer teddy and the body underneath it, his gaze dropped and he sucked in a breath.

"Is it permitted for the slave to tell his mistress she looks fantastic?"

She laughed, loving how he'd got into the mood. "The slave has my permission to give compliments." She snapped her fingers. "My wine."

He strolled over, pure male animal, an admiring heat in his eyes and an appreciative bulge behind his fly.

When he handed her the glass she took a drink. Liquid courage. The courage to ask for what she wanted.

"Come here." She beckoned him closer.

He put the other glass on the dresser and stepped near, until the fronts of their bodies almost touched. Was she imagining it, or could she feel the heat coming off him?

She wanted to plaster her body up against him. Almost moaned with need. But she managed to stay in the role she'd chosen. "Now kiss me," she commanded. "And none of this slow stuff. Kiss me like you mean it, like you can't get enough of me."

His eyes glinted with humor. "I can manage that."

Before she could draw a breath, his hands were on her shoulders, gripping tight, pulling her up toward him. His mouth was on hers. Not teasing and caressing this time, but forceful. His tongue stroked the crease between her lips, inflaming her, and she opened to welcome him in.

Now *this* was a kiss! Heady, passionate, demanding. As she answered back, heat flamed through her body and in an instant she was as aroused as she'd been earlier. No, more aroused. Just like she'd been on that massage table. She thrust her tongue against his, forcing it back into his mouth and following. He tasted like wine, and his kiss broke through her inhibitions even more effectively than alcohol.

Her hips ground against him, seeking out and enjoying every inch of that growing erection. Since she'd first seen him tonight, she'd thought how great he looked in jeans, with his long legs, firm butt, tantalizing package.

But right now, he'd look better out of jeans. And out of his T-shirt.

She pulled back from the kiss and reached between them, fumbling to pull his T-shirt out of his jeans. Then she changed her mind. She wanted to watch. "Take your shirt off."

He yanked it free and pulled it over his head. Not making a production of it; just a guy taking off his shirt.

But the body that was revealed when he tossed that shirt aside was no normal guy's. He was as sculpted as Ann had guessed, and his skin was bronzed with tan. His chest hair was perfect—not sparse but not a hairy mat—and it, too, was sun-glazed, gleaming in the candlelight.

Her breath came fast and shallow, shuddering through her chest, and her nipples were tight and achy. Craving contact. But his chest wasn't enough. She wanted all of him.

"Jeans," she commanded.

"Glad to." His voice was rough, his cheeks flushed. His fingers made quick work of the buckle, then he slid the zipper down and hooked his thumbs into the waist of his jeans.

Anticipation made Ann's mouth dry and her pussy wet.

He shoved his jeans down, revealing navy cotton boxers riding low on lean hips. His cock lifted the waistband away from his skin. He bent to step out of his jeans, then straightened. "More?"

"I want you naked."

"And you?"

Last week he'd seen her nude body, but she felt self-conscious in the presence of such male beauty. Tonight, she was mistress. If she felt more comfortable with her clothes on, she'd leave them on. "Just the robe, for a start." To tease him, she said, "You may take it off me."

He reached out with both hands and let his fingers brush the silk at her shoulders. Then he slid them onto her bare skin in a caress that made her shiver with pleasure. Gently he eased the sides of the robe off her shoulders, fingertips drifting lightly across her skin.

When the robe fell free and slid to the floor, he didn't lift his hands, but continued to caress her upper arms. "Beautiful." He was studying her body and when his gaze lifted to her face, it was intense.

She realized that, ever so subtly, he was drawing her closer. Her flimsily clad stomach brushed against him and she felt the rigid heat beneath his boxers.

Oh yeah, she wanted him. Her sex ached with it.

But she stepped away, taking back control. "Take off your shorts."

He peeled them down and his cock sprang free. It looked so delicious; her mouth pooled with saliva and her pussy flooded. Both of them wanted him inside her.

His skin was paler, his pubic hair thicker, curlier, darker than the hair on his chest. But she barely noticed those details, she was so focused on that long, thick shaft that promised pure pleasure. From the bulging sac at its base, up the thick column ridged with veins, to the proud velvety crown.

She touched him. Couldn't resist wrapping her hand around that pulsing heat. His body tensed, then it was like he forced himself to relax before he said, "That feels good. It's all yours. Take what you want."

What she wanted was orgasm. One for her, one for him. Tonight, he had no reason to hold back, and she was a sexy enough woman to make him come.

"Pull down the covers then lie on the bed, on your back," she told him.

He obeyed and she stood by the bed for a moment, feasting her eyes. His hair and skin went perfectly with her sheets, like she'd picked the man and the bedding to match. He'd stacked his hands behind his head, stretching his already taut torso. His legs were spread in a V that drew her gaze to where they met. Not that the jutting cock didn't do that by itself, rising up his belly.

"Ann?" he said softly. "Tell me what you want."

I want to suck your luscious cock.

Nope, no way she was saying that out loud. He might like it if she talked dirty, but she was too damned inhibited.

She had no trouble with action, though. And she'd pretty much bet he'd get the message.

Ann kneeled on the bed beside him and took his rigid penis in both hands. Then she curled down to lick across the head, a few soft, moist strokes. Mmm, he tasted good, smelled good, made her senses hum with appreciation.

She opened her mouth and slid her lips lower, as far down his shaft as she could go.

Ouch. Her jaw was feeling a lot better but his cock was formidable. She eased back so she wasn't putting so much strain on her jaw. *My dentist would kill me if she saw me now.*

She swirled her tongue around the head of his cock, sucked, moved her lips lower, felt her own body respond just as if he'd touched her. And, speaking of touch . . . She adjusted position so she was kneeling on either side of one of his legs. When she lowered herself, he must have read her mind because he brought his leg up so she could catch it between her thighs. Ride it. Press her damp crotch tight against it. The light fabric of her teddy was the only thing between them, and it added a tantalizing friction.

She loved how he responded to her mouth, letting out sighs of pleasure, going at her pace, rather than trying to force his cock farther in.

"Oh yeah, Ann," he murmured. "That feels so good, the way you suck me."

If felt just fine to her, too. She knew she gave good head, and she loved doing it. Loved the feeling of power. Loved the way her pussy responded, anticipating feeling that strong cock inside her. Fellatio was one of the best ways of bringing herself close to the edge, close enough that climax was almost guaranteed once the man finally entered her.

Just thinking about his perfect cock plunging deep made her moan and rub herself shamelessly against his leg.

She might not be able to take him deeply in her mouth, but she had other tricks in her arsenal to reward and entice her considerate lover. With her lips and tongue she tasted her way around and down his shaft, teasing his balls gently with her fingers as she did.

"Oh, God, yes." He laced his own fingers through her hair, caressing her head but not guiding it.

She sucked one of his balls ever so softly into her mouth and his breath shuddered. She did the same with the other, then worked back up his shaft. Once she reached the head, she wrapped her lips around him and flicked her tongue against that sensitive spot on the underside.

By now any normal man would be close to orgasm, getting

impatient, wanting to throw her onto her back and take control. She knew the signs: balls tightening, breath coming harsh and fast, thrusts becoming uncoordinated. But none of that was happening with Adonis. In fact, his breathing seemed almost measured, like he was deliberately taking deep breaths.

Of course. To calm himself down. That was another thing guys did. Along with all that crazy stuff like running baseball scores in their heads. They were scared of coming too early.

Damned unfair that orgasm came so easily for some people that they had to fight to hold it off. For her the battle went the other way. It took a lot of concentrated effort to build to that peak, hold onto the edge, then tip over into ecstasy.

Edge? What edge? While she'd been busy analyzing, her body had cooled off.

"Ann? You still with me? My turn to eat your sweet pussy?"

Now there was a tempting offer. But this time, she wanted to control the sex. To show him she could be a great lover, give him that orgasm he'd missed out on before.

"Just figuring out what to do to you next, slave," she murmured seductively, then applied her lips to his cock with fresh vigor. *Note to self: Turn brain OFF.*

She concentrated on sensation, the taste and fullness of him in her mouth, the pressure against her clit through the silk of her teddy as she squirmed against his leg. Arousal built again.

She gave his cock a couple of final tongue-flicks across the tip, then crawled up his body so she was sitting across his groin. His erection was under her now and the stimulation against her crotch was even better than from his leg.

In fact, if she slid back and forth so her clit got the pressure it craved, chances were she'd come. But, no, she felt too vulnerable when that happened when the guy lay there watching her.

She glanced at Adonis's face, to gauge his arousal. Saw tousled hair, flushed cheeks. He was staring at her chest. She glanced down to see her breasts clearly visible through the teddy, her nipples pink and hard, begging for attention.

"May I touch?" he asked.

Ah, good. He remembered she was still mistress. A shudder of desire ran through her. "You may." She managed an imperious tone, even though she wanted to whimper, "Please, please, please."

Using his whole hand, he cupped her breast, then stroked around the outside, circling until he'd reached the center. By now her nipple was so tight and hungry, it almost hurt.

At last he touched it, and Ann sighed with a combination of relief and pleasure.

Each gentle squeeze of thumb and forefinger sent sensation throbbing through her sex. Now he was using both hands, caressing and teasing both breasts until she couldn't take it any more. She was *so* ready to have that gorgeous hard-on inside her.

He had a rigid, throbbing cock; she had a wet, aching pussy. And yet the crazy man seemed so fascinated with her breasts he could play with them all night.

Time to take charge again. Reaching between them she unsnapped the crotch of her teddy. Maybe she couldn't come right out and say, *Fuck me*, but she could make her wishes clear. "There's a condom on the bedside table."

"You want . . ." One glance at her face—which no doubt conveyed her frustration—and he said, "Sure, okay." He found the package and held it toward her. "You or me?"

"I'll do it." She liked smoothing protection over a man. Applying a barrier to reassure her that, no matter how intimate the sex might seem, their bodies weren't merging completely.

For her, sex was about orgasm. Nothing more than that. She wasn't a romantic like her girlfriends, looking for emotional connection with a life mate. No, she was a self-sufficient, independent woman with physical needs that deserved to be satisfied.

When she'd sheathed him, she slid her slick pussy back and forth across him a few times, building her arousal again. Then she raised herself on her knees until she could straighten his cock and touch the tip to her opening.

With the other hand, she spread herself so he could slide inside. She'd never felt so stretched, so filled, and the sensation was almost painful. But then her muscles relaxed, her pussy flooded in welcome, and he slid deeper.

When he was all the way in, she sat there, looking down, appreciating everything about the moment. Her body, covered by semi-sheer black fabric, looked mysterious and sexy in the flickering glow of candlelight. And Adonis, spread out beneath her, was as beautiful as she'd ever imagined a man could be.

He smiled up at her. "You feel as good as you look, Ann."

If she did, how could he manage to hold still? She couldn't, not for long. His rigid cock was embedded in her, deeper than she'd ever felt, and her body was taut with sexual tension. She tightened around him, ground down against his pelvis, heightening the sensation.

She expected him to thrust up, but he didn't. She was still in charge of this gorgeous man's body and their sexual satisfaction.

Oh, crap. I give head like a hot damn, but when it comes to intercourse . . . The truth was, she never felt completely in tune with her own body, much less the man's.

"Hey," Adonis said softly. "Everything okay?" His fingers tweaked her nipple, sending a jolt of sensation straight to where their bodies joined.

She clenched involuntarily. "Yeah. Very okay." Then she began to move. Gliding up his cock, to the very top. It felt good, but what she really wanted, needed, was when she slid down and touched base, ground into him. Put pressure on her clit.

Concentrating, trying to read her body's signals, she slid up, ground down again. Reaching for those tantalizing sensations, feeling the tension climbing each time she pressed against him.

Oh, yes. God, she was close. She wanted so badly to come but was scared she wouldn't. It just took one thing—the guy making a weird sound, him moving too slow, sometimes it was just a shift in her body—and she'd lose the edge, never be able to get it back.

Damn! Didn't I say, shut off my brain and stop analyzing?

It had slipped away again. But she wasn't giving up. Adonis was so sexy, maybe she could get it back. She slowed down, started again, and thank God he followed her lead. He even said, "Man, that's good."

She reached for what she'd been feeling, slowly felt it build again. Increased the pace until she was there, so close. If she touched her clit, squeezed it just right, she'd come. But she didn't want to do it front of Adonis. It seemed too needy.

"Beautiful woman," he murmured. "Sexy lover."

Yeah, okay, nice words, but shouldn't we be climaxing now? Do I have to do everything?

The other thing that sometimes worked was for the guy to come himself. Those final deep, almost wrenching thrusts sometimes brought her along with him. Besides, she *had* to make Adonis come, she already owed him one.

But he still seemed content to follow her movements, rather than plunge toward orgasm.

What's wrong with me? Why isn't he as turned on as I am?

She liked it when two people climaxed together. Once she'd come herself, it was hard to fake the enthusiasm necessary to get the guy off. And she had to make her partner come, or she'd feel like an inadequate lover.

She was *so* not giving up on this night. "Adonis," she said desperately, "I want to come. I want *us* to come."

He looked confused. "But we've only got started."

What the hell was he talking about? "You're my slave and I want orgasms." The words grated out through her clenched teeth. "One for me, one for you. *Now*."

"You . . . Okay, I get it."

She slid faster up and down on his cock, ground herself into him almost desperately, and now, finally, he was thrusting the way she needed, driving himself hard into her. His cock rubbed her supersensitive clit and excitement spiraled up again. She reached back to touch his balls. Felt them draw up, heard his breathing rasp. Yes!

Please, please, let me come when he does.

Then his fingers were on her clit, giving her exactly what she needed. Gentle pressure, a stroke, a squeeze.

"Oh, yes!" Exquisite sensation poured through her. Waves of pleasure, of release. Pure physical joy.

She'd barely stopped coming when Adonis thrust even harder and faster and—God, she couldn't believe it—her body tightened again. Climbing that peak of tension toward climax.

His fingers were on her clit again, or had they ever left? And his cock was rocking against her womb and everything inside came apart again as he thrust one final time and they both cried out in release.

As usual, Ann got to work before seven, double espresso in hand.

What wasn't usual was the toasted bagel—okay, maybe she *had* listened when Adonis talked about regular meals—and the fact that she felt amazing.

Terrific sex, and a promise of more on Saturday night. She'd got in a couple of hours of productive work after Adonis left, and then a few hours of sound, satisfied sleep. A perfect night.

As she walked down the hall to her office, she became aware of a strange sound. *Oh my God, am I actually humming?*

"Ann!" a man's voice called behind her.

David. She cut off the hum and turned, smiling brightly. "Hi. Let me put my briefcase down and I'm all set to get started."

He was his usual perfectly groomed self, handsome in that craggy way she found so appealing, but in the afterglow of sex with Adonis it was easier to suppress the usual zing of sexual awareness. Hmm, he seemed stressed, or maybe tired, today. The lines around his eyes and mouth made him look his age, which was almost forty. "Are you all right?"

"I need to talk to you." He sounded grim.

Her cheerful mood disappeared. *Damn. Did I screw something up on our case?*

Ann, you have to double-check everything. There was her mother, frowning. *You know you're not naturally brilliant, and that means you have to work harder.*

"I do!"

"What?" David was staring at her.

Crap. Said it out loud. Not the way to impress him. "I mean—" She thought quickly. "I *do* have time right now. Come on in." She gestured him into her office and he closed the door. When he took one of the guest chairs, she sat in the other rather than going behind her desk.

"What is it?" She popped the plastic top on her takeout coffee container and took a sip, fortifying herself against whatever he had to say.

"I noticed you left early the last three nights." Then he frowned. "Well, not *early*, but early for you."

Damn, she'd thought she was up to date on their work. "I'm sorry. I'll work extra-late tonight if we're getting behind."

"No, that's not—" He broke off. "I'm not saying this right."

Was he dumping her from the case? Didn't he want her on the Healthy Life Clinic file anymore? Quickly she said, "Working on this case means a lot to me. The Charter issues are fascinating. David, what's the problem? I'll fix it, I'll work harder."

He rubbed gray eyes that were already bloodshot. "When you came in this morning, you were humming."

Humming was a crime now? Okay, this was getting ridiculous.

"And when you left last night," he went on, "and the couple of nights before, you looked excited. Like you were anticipating something great."

Evenings with the Foursome, sex with Adonis. "I guess I was." She shook her head, annoyance warring with anxiety. "I'm not following. What does this have to do with my work?"

"Damn it, Ann!" He glared at her. "It's not about the fucking case."

Wow. In the month or so she'd known him, she'd never heard him say the F-word. "Then, what is it about?" she asked cautiously.

"You're seeing someone."

Slowly his meaning sank in.

Holy shit, the man's jealous! The thought was intoxicating. Inappropriately so, but all the same, the feeling was heady.

"I, uh . . ." Seeing? She could have repeated the F-word back to him, because that's exactly what she and Adonis were doing. But that would have been crude. And mean.

She could just imagine Jenny saying, "Go for it, girl, exercise your female power."

No, she wasn't that petty. She nodded cautiously. "Yes, I am."

His gaze was . . . there was only one word for it. Tortured.

Well, hot damn. The married guy's jealous because I, the person who's supposed to only be a coworker, am seeing another man.

How cool was that? Jenny'd be saying, "Tough shit, buddy. You snooze, you lose."

No, that was unfair. Ann understood David's confusion about his marriage, his reasons for not telling her when they'd first met and started to be attracted to each other. She'd suffered enough emotional trauma over him, she could sympathize with him now.

The guy looks pretty sexy when he's tortured.

No, I am not *going to jump him.* Even if that zing of sexual heat was back, and making her blood fizz.

6

"You know we agreed there couldn't be anything between us," Ann reminded them both.

"I know. But I didn't think you'd start seeing someone else." David scrubbed his hands across his temples.

"What *did* you think?" she asked, a little sharply. *That I'd get all angsty and stay celibate? Typical self-centered male.*

Well, if she hadn't gone for a massage and met Adonis, that's precisely what she would be doing. Thank God for Adonis, giving her a lovely distraction and a better sense of perspective on her relationship with David.

Pity she still found the married lawyer attractive, though. Pity he was so damned intellectually fascinating. Pity that—but for him being married and a senior partner at her firm—he'd be her perfect man.

Damn. Maybe another evening or two with Adonis would cure her.

David lifted his head, raked his hand through crisply cut dark curls and stared at her. "What if I left her?"

"L-left? Left your wife?" He'd never suggested this before.

Yes, he'd said their marriage was rocky, but he'd never said he might leave.

David grabbed her hands in a hot, hard grip. "I can't look at you without wanting you. You're so smart and incisive, it's a joy talking to you. You're beautiful and so sexy I want to rip that business suit off that lovely body."

Then he was out of his chair, pulling her up and into his arms. Kissing her. Fiercely, hungrily.

She was so stunned she couldn't respond. His lips were hard, almost too hard, his tongue demanding. She'd yearned for his kiss since she'd met him, but now he was so far ahead of her she couldn't catch up.

Through their clothes, her sex made contact with his hardening erection and began to throb, urging her on.

Her brain answered back. *No! He's still married, damn it. I don't believe in this.*

She wrenched herself away. "David, stop. We can't do this."

His breath came out in harsh pants and he looked disheveled for the first time since she'd met him. "I want you, Ann. I need you."

"I need . . . time to think." Her heart was racing and she felt like she might hyperventilate. "This is, uh, unexpected. I never . . ." She shook her head helplessly.

"I'm sorry. But it's been driving me crazy, thinking of you with someone else." He reached for her hands again, but she took a quick step backward, stumbled, and banged her hip against the corner of her desk before taking refuge behind it.

He stood on the other side, both hands on the desk, leaning toward her. "You're attracted to me, you told me so."

It took all her willpower not to lean toward him, too. She stared into his troubled gray eyes, yearned to smooth the frown line from his forehead. Her body urged her to try out that kiss again, now she was ready for it.

Yes, she was attracted. But she'd also told him she didn't want to come between him and his wife, and that was true, too.

"David, I said I have to think."

"How long?"

"I don't know! As long as it takes. And I've got work to do. This isn't the time and place for this." How dare he do this, after they'd decided they couldn't have a relationship? She'd tried to adjust her thinking, turn over her new leaf, and now he was messing her up all over again. "Go away and . . . let me work," she finished lamely.

He walked to the door, then turned, straightening his jacket and tie. "Just say the word and I'll phone her."

When he walked out, Ann's legs were shaking so badly she collapsed into her leather desk chair. She stared blindly at her computer screen, the stacks of files on her desk. Everything was the same, yet everything had changed. Or, it could, if she said yes to David.

Ann, stop dithering. You know exactly what you have to do. It was her mother, and yes, she did know what Meredith meant. *Concentrate on work. Don't ever let your personal life get in the way of your career.*

What Meredith really meant was, don't *have* a personal life.

But Ann did. And, while her mother would have no sympathy for her current plight, Ann knew who would.

She grabbed her BlackBerry from her briefcase and began a text message. Help! Need emerg 4sum lunch. 2day. 12 @ Las Marg?

It was the first time she'd initiated an emergency lunch. Before, she'd had to rearrange her schedule for her friends' crises. She'd always been the tiniest bit jealous they had such exciting lives, and now she realized how stupid she'd been. She felt like shit.

Physically, too. Her jaw was aching something fierce, and she realized she'd been grinding her teeth. Damn David.

She swallowed a muscle relaxant, sat back in her chair, and took a deep breath. Okay. A few hours, and she could call on the combined wisdom of the Awesome Foursome.

She pulled the Healthy Life Clinic papers out of her briefcase. As she started reading, one hand reached automatically for her coffee. It encountered something else instead. She looked up. Oh, right, the bagel. She took a small bite, chewing gingerly.

Funny how her jaw hadn't hurt last night, after the workout she'd given it with Adonis's scrumptious cock. She nibbled again, and wondered what David's cock was like.

Concentrating on work didn't seem to be in the cards this morning, but she had to try. Especially since she was taking off at lunchtime.

Ann had always had an open-door policy, wanting to be available any time a senior lawyer might need her. Now she looked up nervously every time someone walked by, scared it would be David. Each time the phone rang she jumped, then checked the call display before answering. Finally she gave up, tossed a couple of files in her briefcase, and drove to Las Margaritas, timing her arrival for eleven-thirty, when it opened.

Although she rarely drank on a workday, she ordered a margarita. Eating breakfast came in handy if you were going to start drinking before lunchtime.

Ann, I'm shocked by your behavior.

Tough shit, Mother. You'd be even more shocked if you knew why I was drinking. Gee, what would Meredith Montgomery's response be if she knew her daughter was considering asking a married colleague to leave his wife?

Career-limiting move.

Yeah. Her mother wouldn't worry about Ann's emotions, only the impact on her career. Thank God for the Foursome.

And for tequila. Ann sipped the margarita gratefully. Despite the bagel, the alcohol carried a punch. That, and being away from the office where she might run into David, helped her relax. She pulled out a file and was so immersed she didn't see Jenny until her friend wrapped an arm around her shoulders.

"Hey, Annie, what's up? You okay? Was it a disaster with Adonis? He didn't do anything bad, did he?"

Damn David, anyhow. She'd come into work so mellow after great sex, and he'd ruined her day. "No, definitely not." Remembering made her smile. "It was the opposite of a disaster." She picked up her margarita and took a sip.

Jenny swung into the seat across from her. She was all business in a slim-fitting white shirt over black pants. Not a touch of her trademark pink. No, wait, her earrings had coral beads.

"Lemme guess," Jenny said. "You've fallen for the god and want to marry him and have his babies."

Ann hadn't believed she could laugh, but now she almost spluttered tequila across the table. When she recovered, she said, "Somehow I don't think that's in the cards. Mind you, they'd be beautiful babies if they took after him."

"They'd be beautiful if they took after you, too," Jenny said. "Can't understand why you don't realize how great-looking you are. You're almost as bad as Rina."

"Did I hear my name?" Rina, wearing a burgundy fringed shawl over a loose black top and long skirt, sank into the chair beside Ann. "What am I bad at?"

"Nothing," Ann said. "You're a great musician, a terrific friend and a beautiful woman."

Rina turned to Jenny. "What am I bad at? Ann's obviously not going to tell."

Jen shrugged. "Just, I wish the two of you would see how fantastically beautiful you are."

"Ann may be," Rina said gloomily, "but I'd be beautiful only in some primitive culture that worships fertility goddesses."

Ann exchanged glances with Jenny and, with the tiniest of headshakes, they agreed to drop the subject.

Rina put her hand on Ann's arm. "Can't believe I'm being so selfish. Are you all right? You've never called an emergency lunch before."

"I need advice."

"Then you've come to the right place." It was Suzanne's voice, as she moved past Ann to take the seat beside Jenny. She was in jeans and a long-sleeved tee, her wavy blond hair pulled back in a braid. "We have *loads* of advice. What's up? What did the Greek god do?"

Poor Adonis, now she'd made everyone think he was the root of her troubles. "Nothing bad. Unless you count wanting to kiss forever rather than get down to having sex."

"Not sure about *forever*, but I have nothing against kissing," Jenny said.

"He could kiss me forever and we could have intercourse at the same time," Rina said dreamily. Then, quickly, "I mean, not Adonis and me. Just, in theory, some guy and me."

A waitress in a red T-shirt came over. Jenny ordered a margarita, "Because no one should drink alone," and the others went with sodas.

Ann said, "And a platter of nachos locos," their traditional Las Margaritas meal.

When the waitress had gone, Ann turned to the others. "It's not Adonis. He was great. There was the usual awkwardness of two new people getting together, but it worked out just fine." At the thought of those two orgasms—a new experience for her—a sexy shiver rippled through her body and settled between her thighs.

"If it's not Adonis, then . . ." Rina frowned.

So much for feeling sexy. Ann came down to earth and sighed. "David."

"David? The lawyer? What did the jerk do now?" Suzanne demanded.

Ann took a breath. Suzanne, with her old-fashioned morality, wasn't going to like this. "He figured out I was seeing someone and he was jealous. It made him think."

"Think what?" Jenny asked.

"Think that . . ." Hmm, he hadn't said a lot, but she could fill in the blanks. "I guess it made him realize that he really is interested in me and doesn't want to lose me. He, uh, he's maybe going to split up with his wife."

"Oh my God!" Jenny exclaimed, closely followed by Suzanne's, "Oh no, that's horrible."

Ann glanced at Rina. "Well?"

"I think divorce is sad, but not all marriages are happy." Rina bit her lip. "There aren't any kids, are there?"

Ann shook her head.

"He told you they'd been having problems," Rina went on, toying with her diet soda. "Maybe it was like a trial separation, when he left Toronto to work on the case out here. Once he was away from her, maybe he realized the marriage really was over—"

"*He* realized it?" Suzanne broke in. "What's *she* thinking, back home in Toronto? Have they talked, tried counseling? Does the woman even have a clue what he's thinking?"

Again Ann shook her head. "I don't know. When David dropped this on me this morning, I was upset and—"

"No duh!" Jenny interrupted.

Ann gave her a strained smile. "Yeah. Anyhow, we were in my office. It wasn't the right time to go into it."

"Maybe she cheats on him." Rina darted a glance at Suzanne. "Yes, I think people should take their marriage vows seriously, but there are good reasons to divorce. Maybe David has one. I think Ann needs to find out."

"You're right." Ann stared at Rina. "You're absolutely right. Why didn't I see that myself?" Good God, normally she was the one who said you had to collect all the facts and analyze them before making a decision. "Note to self: Hunt for lost brain!"

"It's not lost," Rina said, making Ann aware she'd **spoken** aloud again. "It's hard to think straight when you've had an emotional shock."

"Yeah, that's why you need us." Jenny wriggled her eyebrows. "We're known for our straight thinking."

"Or at least for analyzing an issue from all angles." Suzanne still looked troubled. "I do agree with Rina. My morality isn't so black and white that I think a couple should stick together forever even if they're miserable. But, Ann, if the man's failed in one relationship, is he a good risk for a new one?"

"Not to mention the rebound effect," Rina threw in.

"And where's the Greek god in all of this?" Jenny demanded.

"Greek god?" It was their waitress, delivering a giant platter of nachos, with cheese, salsa, guacamole, and sour cream. "Did I hear someone say Greek god?"

Jenny nodded toward Ann. "She's seeing one."

The girl smiled, showing a dimple almost as cute as Adonis's. "Lucky you."

When she left, Jenny scooped sour cream and guacamole onto a corn chip and asked, "On the subject of luck, you did get lucky with the god last night, right? After all that kissing?"

Remembering, Ann had to smile. "I told him to can the slow seduction and listen to my needs." She dipped into the nachos herself. If someone put food in front of her, she was delighted to eat it. Her typical problem was dragging herself away from work.

She opened her mouth and tossed the chip in. Thank heavens for tequila and meds.

"How'd he take that?" Jenny asked. "Lots of guys get turned off by a controlling—sorry, I mean strong—woman."

"He already knew she was a lawyer," Suzanne said. "He had to figure that meant strong."

Rina scooped salsa onto a chip, avoiding the sour cream and guacamole. "The bedroom isn't the same as the office." Then she winced. "Sorry. Didn't intend the David reference."

"That's okay. Anyhow, it took Adonis a few minutes to get with the program, then he did great. Told me he was my slave."

"Woo-hoo!" Jenny said. "Sex-slave fantasy."

Ann grinned. "Yeah, exactly."

"There's a certain appeal to that," Suzanne admitted with a grin of her own. "What did you make him do?"

"Kiss me the way I wanted to be kissed, strip, let me control the sex."

"Woman-on-top sex?" Jenny asked.

When Ann nodded, her friend said, "I can see that working for you."

"Polite way of calling me a control freak," Ann said, not taking offense because she'd long ago copped to a guilty plea on that charge.

"Whatever turns you on," Suzanne said.

"So," Rina said eagerly, "was it the best sex you've ever had?"

Ann remembered the last time the Foursome had had this conversation, and she had to shake her head. "No. We were a little out of sync, but it was our first time. We were adjusting to each other." She had to grin. "On the other hand, I came twice. Didn't know my body could do that."

Jenny tilted her head. "Sex slave gave you two O's and yet silk-tie guy still holds the record for best sex?"

Just thinking about that night with Rob made her wet. "He does."

"I remember this story," Suzanne said, leaning forward. "He was a lawyer with a four-poster bed and a great collection of silk ties, right?"

Ann nodded. "One night, when we were undressing at his place, I pulled at his tie and said, 'What is it with men, wanting to be tied up all day?' "

"And that gave him all sorts of ideas," Jenny pitched in. "Like tying you up to his bed."

"My first reaction was panic," Ann remembered. "But mixed in, a tiny dose of fascinated curiosity. He said he'd tie me loosely—" She squeezed her thighs together, tried not to squirm, but, man, was she turned on.

"But he'd be in control," Suzanne objected. "He's dominating, you're submitting. That's so not like you."

Ann reflected. "Yeah, but he gave me control. I made the decision, told him to tie me up. He said he'd untie me any time I wanted. But while I was tied up, it was all about me. Him, making love to me." She hadn't felt like she had to make Rob come—though he had—because she'd barely been able to move. It had given her a sense of freedom she'd never felt before. Or after. "I only had one orgasm, but it was mind-blowing." And right now, if she reached a hand under her skirt and touched herself, she'd come in a flash.

"Okay, I can buy into having a man totally focus on me," Rina said. "But you'd sure have to trust the guy. You'd have to know he'd untie you."

Jenny snorted. "Come on, it's not that big a deal. No bigger than going home with a guy or inviting him to your place. Or even getting into a car with him. If they're going to hurt you, there's not much you can do to stop them."

"Stop, Jen." Rina gave a shiver. "That's frightening."

"You have to trust your judgment." Jenny munched another guacamole-laden chip.

"True," Ann said. And she did, when it came to Adonis. She knew he wouldn't hurt her. He was big, strong, masculine, he did all that rugged outdoorsy guy stuff, he was amazingly sexy—and yet she sensed a deep core of . . . gentleness. He was such a contrast to most of the lawyers she knew. They were either wimpy or blustery—not masculine, not strong, not gentle.

David, however . . . He had that same kind of quiet, masculine confidence. Underneath, was he gentle, too? Fantastic in bed?

"Are you seeing Adonis again?" Rina asked.

Shift gears. Adonis, David, this is too confusing. "Saturday night." And she knew the sex would be even better, because she'd feel more relaxed with him. She sighed and dipped another chip. "But now there's the thing with David, so I'm not sure."

"Hey, Annie?" Jen had that wicked grin on her face. "Way to go, girl. You got two guys."

"You make it sound more fun than it is," Ann said drily.

"How is a sex slave *not* fun? You gotta hang on to Adonis," Jenny said. "At least until you figure out what's going on with David."

"If David tells you all the right things," Suzanne said, "like his wife's been cheating on him for years and refuses to go to marriage counseling, what will you do?"

"I don't know." She put down the chip she'd been about to eat. Her appetite had fled.

"You've been attracted to him from the beginning," Rina said. "If he'd been single, you'd probably have been in bed with him by now."

"There's still the issue of us working for the same firm. At Smythe Levinson it's not prohibited for two lawyers to get involved, but I honestly don't think it's a good idea."

Not a good idea? There was her mother, popping in, arms folded across her chest and an expression of censure on her face. *You're understating the case. Be objective, examine the possible consequences, and you'll see it's an idiotic idea.*

"Well," Suzanne said, "there'd be people—inside and outside the firm—who would take a negative slant on it."

Jen polished off her margarita. "Well, that's their problem. It's your life, Annie."

"But my life's my career. I can't risk my career."

Jenny sighed. "Okay, you got me. I know your career's the most important thing for you."

"It would be even worse if you get together while he's getting a divorce," Rina said softly. "Even if he and his wife were already breaking up, people might think you're the cause."

Crap, the girls are on my mother's *side!* Ann groaned. "You're supposed to be making me feel better."

Suzanne reached across the table to touch her hand. "No, we're here to help you see this clearly."

"Do you want to see it clearly?" Rina asked quietly. "Or do you want to go on emotion and instinct? Does your heart tell you to be with David? Is he *The One?*"

"I don't know." Knowing he was married, she'd tried not to think of him that way.

"If David was The One, would you have had two orgasms with Adonis?" Jenny asked.

"I don't know." Ann rubbed her aching temples. "I don't know anything anymore."

"Yes, you do," Rina said gently. "You know you have to talk to David. And listen carefully, with your mind and your heart."

"Then call us." Jenny winked. "So we can tell you what to do."

Jen was always so brash and upbeat, trying to tease them all into a good mood. More often than not, it worked.

Today, Ann rewarded her attempt with a forced smile. "Why don't you three talk to David and decide for me?"

They all chuckled. But, when they'd paid the bill and were leaving, each of her friends gave Ann a warm hug.

Those hugs reminded her of what was truly important. Loyal friends. No, the girls weren't on her mother's side, they were on hers. They cared, they were trying to help, they'd support her in whatever she decided.

Feeling stronger, she climbed into her Miata, pulled out her cell phone, and dialed David's direct line. "Hi, it's Ann. We need to talk."

"Anytime." He sounded relieved and hopeful.

She was relieved, too. She didn't have answers, but at least she knew the next step to take. As for hope . . . She wasn't sure what to hope for.

"Tonight," she told him. "Out of the office." She had to separate her work life from her personal life, at least geographically. Not at her place, either. Definitely not at his apartment suite at the Sutton Place Hotel. A bar or lounge, then.

"Come to my hotel," he said, cutting into her thoughts.

Did he mean his apartment or the bar? "No." Even if he was referring to the bar, it was too damned close to his bedroom.

"The Hotel Vancouver has a nice lounge," she said. It was spacious, with conversational groupings set at a distance from each other. Nice decor, live music, but not what you'd call romantic. If anyone saw them together, they'd think nothing of two lawyers having a drink a couple of blocks from the office after a long day's work.

"Okay, I'll meet you at eight and we'll walk over."

Ann closed her cell, nervous already. Usually, she solved problems by working out the best-case and worst-case scenarios. All those *possible consequences* Meredith had trained her to consider.

With David, she could imagine too many worst cases but didn't have a clue what the best case would be. She hadn't even kissed the man properly, so how could she possibly know?

But how could she let herself kiss him if he was still married?

And then there was Adonis. She'd had sex with Adonis, and to be honest she'd like to do it again. The two of them would never have a serious relationship; after all, they were complete opposites. Still, a light, sexy liaison had a lot of appeal.

If she and David decided things might get serious between them, she couldn't see Adonis Saturday night. It wouldn't be fair to either man.

Ridiculous to feel sad. After all, she barely knew Adonis.

As for David . . . If he'd been single or divorced when they first met, would she really have let her worries about office relationships get in the way? Maybe not.

So, perhaps in the months down the road, there really was hope for her and David. The thought made her smile.

If the two of them eventually did get together . . . Hmm, would he be as amenable to playing sex slave as Adonis had been?

Once she got back to the office, client phone calls and appointments kept Ann occupied for a few hours. She was researching case law online when her phone rang late in the afternoon. Still reading, she reached out one hand and fumbled for the phone.

Damn, it was David. She'd been trying to put off thinking about him until eight. "Are you calling on your cell? You sound kind of distant."

"I'm in a cab on my way to the airport."

"Airport?" Had she heard him right?

"Something urgent came up on one of my files back in Toronto. A problem with an expert-witness report. Have to be there for an early morning meeting. I'm sorry about tonight."

Damn again. "I wish you'd come and told me in person." She knew she sounded huffy but she had a right. This morning the man had said he'd leave his wife for her!

"Sorry, I only got the call twenty minutes ago. Didn't have time to do anything but check flights and catch a cab."

Okay, maybe he had a valid excuse. "You're not even stopping at the hotel to pick up clothes?"

"No, I . . . I have clothes in Toronto."

Which meant he was staying at the house he shared with his wife. No, she shouldn't leap to conclusions. Maybe he intended to drop by and pick up fresh clothing, go to a hotel. Tell his wife he wanted a divorce . . .

She glanced at the open door of her office, then murmured,

"David, are you going to talk to your w-wife?" Hard to say that word out loud.

"Have you decided, Ann? If you have, then I'll tell Clarice."

And damn for the third time. "No, I wanted to talk to you."

Wait a minute, where does the jerk get off, trying to put this on me?

She straightened tight shoulders. "David, no. This isn't right. *You* have to decide about your marriage. This is between you and your wife." She glanced at the door again. It was almost five and most people were at their own desks, hurriedly winding up their day's tasks. "If you decide to break up, then we'll see if you and I . . . you know. Might have something."

Another sigh, even louder. Then he said, "You're right. But it's tough to leave when I don't know where I'm going."

Normally David was decisive. It was strange, hearing him sound lost. For once, she was the one with more wisdom and insight. "Where you *go*, if you leave a relationship, is to spend some time on your own." Experience—her own and her friends'— told her that. "Figure out who you are and what you want. You can't rush from one woman straight to another."

"You're saying you don't want to be with me?"

"No, I'm saying . . . I don't know. You're married, I can't know how I feel until—unless—you're single." She ran a hand through her hair. "Not to mention, both our careers are at stake. If we did get involved, you'd have to be separated, then we'd have to do it very slowly."

"Damn. You're right again. I'm just impatient. I want to be with you. I've had it with these casual touches, burning gazes. I want you in my arms. My bed."

Oh, God. He had to raise sex. Until now she'd been intellectualizing their conversation but now a throb of heat hit her pussy.

"Don't you want that, Ann?"

Only since the first night we worked late together, when I saw the way your eyes crinkled when you smiled, the way they sparkled with enthusiasm when we discussed the case. When you treated me like an equal. And a woman.

"Y-yes. But—"

He cut her off, voice eager. "So, we could do it, and be discreet at the office."

Could she? Be coworker by day, lover by night? She bit her lip. "Even if no one found out, I'd feel shabby. I meant what I said. You need time on your own to sort out what you want."

"You. I want you."

She wanted him, too. But what were they talking about? What did she want from him? An affair? Marriage?

Talk about getting ahead of myself!

"David, we both need time. Think about it while you're in Toronto and see if you're ready to make a decision. When are you coming back?"

"There are meetings all day tomorrow. Best guess, we'll be working on Saturday. I hope to get back Sunday. Maybe we can get together Sunday night?"

Get together? Now there was a phrase with many meanings. "Same deal as for tonight," she said firmly. "Drinks and talk at the Hotel Vancouver. You'll call me and confirm?"

"As soon as I've booked my flight back. Okay?"

"Sure." No, it was far from okay. She'd live the weekend on tenterhooks. Ann drew a deep breath and her gaze snagged the files on her desk. "I'll carry on with Healthy Life Clinic. Any special instructions?"

"Oh, damn, ask Joanne to check my computer. I was typing a memo to you about some ideas to work on. Forgot to send it, when I got the call from Toronto."

"Sure," she said again. "So, I guess I'll just wait to hear." Hear when he was returning. Hear if he'd left his wife. She ground her teeth then winced as pain radiated through her jaw.

"I'm sorry we couldn't talk in person. But maybe this is for the best. I'll have some time to think. And I'll have—make—an opportunity to see Clarice. We'll—oh, damn, we're at Departures. I have to hang up."

"Okay. I'll see you . . . when I see you, I guess."

After they hung up, she said, "Crap. Just freaking crap." She liked having all the facts, making a decision and moving forward. She didn't want to spend the next few days *waiting!*

She didn't even know how to feel—optimistic, excited, scared, depressed?—until she saw him again.

She groaned, then took a couple of painkillers from her purse and reached for her coffee mug. Her hand brushed the edge of a stack of files and the entire pile began to topple. Dropping the pills, she grabbed for the files just in time to avert disaster. "Klutz."

Ann, it's simply a matter of paying attention. You're not graceful, in fact you're quite the klutz, so you need to concentrate on what you're doing.

Thanks, Mother.

Coping skills. Meredith had tried to teach them to her. Ann wasn't brilliant, so she had to be super organized and work harder than everyone else. She wasn't coordinated, so she had to concentrate harder. When she did, she was fine. In court she'd never once tripped or dropped her files.

She retrieved the pills and reached again, more carefully, for her coffee. Another evening with pills and caffeine and work. This was normal for her; she knew how to do it. She just had to refocus on her priorities before they, like that stack of files, began to topple.

She buzzed Joanne, the paralegal who was working with her and David on Healthy Life Clinic, hoping to catch her before she left work. Joanne answered and Ann repeated what David had said about the memo on his computer screen.

"No problem," a cheerful voice responded. "I'll find it and e-mail it to you before I go, and log David off."

"Print a copy for yourself. Let's get together first thing tomorrow and figure out what we'll tackle while David's away."

"You got it."

Joanne always sounded so upbeat. Maybe because she worked regular hours and had a cute new husband at home. She wasn't ambitious but she did seem satisfied with her life. Ann wouldn't trade lives with her, although, right now, she had to admit to a touch of envy.

She squared her shoulders. Okay, a free evening. Think how much she could get accomplished.

But by eight her eyes were tired, her head ached despite the pills, and her stomach had long ago digested the nachos and was growling. Not only that, but—despite knowing her top priority was her career—she felt lonely at the thought of having nothing better to do than work all night. Or go home to bed, alone.

Last night, her bed hadn't been a lonely place. Maybe if she phoned Adonis, he'd come over and play sex slave again.

No, tempting as that was, she was more in the mood for relaxing company than hot sex. She could call Suzanne or Rina or Jenny, but this week she'd already taken enough time out of their busy lives.

All the same, just thinking of them made her feel better. For the first time in her life, she had friends. Real friends, not just fellow students, colleagues, acquaintances.

She e-mailed them.

Guess what? David went to Toronto! We were going to talk tonight, but he got an emergency call on a case, and now he's gone. I told him he has to decide what he's doing with his wife, and he agreed. So he'll MAYBE decide and talk to her this weekend. And he'll MAYBE be back Sunday and tell me. Aarghh!

In the meantime, I don't know if he's screwing her or divorcing her.

Crude, but that's how she felt, and her friends would understand. Slowly she typed on.

I'd been thinking I should cancel Adonis on Saturday, but
maybe not. I need the distraction! I need the sex <g>.
Until David decides what he's doing, I have a perfect right
to see another man. A perfect man. No, make that a perfect sex slave. <VBG>

No, she wasn't in fact VBG'ing, she felt let down and depressed. But she wanted to end on an upbeat note, so her
friends wouldn't worry about her.

Okay, now what? Haul some work home, in hopes the drive
would clear her head and restore her energy? Or wander the office corridors, see if anyone else was working late and felt like a
drink?

Or phone her mother?

7

It was just past eleven in Toronto; Meredith would still be up. The woman easily got by on about four hours of sleep a night, a trait Ann wished she'd inherited.

They hadn't talked in two or three weeks, so it was time to catch up.

Her mother might not be the warmest person in the world, but she was Ann's only family, and a voice in the night was better than feeling all alone. Besides, Meredith could always be counted on to get Ann back on track any time she even thought of drifting off.

"Ann. What a nice surprise," her mother said crisply, sounding like it was seven in the morning rather than late evening.

"Is this a good time?"

"Perfect. I just got home from a Bar Association event."

She imagined her mother in her tailored suit—a more expensive version of Ann's own—bending down to ease off her Ferragamo pumps. "Anything interesting?"

A dry chuckle. "You'd have to ask my audience. I was the guest speaker."

"Then of course it was interesting." And it was true. Her mother had a brilliant mind and was a highly effective presenter, whether in the courtroom or at a professional function.

"I'll e-mail you a copy. Maybe it will persuade you to follow me into my area of practice."

It wouldn't. No way would she ever try to compete with Meredith. "I'd love to read it."

"What are you working on now?"

She told her mother a bit about the Healthy Life Clinic case, knowing everything she said would be held in the strictest of confidence, and ended with, "Charter law is intriguing."

"Hmm. It requires a sharp intellect, an understanding of politics and policy issues, and the barrister's skills to argue a case all the way up to the Supreme Court. Yes, that could well be the career path for you."

Ann appreciated the compliment, although her mother never called her positive comments compliments or the negative ones criticisms. To her, she was objectively analyzing her daughter's strengths and weaknesses.

And trust Meredith to take a casual comment and start building a career from it.

Still, Ann had never felt so intellectually stimulated by her other cases. Did her mother always have to be right? "Maybe I'll explore the possibilities." She felt a ripple of excitement. This was what she'd wanted—a niche of her own within the huge profession of law.

"I'll talk to some people here, send you some information. You'd move, of course."

"Uh, move?"

"The best Charter firms are in Ottawa and Toronto. Of course, you could transfer to the Toronto branch of Smythe Levinson and continue working with David Wilkins, since the two of you get along so well."

Damn, was I gushing too much? Does she suspect?

"Would he put in a word for you?" her mother asked.

"He might," she said wryly.

As if things aren't complicated enough! If he stays married, could the two of us work together in Toronto? If he and his wife break up . . . God, how many times has Mother told me that career decisions come first, and should never be affected by personal concerns like relationships or geographic preferences?

When Ann had been called to the Bar and accepted the best offer—with Smythe Levinson in Vancouver—it had been a career decision. She'd figured she'd stay two or three years. But it had been four, and she liked it here. Honestly, though, her reasons for staying were personal.

The Foursome. The first friends she'd ever had. Who else could she laugh and joke and let down her hair with? Who else would have helped her through this morning's trauma?

Then there was Vancouver itself. She liked summer dinners outside, with the scent of flowers and ocean. The magnolia trees that bloomed in the center of the business district. And she *loved* the rarity of snow and freezing winds, things she'd hated when she grew up in Toronto.

"I like the West Coast," she said.

But David is based in Toronto. If the two of us . . . Crap, I'm so confused.

"I've never understood that," her mother was saying. "Damn lotusland. It's so laid-back. It doesn't suit you."

Meredith was probably right. "I'll think about it," Ann said.

A sigh. "I wish you'd move back."

Was it possible her mother missed her? That she, too, sometimes longed for a peaceful evening together? All through school, Meredith had helped her with homework. In Ann's time as an undergrad and at law school, they'd shared the home office, sometimes each working on her own project, sometimes discussing what they were doing.

Not the conventional mother-daughter relationship, but it's

what her mother offered, and Ann had long ago learned not to expect hugs and fresh-baked cookies from Meredith.

Every relationship was different. A wise person appreciated the good parts and didn't look for more than the other person could give.

"I really will think about it," Ann said. "Now, tell me more about this speech you gave."

She settled back in her office chair, vaguely aware of her stomach rumbling, but happy for this across-the-country connection with her mother.

On Saturday, after a day at Pure Indulgence, Adonis went for a run by the ocean, then enjoyed a long shower. For dinner he stir-fried some veggies, tossed in peanut butter and soy, and microwaved some leftover brown rice. He ate by the open window, imagining how the evening with Ann might go, and getting turned on.

Last time had been good, although he'd never felt like they'd really been in sync. Strange, because Ann was so hot, and the attraction between them so strong. But when it came to lovemaking, he liked slow and sensual, and she seemed more orgasm-driven.

He'd been pissed about that "schedule two hours for sex" thing, but she'd explained she had to work. Then, playing sex slave had been fun; he had nothing against a woman being in control, taking what she needed. But there'd been times she'd seemed to disconnect. Like she was analyzing rather than giving herself up to the moment and sinking into the sensations and emotions. It made him feel distanced.

But after all, it had been their first time. Tonight would be even better. The idea brought a heavy heat to his groin.

She didn't know anything about tantric sex, but he'd yet to meet the woman who didn't love it once she'd learned a few of the principles. With that in mind, he packed a few items in a bag, then started to walk to Ann's place.

Sex was easy. He could find it whenever he wanted. When he'd been a horny kid, he'd been quick to grab all the riches offered by eager girls. And he'd learned to appreciate quality.

A sixth sense told him that he and Ann, together, might be real quality. If she let herself open up. And slow down.

On the subject of quality, the woman who opened the door to him definitely looked the part. All sexy and sophisticated, her silky black robe worn loose over a lacy teddy in a shade of golden-brown that went with her eyes. It reminded him of Metaxa, the Greek brandy his father shared with him on special occasions. But it packed way more punch.

He leaned forward, touched his lips to hers, and waited to see how she'd respond.

Her kiss was brief, almost automatic. He should've realized she was tense from the tight way she held her shoulders.

When she stepped back to let him in, he said, "You okay? Headache? Feeling stressed?"

"I'm a little stressed," she said slowly, like it was difficult to admit. As if the groove between her eyebrows wasn't a giveaway.

"About work? Or about us? Having second thoughts?"

"Why should I have second thoughts?" she snapped. Then she sighed and gazed up at him, brows drawn together, the frown line still there. "There's nothing wrong with what we're doing. Nothing. Right?"

What was she talking about? Then a possibility dawned on him. That first afternoon, she'd asked if he was seeing anyone—which he wasn't, since his last girlfriend had gone back to university in Alberta. He'd assumed that meant Ann was unattached, too.

"Are you involved with someone else?" he asked. He wasn't

uptight about monogamy, but it was his preference. A relationship, even a short-term one, took time, energy, focus.

"No, I wouldn't cheat on a boyfriend." She shook her head vigorously, but the frown line was still there.

Okay, he was officially confused. Ann looked like pure sex but wasn't giving out signals to match. Maybe she'd just come from work, needed to unwind and get in the mood. She'd told him wine helped her relax, so he handed her one of the two bags he carried.

She glanced inside and gave a wry smile. "Thanks. You know me too well."

He chuckled. That *so* was not the case. "I'd like to."

She made a noncommittal sound, then nodded toward the other bag. "You brought two bottles? You thought I'd need that much alcohol?"

From the way she was acting, chances were she'd pass out before she loosened up. "No, I brought some things I thought we might enjoy."

"Sex toys?" Something sparked in her eyes, something both wary and excited.

"Not exactly." Jeez, was she into that stuff? What would she like? Handcuffs and whips, dildos and vibrators? He wasn't much of a toy guy himself. He pretty much figured one man and one woman were all you needed, if both were imaginative, caring, and in tune with their senses.

Ann reached out, surprising him, and tugged the second bag away. She dipped a hand inside and brought out a length of soft cotton cloth. "Huh?"

He retrieved the bag before she could explore further. "It's a blindfold. I thought—" He was about to go on, to tell her it wasn't for kinky stuff, but she cut him off.

"A blindfold?" She stared at it, obviously fascinated, then shook her head. "You're not blindfolding me and tying me up. I don't know you well enough."

O-kay. So, if she did know him well enough, she'd be into being tied up?

He wasn't. Or at least he didn't think he was. He didn't mind one partner taking the lead, but he liked sex where both participated fully.

On the other hand, making love was about sensation. Enhancing your own body's ability to sense, and stimulating your partner's senses. That's why the blindfold. So that the other items he'd brought would arouse senses other than sight.

If Ann wanted to be tied up as well as blindfolded . . . Yeah, he could imagine getting into that. Not because of the domination aspect; that was a turnoff. But he could envision her spread out on the bed in that lacy teddy, him stroking a feather across her nipple and watching it bud, all her sensations focusing in that one part of her body.

The thought focused his own sensations, too, and arousal made his cock swell.

"Adonis? Did you hear me? I'm not letting you tie me up."

Not yet. But if they kept seeing each other, if she trusted him, maybe they'd try it. She could tie him up first. He could just imagine how it would feel. In fact . . . "Want to tie me up?"

No frown line now. Just wide, bright eyes. She swallowed, loudly enough to be audible. He tracked the swallow down her slender throat, saw the tops of her breasts lift as her breathing quickened. It surprised him when she shook her head. She muttered something that sounded like, "Talk about performance pressure."

Could that be right? "Sorry, didn't quite catch that."

"Nothing. So, what else is in that bag?"

To show her would ruin the effect later. "Good stuff," he reassured her. "Nothing to hurt you. Now, why don't we open that wine?"

As she walked toward the kitchen, he thought this was just like the first time. Her all edgy, both of them feeling the attraction, but neither sure about making the first move. "Your shoulders are tight," he said as he followed her. "Been working today?"

"About ten hours. That's actually a short day for me." She turned to him, rotating her head gingerly. "Can you recommend a massage therapist? The stretches help but I could use another massage." Then she gave a little grin and her eyes gleamed. "I might be safest with a woman this time."

"Mmm. And you figure safe is a good thing?"

"Depends what I'm looking for." The gleam turned into a spark that sizzled the air between them.

What did she want tonight? A fast, hard kiss? A sex slave?

He knew what he wanted. To touch her. First, to ease her pain, help her relax. Then, to awaken her sensuality, stimulate her sexuality. "Let me give you a massage," he offered softly. "Now."

She frowned and the mood turned from one of possibility to discordance again. "No, that's not fair. This is, uh, social. Massage is your job, and you should be paid for what you do. Though, I guess I could—"

Pay him? "No!" he broke in. "I want to."

"Adonis, you don't have to massage me to have sex with me."

He rested his hands lightly on her shoulders, hoping touch could communicate better than they were doing with words. "Ann, I'd enjoy it. I love helping people feel better." And he purely loved touching her beautiful body.

Her shoulders tensed and her frown deepened.

Shit. "Okay, what did I say wrong now?"

"I'm not a charity case," she said stiffly. "You don't have to massage away my headache or give me orgasms to relieve my stress."

His hands tightened, then he pulled them away and glared at her. "Jesus, woman! I like you, I'm attracted to you. I want us to share our bodies, get to know each other. If you have a headache, of course I want to help you get rid of it."

"But that's not why you're here."

It wasn't? "OK, why am I here?"

That frown line was back. "For sex."

He frowned, too. Did she think all he wanted from her was sex? Damn, that was insulting to both of them.

Or was she saying that's all she wanted from him? His blood heated, this time with anger.

On Wednesday night, she'd only given him a couple of hours. He'd accepted that she had some important work that had to be done by morning.

But maybe that was all the time she'd wanted to spend with him. Just enough to play a sex game and get two orgasms. When he was young he'd had no objection to a girl using him for his body, but that had grown stale long ago. Now, he had more pride. Screw Ann, he was leaving.

But maybe he was jumping to a conclusion.

Deliberately he took a couple of slow breaths. "Is that what you want?" he asked, struggling to keep his voice level. "Just sex?"

"I, uh . . . Well, that's what got us together, right? Sexual attraction?"

Didn't they have more than that? Didn't she want more? "That's all you want in a relationship? All you want with me?"

"I . . ." She paused again. "This is new. I've never been with someone like you."

"Someone like me?" Was he so different than her past lovers?

She shrugged. "Someone I barely know, someone who isn't a lawyer." Tiny laugh lines crinkled beside her eyes and mouth. "Someone who looks like the Greek god he's named for."

"Crap, I'm no god." He sighed. "So, you usually date lawyers?"

"Mostly. A university poli sci teacher once. Typically, I get to know them, we connect on an intellectual level, then it may head into sex."

Oh, great. She thought he was dumb.

"Not," she said hurriedly, "that you and I wouldn't necessarily connect that way. I mean, I'm sure it takes brains to do the massage therapy course. You clearly know a lot more about anatomy and physiology, massage, stress relief, and so on, than I do."

His annoyance eased and he reached for her hand. "You're a nice woman, Ann."

"Me?" Her brows lifted in surprise. "Nice? What do you mean? I'm a lawyer."

He had to laugh. "And those two are mutually exclusive?"

She rolled her eyes. "A lot of people think so. Glad to know you're more broad-minded."

Man, she looked so damned cute when she rolled her eyes like that. His tension was rapidly dissolving, and his hopes about their relationship rising. And with them, his cock.

She turned to find her corkscrew. "Why do you say I'm nice?"

"You realized you might have hurt my feelings, and tried to make me feel better."

She shrugged, and he watched that tantalizing strip of naked skin between her short hair and the drooping neckline of her robe. A bare nape. He figured it was usually covered by the collars of those business suits she wore. He leaned down, blew gently.

She shivered, her hand jerked, and the cork popped free.

He reached past her to lift down the glasses she'd used before, taking the opportunity to let his body brush hers, and heard her soft sigh.

"I should have asked if you prefer red or white wine," he said. He'd played it safe, got the same wine as last time.

"Yes." She turned to him with a smile. "I like wine, whatever color. I also like margaritas and mojitos and martinis." The smile became a grin that made her look mischievous and irresistible. "Hey, I never thought. M drinks. Even wine starts with an upside down M."

"Massage starts with an M, too," he pointed out. "Why don't we take the wine into your bedroom and you give me a chance to get rid of that headache?"

She studied him long and hard, through slightly narrowed eyes, like she was assessing his offer. "If you're sure. I don't want to take advantage of you."

"It'll help us both loosen up," he promised. "Even better than wine."

She handed him a glass and clicked hers to it. "To loosening up." Then she led the way to that stylish, sexy bedroom and peeled back the spread. "Guess you want me lying facedown?"

"No, faceup."

"Oh, I see." She shot him a cynical glance. "It's *that* kind of massage. I thought you were going to work on my shoulders and neck."

"I am. But I don't want you lying facedown without a proper massage table. It puts too much strain on your neck." He stripped the spread all the way off the bed. "Take off your robe and lie with your head at the foot of the bed."

She took a couple of healthy swallows of wine, then put the glass down and did as he'd asked. That brandy-colored lace teddy was a little darker than her skin, and it highlighted her curves to perfection.

Just looking at her made him hot.

Okay, this wasn't about his sexual needs, but about easing her aches and helping her unwind.

A little mood-setting could only help. Adonis lit the candles on her dresser and clicked off the lamp. He turned to her sound system and found a short stack of CDs. The Diana Krall they'd listened to before, a couple of R. Carlos Nakai albums—nice that she'd liked the music well enough to go out and buy it— and three recordings of the Vancouver Operatic Society.

He slipped a Nakai disk into her player. "Do you mind if I get oil on the sheets? It'll wash out, but maybe you'd rather lie on a towel?"

"Oil?" She raised up, winced, and lay flat again. "I don't have any massage oil."

"I came prepared."

"Really?" Those finely arched brows lifted again. "That bag of tricks of yours?"

"Yeah." He reached into the bag for the oil. "It's not giant dildos and vibrators and handcuffs." He glanced at her to check her reaction. "Sorry."

"Mmm." She seemed to be reserving judgment.

"I'm going to peel your straps down so I don't get oil on this pretty teddy."

"You know it's called a teddy?"

"Three older sisters. I've probably heard more discussions of female lingerie than you have. My dad's only rule was, not at the dinner table. He had to be free to walk out of the room."

"But you stayed and listened?" Her lips twitched. "Kinky boy."

Gently he peeled down one strap, letting his fingers drift across her soft skin. "Sensible boy. I figured the information would come in handy one day."

He lowered the other strap, again with a caress. Under the lace, her nipples were budding. And under his jeans, his cock was hardening.

"I could take the teddy off," she said, her voice husky.

And he could strip off his clothes and plunge into her, as his woody was urging him to do. But no, that's not what he wanted with Ann. She deserved time, gentleness, quality. "Later," he told her. "You're distracting enough like this. There's lots of time."

She frowned. "Well, I do have to get back to work in a couple of hours."

"What?" He paused in the act of opening the massage oil. "You're going to work on Saturday night?"

"I can't quit for the day. I have too much to do."

His hand clenched on the bottle of oil. Same pattern as Wednesday.

Fuck. She didn't want to get to know him, have any conversation, intellectual or otherwise. Her planner had a slot marked "Adonis: sex." She wasn't prepared to give him the six hours he'd asked for; all she wanted was quickie orgasms.

Okay, he was pissed. Time to blow this joint. He sure as hell deserved better than this.

Except, he also felt challenged. A woman who preferred middle-of-the-night work to his erotic company? She was nuts, and he could prove it to her.

But why should he? She'd insulted him.

His throbbing erection urged him not to quit now. His male ego was fighting a "go"/"no, stay" battle.

"Adonis?" she said. "I'm sorry, did I mislead you?" She sat up and turned to him, frowning. "When we talked about getting together tonight, I thought we both meant the same as on Wednesday. Great sex, and that's it."

Slam-bang sex didn't qualify as great in his mind, but he kept quiet.

"I really can't afford to take more time off work. There's a big case I'm involved in, as well as all the regular stuff and—" She broke off, looking upset and guilty. "There are only so many hours in the day."

He sighed. It seemed she hadn't meant to offend him, she was just so damned focused on her job. "What's the big case that's so important?" he said, voice rough at the edges.

Her eyebrows flew up as if she was surprised he'd asked.

"It's a Charter case. You know, the Canadian Charter of Rights and Freedoms?"

"Yeah, I've heard of it." Jeez, she really did think he was stupid. He was so tempted to leave, but it seemed kind of childish. Storming out because his feelings were hurt. He could be adult about this. "What's the case, and which side do you represent?"

"I'll tell you the generalities. You understand I can't reveal anything confidential, or talk about our legal arguments?"

He barely refrained from saying, "Well, duh." Instead he said, "Confidentiality applies to my work, too."

She flushed. "Sorry, of course it does. Anyhow, the firm represents a medical clinic that's into promoting healthy life choices. They've been refusing some treatments to patients, and a few patients have started a class-action suit, saying they're being denied equality rights under the Charter." Her face was animated, and so was her voice.

"You really love your work," he said, surprised. He'd assumed from her stress level that she was in a job she didn't enjoy.

"I do. Especially this Charter case. It's fascinating."

Hmm. His sister Andie worked crazy hours, too, but usually came away happy and energized. Why didn't the same thing happen with Ann? Maybe it was all the other stuff, like not eating regular meals, not getting exercise, drinking too much coffee. Working all night.

Did she see the irony, in representing doctors who promoted healthy life choices?

Obviously not. And if he pointed it out, or lectured her about living a balanced life, she'd probably toss him out right now. A few minutes ago he'd have gone gladly, but, now he wanted to stay. The woman frustrated him, but, damn, she intrigued him, too. "Lie down again," he said.

As she obeyed, he said, "Close your eyes."

"Why?" The muscles around her eyes tensed.

He grinned. "No, I'm not going to blindfold you. It's just nice to let your eyes relax. Let all your muscles relax."

"All right." Her eyes closed but the muscles around them twitched, like she was forcing herself to hold her lids down.

Yeah, he could relate. His own body was still full of tension. He opened the bottle of oil and let a couple drops drip onto his index finger, then lifted his finger and breathed deeply, drawing the scent in. He exhaled, focusing on letting out stress. Breathed again, drawing in the erotic aroma. Breathed out, exhaling tension. Okay, that was better.

"Adonis?" she said nervously.

He held his finger under her nose. "Take a deep breath. What do you smell?"

"Mmm, that's nice." Her eyes opened, then shut again, probably because she realized vision wouldn't answer his question. She sniffed again. "Flowery, kind of sultry and exotic. Like I imagine tropical nights would smell. What is it?"

"Jasmine, neroli, and rose."

"Neroli?"

"Orange blossom."

"It's different than the lavender one you used last time."

Tonight's had aphrodisiac qualities. "Different scents for different moods," he said lightly. "How's it make you feel?"

She breathed deeply, and he could see her shoulders lowering, the tension beginning to flow out. Her eyelids had stopped twitching. "Like I'm lying in a tropical garden on a warm, sultry night." A smile flickered. "With a Native American playing a flute."

He smiled, too. The music wasn't the best music to match the scent, but her CD collection didn't offer many options. Besides, the scent and the sound weren't disharmonious, they were kind of intriguing.

He sat on the floor behind her head. After dripping a little oil into one palm, he rubbed his hands together. "I'm going to start with your shoulders. Okay?"

She nodded, so he began to touch her. Smoothing, soothing, stroking, then gradually deepening his touch. Under his hands, he felt her muscles warm and soften. Her breathing slowed and she let out a sigh of pleasure. Her nipples were no longer beaded and he could see rosy-brown areolas through the lace.

His penis was semierect. Yes, he was aware of Ann as a sexy woman. But for now he went with the flow, enjoying the massage. This was what he'd become used to with a sex partner. Letting desire ebb and flow, enjoying the process rather than striving to achieve a result.

He tried to send Ann messages through his fingers. Relax, loosen up, trust me. Listen to your body, trust your beautiful body. Treat it well. Let me treat it well.

After a while, he rose to his knees. "I'm going to slide my hands under your shoulders," he said softly, "and work your back. Don't lift, don't try to help me, just settle into my hands."

He eased his hands under her, feeling her bones and muscles adjust to his presence. Deftly he located tight spots, kneaded out the knots, coaxed all her tired, strained muscles to loosen and stretch.

"Feels so good," she murmured. "Thank you, Adonis."

"You're welcome." He leaned down and pressed his lips to her forehead. One brief touch, nothing to change her peaceful mood.

He had worked down her back as far as he could reach, almost to her slim waist. Now he massaged his way back up again and started on her slender neck. He squeezed and kneaded, trying to gauge her reaction. He didn't want to hurt her, but if the massage was too light it wouldn't have a lasting effect. "How does this feel?" he whispered, close to her ear.

She gave a shiver. "Perfect. Don't ever stop."

He chuckled softly and kept easing out the stresses in her neck. When her muscles seemed as warm and soft as butter, he asked, "Is it all right if I massage your face?"

"My face?" Her eyes popped open. "Why?"

"Don't you ever rub your temples when you have a headache?"

She closed her eyes again, and they crinkled up as she smiled. "Enough to wear grooves. Can't you see them?"

All he saw was soft, delicate skin fringed by silky hair. Still, he knew where to press. "You mean here?"

"Those are the ones."

He gently massaged her temples, her forehead. Then he settled his hands lightly so his thumbs were under her jaw on each side and his fingers rested on her cheekbones. He stroked outward toward her ears, then back in, over and over again, a little deeper each time.

She sighed, murmured something wordless, and he moved on to work her jaw.

When the massage was done, Adonis stroked her face softly, then even more gently. He hoped he could ease Ann from relaxation to a higher level of sensory awareness. Bending close to one ear, he murmured, "Are you listening to the music?"

"Mmm. Dimly. I'm kind of drifting. Headache's gone. Thank you."

"My pleasure. Now, focus on the music. Tell me what you hear."

Her brows lifted, then she must have decided to humor him. "It's just one flute but the sound is full and resonant. Kind of . . . round, if that makes sense." She smiled. "My friend Rina would do better at this. She's a musician."

"There's no better or worse. Just concentrate on the music."

"Sometimes it's pure and sometimes it vibrates. It climbs and twists, then it unwinds and comes down again."

"I hadn't thought of it that way before." It was a good description of lovemaking too, the way he liked to do it when the mood was right, and time limitless. He held his hands just above the skin of her temples and forehead and stroked the air, as if he was touching her. "Tune into your body and your sensations. What are you feeling?"

"Warm and soft, kind of melted like the oil. My forehead's tingly, in a nice way. Are you doing something? It almost feels like you're touching me, but not quite."

"My hands are over the surface of your skin. Some people call it energy healing, or aura healing. It helps with stress."

"You think you can heal me without touching me," she said skeptically.

"You're the one who feels it," he reminded her.

He eased his hands away and reached into the bag he'd brought. Should he blindfold her? No, she might tense up again. "Don't open your eyes," he murmured as he took out a small bunch of red seedless grapes. He broke one off and held it against her lips. "Smell, feel. What is it?"

She smiled against the grape. "Not your finger, not your cock."

"You're picking the first things that come to mind. Concentrate, smell."

"I smell something but it's not strong and I have no idea what it is."

"Open your lips and let me slide it in. I promise it'll be nice."

Her eyelids twitched but she kept them closed and opened her mouth.

He slid the grape in. "Don't bite down."

Her mouth worked as she rolled it around. "Grape," she said triumphantly.

"What does it taste like? Now you can bite."

She bit, chewed. "Mmm, good. Sweet, intense, with a tart edge. Probably red rather than green. Am I right?"

"Ann, it's not about right and wrong. It's about sensing. Just sensing." He fed her a couple more, then she said, "If you're playing slave again, I think you should be peeling these."

He chuckled. Then he took something else and held it to her nose. "Try this. Smell." He stroked it down her cheek until it rested on her lips.

"Chocolate," she said promptly. "It's a chocolate." Her tongue came out and licked, cat-like and delicate. Sensual and sexy. She licked again. "Dark chocolate. My favorite."

His cock envied the chocolate, but Adonis knew how to be patient. Besides, Ann was going along with him, tuning into her senses and responding. "Take it in, find out what it is."

She opened and he slid the chocolate in. Her jaw moved as she bit down cautiously. Then surprise and delight lit her face. She chewed, obviously savoring the treat. That pretty pink tongue came out and licked her lips. "Chocolate-covered cherry. I'd say it's from Purdy's."

"How did you know that?"

"Joanne, a woman I work with, buys treats there every week or so." Eyes still closed, she smiled up at him. "Got another?"

"I dunno," he teased. "Did you eat dinner? I don't think you should get dessert if you didn't finish your dinner."

"I had some crackers and cheese while I worked." Her lips twitched. "Then of course there was wine and some grapes."

He laughed, loving that sensual mouth of hers.

"I guess it'll do." He eased another chocolate between her lips. Watching her eat the things was more sensual and enjoyable than eating them himself. "Ready for something else?"

"Mmm. Only if it's better than chocolate cherries."

"You'll have to tell me."

Her nostrils flared a little, her lips twitched. She was expecting more food.

8

Adonis decided to fool her. He picked up a peacock feather, soft and fringed at the tip. He traced it lightly across Ann's throat. She shivered, drew in a breath. He let it drift down her chest. In the candlelight, the iridescent greens and blues gleamed.

"You're touching me," she said. "But it's not your hand. Not that energy-aura thing, either. It feels different."

"Good?" He flicked the feather in a fast, darting circle around her breast, then back and forth across her nipple. Her flesh puckered and began to bead, giving him his answer.

"Mmm, I'm not sure." Her voice had gone kind of purry and her eyelids didn't twitch. She wasn't even tempted to look. "I need to do a comparison test. Fingers on one breast, and whatever that is on the other."

He palmed her breast, cupped and squeezed it. Then he began to circle her areola with one finger. With his other hand he used the feather to tease her other breast. As he did, he felt the shift in his own body. The same one she was experiencing. From sensual awareness to arousal.

Ann's head went back, her chest arched. "Hands win. I want both of them."

He tossed the feather aside and cupped both breasts, his hands delighting in the soft, full, utterly feminine warmth of her. But there was something else he wanted too. In tantric sex, lovers gazed into each other's eyes, deepening the connection between them.

Ann's eyes had been closed too long. He wanted to see those green and gold flecks sparkle in the flickering candlelight. He wanted to look inside her and imagine all the things her lovely body and complicated mind might hold. "Open your eyes."

"Well, finally," she said in a teasing tone. Her lids lifted and she blinked a couple of times, squinted, blinked again. Then she focused on him, with a lazy smile. "Okay, Adonis, my eyes are open, so how about giving me something special to look at? Why don't you take your shirt off?" She reached a hand out and latched onto the top button.

Tonight he wore a white cotton shirt, the sleeves rolled up his forearms. He was warm from the exertion of the massage, and his own arousal. But at the moment he wanted her looking into his eyes, not at his torso. He caught her hand in his. "Just look at me for a moment."

"The scenery would be even better with your shirt off."

"Look into my eyes."

"Why?"

"It helps two people connect."

"You are into some weird stuff tonight."

He touched a finger to her bottom lip. "You liked the chocolate cherries."

"Fine." Her gaze met his for all of about six seconds, then darted away. "Now, I either want your shirt off, or another cherry."

Why were so many people uncomfortable with looking into

each other's eyes? Windows into the soul, someone had said. He didn't mind sharing his soul with Ann, but she was still guarding hers.

Again he thought of that slot in her planner: "Adonis: sex." What would it take to get her to move past that?

"Adonis?" Her hand struggled within his.

He sighed. Maybe he was hoping for too much, too fast. She'd let down her guard enough to close her eyes and trust him while he massaged and fed her. It was progress.

"Okay." He released her hand. "Shirt off."

She worked the buttons free, parted the sides, then he stood and slipped out of the shirt. He took a moment to replace the now-finished Nakai CD with the Diana Krall one. When he turned back to the bed, Ann was lying on her side, head propped on one hand, studying him. "Take it all off," she said, her voice husky and seductive.

He peeled off his jeans and boxers, releasing his erection, then sat cross-legged on the bed. He was hard, no question he wanted her, but he was in control of his body. There was a lot he wanted from this woman. Far more than quick and dirty sex. "Come sit on my lap?"

"How? Won't I be heavy?"

"You're not heavy. Here, like this."

He helped her ease down so she was half-kneeling, half-sitting, some of her weight across his thighs and the rest on her knees and lower legs. Tantric practitioners called the position yab-yom. His arms circled her waist and hers rested on his shoulders.

She glanced past him at the wall. "It's like a Kama Sutra position."

"Tantric sex has a lot in common with Kama Sutra."

She stiffened. "Tantric sex? You're really into that stuff?"

"It gave me a whole different idea of what lovemaking could be."

"Right," she said flatly. "Better. You said that last time." She cleared her throat. "So, you travel all over learning massage *and* sex techniques too? You're an expert on tantric sex?"

He shook his head. "God, far from an expert. When I was in India, I had a lover who was into it. She taught me some things, and I realized I'd only experienced a tiny bit of what lovemaking could really be like."

His and Ann's crotches were snuggled up together so the lace of her teddy brushed his naked cock. Despite the intimacy of the position, her body was stiff in his arms. She sounded cool and defensive when she said, "A tiny bit? I thought Wednesday night was pretty good."

"Wednesday was really nice."

"Nice? It just felt *nice*?" Now she was gazing into his eyes. But more with outrage than that sense of intimate connection he was looking for.

"*Really* nice. But orgasm can be more powerful for a guy if he holds it off longer."

"Longer?" She frowned. "You came too soon? And here I thought—" She broke off.

"Thought what?"

"You were never going to come. You weren't turned on enough. I felt inadequate because I wasn't making you come."

"Jesus, Ann. You really are goal-oriented." He'd been right about what he thought he heard earlier. She *had* said, "Talk about performance pressure."

Her eyes narrowed. "Oh sure, tell me you don't care if you climax."

"It's nice but not essential." They were gazing into each other's eyes the way he'd wanted, struggling for an understanding that clearly eluded both of them. "I used to be goal-oriented," he said. "With the goal being orgasm. But I've learned sex can be about so much more than that. It's the process that's important, more than the result."

Her lashes flicked down, then up again. "So, you're saying, you make love for a long time, enjoy the process, and hold off orgasm. Like, for how long?" She didn't sound upset anymore, but definitely skeptical.

He touched her shoulders delicately, exploring the skin he'd so recently massaged. Jasmine-scented skin that glowed from the oil he'd used. "Who measures time when you're making love?"

"A lot of people. People measure things." She glanced down at his cock, then back up, making him aware he was only semi-erect.

Was she thinking one or both of them was inadequate because he didn't have a raging woody? He shoved the thought away and answered her original question. "How long? I don't know. Hours, sometimes."

"Hours." She wrapped a hand around him. "You're saying you can go hours before you come."

His cock throbbed and swelled, sensation rippling through his body. He nodded, drifting the tip of one finger up her neck as he did, and watching her shiver.

"Why would you want to?" She circled him with her thumb and middle finger and began to stroke up and down, and with each stroke he expanded.

"So I can enjoy being with my lover. So we can touch, explore, experience each other fully." He caught the bottom of her ear between thumb and index finger, just below the simple gold earring she wore. "Awaken our entire bodies to pleasure, not just our genitals."

"Can you honestly say you don't care if you climax?" She stroked faster.

"Sometimes." Her clever hand was definitely tapping into his sexual energy and he was about as hard as he could get.

At her skeptical glance downward, he chuckled. "Okay, I

usually do like to climax and ejaculate. But it's no big deal if I don't."

Her hand stopped and her eyes glittered warningly. "Is it a big deal if *she* doesn't?"

"If she wants to, then she should have however many orgasms she wants." He traced the outer line of her earlobe.

She shook her head, dislodging his finger. "You'll make sure your lover gets as many orgasms as she wants, but you don't care if you come?"

"Pretty much."

He could tell there were about a dozen things she wanted to say, but she settled for, "One will do, but two would be nice. And, whether or not you care if you come, I'd like it if you did." She caught him, just below the head of his cock, squeezed gently, then began to stroke again.

He gave her a mock salute. "Okay, if you're going to set the rules of the game, I guess I'll just have to follow orders."

"Rules?" Her hand paused. Then her face lit up. "You're right, we need rules."

"Rules for having sex? You're crazy." He went back to caressing the rim of her earlobe, then let his finger drift into the center.

Without seeming aware she did it, she arched her neck and leaned into his hand like a cat asking to be stroked. "If I am, then you are, too. You already have all these tantric sex rules about taking things slow and not focusing on climax. Well, I think those rules are crazy. I want rules of my own."

"And what would yours be? You always get one, preferably two, orgasms?"

She grinned. "That's a pretty good rule. But I like rules that are fair. You get an orgasm, too." A finger circled the head of his penis, her touch silky and tantalizing.

"If you get two, I should have two as well."

Her eyes widened. "You can do that? In what time period?"

"Damn, woman." He chuckled. "There you go, clock-watching again." He spread his fingers, threaded them through the hair behind her ears, lifting it away from her head, then letting it fall back.

"Mmm. Nice." Then she gave a heavy sigh. "But we're so different, could we ever agree on how to have sex?" She was just holding his penis now, but her warm hand felt good.

"We didn't do so badly last time," he reminded her. All the same, she could be right. He was positive his way was best. Yet he could see how a clock-watching, goal-oriented woman like her would have trouble accepting tantric sex.

She grinned impishly. "Last time you let me do it my way."

Yeah, and she'd got off on that sex-slave thing. He had, too, but there were so many more things he wanted to teach her. If he had his way, she'd soon be booking way more than two hours for sex with him!

"You said you want rules that are fair," he reminded her as he stroked her nape. "So how about we take turns?"

"Turns? What do you mean?"

"Take turns deciding how we're going to have sex." He wasn't a dummy when it came to strategy, and it was unrealistic to think they'd be making love for much longer tonight. So he said, "I'll even give you two in a row."

"Two what? Orgasms?" Her eyes sparkled.

"One-track mind. Yeah, that, too. What I meant was, turns. On Wednesday you were in charge, you were on top, and you can do it again tonight if you want."

"Be on top?"

"Be wherever you want to be. This time, you decide how we make love." He waited for her to point out that he'd controlled the last hour and a half, but she didn't. "Next time, I get to choose."

"So the rule is, taking turns on top." She gave his penis a gentle squeeze.

"Sure, if you want to put it that way. And tonight's your turn."

"I can definitely get into that. Okay, let's get started."

For him, they'd started when they first touched. Or maybe first laid eyes on each other at her door. But he knew by now Ann viewed sex differently. Everything he'd done up to now had confused her, but now she knew where she stood. Firmly in the driver's seat.

"Your wish is my command," he told her.

She didn't respond.

"Come on, Ann. I bet you know what you want. Tell me."

"I don't want to sound crude. Or needy."

"You couldn't. Tell me what would feel good. How about I lick you all over?"

She gave a nervous giggle. "Licking's good. But maybe not *all* over. You could focus on, uh, the erogenous zones."

One day it'd be his turn and he really would lick her all over. For now, he'd obey her command. But, if she wasn't going to come out and say, "go down on me," then he was going to torture her a little. "Lie down. Head at the top of the bed on the pillow."

She released his cock and scrambled to do it, lying with her long legs suggestively apart.

He blanketed her with his body.

"Adonis, I—"

He cut her off by dipping the tip of his tongue in her left ear. "Ear," he whispered, breathing warm air onto the damp spot. "Erogenous zone." He ran his tongue around the outside, then dipped in again.

She squirmed underneath him and he shifted position so his cock was between her legs, pressing against the lace at her crotch. Lazily he toyed with her ear while his hips made small movements and her hips twisted in response. She was hot, growing wet against him, and the soft firmness of her curvy body was getting to him.

"I want—" she started.

This time he interrupted by touching his lips to hers. "I know. Erogenous zones. Mouth, tongue." He proved his point by nibbling around her lips, then swirling his tongue into her mouth, at first teasing, then passionate and demanding.

She answered the demand, kissing back hungrily, arching her body against his.

He felt the stimulation all the way down. Lace against chest hair, nipples poking him, soft legs writhing against his. Hot, wet lace against his throbbing cock.

Her hands grasped his butt, pulling him against her almost desperately.

"Adonis!" She tore her mouth from his, released his backside, and grabbed on to his shoulders. "There's another erogenous zone."

He raised up on his elbows. "Oh, yeah. Throat, inside of the elbows, back of the knees."

"I'm supposed to be in control. You're not doing what I told you."

"You said to lick your erogenous zones."

"You know what I mean," she said, sounding frustrated.

"Maybe you have to be more specific," he teased.

"Fine." She took a breath, then stared into his eyes. "Eat my pussy. Is that specific enough for you?" Her eyes were glittering, and he could tell that speaking so bluntly was turning her on.

"Okay, I'll eat you. And then what?"

The glitter was brighter. "Fuck me. In the pussy. With your cock. Make me come."

She wasn't the only one getting hot. It was like a wet dream to hear those words coming out of that lush mouth. "Your wish is my command."

He eased down her body, unsnapped the crotch of her teddy, and pulled the fabric aside. Her labia were swollen and moist petals. Tantric imagery compared a woman's sex to a lotus flower, and Ann was a lovely rosy blossom.

Gently he tugged on her legs, pulling her down the bed, then he kneeled on the floor. With one finger he parted her lips, then ran his tongue around the outer ones, at first slow and easy, then harder, faster, feeling her grow wetter. She tasted sweet and musky, and smelled of sexual heat.

His tongue explored her inner lips, then dipped inside her vagina as her mound thrust toward him, demanding more. He eased back for a moment, found a pillow, and maneuvered it under her bottom. Now he had better access, and there'd be less strain on her back.

He tasted her again, flicked his tongue against her clitoris, which was peeping out from its hood. A long shudder moved through her body, and she moaned, "Yes, that's so good."

It felt and tasted good to him, too. His cock, pressed against the end of the bed, was as aroused as her clit.

Easing one finger inside, then another, he felt her body clenching around him, her juices flowing. He circled inside her, doing the clock. Touching twelve, three, six, and nine, enjoying her pleasure as she writhed faster.

"Adonis, I'm so close," she panted. "Suck me."

As his fingers found her G-spot, he applied his mouth to her clit, swirling his tongue, flicking and teasing until she groaned, then closing his lips on her and sucking gently.

Her knees were up and her thighs clamped his head, holding him there. Then she said, "Oh! Oh, yes," and began to spasm, her inner walls gripping his fingers in rhythmic contractions.

Gradually the motions slowed and her knees relaxed, releasing his head.

He fumbled for a condom and sheathed himself. Then he licked her labia again, tasting her musk, feeling her tremble.

"Now," she said, voice a breathy whisper. "Fuck me now, Adonis."

He shoved another pillow under her, lifting her lower body high, then slid into her in one long, easy glide. Balancing his weight on his knees and forearms, he leaned forward to kiss her. Her lips parted and she took his mouth hungrily. Her fingers threaded through his hair, her legs came up and crossed over to hook around his thighs as he began to pump into her.

"You have a beautiful pussy, outside and in," he murmured. Tight and wet, full of sensation. He loved gliding in and out of her, changing the angle slightly with each thrust.

"Are you wearing a condom?" she gasped.

"Yeah, of course."

"It f-feels different."

"Textured. Little bumps and spirals," he said between thrusts. "Is it okay?"

"Good, really good. I l-like t-texture." Her voice kept breaking.

Her eyes were squeezed shut and he wished she'd open them, but her whole face was tight with concentration. This was a woman who worked hard at orgasm, like she did at her job.

Well, anyone who worked that damned hard deserved a reward. He rested his face against the curve of her neck, breathed in the scent of that aphrodisiac massage oil. Kissed and nibbled her soft skin. Felt the press of her breasts, the grinding thrust of her hips as he stroked into her harder and deeper.

Her head thrashed, she gasped a little stream of "ohs," letting him know she was close.

"Yeah, Ann, feel me in you. Let me fill you up." He shifted his angle to better stimulate her G-spot and the "ohs" got faster and became an "Oh, God!"

Reaching between them, he found her clit, then he let himself go, plunging hard and fast, driving them both toward climax. When he poured himself into her, she was already shuddering in spasms around him.

Her eyes were still closed. Shutting him out.

Despite the blistering orgasm, he wasn't satisfied.

And he knew it wasn't just about sex, tantric or otherwise. He wanted Ann Montgomery to let him in. Into her mind, maybe even into her heart. She was special. Instinct told him that. Even as reason said they were opposites, she was too high-maintenance, she'd never let a guy like him get close.

After their breathing had slowed, he kissed her softly on the forehead, then withdrew and went to deal with the condom.

As he washed his hands, he studied his reflection in the mirror above the sink. Hair tousled, cheeks flushed, he looked like he'd had great sex. Except for his troubled eyes, which told a different story.

Next time—if they both decided there'd be a next time—it would be his turn "on top," as she called it. He could ask for what he wanted. See if he had a chance of breaking down the barriers she'd flung up.

One thing he'd learned tonight, though. Her behavior told him it wasn't just him. He'd be prepared to bet she had never let a man get truly intimate.

Oh, yeah, he wanted a next time. There was more to this woman than the workaholic lawyer who needed to schedule and control sex.

Well, of course there was. She had friends, one of whom had given her a stuffed cat. Friendships took time and emotional investment.

Did Ann invest more in her friendships than in her sexual relationships? If so, why? And could she be persuaded to change her mind?

He could be pretty damned persuasive.

Humming, he went back to the bedroom. She'd risen and was belting her black robe.

"Thanks, Adonis," she said, coming to him and stretching up to give him a quick kiss. "That was terrific." It was a dismissal. A polite one, but a dismissal all the same.

"And now you want to get back to work." Next time, he told himself, as he gathered the things he'd brought. When he picked up the bottle of oil, she said, "Can I keep it?"

A good sign. He handed it to her. "Sounds like a pretty demanding job you have."

She wrinkled her nose. "The thing is, I'm not brilliant. For me, it's always taken hard work to excel. My mother picked up on that when I was still in kindergarten. There was another girl who was brighter than me, but Mother helped me realize I could be at the top of the class if I put in enough work." An impish grin flashed. "I may not be the smartest, but I try harder."

He imagined a serious little girl, rushing home from school so she could study. Trying to impress a mom who'd told her she wasn't supersmart. "Did your mom teach you to play, too?"

"Of course. Word games, math and science puzzles."

"No playing with dolls or climbing trees?" He glanced around, trying to find his boxers.

Ann bent down to look under the end of the bed and came up with his shorts, which she handed over. "Too frivolous." A wistful expression flashed across her face, to be replaced by a knowing one. "You're on about a balanced life again, aren't you?"

"Caught me." He flashed a quick grin. "Just doesn't seem healthy, working all the time."

"I do have a long dinner with my girlfriends every Monday." She shrugged, then said wryly, "Yeah, Adonis, I've been working like a fiend forever. I don't know what else I'd do with my time anyway."

He caught her chin between his thumb and index finger, gazed into her eyes, and winked. "Tantric sex?"

She chuckled and pulled away. "You never give up." She tossed his T-shirt at him. "What do you do with *your* spare time? Aside, that is, from hours and hours of tantric sex."

"Camping trips, kayaking, work out at the gym. Hang out with my family, my friends. Read a book, meditate, go for a long walk." He drew a breath. "Babysit my niece and nephews. Go to a movie, sometimes the opera. Mom loves opera, Dad hates it. She kept dragging me along until I grew to appreciate it." He snapped his fingers. "Hey, you like opera, too. I saw your CDs."

"My friend Rina plays clarinet with the operatic society."

"And you go to the performances?"

She shook her head. "Not usually. But I do support her by buying CDs."

"It'd mean more to her if you were there."

She stared at him. "I never thought of it that way. But I'm always so busy."

Too busy to support a friend? He didn't say the words, but she flushed and said, "Any time one of us really needs the others, we're there for each other."

"I'm sure you are." Yeah, he could see Ann being someone you could depend on in a crisis. Just not a person who'd shove work aside for activities she didn't see as necessary.

Now he knew exactly what he wanted to do with her. "My turn next, right?"

She gave him a cautious glance. "That's the rule. But I'm not sure I'm ready for tantric stuff."

He shook his head. "Blow off the afternoon tomorrow and come kayaking."

"Do what?" She looked almost horrified.

"It's Sunday. Day of rest." When she opened her mouth for what he knew would be a protest, he held up a hand to stop her. "Yeah, you never rest. But try it. Work all morning, then come out and play."

"Kayaking? In one of those tiny boats, right down in the water? I'm a klutz; I'd tip the boat."

"I doubt it. But even if you did, I wouldn't let you drown. We'd just have to come home and find some way of warming up." He gave her his best sexy grin, the one that created the dimple his sisters always teased him about. "All work, no play, you know what'll come of that." He smoothed her frown line.

Her gaze dropped. "Am I really that dull?" she asked softly.

He gripped her chin again, and waited until she raised her eyes to meet his. "You're beautiful and sexy and fascinating. You've got layers, Ann, and I bet you haven't discovered half of them yourself."

The corner of her lip twitched. "I'm an onion and you want to peel me?"

"I want us to peel you together."

Her lip twitched again. "It'd be easier if you just wanted sex."

He chuckled, knowing he was getting to her. "But not half as much fun."

"What if I said I could free up the afternoon for sex tomorrow? It's your turn, I guess maybe we could try the tantric thing."

His cock pulsed. Man, that idea was tempting. But so was kayaking.

Ann was watching his face closely, and he sensed it was a test. He didn't know what answer she was looking for, but he gave her the truth. "I'd rather go kayaking."

Her frown line was back. "Sex with me is that bad?"

"God, no, it's great. But spending the afternoon outside with you, talking and getting to know each other, would be that good."

The moment Adonis left, Ann e-mailed her friends. Help! Adonis is taking me KAYAKING!!! Am I losing my freaking MIND???

Not expecting a response until morning, she was surprised when Jenny replied immediately: KAYAKING???? Ann Montgomery's going KAYAKING??? Physical activity? Outside? OK, I'm gonna call the straitjacket dudes.

Ann e-mailed back: What are you doing on the computer at midnight?

Jenny responded: Just got back from an evening at Scott's. Now that the family knows I'm dating him, they've stuck me with a midnight curfew. Rats! Could stay out later when I was pretending it was interviews. Can you believe, half the time Auntie or Granny waits up, and tries to make me a cup of tea?

When Ann was Jen's age, she'd lived at home, too, attending law school. Curfews hadn't been an issue because she'd spent most evenings either at the law library or at home working.

So what's with this kayaking stuff? Jenny asked.

Adonis says my life needs balance, Ann responded.

Jenny's reply read: No duh! But why're you listening to this guy? You've never listened to us about this.

True. It had become one of their "agree to disagree, and leave it alone" subjects. Like Rina's body-image issue.

He's persuasive. She couldn't tell Jenny about their "taking turns on top" rule, not until the Foursome was together on

Monday. And we'd just had great sex, I was in that postorgas-mic glow state. Not responsible for my actions. Honesty made her go on. OK, the idea intrigued me. Like playing hooky. And he said he wanted us to get to know each other.

Her fingers paused, then slowly she went on. He seems to like me for more than just sex. She still didn't know whether to be offended or flattered that he'd chosen kayaking over sex. Jenny's answer flew back. Well, of course he does! You're smart and fun and perceptive, not to mention gorgeous.

Nothing like a loyal friend. He's the gorgeous one. As for me being fun . . . Well, I doubt he's into the same kind of fun the Foursome is. Our fun is pretty much girl-talk. But I guess we'll find out. If we're not compatible outside of bed, the silver lining is, I'll never have to kayak again! We'll just stay in bed. BTW, did I mention we have RULES?

Jen and Scott had the Fantasy Rules, Suzanne and Jaxon had the Champagne Rules. It was so cool to have rules, too.

Jenny came back with, Rules? Sex rules? Gimme deets, girl!

Ann smiled gleefully. Foursome Rules prevail. Can't spill until we're all together. I'll tell you Monday.

Mean, mean, mean, Jenny responded. So this means Adonis has beaten out David?

Well, damn. How about that? She'd forgotten about David for the entire evening. Though she'd been conflicted in the be-ginning, Adonis had got her all mellow with that scented mas-sage oil. Nor had David come to mind during those two terrific orgasms, or the conversation about sex rules. And since then, she'd been obsessing about kayaking.

I haven't heard from David. He may come back tomorrow and if he does, we'll talk.

Jen said, Think he's breaking up with his wife? What'll you do then? He's, like, your dream guy, right?

She groaned. Jen, I don't know. I just don't know. Aagh!

Don't let him pressure you. It's your heart. Give it time, it'll tell you what's best for you.

Thanks, Ann typed. That's really good advice.

As she closed her e-mail, she felt much better. Of course she had time.

9

Not only was Ann petrified about the idea of kayaking, but she didn't have the slightest idea what to wear. "Clothes to drown in," she muttered late Sunday morning as she studied the meager contents of her closet.

Adonis was a jeans guy, so she'd be a jeans girl. She had a fun, rhinestoned pair she wore when the Foursome did something special—like attend the firefighter calendar competition where Jenny'd met Scott. Then she had the comfy old pair she wore at home.

Jen, who adored sparkly stuff, would have voted for the rhinestones, but Ann went with the plain ones. Socks, sneakers, and a T-shirt that sported the Shakespeare quote, "The first thing we do, let's kill all the lawyers."

She stared in the mirror. Dull. Maybe she should've gone with rhinestones.

Rhinestones are tacky, and that T-shirt is disrespectful of everything we're both working to achieve.

Well, Mother, then just be glad you're not here to see me.

Ann snickered. *Of course if you were, you'd be way more pissed about me goofing off, than what I wear to do it.*

She found the pink mini-backpack Jenny had once given her—far more Jen's style than her own, but she didn't have anything else—and tossed in a windbreaker, a water bottle, her wallet, and the necessary odds and ends.

If David flew back into town today and they got together later, she'd definitely have to come up with a more impressive outfit than jeans and a girlie backpack.

Oh, God. Kayaking. Adonis. David. What a crazy day.

That's what you get for losing your focus, Ann. If you'd just stick to work, you wouldn't have these problems. Haven't I always told you—

The door buzzer cut her mother off. Ann took a deep breath, tried to quell the butterflies in her tummy, and told Adonis, "I'll be right down."

He wore jeans too—oh, God, faded old ones that very nicely highlighted his very nice package. His tucked-in T-shirt was a soft blue that made his skin look even darker. On his feet were a pair of rubber-soled, Velcro-fastened sandals.

"Hey, you." He read her shirt and laughed. "Thought I had a date with a lawyer, but maybe you killed her off?"

"Is this okay? I didn't know what to wear."

"You look great." He pulled her to him for a quick, warm kiss that made her pulse race, then thrust her away and stared some more. "How do you always manage to do that?"

"Do what?"

"Whether it's a business suit, a teddy, or jeans, you look like a movie star."

Sweet, but his sisters should have told him not to go overboard with the compliments. "Yeah, sure. If I look good at all, it's my mother's influence. Her bone structure and her instructions on good taste." She glanced down at her chest. "Not that she likes lawyer jokes."

"Ah. She's a lawyer, too," he said, as if he'd gotten the answer to an unasked question.

She nodded. "A very successful one. In Toronto. She does intellectual-property law. Things like patents, trademarks, copyright."

"Sounds kind of dull. Compared to that Charter stuff you were talking about."

Surprised, Ann beamed at him. He thought her work was interesting? How cool!

"Okay, let's go," he said.

He'd distracted her, but now her anxiety returned. "I'm really not sure about this."

"Relax. I'll look after you. It's not torture, it's just kayaking."

"Your definition of torture's different than mine." But she couldn't help smiling. "All right, where's your car?"

He held out his hand. "I've booked a kayak from a place on the Island. We can walk."

Granville Island was only fifteen minutes from her place, but she'd never walked there. In fact, she rarely went there. The market shops didn't open until long after she'd gone to work, and closed well before she drove home.

She put her hand into Adonis's. "If you let me drown, my mother will sue your pants off," she joked, though she worried less about drowning than about making a fool of herself.

All the same, as they headed toward the seawall, she felt an unusual sense of adventure. The September sunshine, playing hooky, his company—she was on top of the world.

He squeezed her hand tight, walking in a long-legged saunter that had her hurrying to keep up. The seawall path was busy but he steered them among the people, dogs, and baby buggies. To her left, condo and town house balconies were bright with late summer flowers; to her right, sunlight sparkled off the ocean and a couple of kayakers paddled by. She'd lived in her place for two years but never noticed these things before.

"So your mom's an intellectual-property lawyer," Adonis said.

"Internationally renowned." Ann heard the pride in her voice. "She's always traveling to consult and speak at conferences."

"Impressive."

"Oh, yeah! She picked her niche early on, and had the foresight to choose a field that's really taken off. Especially with the Internet."

She felt a moment's envy. Meredith had vision as well as dedication. In comparison, Ann felt like she was stumbling around. Sure, she was on the partnership track, but she hadn't settled on an area of specialty. Was Charter law old hat, now the legislation had been in place for a quarter century? Her mother had said it was a good fit, but was that because she knew Ann didn't have Meredith's level of smarts?

"You're thinking about work," Adonis said.

She shot him a surprised glance. "How can you tell?"

"Tension in your shoulders. Your hand stopped holding mine and just sat there."

"Communicating without saying a word again?" She gripped his hand to let him know she was back.

"You do it so well. Want to talk about the work thing?"

"Just wishing I had as clear a direction in mind as Mother did at my age."

"You're not exactly old yet. And what's your dad think about all this career stuff?"

There was an edge to his normally tranquil voice. What was that all about?

"Don't have a father," she said, as she had hundreds of times before.

"Oh?" He glanced at her and she could see he wasn't sure if he should ask.

"I never had a dad. My mother raised me alone."

"Sorry." He squeezed her hand. "That must've been tough."

"It was okay." Her mother had always said they were better off, just the two of them.

Adonis released her hand and put his arm around her. "Okay, but not great."

His touch was so comforting, his words so understanding, she found herself talking about something she'd almost never put into words. "Mother tried so hard. She said we didn't need anyone else. Kept lecturing me about how a woman needs a man like a fish needs a bicycle."

He laughed softly. "My mom says that, too. She's been married to dad for going on forty years, but she says a relationship has to be about *want*. Never about need."

"Hmm. She has a different interpretation of that saying than my mother does." Ann sighed. "Mother did her best to prove we didn't need a man. All the same, I felt like I was missing out on something."

"Of course you were. Parents are—" He shrugged. "Not perfect. Annoying sometimes." There was that edge again. It seemed even mellow Adonis had parent issues. "But they love you, and kids need that. If you have two parents, you have twice as much love. Your mom may not have needed or wanted a husband, but I bet as a little girl you wanted a dad."

Want, not need. Yes, there was a difference. When she'd studied at classmates' houses, sometimes the dads would come home. With hugs and kisses for their children.

She'd so badly wanted a daddy's hug.

"Yeah, I wanted a father," she admitted softly. Why did Adonis have this impact, making her want to talk about things she avoided even thinking about? "Maybe sometimes I still do."

Was Jenny right in saying she was attracted to older men because subconsciously she was looking for a man she could look up to, go to for advice and approval? Someone to counterbalance the strength of her mother's influence?

She studied the other people who were out walking. Families, single parents, couples, a few people on their own. Sure, if you had more people in your life, you probably did get more love. But there was also more potential for tension, conflict. Bottom line, if you wanted to make it in the world, better to do it on your own, without having to take anyone else into consideration.

Her mother could have gone further earlier in her career, if she hadn't had Ann. Meredith had never come right out and said so, but Ann had always known it.

"You never even met your dad?" Adonis asked, pulling her closer.

He sure was a touchy-feely guy. The opposite of her. Of her mother. But, strangely, she enjoyed it. His openness even made her want to open up a little herself. She put her arm around his slim waist. "Never even knew who he was."

Adonis broke stride. "You don't even know his name?" he said disbelievingly. Then, "Sorry. Mom's told me about hippie days, free love. I don't mean to put your mom down if she didn't know who he was. Or, did she decide to have a kid on her own, and use a sperm donor?"

Sperm donor? Like ambitious Meredith would have *chosen* to get pregnant?

"You so don't know my mother," she said. "No, not a sperm donor." The pregnancy had to have been unwanted. She didn't know why her mother hadn't chosen abortion, but she could guess why she'd ruled out adoption. Duty and perfectionism. Who could raise a child as well as superefficient Meredith Montgomery?

"She hasn't told you anything about him?"

How many times had Ann asked, before finally giving up? She shook her head.

"That's not fair to you."

Yeah, tell me about it. She shrugged a shrug that was the product of years of hurt and rationalization. "It upset her to think about him."

"Who cares? She's a parent, she can deal with a little upset. She's the one who had the bad judgment to get involved with the guy. I figure, you have a right to know who your father was. For better or worse."

Maybe she did. She felt like she did. But Adonis didn't know her mother.

Ann Montgomery, there is not one single thing you need to know about your biological father. You have me, and that's all you need.

Once Meredith had an idea fixed in her head, she wasn't about to change her mind.

"I know," Adonis said. "It's hard to challenge your parents after they drum into your head how you're supposed to respect them."

Again, he'd understood. Feeling grateful, she hugged his waist. She could feel his muscles shift as he walked. Gratitude slid toward sexual awareness.

Here she was, strolling the seawall with her very own Greek god. Her shoulders straightened, and she realized how many women were casting envious glances in her direction. She wanted to tell them, "Not only is he hot, he's actually nice."

When was the last time she'd done something like this—strolled casually along, linked together with a guy? Could she even remember doing it?

She moved her arm so she could hook her thumb into the back pocket of his jeans. Her hand curved down over his butt, to feel the play of those strong muscles as he walked.

He reciprocated, his big hand covering one entire cheek of

what was nowhere near as firm a backside. His hip nudged hers and she remembered what he looked like naked. The things they'd done together. The way her body responded to him.

Her nipples tightened. "What did you stroke me with last night?" she asked, glancing sideways at him.

He grinned. "My hands, my tongue. Was there something else?"

"Something soft and kind of wispy. Silk fringe on a scarf, maybe?"

"A peacock feather."

"Really? Why? I mean, why not just use"—she shot him a teasing glance—"your hands, your tongue?"

"Different sensations are fun. They make your body more aware."

Her body was certainly aware of him now. In fact, she could think of an activity or two that she'd enjoy a whole lot more than kayaking. "Mmm, that sounds appealing. What do you say we go back to my place and experiment with different sensations?" she asked suggestively.

He released her butt and drifted his fingers down her arm, skimming the surface.

She gave a shiver of pleasure. "Yes. Like that."

He chuckled. "Later. It's too nice a day to be inside."

A man who turned down sex. This habit of his was getting annoying. Insulted, she let go of him and ran her fingers through her hair. "Fine. It's your turn on top. You chose kayaking, so that's what we'll do."

He caught her hand, swung it between them. "Trust me. You'll love it."

She wondered if he was really as simple and straightforward as he seemed, or if he'd learned—from all those sisters—that it was best to ignore a woman's bad moods.

"Let's take a picnic," he said. "We can pick some things up at the market."

It was hard to stay miffed when the huge market building was such a cheerful bustle, bright with mounds of fresh produce, the air heady with the scent of a dozen different foods baking. Adonis was fun to shop with, as they agreed on Italian bread warm from the oven, cheese and olives, grapes and apples, chilled fruit drinks.

Having skipped breakfast in favor of work, Ann's mouth was watering. When they passed a doughnut place, she couldn't resist and ordered a double chocolate. "Want one?" she asked Adonis, expecting a lecture on health food.

"Sure."

"Aha. You do eat junk food."

"Been known to happen."

Munching their doughnuts, they walked out of the market and past a building where a shop displaying arts and crafts called out to Ann. How could she have ignored this fabulous place for so long?

Boats were docked on the west side of Granville Island. Adonis led her toward racks of brightly colored kayaks, gleaming in the sun. She eyed them nervously.

Ann, you have to realize you're not the athletic type. Don't worry about it; that kind of thing is a waste of time anyhow.

Trust Meredith to get in a double-whammy. *Yeah, sure. I'm a klutz, and I'm a fool for wasting my time this way. Thanks a lot, Mother!*

"I did mention I'm not the most coordinated person in the world, didn't I?"

"You'll be fine. I booked a double kayak. It's easier, until you get the hang of it."

Until? Like, she'd be doing this again? "You should know, I don't swim."

"You don't? How can you live by the ocean and not swim?"

"I grew up in Toronto. I've never been swimming in my life."

He grinned. "And you'd rather not start with today? Okay, no tipping allowed."

"But what if we do?"

"You'll be wearing a life vest, and I'll be there to rescue you." He gave an exasperated sigh. "God, Ann, just relax."

She held back a nervous giggle. *Okay, even Mr. Cool, Calm, and Collected can get irked.*

They walked into an outdoors store that had clothing and equipment for activities Ann would rather not contemplate. It was probably Adonis's second home.

He opened his pack and handed her a bag bearing the store's logo. "Go into the restroom and change into these. I picked them up when I reserved the kayak."

"Uh?" She glanced inside, to find black legging-style pants that looked an awful lot like yoga pants, and an olive-green T-shirt, both in a lightweight fabric.

"You get wet in a kayak. That fabric repels water." He winked. "And wicks away perspiration when you get all hot and sweaty from paddling."

"But you're wearing jeans."

He touched his pack. "I'm going to change, too."

"Oh, okay. How much do I owe you?"

He shook his head. "They're a gift."

"Really?" No guy had ever given her anything but the conventional flowers and candy before. "Thanks, Adonis."

In the small restroom, she slipped into her new outfit. He'd got the sizes right; the clothes hugged her curves without binding. The color of the tee even brought out the green in her eyes. The guy really had learned a lot from his sisters, and no doubt girlfriends as well.

When she stepped out of the restroom, there was Adonis in his own kayak gear. He wore the same kind of pants as she did, and oh man, did they showcase the package underneath. Hard to raise her eyes above his waist, but she managed, only to gape at the muscles revealed by the formfitting white tank top.

Okay, maybe there was something to be said for kayaking.

Her clothing was thin for the September weather, but seeing Adonis made her skin heat up.

"You look great," he told her, and the sexy gleam in his eyes warmed her even more.

He took the clothes she'd been wearing and stowed them in his pack. Then she followed him and one of the staff, a skinny guy with long hair in a ponytail, out to the wharf. The staff guy deftly lifted a red kayak from a rack, and he and Adonis stowed the gear in compartments.

Serious nerves were setting in now, and she began to shiver.

"Shoes and socks off," Adonis told her. "They'll only get soaked."

She obeyed, fingers fumbling with the laces, bare feet not appreciating the cool air.

Adonis put an arm around her. "You'll warm up when we get paddling."

The ponytailed guy handed them both life vests. They were not the height of fashion, and Ann wasn't sure how to fasten hers.

Adonis assisted her, his hands brushing her breasts unnecessarily. A wasted effort, because at the moment she was more concerned with survival than sex.

Feeling even clumsier in the bulky vest, she eyed the craft bobbing in the water. It was long and narrow and looked flimsy and unstable. Not to mention uncomfortable.

"You sit up front," Adonis said, indicating one of the oval holes.

Good thing he'd pointed. She'd never have known front from back. While both men steadied the kayak, she lowered herself gingerly until she was sitting on something that was supposed to pass for a seat, with her legs stretched out in front of her.

Yup. Definitely uncomfortable. She wriggled around, trying to adjust her position, and the boat dipped alarmingly.

"Keep your movements slow and small," Adonis said. "Try to keep your upper body steady." He handed her a paddle, a stick with a blade on each end. "Rest that across the kayak. Don't worry about using it until I get us clear of the marina and into open water."

Open water. That had a scary ring.

She didn't dare look around for fear of unbalancing the kayak, but could tell he was getting in behind her. The boat lurched, then steadied. Good God, they were right down in the water, the sides of the boat only a few inches above the surface.

And then they were moving forward, away from the wharf, as Adonis called good-bye to the attendant.

Her peripheral vision picked up the tip of Adonis's oar dipping smoothly into the dark water first on one side, then the other, in a steady rhythm. The boat moved more smoothly than she'd expected, with only a slight rocking motion.

She had no idea how he was steering, but somehow he maneuvered around other craft and before she knew it they were passing by the deck of Bridges restaurant. A few weeks ago the Foursome had eaten dinner there, paying no attention to the water traffic passing by.

"I'd rather be up there than down here," she said.

He chuckled, as if she was making a joke.

What the hell was she doing here? The outdoors and any kind of sport were utterly foreign to her. Yeah, it was appealingly masculine that Adonis was good at all this, but it reinforced that they were opposites. She should be working, waiting for David to fly back from Toronto and perhaps tell her his marriage was over.

"I can't be out too long," she called back to Adonis. "I have tentative plans for tonight."

One of the cute water taxis that went back and forth across

False Creek scooted past them and the pilot waved. Cautiously, remembering to keep her upper body stable, Ann lifted a hand and waved back as Adonis said, "Me, too. Dinner with my family."

"Oh? Is that a regular Sunday-night thing?" She knew Suzanne's and Jenny's families both made a big deal out of Sunday dinner.

"For sure. Mom puts on a big spread for family, friends, whoever drops by."

"She cooks for all those people?" Good God! Hadn't women's lib had any impact on the woman?

"She's always loved to cook. We tell her she should open her own restaurant."

"Why hasn't she?" Didn't she believe women should have careers?

"Says that would turn cooking into something she *has* to do, rather than something she *wants* to do."

This was the same woman who'd said a relationship should be about want, not need. "Sounds like she's big on *want*, your mom."

"Yeah. Calls herself a child of the sixties. She always told us, you gotta figure out what you want, then go for it."

"My mother said pretty much the same thing," Ann mused. And yet, Meredith would have looked down on Adonis's mom's choices. It wasn't good enough for a woman to be a wife and mother. "Does your mom have a job outside the home?"

"She's had part-time ones, but mostly she's been involved with school activities. First with us, then the grandkids." They'd reached the downtown side of False Creek, and he steered the kayak so he was paddling parallel to the shore. "Okay, time to pull your weight, Lawyer-girl."

Lawyer-girl? She wasn't a girl, she was a woman. If the phrase had come from another person she might've been annoyed, but Adonis—raised by all those women—didn't seem to have a chauvinistic bone in his body. He was using the term the same way Jenny used "Annie." An affectionate tease.

"What do I do?" she asked.

"Alternate from side to side in a smooth, steady rhythm. Let the edge of the blade slice into the water, not going too deep but not skimming the surface, either. Watch me."

She craned to see over her shoulder as he demonstrated a slow stroke.

"That means," he went on, "as you switch from side to side you may need to shift the position of the paddle in your hands a little, so the edge cuts in right. Give it a try."

Gingerly Ann let go the edges of the kayak and tried to work the paddle. As she'd suspected, it was a lot harder than he made it look.

She clipped the top of a little wave and almost lost the paddle. Cold water cascaded into her lap. When he'd been paddling, she'd stayed dry as a bone; now she saw why he'd said she'd get wet. When she switched to the other side, she dug so deep the paddle stuck in the ocean. Then it wrenched free, the kayak rocked violently, and she dropped the paddle to grab on to the edges of the boat.

The paddle fell on an angle across the kayak and she caught it before it could slide into the ocean. "I stink at this," she said grimly.

"Try again," Adonis said. "It takes a while to get the feel of it. And don't put so much effort behind it or you'll get sore shoulders really quickly."

She floundered for a few more strokes and he reminded her to try to get a rhythm going.

This is as bad as freaking yoga! She opened her mouth to tell him to turn them around and head back, then closed it. For some reason, she didn't want him to think badly of her. Biting her lip, she kept trying, and her stroke did even out a little. The kayak actually began to move forward.

Then it went faster, and she realized Adonis was paddling, too, trying to time his strokes to her awkward ones. "I told you I'd be hopeless at this," she grumbled, embarrassed.

"You're not going to be perfect first time out," he said. "Relax, have fun. Enjoy the ocean, the fresh air."

Have fun? Is the man insane?

And yet, as the kayak glided past English Bay, the beach well populated on this sunny Sunday afternoon, she started to again feel the unusual thrill of playing hooky. If anyone on the beach noticed the kayak and thought, "That woman looks like Ann Montgomery," they'd quickly decide it couldn't be because Ann would be busy working on legal files.

Poor Ann. Such a dull person, with such a boring life.

That's ridiculous, Ann. They'll all envy you as you rise through the ranks of the legal profession. You'll make me, and yourself, proud.

Take a hike, Mother. This kayak's too small for three people!

Ann definitely wasn't chilled any more; in fact, her shoulders were starting to burn from effort. To take her mind off the ache, she called to Adonis, "Tell me about your sisters."

"From oldest to youngest, they're Andie and Phil, christened Andromeda and Philomena, then Zoë, which is a Greek name, too. Mom really got into that Greek stuff."

"I'll say." She'd always thought Ann was too plain a name. Now she thanked God she wasn't named Andromeda. "Because she married your dad?"

"Even before that. She saw this movie, *The Moonspinners*, as a teenager. It starred Hayley Mills and Peter McEnery. A romantic suspense thing set on a Greek island. After that, she dreamed of going to Greece, and, after high school, she did. Backpacking around, working in restaurants. Went to Crete, met my dad."

"You even know the names of the actors in the movie?"

He chuckled. "Family stories. You know how they get repeated. She's even made us watch the movie."

Family stories. Her mother hadn't shared many. "You were talking about your sisters?"

"Right. Andie's single, a research biologist at UBC. Phil is married, has a teenage daughter and a younger son. She's a civil engineer with the City of Vancouver. Zoë's married too, with a baby. She's an assistant manager at Diva, the restaurant at the Metropolitan Hotel."

"Those are some high-powered jobs."

"Yeah. Especially considering that Dad is a tile-layer. But both Mom and Dad encouraged us to—" Either his voice trailed off, or he'd broken off in the middle of the sentence.

"Sorry? To what?"

"Mom told us to find our bliss and go for it. Dad wants everything for his kids. Careers, relationships, children."

"You said Andie's not married?"

"Yeah, he gets on her case about that. She says she doesn't hate the idea, she's just waiting for the right man. Figured maybe when Phil made him a grandpa, he'd ease off on Andie, but no way."

"I doubt parents ever ease off. Not if my mother's any example."

"I'm afraid you're right." Hard to tell, out here on the ocean, but it seemed to her he sounded bitter.

Tentatively, she asked, "Does everyone pretty much get along?"

He gave a wry laugh. "Like any family. We have our squabbles but we all love each other. Mom's the heart, the nurturer. Dad's not much of a talker, but you can see how happy he is when he sits at the head of that big table on Sunday nights."

"I'm a little envious," Ann confessed. "I have three close girlfriends, but almost no relatives." Only grandparents whom she never saw any more.

"Any time you want family, feel free to borrow mine. Hey, come for dinner tonight." Before she could remind him of her tentative plans, he said, "If that other thing falls through."

Blow off the afternoon kayaking and the evening at dinner with a family out of *My Big Fat Greek Wedding*? Nope, not gonna happen. Still, she said, "Thanks for the invitation."

Her shoulders really hurt now. She tried to stretch them without losing her rhythm.

"Take a break," he said. "Let me do the work."

A woman should always pull her weight. Never rely on a man. And yet, she was out of shape and tired, and he was obviously in great shape. *Oh hell, it's Sunday afternoon. I can suspend the mother-rules and just enjoy.*

So she rested the paddle across the kayak and leaned back, careful to remain stable, to make only the slowest of movements. Cautiously she wriggled her legs to relieve the tension in them, rotated her shoulders. The sun beating down on her felt heavenly—and it was a pleasant contrast to the cool puddle she was sitting in. Because she didn't have Adonis's paddling technique, water had continually run down the paddle to drip on her.

Adonis's sure strokes drove the kayak forward with no loss of speed, illustrating how token her efforts had been. All the same, she'd tried something new, hadn't tipped the boat, and felt proud.

Take that, Mother. I may not be super-coordinated, but I'm not hopeless either.

To her right, Stanley Park slipped by. Beaches, trees, the seawall path cluttered with walkers, cyclists and Rollerbladers. Dogs and their owners. Two police officers on horseback.

She let a hand trail over the side of the boat and felt cold water sliding past. If they tipped, it would be freezing. But Adonis wasn't going to let them.

This was the modern version of a scene from one of those

period-piece romantic movies, in which the gentleman, dressed in formal clothes, rowed the lady around the lake. The lady was, of course, clad in a long, ruffled dress and held a parasol to shield her delicate skin from the sun.

Oh, crap, forgot the sunscreen. What an idiot! Note to self: Apply tons of lotion tonight.

If she got together with David, she'd have a fresh crop of freckles. He'd know she'd been doing something other than working.

They'd reached the western point of the park, where a jagged rock rose dramatically—and phallically—from the ocean, topped by a fringe of green branches growing from a gnarled tree. "What's the name of that rock?" Ann knew she'd heard it, but she spent almost no time playing tourist in her adopted city.

"Siwash Rock."

As they drew closer, she saw that gulls perched on it, along with sleek black birds with long necks. "And the black birds?"

"Cormorants."

She lifted the paddle and tried to pick up Adonis's rhythm. After the rest, it took her a moment to get back into the pattern, but then her muscles loosened and the paddling came easier.

This was so unlike her, the whole thing felt like a dream.

A good one, to her surprise. She and Adonis, their strokes synchronized, paddled in silence and harmony, urging the tiny kayak through the sun-sparkled water. Overhead, blue sky, a few fluffy clouds, a couple of gulls riding air currents.

Peaceful, yet invigorating at the same time.

They passed under the Lion's Gate Bridge and she didn't envy all those people in their cars, hurrying to get somewhere.

"Great blue heron by the beach," Adonis said softly.

She glanced over to see a storklike creature standing on one leg, unmoving as it watched the water. A couple dozen birds, swimming together, gazed at them as the kayak passed by.

"Ducks," she said. "Different kinds?"

"Mallards and wood ducks, males and females. The wood ducks are the ones with the funny-shaped head, kind of like a bike helmet."

"Is there anything you don't know about the great outdoors?"

"I like to know what I'm seeing, and I spend a lot of time outside." He chuckled. "At least when it's warm. I'm not so keen on cold, rainy days."

"Me, either."

"Aren't you too busy to notice the weather, Lawyer-girl?" He said it lightly, teasingly.

"I do get outside on occasion."

"Walking to the courthouse?"

She turned, which made her paddle go off balance and splash more chilly water down her front. "Having dinner with my friends. We like eating outside."

"Me, too."

"See, I'm not *all* work."

"Yeah, and even when you do work, you wear a teddy under your business suit. Right?"

She flushed. "They make me feel feminine."

"Which you definitely are." His smile widened and even from a few feet away she could see the dimple flash. "You're a woman of layers, Ann. It's fun getting to know you."

"Uh, thanks." Flushing from the compliment, she faced front again and tried to find her paddling rhythm.

From behind her a sexy voice asked, "You wearing one of those teddies today?"

Of course she was. A sleek flesh-toned one. She tossed her head—wishing, for once, that she had long hair like her girlfriends. "That's for me to know and you to find out."

Not that he would. After all, it wasn't like they could find a private spot in Stanley Park on a sunny Sunday afternoon. But then she remembered one of Suzanne's stories, about how she and Jaxon had made out in the middle of the very same park. Hmm . . .

I could get arrested! Disbarred!

I could have an orgasm.

"Getting hungry?" he asked.

At the thought of having sex with him? "You bet," she answered, then her stomach rumbled, reminding her that all she'd had to eat today was a doughnut. "Is there somewhere we can stop for our picnic?"

"Up here. Stop paddling and I'll steer us in."

They were at the stretch of park where the statue of a female swimmer in a wetsuit perched on a rock. The kayak glided smoothly toward a rocky beach until the point nudged the shore. No dock. Hmm.

Adonis stepped out in his sandals, pants rolled up his calves, and splashed past her to shore. He straddled the front of the kayak and sat on it to steady it. "Hand me your paddle. Then climb out. Careful, the footing's uneven."

She rolled her own pants, then rose to a crouch, hanging on to both sides of the boat. Trying to stay balanced, she eased one foot into the icy water, then the other.

Her tender bare feet encountered hard, uneven stones. "Ouch. Crap! Freaking rocks!"

She tried to walk, but stepped on a sharp stone and lost her balance. She was teetering when Adonis stepped forward to catch her. "City girl." He smiled. "Need to toughen you up." He hoisted her into his arms and walked out of the water and up the beach, carrying her as easily as if she were pint-size like Jenny rather than a solid hundred and thirty pounds.

She barely had a chance to appreciate his strength, his sunny, musky scent, before he plunked her down on a log. The breeze off the ocean hit her damp clothing and she shivered.

He'd been holding one end of the rope that tied to the kayak, and now he went back to ease the boat up the rocky beach, where he tied the rope to a sturdy tree.

As he started removing their things from the storage compartments, he said over his shoulder, "We can picnic here, with the view, or look for a more private spot up in the trees."

The view over to the North Shore was great, but the seawall walk went right past the beach. Definitely not secluded. "I vote for the trees." God knows what she had in mind, but privacy at least let her contemplate the possibilities.

He walked over, looking sexy as hell in the clingy kayaking gear, and handed her her dry clothes, socks, and shoes. "There's a thicket of trees over there. You can change and warm up."

She hurried to do so, relieved to find her teddy was barely damp. The cotton T-shirt and jeans felt snug and warm, and her feet appreciated the socks and shoes. Feeling much better, she went to rejoin Adonis, and found he'd traded his kayak pants for jeans.

Either he'd been here before or he had good instincts. Across the road, he found a narrow trail leading into the forest. Sunlight filtered through the branches high above them and the air smelled woodsy and green. She drew in a big lungful and let it out slowly, feeling a sense of peace seep through her. This taste of Adonis's world was delicious.

They came to a small clearing where patchy grass and moss covered the ground. She took off her shoes, feeling the warm, rough grass through her socks.

"Should've thought to bring a blanket or towel," he said. But in the next moment he was stripping off his tank top. "Here, you can sit on this."

He bent to spread it on the rough ground.

Ann was powerless to do anything but stare. Half-naked, highlighted by sunshine against a backdrop of dark green forest, Adonis looked like a nature god. If only he'd take off his jeans, the illusion would be complete.

He can't, it's a public park.

But we didn't meet anyone else in the time we've been walk-ing this trail.

Which is all of maybe five minutes. Anyone could come across us.

Suzanne and Jaxon would do it.

Yeah, but I'm not as gutsy as Suzanne.

Ann sighed and tugged her backpack off her shoulders. "I have a jacket, too." She unzipped the bag.

"You're not going to peel off your T-shirt?"

His wicked tone made her pause. "Peel off . . ." Her teddy wasn't much skimpier than the underwear-style summer tops a lot of young women wore in public. "You just want to find out what I'm wearing under it."

"Damn right I do." When she went closer and squinted against the sun to see his face, she read the sexual heat in his eyes.

Heat that put the September sun to shame. Heat that told her he was definitely a man, not some illusory god. Heat that brought an echoing burn in her own body.

She raised a hand, unable to resist touching that firm, bronzed skin. His shoulder first, strong and supple and warm, then down his upper arm where the muscles bunched. Across his forearm, her fingers drifting through hair tipped in gold. To his hand, which she clasped in hers.

Then she gazed up at him, meeting the heat in his eyes and answering back with a sultry smile. "What will you give me if I take my T-shirt off?"

"What do you want?"

Her body, throbbing with arousal, knew the answer. Adonis was completely unlike any man she'd gone out with before, but this nature-boy stuff turned her on. His quiet competence, his depth of knowledge, the way he shared his enjoyment of a world she'd barely noticed.

Not to mention all those golden-brown muscles, the streaky wind-tousled hair, those gleaming eyes the color of melted chocolate.

"What do I want?" She tugged her T-shirt out of her jeans and lifted it far enough so he could see a couple of inches of the teddy underneath. "Sex, here and now." Her voice came out breathy from nerves.

10

I don't really mean it. Do I? We can't do it here, can we? No, he'll turn me down. Of course he will.

"Keep stripping," he drawled.

With clumsy fingers, she did. She pulled the shirt over her head, tossed it aside, and shook back her hair before she dared to look at him.

He was studying her, nodding approval. "Nice. Jeans and a teddy. Suits you." His voice was husky and his gaze stroked heat down her body, arousing her as if he'd touched her. She knew without looking that her nipples were poking against the thin fabric. Her sex was swollen and sensitive inside the constricting jeans.

"Thanks," she choked out.

"Didn't know you were such a risk taker. You really want to do this?"

She'd challenged him; now he was challenging right back. Did she really mean it, that she wanted them to have sex where anyone could walk by?

Outrageous. Ann Montgomery, I can't believe my daughter would even contemplate such a thing.

Outrageous? Interesting choice of word, Mother. Reminds me of Suzanne's and Jenny's adventures. And you know what that makes me think? That I damn well deserve a turn, too!

She sucked in a breath, let the air out. "I'm not kidding." She tried for a seductive smile. "You up for it?"

His gaze was heated. "There's hard evidence in front of your eyes, Lawyer-girl."

She glanced down his body. Earlier, she'd admired how those faded, worn, loose-fitting jeans looked on his rangy body. Now they weren't at all loose under the fly, and they looked even better. Her breath caught, her pussy clenched with need.

Boldly she stepped forward so the front of her body brushed his. Her breasts, clad in the flimsiest of fabric, against his hot, hard, naked chest. The fly of her jeans against his. She wriggled her hips, pressing closer against his rigid column.

She started to raise her arms so she could touch him, but he caught her hands in his, holding them down at their sides. Then he leaned down. She arched up and their lips met. Softly, closed-lipped, a tender hello. A temptation, a tease that made her want more.

"You have the sexiest mouth I've ever seen," he said.

"Me?" He sure was good for her ego, as well as her hormones.

"Drives a man crazy, thinking about what you could do with that mouth."

She tilted her head, sent him what she hoped was a seductive smile. "And just what do you want me to do with it?"

"Everything. But for now, how about . . ."

This time, when his lips came down on hers, she parted her mouth slightly. Hoped he'd deepen the kiss, turn up the heat. Instead he darted out his tongue to caress her bottom lip, then retreated. Came back to do her top lip. Kept going, finding a different spot each time. A lick, a nip, a gentle sucking pressure; she never knew what was coming next.

He was seducing her mouth, and he hadn't even ventured inside it yet. And each touch resonated in her swollen sex.

She answered back, finding surprising pleasure in just caressing, nibbling, tasting his firm lips. Then she upped the ante and flicked her tongue between them, touching the tip of his tongue with hers, then retreating.

He followed, and she lost all thought of time as they lazily explored each other's mouths. The fronts of their bodies took up their own dance of touch—pressing, shifting, rubbing.

Wanting to tangle her fingers in that sun-streaked hair, caress his strong back, Ann tried to free her hands, but Adonis held them firmly. Gradually she realized he was right. This way, their attention focused on different kinds of touch. The interplay of lips and tongues, the constant exchange of messages between chests, thighs, groins.

Every single subtle movement became more intense, more arousing. Every cell in her body was aware. Deliciously sensitized.

She'd never felt like this before, both hungry with need and content to keep on touching the way they were, not rushing into sex.

His mouth eased away from hers and he said, "Ann? Look at me."

She glanced up. Found deep brown eyes gazing at her, filled with heat and . . . Was that affection? Lust, she'd expected, but not this warmth and sincerity that seemed to gaze right inside of her, search out all her secrets.

That gaze made her wish she was the kind of woman he really wanted. Serene, balanced, in tune with nature and with herself.

Feeling inadequate, she did what she knew how to do best,

and took control. She tugged her hands free and reached up to pull his head down. "I said sex *now*. Not three days from now."

Did she hear him sigh as she closed her eyes? But when she pressed her mouth hungrily to his, he responded. His hands cupped her bottom, pulling her hard against him.

Then he was maneuvering her backward into the trees until she came up against one. Behind her, the bark was rough but not uncomfortable. She glanced up, saw leafy green branches high above, a canopy that let only a flicker of sunshine through.

Adonis reached between them to undo her jeans and slide his hand down the front. She eased the sides of the pants down to allow him better access, too desperate to be embarrassed that she was soaking wet. And aching for release.

He found the snap that secured her teddy and undid that, too, and now there was nothing between his deft fingers and her needy sex. She was close to tumbling over the edge. If he'd just—Oh God, yes! Like that!

Two long fingers slid inside her and she clenched on them as his thumb stroked her clit, back and forth. Jesus, she was going to come. This quickly, with just a couple of strokes from his fingers. It was never this easy for her, surely she couldn't—

Crap. Lost it.

Besides, they didn't have all day to fool around. The trees at the edge of the clearing provided only partial concealment. Someone might follow the same trail they had, walk into the clearing, glance into the surrounding trees, and see them.

If they were going to have real sex, they needed to get on with it. She pulled away from him. "Do you have a condom?" She hadn't thought to put any in her bag.

"You in a hurry?"

"Yes. Someone might come."

"Damn well hope so," he said fervently.

"We've pushed our luck already."

"Guess so." He pulled a condom from his pocket, started to unzip his jeans, then paused. "You want to do this?"

"Yes." Her fascinated gaze was on the opening of his jeans, the curly brown hair dusting his taut belly. She parted the opening, saw the engorged head of his penis and realized he wasn't wearing underwear. Hurriedly she finished unzipping his fly, then she was grasping him in her hand. God, the man had the biggest, best, most gorgeous cock she'd ever seen. He looked so delicious she wanted to eat him up. But they didn't have time.

She ripped open the wrapper and struggled to spread the condom over him, her fingers clumsy with haste. "How are we going to—?"

He cut off her question by pulling her jeans down her legs. The moment she stepped out of them, he scooped her up, hands supporting her thighs and butt. "Like this."

Automatically her legs wrapped around him and her arms clung to his shoulders. She gasped as her pussy came into contact with his cock. "You can't hold me up." Sure, he was a strong guy, but she was no featherweight.

"Stop worrying. Come on, Ann, you're the one who's in such a hurry."

Anyone might come along at any moment. The thought was terrifying—but sexy. This couldn't really be her, the control-freak lawyer. It must be a dream.

Yes, of course, that was the answer. She'd dreamed this entire out-of-character afternoon. So she might as well make the most of it.

"Yeah, I'm in a hurry," she purred. "In a hurry to have you inside me." She reached between them, shifted position, clasped his penis, and guided it to her entry. "Inside me, hard and fast. Think you can do that?"

"Oh, yeah, I can do that."

And he did. So hard and fast he took her breath away. Then again, making her gasp.

Then, suddenly, he was lifting her, pulling out, putting her down. Grabbing her jeans, then tugging her deeper into the trees. "Someone's coming."

Well, just freaking crap.

He was right, she heard voices, laughter. She started to step into her jeans but Adonis put a hand on her shoulder. "It's okay, they're going away."

Yes, the voices were growing fainter. All the same, she'd woken up to reality. This was no dream; they really could get caught. She put a foot into one leg of her jeans. "That was scary."

"What do you think you're doing?"

"Getting dressed. This was a crazy idea." But damn, her body ached with sexual frustration.

"Crazy or not, we're gonna do it."

His determined tone brought her head up. "Adonis, we—" She broke off at the sight of him. Jeans shoved down his legs, jutting erection, gorgeous naked torso, and an expression that told her he wasn't taking no for an answer.

She hated domineering men. So why did her pussy throb, her heartbeat quicken?

Because he wants me. That badly. For once, he's not saying "slow down." He wants full steam ahead. And I want him the same way.

Before she could say a word, he'd picked her up again and automatically she reached down to ease him inside. All the arousal she'd felt before came rushing back, and by the time he'd plunged deep inside her she was with him. Completely.

He pulled out, thrust back. Then again, harder and faster, and all she could do was cling helplessly as he plunged into her, each cell inside her screaming out with pleasure.

When his mouth closed on hers she realized she'd been panting and moaning. *Have to be quiet. Someone might hear.*

His kiss took care of that, his tongue sweeping into her mouth in a sweet invasion that echoed what his cock was doing.

She wriggled her hips, trying to find the perfect angle to get the stimulation she needed.

He tore his mouth away. "Touch your clit."

Shocked, she sputtered, "Wh-what?"

"You need your clit stimulated to come."

How on earth did he know that?

"My hands are occupied right now," he said, "but you can do it."

I can't. It's too embarrassing. Almost like . . . masturbating in front of him.

A bolt of pure, shocking arousal shot through her. Once, the Foursome had talked about a fantasy of a man and woman touching themselves in front of each other. Bringing themselves to orgasm. They'd admitted to being too inhibited to try it, but she'd thought how sexy it would be.

And now he'd told her to touch herself. She reached down, fingered that aching bud. Her body was overwhelmed by sensation: his cock thrusting, his balls slapping against her, her own fingers. Slick heat, tantalizing movement. "Oh, God, I'm so close. Adonis, you have to come. Come now!"

"Oh, yeah!" He thrust even harder; she felt his testicles tighten. Sensation built higher, unbelievably higher. Cresting forever. All she could do was ride it helplessly until it crashed in waves of pleasure that shuddered through her as Adonis gave that final thrust of climax.

She'd buried her face against his shoulder. His mouth was in her hair, his chest heaved against hers. Her arms were so weak she could barely cling to him. How could he still manage to hold her up? So strong, this amazing lover of hers.

That's when she heard voices. Along with rustles, snaps of twigs, a dog barking.

"Fuck," Adonis said, and they separated hurriedly.

The voices got louder and Ann tried to force trembling legs into her jeans. Adonis yanked up his own and started to zip them.

"Pretty spot," a male voice said.

Zipping her own jeans, Ann peeked around Adonis through a screen of trees and saw a young couple with a little boy and a fox terrier enter the clearing.

"Looks like someone's already here." The woman gestured to the clothes, packs, and Granville Island bags scattered on the grass. "I wonder where they are?"

"Our cue," Adonis muttered. He walked through the trees, then stepped from their shadow into the clearing. "Hi," he called out as Ann followed him.

"Oh, hi," the man said. "You folks coming or going?"

Adonis, voice shaky like he was holding back a laugh, said, "Just c-coming. For a picnic."

"Well, maybe we could share this beautiful—" the man started.

"No, honey," his wife broke in, her gaze going from Adonis to Ann and back again. "We'll find another place."

"Have a nice day," Ann called to them as they walked away. She turned to Adonis. "We scared them off."

"They must've figured we were crazed sex maniacs."

She giggled, feeling more free and easy than she could remember. "They'd be right." Wow, that sex had been amazing. She thought back to the expression on the woman's face. More wistful than shocked. And admiring, when it had returned to Adonis.

"Hungry?" he asked.

Another giggle. "*She* was. Me, I'm pretty much satisfied."

Then she raised her eyebrows in pretend surprise. "Oh, you meant food. Yeah, I do seem to have worked up an appetite."

While she spread her damp kayak clothes out to dry, Adonis unpacked the snacks. Soon they were eating with gusto. Simple food, but great. The September sun was warm, the air all green and fresh.

"I love eating outside," she said.

"You said you and your friends do that."

She nodded. "Yes. The Awesome Foursome."

"Cute name. Tell me about them."

With other dates and lovers, the main topics of conversation had been work-oriented. No one had ever asked her about the Foursome before, and once she got started she relished talking about her friends.

When she paused to drink some cranberry juice, Adonis said, "You get together once a week? That's a big time commitment for you."

"They're worth it. Our friendship is worth it."

"They really matter to you."

Did he emphasize "they," and was that a hurt look on his face? She knew he'd been annoyed that she'd scheduled him into narrow time slots. But she'd just met him, and the Foursome was different. She wanted him to understand. "I've known them less than two years but they've become hugely important to me." She leaned toward him, speaking earnestly. "The thing is, I never had friends before."

"Really?" Now he looked more sympathetic than hurt. "You did say your mom taught you to work, not play."

"She helped me learn the tools for getting ahead."

"Yeah, but don't you think it's important to have fun along the way? I can't believe a bright, pretty girl like you didn't have friends." He popped an olive into her mouth.

She chewed, swallowed. "There were other smart girls I did

homework with. In high school the kids in the Future Lawyers club got together to discuss cases and legal issues. In law school of course I had a study group."

"Sounds pretty damn heavy. Not sure I would've liked you back then."

Trying not to feel hurt, she pointed out, "I'm the same woman."

He studied her and a slow grin grew on his face, his dimple flashed. "Nah. That Awesome Foursome's been a good influence. Look at you now." His gaze tracked down from her face—which she knew was flushed and freckled from the sun—to her breasts, which she now realized were clearly outlined by the sheer flesh-colored teddy.

No wonder that other woman had dragged her husband and kid away.

"I was all-work, no-play," she said softly. "Until I met Suzanne and Jenny and Rina. They taught me how to kick back, to gossip and laugh and just hang out."

"Good for them." He picked up another olive and held it to her mouth. When she opened her lips, he said, "Close your eyes."

"Too late. I've already seen it's an olive."

"Yeah, but close your eyes and taste it. Really taste it. Think of an olive tree in Greece, because this is a Kalamata olive. Imagine the sunshine pouring down as the fruit slowly ripens. An old man in black spreading his net under the tree, then coming to collect the olives. Curing them in brine until the dark skin takes on that deep purple color."

As he spoke, she let the images form in her head. How often had she eaten olives, aware that she liked them but never thinking of where they'd come from, all the steps that had brought that olive from the tree to her mouth?

And she realized something else. She'd learned a lot from the Foursome, but Adonis had taught her a lesson or two, as well. Should she tell him? She'd been trained never to give up information that could give the other side power—in a legal case or in a relationship. But she trusted this man, who seemed wise for his age.

"I love the olive story," she said. "And this whole day. The girls couldn't have got me out here on a Sunday afternoon," she admitted. "If one of them had a crisis, of course I'd be there, but I wouldn't take time just to goof off."

The dimple flashed again. "You're saying I'm a good influence, too? I like that."

A good influence? Her mother's expression was horrified. *Ann, look at yourself. You're half-naked in public, you could have been caught in flagrante delicto. And even more important, you're willfully neglecting your career.*

Haven't you ever heard of balance, Mother? Okay, that's weird, I'm parroting Adonis.

Of course. But all the balls you balance should further your career.

Adonis's balls are way more fun!

"Ann? You okay?"

She snapped back, to see Adonis's concerned face.

"Just thinking that you and my mother would *so* not get along."

"I guess—" He broke off as three older women wearing hiking shorts and shoes and carrying backpacks, came out of the trees.

Ann quickly crossed her arms over her breasts in the revealing teddy.

They all exchanged "hellos" and "nice days" and the women went on their way.

"Guess it's true," Adonis said, "about me and your mom. Too bad. Seems like we both want what's best for you."

Surprised, she smiled at him. "She does, you're right. My

girlfriends say she's rigid and controlling, that her ideas are crazy. But it's what worked for her, and she wants the same for me. It's her way of loving me."

He nodded. "I can see that." A corner of his mouth tilted, but without humor. "She reminds me of my dad."

"In what way?"

"I said he was a tile-layer, right? He's built his own business, based on skills he learned from his dad back on Crete, and he takes pride in his work."

She was beginning to see. "He wanted you to follow in his footsteps?"

"Bingo." He snapped his fingers. "Except it's *wants*, not *wanted*. Says massage is work for girls. I should have a real man's job. Wish he'd just accept me the way I am." Then he shook his head. "Let's not talk about this stuff, on a great day like this."

Hmm. It seemed they'd hit on a topic that made Mr. Balance feel off balance.

Adonis tore off some more bread, put a slice of cheese on it, and handed it to her. Curious though she was, she'd accept his none-too-subtle hint. *Note to self: File it away for future reference, to ask again.*

"How's your back doing?" Adonis asked. "Sore from the kayaking? I could give you—"

The cell phone in her pack rang, cutting him off. David! She'd completely forgotten.

What in freaking hell am I doing?

"Sorry," she muttered to Adonis, feeling shitty. "I have to take this."

She opened the phone. "Hello?"

"Ann, it's David. I'm still in Toronto."

"Oh." She wasn't sure whether to be disappointed or relieved. Talking to David after she'd just had sex with Adonis was . . . complicated.

"Yes, it's more complicated than I'd anticipated."

She stifled an ironic laugh at his use of the same word she'd just been thinking. "You're not coming back tonight?"

"No. There's another meeting in the morning, then I'll see. Ann, I can't stop thinking about you."

What about his wife? Had they talked? Why wasn't he saying anything about her?

She glanced at Adonis, who had stretched out, eyes closed.

Okay, I really am insane. How can I do this? After all, I'm plain old Ann, not some femme fatale who can juggle two men while painting her toenails.

"Have you, uh, had that conversation we'd discussed?" she asked David.

"Conversation?" He paused. "You're with someone?"

"Yes."

"Oh. I assumed you'd be in the office, alone."

"Well, I'm not," she snapped, feeling less guilty by the moment. *If he's going to take me for granted, I should damn well tell him I'm picnicking with a half-naked nature god.* "So, back to that matter we were talking about?"

"I've been so busy, I haven't had a chance to talk to her. Maybe tonight."

She sighed with frustration, not caring if he heard.

"If I can make it back tomorrow," he said, "can we get together for a late dinner?"

IF he can make it back? IF he manages to clear time in his busy schedule to talk to his wife and decide IF he wants to leave her?

"I already have plans," she said shortly. Tomorrow was Monday. Foursome night.

"You can't change them?" His voice softened. "Ann, I really want to see you."

Oh, man...

She could shift dinner. Her friends would understand. On

the other hand, what message would it send him? He had to re-spect her time and priorities. She couldn't let him think she'd rearrange her life to accommodate him.

Especially if I'm not impressed with his freaking priorities. Yes, work was important—she of all people could relate to that—but she was important too. And so was his decision about his marriage.

"Ann? Still there?"

"No, I can't change my plans. Especially if you're not sure of yours."

"Fair enough." He sighed. "Damn, this is a real mess, isn't it?"

And whose fault is that? We struck a deal to be "just col-leagues" and you went and changed things. "Let me know when you know anything," she said grimly, then hung up.

She groaned. Yeah, it was a mess. *My whole damn life is a mess.*

"Problems?" It was Adonis's voice.

Damn. Forgot he was listening. What am I thinking? I can't handle this.

She turned to see him lying there, arms pillowed behind his head, eyes still closed, and sighed. "No. Yes. I don't know."

He sat up. "Couldn't help hearing, sounds like your plans for tonight fell through."

"They did," she said grimly.

"That dinner invitation still stands."

Would it, if he knew she'd been talking to a guy she might eventually dump him for?

Like the Greek god's going to pine over little old me? In what parallel universe?

"Aw, come on," he teased, "blow off the rest of the day."

She forced a smile. Right now, the last thing she felt like being was sociable, but did she want to spend the rest of the day moping and fuming and trying to work? "I'm tempted, but I do have a lot to do. Let me think about it."

"Okay." He rose. "Time to head back."

In silence they packed up their stuff. Damn David for spoiling the wonderful mood.

Nope, not fair. I let him spoil it. If I'd told him we couldn't get involved, I could enjoy this beautiful afternoon with no interruptions and no guilt.

But in so many ways, David's perfect for me. We could be partners in work, as well as in life. If he does leave his wife.

Could we ever be partners in play? Would he have monkey sex with me in the woods? Tell me stories about olives? Adonis and I don't have a future, but he's taught me I'm not all-work after all.

Oh, freaking hell!

They changed back into their kayaking gear—hers dry now, thanks to the sun—and once she'd managed to get into the skittery craft, the paddling came easier. She didn't splash herself as often, and concentrating on the rhythm helped her relax. Adonis seemed content with silence, but she needed distraction.

"Tell me about the birds and trees, and all the things we're passing on the shore," she said, and he complied.

When they were back at Granville Island and had returned the kayak and changed once more, Adonis asked, "What about dinner? Come on, it'll be fun."

The chances of being able to work productively were pretty much nil. And she didn't feel like being alone with her thoughts. Would she be taking advantage of Adonis's kindness?

She'd never sleep with two men at the same time, and she wasn't even dating David. Yet, she felt weird.

I need the girls! Wish I could text message them and ask them what to do.

Jen would say go for it. Rina would ask what her heart told

her to do. Suzanne would say . . . Oh, who knew what Suzanne might say? She could be awfully preachy sometimes.

"It's not that complicated a question," Adonis said, jarring her out of her internal debate.

Little does he know!

But he should. Yeah, she knew what Suzanne would say. Be honest with the man.

"Adonis, there's something I need to tell you." She glanced around, found a wooden bench out of the way of foot traffic, and gestured toward it.

When they were seated side by side, he said, "Sounds serious. Is this what's behind all those trances you go off into?"

"Some of them." Her lips twitched. "Though sometimes it's my mother. But yeah, I do have another issue in my life. Uh, actually, another guy."

His body jerked and he frowned. "Hey, you said you weren't seeing anyone."

"I'm not. Yet. And maybe never."

The frown turned into a scowl. "That doesn't make sense."

"There's a man, a lawyer at work. We were attracted to each other when we met, but, uh, there were reasons we couldn't get together. So we decided we'd just be colleagues, and I was dealing with that. But now the reasons might go away."

Adonis thrust himself up from the bench, startling a half-dozen pigeons that had settled near their feet. He glared down at her. "You sleeping with this guy, too?"

She shook her head vigorously. "I wouldn't. We've never even—Well, he did kiss me once but I broke it off."

Adonis paced a few steps away, his strides urgent and rough. Then he stood, hands in his pockets, back to her. Over his shoulder, he said, "What happens if those reasons go away?"

She wasn't sure whether to remain sitting or go to him. "I don't know."

"So you're just killing time with me." He swung around to face her, and his expression was as harsh as his voice.

Okay, what's happening here? This is Mr. Mellow. Why's he reacting so strongly?

"That's not fair," she said softly. "Adonis, I like you, we have a good time together." She got up and walked over to him. "Didn't you say you leave town each winter and go someplace sunny? I could say you're killing time with me. We both know this is a short-term thing."

His brow wrinkled and his frown was almost puzzled. "I guess you're right."

"You *are* planning to leave, aren't you? Even if you and I continue to see each other for the next few weeks?"

"Well . . . sure. I mean, I always go someplace warm for winter. It's nothing personal."

She nodded. "I know." Even as she spoke the words, she felt a twinge of regret. She'd miss him. He was a good guy as well as an extraordinary lover.

"Guess you're a pretty good lawyer," he said grudgingly. "You build a persuasive case."

They studied each other, neither speaking. Then she said, "So, are we okay?"

"Sure." His tone wasn't convincing.

"I'll head home. Let you get to your family's for dinner."

"Dinner. Right." He studied her, and said almost grudgingly, "Short-term friends are welcome too."

"You don't want me . You're still upset."

"Upset?" He huffed. "I'm not upset over some guy you might someday get involved with. Give me a break. Look, come for dinner."

"I don't think it's such a good idea."

"Jesus, Ann, don't get all heavy about this. It's good we cleared the air, talked about where things stand."

Yeah, sure, and that's why you sound so exasperated.

Still, she tried to take him at his word. "We know we're both on the same track, about this being a casual thing."

"Right."

The air might be clear, but it didn't exactly feel light. "Thanks anyhow, but I'll give dinner a pass."

"Sure."

11

Then Adonis shook his head and sighed. "Hell. We're friends, it's just dinner. Can't believe you've got me obsessing the way you do."

Her spirits lifted a smidgeon. "Can't have that. I do enough obsessing for any two normal people."

"Try, a dozen people," he teased, and finally his tone was light and easy.

"Okay, I'm coming for dinner. But I need to go home and change."

"You're fine like that. It's casual."

All the same, she couldn't imagine going to anyone's home for Sunday dinner wearing a "kill all the lawyers" T-shirt. "Trust me, I need to change, or I'll spend the evening *obsessing* about it. So, should we get your car then go back to my place? It'll only take me a minute."

"Don't have a car."

"You don't have a *car*?" How could anyone survive without a car? Every lawyer she knew had a car, and so did her girlfriends.

He chuckled. "Believe it or not, lots of Vancouverites get by without cars." He took her hand and tugged her toward the seawall. "I walk most places. Occasionally get a lift or hop a bus. I'm not usually going far. Besides, what'd I do with a car those months I'm out of town?"

In Vancouver, he didn't go far. But each winter, he went to a whole different country.

"Gather you *need* a car?" he said.

Okay, he'd caught her. She gave him a rueful grin. "Mostly I drive to and from work. It'd be cheaper to take the bus or even cab it. But the truth is, I love my car."

A smile spread over his face. "You love it?" When they'd started walking, he'd held her hand passively, but now he linked his fingers in hers.

She nodded, feeling foolish. But damn it, she did love her car.

"Okay," he said. "We'll take your wheels. And I'm not even going to ask what kind of car you drive. I want to be surprised."

"Do you own *anything*?" she asked. "Or are you totally into this snowbird thing?"

"Snowbird? What's that?"

"You haven't heard that term? People who leave the cold behind and go some place like Florida in winter. They tend to be retired or semiretired."

"Great. I'm twenty-four and you're making me sound ancient. Anyhow, no, I don't own much. Where would I store stuff when I was away?"

"Uh, your apartment?" So she was right. He *was* younger, by four years.

"Don't have one I keep year-round. Why pay rent when I'm not here? When I get back to town, I crash at my parents' or a friend's for a week or two until I find a furnished place to rent."

She glanced at the upscale town houses and apartments they

were passing, with expensive patio furniture, barbecues, and flower boxes on the balconies. Didn't Adonis have any desire to own a home of his own?

Of course, despite his experience and maturity—in at least some areas—he was still young. At his age, she'd still lived with her mother, as a lot of young adults did these days.

"Wouldn't it be easier just to live with your parents?" she asked.

"I love my folks, but I want my independence."

She could relate to that. "Me, too."

"From the hours you put in, you could probably live in your office."

She poked an elbow in his ribs. "Some of us actually enjoy our jobs enough that we want to work full-time." Not to mention, having the ambition to want to build a successful career.

"I love my work, but there are so many other things I enjoy, too." He poked her back. "Like this afternoon." Then he said, "Do you always work this hard, or are the extra-long hours because of the Charter case?"

"I always put in long hours. Billable hours really matter, if I'm going to make partner and keep moving ahead. Usually the work's interesting, and this case in particular fascinates me."

"You said patients are being denied treatment? And you represent the doctors who are doing it? 'Scuse me for saying, but it doesn't sound like you're on the side of the angels here."

She thought about what she could tell him without violating confidentiality. The bare bones had already been made public in papers filed with the court, not to mention newspaper articles. "They're denying surgery to patients who are seriously overweight and are either chronic drinkers or chronic smokers. Unless they mend their bad habits."

"Oh yeah, I've heard about that. Because the chances of recovery are way lower. Plus the patients are just going to wear out their hearts, kidneys, whatever, all over again. Right?"

"Exactly."

"Makes sense to me. So, what's the argument on the patients' side?"

"The Charter and the Canada Health Act require that everyone be treated equally. The Canada Health Act is the source of funding for our provincial health insurance plan, and the funding is dependent on there being equality for all insured."

"And these patients are insured under the plan? They didn't opt for private health services?"

"That's right."

He really got it. Not only that, he encouraged her to go on, seemed genuinely interested, and asked a couple of insightful questions. When they reached the door of her condo building, she said, "I've really run on about this. I'm surprised you let me. After all, it's work, and you disapprove of me working so hard."

"Doesn't mean I'm not interested in what you do. Especially when it's something that gets you excited." He winked. "I'm all for you getting excited." He let go of her hand and reached for her shoulders. When he lowered his head, she knew he intended to kiss her.

She couldn't. Despite their clearing the air, she still felt unsettled about the David thing. Sidestepping him, she said, "I'm sweaty. I need to change."

"Need a shower?" He wriggled his eyebrows suggestively.

She did, but not a sexy one. "No, I . . ." She forced herself to meet his gaze. "I'm sorry, I'm not in the mood right now."

"O-kay." He gazed at her for a moment, then shrugged. "No problem."

Really? He could take sexual rejection that easily? Most men saw it as a challenge, and tried any and all means to change a woman's mind. And she'd told him there was another man she was interested in. Typically, that would rouse an insecure guy's competitive instincts.

This was one of the times when he came across as more mature than his years.

Of course, maybe he wasn't all that keen on having sex with her at the moment, either. He hadn't seemed happy about her having another potential lover in the wings.

Complicated. Everything was so damn complicated.

"Come on up," she said. "You can have a cold drink while I get ready."

She left him in the kitchen, then dashed to the bedroom and closed the door. As she took a quick shower, she tried to figure out what to wear. Nothing that required pantyhose—that would be silly, with him dressed so casually. Sequined jeans didn't seem right for his parents' house.

Let's face it—I'm not a casual person. No wonder I don't have the wardrobe for tonight.

Tossing a pair of navy work pants and a long-sleeved sage-green shirt on the bed, she figured she'd look boring as hell. Too bad she didn't have something fun to add, like the kind of earrings her girlfriends wore. She opened the drawer that held her teddies.

Ooh, now there was an idea. She chose one that was flower-printed. If she left the top few buttons of her blouse undone, she'd still be decent but the occasional flash of coral blossoms and green leaves would add interest.

When she stepped through the door and Adonis turned to her, the expression in his eyes said she'd succeeded. "Man, you did it again," he said.

Nervously, she touched an ear. "I need to buy earrings." The outfit would be so much better with fun ones that brushed her neck, rather than these plain gold studs.

"Uh, you mean, now?"

God, she was coming across like a nutbar. She shook her head. "No, I just . . . In general. I have the most boring earrings."

"Pretty teddy, though."

"The flowers look okay? I don't usually wear flowery stuff. It can be awfully girlie."

He shook his head. "Your pink backpack's girlie. That teddy's sensual. Besides, I can't imagine you looking girlie, you're more the classic type."

"Classic? Uh, thanks."

"Ready to go?"

The whole time they'd been in her apartment, he hadn't touched her. She was relieved he hadn't pressed the sex issue, but she'd become used to his warm, almost constant touches and missed them now. She took a jacket from a closet by the door, slung a purse over her shoulder, and said, "My car's in the underground parking garage."

Once they were in the elevator, she couldn't stop herself from reaching for his hand. His fingers promptly intertwined with hers.

In the parking area, she guided Adonis past the SUVs and minivans, the Mercedeses, BMWs, and Lexuses. When she pressed the remote on her key ring, her red Miata chirped in greeting.

He chuckled as they walked over to it. "Now *this* is girlie." He glanced at her. "So Lawyer-girl's into sports cars."

"I know. It's out of character."

After a moment's reflection, he said, "Nuh-uh. You *love* this car. It's the only thing I've ever heard you say you love. So it's the most *in* character thing about you. This cute little car, those sexy teddies, and that Awesome Foursome of yours."

"And my job," she reminded him.

"At least when it excites you and doesn't stress you out."

She slid into the driver's seat and released the two clamps that held the soft top in place at the front.

Adonis hooked a strong arm into the top and eased it back,

then slid in beside her. "Not too many top-down days left this year."

"I'll be putting the top up and leaving it there, and you'll be going someplace warm. Yeah, I can see the appeal in that."

"You, too, could—"

"No way." She shook her head. "Not if I want a career."

She turned the key and the engine roared to life. "Poor car," she said. "Mostly it just goes to and from the office. It might seem like a waste, but I honestly enjoy those ten-minute rides with the wind in my hair. Makes me feel like a different person."

"Or like the real you."

She shook her head. As she pulled onto the street, she asked, "Where are we heading?"

"East Van. The area around Commercial Drive. There's a bit of a Greek community."

"Tell me more about your parents. I don't even know their names."

"My folks." He grinned. "In a nutshell, hippie earth mother met macho Greek male, and they've been trying to figure each other out for going on forty years. Dad is Spiros Stefanakis, Mom is Irene Reeves. Never took Dad's surname and to this day it pisses him off."

"Wow. If they're so different . . ."

"What got them together? Attraction of opposites. Hormones. But it grew into love. There are a lot of things they don't agree on, but they respect each other. They've learned to compromise. And that hormone stuff is still there."

"They're still . . . ?"

"Hot for each other? Yeah. It was embarrassing as hell when I was a teenager, but Mom had a couple of frank talks with me. Told me sex is natural, not something to tell dirty jokes about.

That physical love between a man and a woman is a beautiful thing."

"Wow. My mother told me, boys only want one thing from a girl, they're guided by their penises, and I shouldn't believe a word they said."

"Yeah, well."

"You agree with her?" She shot him a glance.

He grinned. "About teenage boys. Self-control isn't their best thing."

"She also said, none of that changed much when they grew up."

"Okay, now that's harsh. Did you believe that stuff?"

No, she didn't think all males were ruled by their cocks. And sex was a natural human need. But... "I guess I have some trust issues," she admitted. "Like, it surprised me when I told you I wasn't in the mood, and you backed off. A lot of men would have pressed."

"That's shitty."

"Yeah. And it's less about wanting sex than a power thing. I insult a guy's fragile male ego, he has to find some way of getting back at me." And she'd doubly insulted Adonis, first by mentioning David and then by turning down sex.

"Sex should never be about power."

She raised her eyebrows. "Remember our Rules? Taking turns on top?"

He shifted position so his left arm brushed her right one. "That's sex play. And we both opted in. No one's trying to manipulate or overpower the other."

She turned onto Cambie. "What's the best route to take?"

"Go up to Broadway and turn left."

Ann got over into the left-hand lane, then realized Broadway was a "no left turn."

"Sorry," he said. "I'm not used to coming here in a car. Usually I walk."

"Out to Commercial Drive?" The idea was inconceivable.

"It's only four or five miles." He glanced at her, dimple flashing. "Let me guess. You've never walked five miles in your life."

"Maybe if you took all the steps I walked in a year—to the courthouse and back—they'd add up to that." She groaned. "I should get in better shape, but I honestly don't have time."

"Being in shape gives you more energy."

"Caffeine gives me energy."

"Wrong kind," he said.

Kind of like how she was feeling now. Energized, but by nerves. When was the last time she'd met new people in a social situation? Everything she did, except with the Foursome, was work-related. "What are they going to think?" she asked. "About you bringing me home? I mean, will they wonder if . . . ?"

"If you're my girlfriend?"

Girlfriend. Her mother had always said the terms "girl-friend" and "boyfriend" were ridiculous for people who'd passed their teens. Jen and Suzanne and Rina used the words and were specific about what they meant. They implied "dat-ing," another precise term that meant being involved. More than just "hooking up" or "getting together." More than just sex.

Something like picnicking and kayaking? Going to dinner with the family?

"What will you tell them?" she asked, curious to hear his response.

"I'll introduce you as my friend. They can draw whatever conclusions they like."

"How should I behave?"

He gave a snort of laughter. "However you want to."

"That's not very helpful."

"It's just dinner, Ann. Casual, relaxed. Don't stress over it, there's no code of behavior. Be yourself, don't *obsess* about being perfect."

"If I promise not to *obsess*, can I at least take flowers?"

He agreed, and they stopped at a market where, with his advice, she chose a large bouquet of bright mixed blossoms. Then she followed his directions until they'd pulled up in front of a big house with a large maple tree in the front yard. In structure, it was a typical old-fashioned family home, but the color scheme was pure Mediterranean, with vivid blue and turquoise accented by white trim and tubs of red geraniums on the porch.

"You grew up here?" she asked.

"Yeah. Mom and Dad have outgrown the house, but they refuse to sell it." He gestured to the maple. "That was smaller, and I used to climb it."

As Ann walked up the steps to the rambling porch, she thought that the house—barring its exotic paint job—was straight out of a family sitcom. Not that she'd been allowed to watch such time-wasters, but occasionally, at a classmate's house, they'd snuck a break from studying.

She'd grown up in apartments. A small one at first, then a fancier one as her mother's career took off. Yards were another time-waster, according to Meredith. Besides, if Ann had ever tried to climb a tree, klutz that she was, she'd probably have broken her neck.

Didn't do so badly at kayaking, though. Even a klutz can learn, with a supportive teacher.

Adonis opened the front door without knocking, and ushered her in. He was promptly tackled by a small, flying figure that appeared to be male. The kid grabbed him around the knees, crying, "Uncle Donny, Uncle Donny."

Donny?

Adonis swept the kid up and swung him around. "Hey, Colin. How's it going?"

"Hi," a female voice said. "I'm Phil, the whirling dervish's mom. Welcome to bedlam."

Ann turned to see a tall, slim woman wearing black jeans and a long-sleeved red rugby shirt. She had strong features, dark brown hair pulled back in a ponytail, and curious brown eyes.

"Ann Montgomery." Ann held out her hand. "A friend of Adonis's. I hope it's all right that I'm here."

Phil shook firmly. "Friends are always welcome."

Ann held out the bouquet but Phil waved it away. "Mom's the hostess, not me. She's in the kitchen. Just go barge in." She gestured toward an open doorway, through which came a clamor of voices.

"Uh . . . ? Barge in?"

I'd rather present a case in the BC Court of Appeal than invade a kitchen filled with strangers.

Phil turned to her brother, who'd finally put Colin down, and gave him a quick hug. "Hey, Donny, Ann's not the barging type. Go introduce her around. I have to get my kid washed up, he's been playing in the garden."

She grabbed her son's hand and dragged him away, touching Ann's arm in passing. "We won't bite, honest. Not even Colin."

"Do I look that scared?" Ann murmured to Adonis.

"Yeah, kind of." He tweaked her nose. "Though the sunburn and freckles camouflage it."

He took her hand and, much as Phil had done with Colin, tugged her along behind him as he walked toward the kitchen door.

Ann pulled her hand free and hung back, letting him go through first, then watched as what seemed like dozens of people came to hug him.

Family. Something she'd never had.

Adonis began to introduce her but she was so intimidated by the number of people who filled the spacious kitchen, she couldn't concentrate. His mother, though, stood out.

Irene Reeves had presence of a completely different sort than Ann's mother. She had loosely flowing honey-blond hair, and was dressed in faded jeans and an embroidered Indian cotton blouse—the loose, peasant style Rina often wore. She looked like the hippie Adonis said she'd been. Even without a scrap of makeup, her face was serene and lovely, her blue eyes crinkling in a smile.

She handed the wooden spoon she was holding to Adonis, said, "Mind the soup," then rested her hands on Ann's shoulders and gazed into her face. "Welcome, Ann. I'm glad Adonis brought you." She squeezed lightly then let go.

"Thank you." It was all Ann could do not to stutter. The greeting had caught her off guard. It seemed Irene was a toucher like her son, and completely unlike Ann's own mother.

Ann passed over the flowers.

"Lovely. Thanks so much, dear." Irene went to find a vase, leaving Adonis dealing with whatever was cooking on the stove.

Ann leaned over to look, and sniff. "Yum. What is that?"

He took the pot off the stove and stirred in lemon peel, parsley, butter, and what seemed to be lemon juice. "Avgolemono soup. Chicken broth, egg, rice, seasonings, and lots of lemon." He turned the heat to low and put the pot back on the stove.

The natural way he moved made Ann ask, "Do you cook?"

"Sure. Nothing too fancy, but I like it. It's sensual. Colors, textures, flavors, odors."

Sensual. A word that seemed to describe much of what Adonis did, and valued.

"Ann." A hand touched her arm. "I'm Zoë. Come talk to Andie and me."

She turned to see the youngest of the women in the kitchen. Zoë was full-figured and had short sandy hair. Her smile was friendly.

Reluctant to leave the security of Adonis's side, Ann forced herself to smile, too, and follow Zoë to the table. Zoë and Andie were chopping onions, cucumbers, green peppers, and tomatoes—Greek salad ingredients.

Andie had striking features, Mediterranean coloring, black hair worn straight and shining to her shoulders. Ann guessed she was the one who most took after their father.

Phil came next, then Zoë, with Adonis most resembling their mother, as if Irene's contribution had finally overcome her husband's powerful genes.

From what Adonis had said about his sisters, it seemed like career ambition worked down the ladder, too, with Andie, the eldest, being the most career-oriented and Adonis the one who chose to work only part-time.

"I'd like to help," Ann said, "but I'm hopeless in the kitchen. Is there something I can do that doesn't involve knives or sauces?"

"You can crumble feta." Andie winked. "Can't get in too much trouble with that." She passed over a bowl and a big block of cheese.

Ann smiled in gratitude, went to wash her hands, then returned to her seat. As she began to crumble cheese between her fingers, she glanced at Zoë, who was chopping tomatoes in a blur of flashing silver. "Adonis says you're assistant manager at Diva at the Met?"

Zoë's eyes twinkled at Ann over the still-flashing knife. "Don't be too impressed by the title. In truth, it just means Girl Friday."

"That's crap," Andie said crisply. "The way you're going, you'll soon manage a restaurant of your own."

"If I *want* to," Zoë said. To Ann, she said, "I've been seriously into food since I was a kid. Helped Mom in the kitchen, worked at McDonald's, moved on to waitress, short-order cook, then sous chef. I take restaurant management courses, too."

Ann gestured at the rapidly growing salad. "I'm surprised you didn't choose a Greek restaurant."

"I need a variety of experience. I may end up with Greek, though." She grinned at her sister. "Yeah, maybe my own restaurant. But definitely not now, with a four-month-old."

"How do you manage a job like that, with a baby?" Ann asked.

"Married the right guy. Mario's a Web site designer and he works at home. He can arrange his work and appointments around my job. Most of the time, at least one of us is home with Matt. And when we do need a sitter we have a huge family to draw on."

"Especially Phil's thirteen-year-old, Caitlin," Andie said. "She's had lots of experience looking after her brother Colin, and she adores Matt."

Zoë stood up and slid the last of the tomatoes from the wooden cutting board into the huge salad bowl, added olive oil, chopped herbs, and Ann's feta, and then tossed the salad.

When Ann went to wash her hands, she realized Adonis had left the kitchen. Irene was there, though, reaching into the oven. Ann held the door for her as she extracted a big pan of something fragrant. Ann sniffed appreciatively. "Moussaka?"

Irene flashed her a smile. "Right. Hope you're not vegetarian, there's lamb in it."

"I am *so* not vegetarian," Ann said fervently. "It smells delicious."

"The recipe came from Spiros's mother." Irene glanced around the kitchen. "Okay, I think we're set. Andie, want to get the wine?"

Andie got up. "Ann, you drink red?"

"Absolutely."

Andie disappeared, then came back juggling four liter bottles. Unlabeled. Deftly she pulled a cork and poured into a glass tumbler, which she handed to Ann.

Ann took a cautious sip. The wine must've been in the basement, because it was cooler than room temperature. The taste was bold and full, on the dry side. It reminded her of the kind of wine the Foursome drank at Athene's Greek restaurant in the winter.

"Not too 'in your face' for you?" Zoë asked.

Ann shook her head. "I like it. Is it Greek?"

"As Greek as Dad can make it, here in Vancouver."

"Your father makes it?"

"In the basement," Andie said. "The man doesn't cook, but he makes decent wine." She picked up some tumblers. "Can you carry some, too?"

Ann felt a fresh onset of nerves at the thought of sitting down with the entire family.

The dining-room table was a monster. On one side sat Andie, Phil and her husband George, young Colin, and thirteen-year-old Caitlin with Zoë's baby on her lap. Adonis and Ann were on the other side, with Zoë and her husband Mario. At one end of the table was Irene Reeves, and at the other a powerful-looking man who had to be Spiros Stefanakis.

Ann nudged Adonis and whispered, "Introduce me to your father?"

"Oh, you haven't met? Dad, this is—"

The front door opened and a dark, extraordinarily handsome young man dashed in. "Am I too late? Do you have room for one more?"

Ann stared at him, puzzled. He sure didn't look Greek. She'd have said Indo-Canadian, from his coloring.

Irene stood and gave him a quick hug. "Jag, dear, you know we always have room for you. Go, get silverware and a plate. Adonis, get another chair."

As Adonis obeyed, Ann leaned toward Zoë, who was on her left. "Who's Jag?"

"He's almost another sibling. He and Donny have been

friends since elementary school. He's an only child. His parents are importers and travel a lot, so he often shows up here on Sunday night for food and company."

Oh, great. Not only Adonis's family; she was going to meet his best friend too.

Adonis placed the chair so Jag would be sitting between him and his mom, and everyone else on their side of the table shuffled down. When Adonis sat, Ann realized they were now thigh to thigh. When she reached for her wine tumbler, her shirt brushed his bare forearm. Every slightest touch sent up a tingle that reminded her that, while they'd been acting like casual friends, just a few hours ago he'd been inside her.

And, whether or not it made sense, she wanted him there again. Before the night was out.

Adonis reached for his tumbler, using the excuse to lean away from Ann. Damn, the woman was getting to him. If that stuff about pheromones was to be believed, he was supersusceptible to the ones she sent out. As well as to the warm press of her thigh through those thin pants, the tickle of her sleeve against his bare skin.

Naked under his jeans, his cock woke with a twitch.

Shit, he couldn't let this happen. Not at his parents' dinner table.

Jag came back from the kitchen with silverware, a plate, and a glass, and Adonis said, "Sit here." He offered his own chair, shifting his place setting one to the right so he was back beside his mom.

Ann shot him a puzzled glance, then smiled at his friend. "Hi. I'm Ann Montgomery."

"So pleased to meet you. I'm Jagdeep Singh, but call me Jag. Easy to remember." He flashed a dazzling smile, the one that tended to make women fall all over him. "Just think classy and fast."

Ann laughed and reached out to shake his hand. Jag held on way too long.

Damn, on second thought, maybe it wasn't such a good idea putting Jag thigh to thigh with lovely, sexy Ann. He didn't need more damned competition.

"Adonis!" His dad's voice broke into his thoughts. "Where are your manners? You invite a guest, then don't introduce us?"

"Sorry." He'd assumed his sisters would take care of everything. He'd just known he needed a little distance from Ann, to try and sort out his feelings. Not that Colin had given him a chance to do anything but play with his Game Boy. "Dad, this is my friend, Ann Montgomery. We went kayaking this afternoon so I invited her along for dinner. Ann, this is my father, Spiros Stefanakis."

His father, who could be charming himself, gave a warm smile. In his flawless but slightly accented English, he said, "Ann, welcome to my house."

"Yours?" Irene said drily.

Her husband gave a wry chuckle. "She lets me get away with nothing, this wife of mine. The truth is, it's her house. She rules it, and doesn't let me forget it for a moment."

"Not that your mother was any different," Andie teased.

"Ha! You are so right. But she, at least, had the grace to let my father believe he was in charge." He shot an affectionate look down to the other end of the table.

"Chauvinistic world you grew up in," his mom shot back. "You're lucky I got you out of there."

"Lucky indeed," he said genially. Then he turned back to Ann. "It is a man's greatest luck to find the right woman." He glanced toward Phil's and Zoë's husbands. "Yes?"

Both men hurried to agree as their wives chuckled.

"And," his dad went on, "it is right for a woman to be married and have children." He focused on Andie. "Yes?"

"When the time is right." She stared him down.

Everyone started to pass dishes around and several conversations started up. On Adonis's left, Jag and Ann were getting to know each other. On his right, his mom was helping Caitlin deal with baby Matt.

Fine, he didn't want to talk to anyone, anyway. The truth is, he was in a shitty mood.

All because Ann had said she was interested in another man.

He'd put up a good front, said the proper things. Things he *should* believe. After all, the woman was right, he'd be leaving for the tropics soon. It was a stupid time to start a relationship. Besides, she was older, a lawyer. He wasn't the kind of guy she'd ever get serious about.

So, why did he care?

Injured pride? That she might prefer another man over him? Nah, couldn't be. Hell, he'd been dating Sonji when he introduced her to his friend Damon, and now the two were married. He'd been best man at the wedding and not felt an ounce of jealousy.

No, it was Ann.

From the moment he'd met her, she'd been different than the others. And damned if he could figure out why. She was pretty and smart, endearing and frustrating, sexy and moody—in other words, just the same as every other woman he'd been involved with.

Except, when he was with her he felt different. Her particular blend of strength and vulnerability touched his heart in a way no other woman had.

He wasn't actually falling for her, was he?

He'd been fond of a lot of women, but only once had he actually fallen in love. It was in high school and Lina'd been class president and valedictorian. They'd dated for two years and he'd dreamed of a future with her, but she was more practical.

She told him she loved him, but said their paths were heading in opposite directions.

She'd been success-bound, like Ann. Driven. And he wasn't looking to leave his mark on the world, or at least not in the way people meant when they used that phrase. He wanted to heal others, love and be loved, be healthy and happy. What could be better than that?

"Adonis?" His mom touched his arm. "You feeling okay? You're not eating."

He found a smile for her. "I'm fine. Guess I had too much for lunch." He dutifully spooned some moussaka onto his plate and tasted it.

"It's okay I put lamb in it, isn't it? I know you like your vegetarian food."

"It's fine, Mom. Yeah, I think vegetarian's healthier, but I'm not a purist. Meat's good from time to time." He winked. "Especially if you're the cook."

Irene glanced past him. "That's a clever woman you brought home."

He didn't turn to look. He could hear Ann's voice—animated the way it got when she was excited—as she talked to Jag and Andie about a case she'd worked on. "She is."

"How'd you two meet?"

"She came for a massage, we got to be friends."

"Ann's not the usual kind of woman you date," she said softly.

"Oh, come on, I don't date bimbos." He toyed with his food, forced himself to eat.

"Good God, I hope not. I'd have done a poor job as a mother if you did. I just mean, she's really focused on her career."

"Yeah," he said gloomily. "Ann's mom—a single parent—is like that, too, and I think puts a lot of pressure on her." He shrugged. "Anyhow, we're just friends. No point thinking of anything more when I'll be leaving the country soon."

She sighed. "Believe me, I understand your love of the sun. But how long are you going to keep doing this, Adonis? Playing gypsy every winter?"

"Why would I stop?"

Her gaze was steady, maybe a little sad. "Only you can answer that question."

12

Across the table, Caitlin was asking Ann questions about being a lawyer.

Adonis turned so he could watch Ann as she responded. He guessed she had little experience with kids, but she was a natural with Caitlin. Didn't talk down to her, gave her thoughtful answers. His niece's eyes sparkled with enthusiasm.

His mom leaned forward. "Ann, how is it for women in the legal profession now? Is there much discrimination?"

Ann directed her open gaze on her. "Not overtly. In fact, there are places where being female is an advantage. For example, getting appointed to the Bench. Female, ethnic, and disabled, and you're a shoo-in." As everyone chuckled, she shook her head quickly. "I'm sorry, it's a silly joke. While there's a grain of truth to it, it doesn't mean the more recent appointments are any less deserving. What it indicates, is a realization that the Bench should be as diverse in composition as our society is."

"Well said," his mom responded. "The old white boys have

had their day. But in the profession itself? There are still problems?"

"Not so much, for a woman who devotes herself to the job. But if a woman has other priorities as well, it can be hard to compete with the men. The practice of law—at least for top-rank lawyers—demands a huge commitment of time and energy. If a woman takes maternity leave, she'll fall behind. If she goes home at a reasonable hour to be with her family, takes time off when a kid's sick, it's hard to compete. Success is about billable hours and bringing in clients."

"Personally," his mom said briskly, "I'd far rather consult a lawyer who's a well-rounded human being and participates in society, not a workaholic who's always closeted in a law office."

Adonis wanted to applaud.

An expression of surprise crossed Ann's face. "I hadn't thought of it that way."

Irene leaned her elbows on the table. "It's like what you said about the Bench. Who wants an old-white-boy judge who's never stepped outside the law office to see the real world? A man who's never lived, never watched kids grow up, never opened his mind beyond its narrow, prejudiced little niche. Better a multicultural woman who has clients from many backgrounds and walks of life, who has kids and a home, who knows what life today is really all about for the people who *live* it, not the ones who shut themselves away from it."

"Our mom, the feminist," Zoë joked.

"Tell me you disagree," Irene challenged.

"Of course not. It just gets kind of heavy. I mean, your generation did its thing, and I'm glad because my generation reaps the benefits. But do we have to hear about it all the time?"

Ann laughed. "Exactly what I've thought about my mother, but never dared say."

"Your mom's a libber, too?" Irene asked.

"Oh, yeah." Ann took a gulp of wine, draining her tumbler, and Jag picked up the bottle and refilled it. "She marched and burned her bra with the best of them."

"Those were the days." Irene had a nostalgic smile on her face. "We wanted to change the world, and we did—even if progress has been slower than we all hoped. But we were young, idealistic, naïve." She grinned. "Damn, we had fun!"

"Fun?" Ann tilted her head. "I don't think my mother was so much into the fun aspect." She took another drink. "She doesn't consider fun a worthwhile activity."

Caitlin giggled and Adonis realized Ann was getting a little tipsy.

"Well," his mom said, "I guess life is always a combination of work and play, and we each find the mix that's best for us. It changes too, at different stages in life."

"When you're a child, you play all the time." The voice that broke in was his dad's. Adonis hadn't realized he was even listening to this conversation. "Then as you get older, you learn about responsibility. You become an adult, get a real job, stop frittering your life away."

Crap. Of course his dad was staring at him as he spoke. They were back to the same stupid issue.

"Donny doesn't have to grow up yet," Phil defended him. "He's still a kid."

"Yeah," Jag broke in. "We're boys, it's still playtime for us."

His father ignored Jag and spoke directly to Adonis. "How many more years are you going to play?"

"I'm not playing," he said evenly. "I have a job that I love."

"You don't even work full-time, and you have a girl's job."

"Spiros!" Irene broke in. "There's no such thing as men's jobs and women's jobs."

"Hah. This one"—he pointed at Ann—"she does real work.

Contributes to society, builds a career. Like my—our—daughters do. Them, I am proud of. It's only Adonis—my one *son*—who plays the child."

Adonis shook his head. He didn't even get angry anymore, just felt the familiar ache of hurt. He'd been taught to respect his father, and he did. He just wished his dad could damn well respect him back.

All the words had been flung back and forth, time and time again. He knew what came next in the script. Mom would defend him, say he did contribute to society, that massage was as important as tile-laying. At which point his dad would get huffy and—

To his surprise, the next voice was Ann's. "Adonis makes a valuable contribution to society. He's a healer."

"If he was a doctor, I would agree." His father gave a snort. "Not this touchy-feely massage stuff."

"It heals, too," Ann said. "And he has a gift for it. You both work with your hands; perhaps he inherited that gift from you."

Another snort, but not quite so strong this time.

Irene said, "Yes, from both of us. Your hands, Spiros, and my talent for nurturing." She glanced around the table. "Look at us, each a product of our parents' genes, and yet unique. What's important is to be true to your own nature. To love your life, and the people in it." Her gaze went around the table, pausing on each person and ending on Ann.

Adonis realized Ann was staring at his mom with a look that bordered on bewilderment. "My mother's built a life she loves," she said softly.

Ah, now he understood her expression. She'd been comparing his mother to her own.

"It suits her," Ann went on. "I think her nature is more oriented toward work than people. She has colleagues, but nothing like this." She gestured around the table.

His mom smiled at her. "No big family? But all the same, she has the most important thing. A wonderful child to love."

"Me? But she—" Ann broke off suddenly, as if she'd become aware she was revealing personal details in front of a bunch of strangers. That was the thing about his family. They pretty much adopted her. It must be a rare feeling for Ann. She flashed a quick, almost shy smile. "Yes, you're right. Mother loves me."

"And you love her, and you've blessed her life," his mom said with certainty.

"Blessed?" Ann's nose wrinkled up. "I'm afraid I'm often more of a disappointment than a blessing. She has such high expectations."

"I'm not talking about expectations," Irene said. "A child opens up a parent's heart. It's a true blessing to have a child to love. Right, Spiros?"

"Mmph. More of a blessing when the child lives up to expectations." He shot a piercing glance at Adonis, then his face softened. "Okay, Irene, you're right."

Yeah, his dad loved him. Would he have loved him more if he'd become a tile-layer?

Maybe not, but he might have, just once, said he was proud of his son.

Adonis reached for his wine tumbler and found it was empty. When he went to grab the bottle, he found Ann's hand already there. He shot her a rueful glance. "I'll do the honors."

After he'd poured for her, he had second thoughts about refilling his own glass. She was getting sloshed and someone would have to drive that little car of hers.

Conversation flowed as easily as wine for the rest of the meal, as if everyone had made a silent pact to avoid awkward subjects. Adonis was quieter than usual, sitting back and listening to Ann's unaccustomed laugh, watching the flush deepen across her sunburned cheeks and nose. Thinking how cute and fun and sexy she looked.

She fit in here.

This other man she was interested in was a lawyer. He'd be her age, maybe older. Someone she'd enjoy talking to about all those cases that got her so excited. But could he give her an afternoon like they'd had? A family that took her in as if she belonged?

Well, she did belong.

Caitlin had even dumped Matt on her lap and Ann didn't seem the least bit upset about him slobbering milky drool all over that crisp green shirt.

Damn, this woman should have babies, a family, evenings like this, followed by hours of the most erotic lovemaking imaginable. She shouldn't be locked up in an office all the time.

Maybe she sensed him watching because she looked up from kissing Matt's soft curls and gave him a smile so warm it took his breath away. "I love your family," she mouthed.

Love.

Not a word she flung about. She loved her friends, her car, and a challenging legal case. She loved sexy teddies that made her feel feminine. And she loved his family.

Yeah, she was halfway drunk. Uninhibited. All the more likely to be telling the truth.

He wasn't the least bit drunk, but his heart was telling him this scene was right. Except, she should damn well be sitting beside him, not Jag. And that baby on her lap should be theirs.

Oh, man, where the hell did that come from? But, more importantly, did he mean it?

"Adonis?" His mom's voice was soft, but still penetrated the din of conversation.

He turned her way. "Yeah?"

"She's special."

"I know."

"Don't let her get away."

"I might not have a choice."

Blue eyes regarded him steadily. "Maybe this is the time."

"What time?"

"The time to settle down. I know you're young, but when something's right, it's right."

"You really see it?" he murmured. "Ann and me? We're so different."

Her lips curled up bit by bit until she was laughing. When she stopped, she said, "Different? You say this to Irene Reeves, the woman who's lived with and loved Spiros Stefanakis for thirty-eight years?"

"Good point. But I'm not sure Ann would see it your way. I'm not even sure I do."

"Don't rush into anything. But don't be too hasty to throw away something that—" She shrugged, gestured around the table. "That feels this good."

Her words resonated in his mind as everyone pitched in to clear up the dishes and leftovers. As Zoë, the brand-new expert on babies, sponged the milk stain out of Ann's blouse. As his mom handed an unprotesting Ann containers of leftovers to take home.

He and Ann walked out into night air that was showing the first crispness of autumn, and he tucked her hand through his arm to steady her as they went down the steps.

"I've had too much to drink," she said with a hiccup. "Are you okay to drive?"

"I'm fine."

"That was fun," she said wonderingly as he helped her climb into the passenger seat. "So much fun. Your family's wonderful. Especially Irene."

"Yeah, Mom's the best."

He went around to the driver's side and slid the seat back about a foot as she said, "She made me see it differently, about my mother."

"It?" He turned the key in the ignition, the engine roared to life, and he pulled away from the curb.

Ann hiccuped again, then giggled. "Sorry, I'm not being very arcit . . . ar-tic-u-late. I mean, about being a blessing. You see, I was unplanned and unwanted. I screwed up my mother's plans, set her career back, made things harder on her."

"She and your father are the ones who screwed things up."

"Yeah, but—" She waved a hand. "That's not my point. My point is . . . Uh, I've forgotten it. You made me forget. What was I saying?"

"Being a blessing, versus screwing up your mother's life."

"Right. So, even if I screwed things up in one way, maybe I was a blessing, too, because I gave her someone to love. To share her life with. Otherwise, she'd have been all alone."

"You're right." He loved his mom for helping her see it. "Her life wouldn't have been anywhere near as rich without you in it." And what would his be like, if he lost Ann?

"Alone is sad," Ann said. "I'm alone. I have her, but she's in Toronto."

"You have friends."

She brightened. "Yes, there's the Foursome. Thank God for them."

It hurt that she hadn't mentioned him. But why would she, when she thought of him as short term? Trying to get past his feelings, he said, "If you didn't work so hard, you'd have more time for relationships. One day, marriage and kids."

"I can't. I mean . . ." She was quiet a few seconds then said, "Matt's so great. I don't think I've ever held a baby before."

"Discovering a few maternal instincts?"

"I guess maybe I . . . Oh, crap! How can I? A woman can't

have a successful career in law if she's always running home to look after a baby."

"If it's important, you figure it out. Like my sisters do with their husbands."

She didn't respond. When he glanced over, he saw her eyes were shut. Had she dozed off? Weird day. Weird evening. He wondered what would happen when they arrived at her place.

"I need a drink," she announced, opening her eyes again.

"You've already had a lot of wine."

"I'm depressed," she said dramatically, "and I need a drink. A marini. No, I mean, mar-ti-ni. A pretty one. Girlie one."

Jesus. The alcohol was really getting to her.

All the same, seeing the in-control lawyer acting so silly was kind of cute. It made him feel mushy-hearted and protective.

What would one more drink hurt, if he was there to look after her? Except, booze magnified a person's mood. If she really was depressed . . . "Why are you depressed?"

She flung out a hand. "Everyone *handles* things better than me."

"Handles things? What things?"

"*Every*thing. Life. Your mom does, your sisters, my girlfriends. Even my mother. *She* had a career and a kid. Why can't I?"

"Uh, no reason that I can see. If that's what you want."

"What if I do?" She'd unclipped her seatbelt and was leaning toward him, her wine-scented breath brushing his cheek.

He pictured her holding Matt, talking seriously to Caitlin, teasing Colin about his third helping of avgolemono soup. "Then you'll do it, and you'll be a great mom."

"I will?" She sounded astonished.

"You're a natural."

"A natural mom? You're kidding. Aren't you?" Her tone went wistful.

"Nope."

"You are . . ." She shook her head, the movement exaggerated. "You are just the sweetest man alive. You know what?"

"You want a martini?"

"No. I want you."

She twisted sideways in her seat and scrabbled with the zipper of his jeans. As her fingers brushed the denim, his cock surged to attention. "Ann! What are you doing?"

His erection sprang free and her hand captured it. She giggled. "Isn't it obvious?"

She squeezed him, her hand warm and soft and tight around him. He wanted to pump. Forced himself to hold back. Then she bent over further and took him in her mouth.

"Oh, my God." The car swerved toward the curb and he yanked at the wheel. "You're going to make me drive off the road."

She lifted her head, hand still clasping him at the base. "You're a good driver. Good kayaker. Good massager. Oops, guess that's masseur." She stroked her hand up and down his cock. "Good lover," she purred.

Then she lowered her head again and he gripped the steering wheel with both hands. Her head was crammed in his lap, soft hair tickling his belly as the heat of her mouth encompassed him. She sucked, ran her tongue under the head of his cock and found that specially sensitive spot, and he groaned with pleasure.

She closed her teeth on him ever so gently and he jerked, the car hit a bump, and she quickly pulled back. "Be careful! I almost bit you."

"This is crazy. We can't do it, it's too dangerous."

But her mouth was back on him.

He could pull over to the side of the road, but they were on Broadway, a busy street. Someone would drive by and see them. Tempted as he was, this had to wait.

Hell, wasn't he the guy who believed that lots of foreplay made for better orgasms? The guy who was supposed to know how to control himself?

Man, but this woman got to him.

Reluctantly he gripped her shoulder and tugged. "Sit up. I'm gonna take a rain check."

"You're turning down a blow job?" Her face was scrunched up in disbelief. "Freaking spoilsport." She flung herself back in the passenger seat, folding her arms across her chest.

Ann was pissed at him, and so was his raging erection. And here he was, driving on a main road with his naked penis sticking up for anyone in a passing car to see.

Steering with one hand, he managed to pull out his shirt and drape it over his lap. Then he drove the last mile or two to her place, beeped the remote to open the parking gate, and parked the Miata. He eased his hopeful woody back in his jeans.

"Come on, Ann, it's time for bed."

She shot him a nasty look. "So *now* you want me."

Women. Patiently he said, "I always want you. Now's just a better time than when we're driving in traffic."

"Fine. Be that way."

When he helped her out of the car, her legs were rubbery, and he had to loop an arm around her waist to hold her up.

In the elevator she studied her reflection, head tilting left then right, frowning. "Do you like this teddy?"

"Oh, yeah."

"You can't really see it." She fumbled with her shirt buttons, undoing them down to the bottom, then pulled her shirt open. "Do you like it better than the one I wore this afternoon?"

The elevator dinged and he grabbed the sides of her shirt and held them together as the doors opened. "I like them both. I like all your teddies."

"You're covering me up. You don't like it. You don't think I look pretty."

"Jesus, woman, you're hammered. Let's get into your apartment, okay?"

He steered her down the hallway, unlocked the door, then nudged her inside. After he closed and locked the door behind them, he saw she'd collapsed on the couch. "What am I going to do with you?"

She squinted up at him, eyes bleary. "Tell me I'm pretty. Even if you have to *lie*. A girl likes to hear these things."

If she remembered this tomorrow, she'd die of embarrassment. The thought made his lips curve. "You're pretty, and that's the truth. Lovely, sexy."

He kneeled beside the couch, hooking one arm under her shoulders, one under her knees, and lifted her. "Time for bed."

"You *do* want me." Her arms twined around his neck, thrust through his hair, tried to pull his head down.

Carrying her into the bedroom, he tripped over a rug, stumbled a few steps, then lost his balance and dumped her unceremoniously on the bed. "I want you. But when you're sober." He clicked on a bedside lamp.

"But I want you *now*." She bounced up again and sat on the edge of the bed, reaching for the waist of his jeans. "It's not gen-tle-man-ly to turn down a lady."

"Oh, God," he groaned as her fingers dragged the zipper open, brushing against his erection.

She yanked his jeans down and his cock was in her hands, then her mouth. God, this crazy woman made him hot. He pulled back. "We need to get you out of your clothes."

"Yes, please. You know what, Adonis?" She began to peel off her shirt but one hand got tangled in a sleeve, so he finished the job for her.

"No, what?"

He undid her pants and pulled them down, and there she was, sitting on the bed in just that flowered teddy. He wanted her so badly. But she was drunk, not responsible.

"What?" he repeated.

"You're a really good lover." She nodded solemnly. "The only man who's ever given me more than one orgasm."

Wow. That was pretty cool.

She scooted up the bed and lay down, legs open, arms reaching for him. "So, take off your clothes and come here. I want more. Orgasms."

Maybe he'd give her a kiss. Just so she didn't feel rejected. He eased down to blanket her. Her arms were stronger than he'd realized, as they clamped around him and pulled him tighter. Wriggling underneath him, she adjusted position so the tip of his cock was pressing against the crotch of her teddy. All he had to do was undo the snap, thrust inside . . .

Her hands tangled in his hair, pulled his face to hers, then she was kissing him hungrily and he couldn't help but respond. Her chest rose and fell quickly under him and her hips twisted as she thrust against him.

She broke from the kiss, panting, "It's my turn on top and I know what I want. I want to come. You give me such good orgasms. Eat me, Adonis, eat my pussy. Then, after, I'll make you come. In my mouth. I want you in my mouth."

His cock surged against her, but he forced himself to say, "Not tonight. You've had too much to drink."

"I feel good. Un-in-hi-bi-ted. I like it."

"You can be uninhibited without being plastered."

"Who says?" she asked indignantly, and he had to stifle a chuckle.

No way could he resist any longer. He began to kiss his way down her body, teasing her taut nipples through the silky fabric of her teddy.

"Not nipples. Eat my pussy," she demanded.

Okay, so much for foreplay. Besides, the sooner he gave her an orgasm, the sooner he'd be inside that hot, sweet mouth of hers.

Her sex was full and moist against her teddy. He slipped open the fastener, releasing all that warm, rosy flesh to his waiting tongue, and began to lick. Delicately at first, then as she writhed and whimpered in need, he sped up, pressed harder.

One finger slid inside her, then another. His tongue kept slicking against her labia, tasting her juices. A thumb teased her swollen clit.

"Yes," she breathed, "just like that. You do it so well."

Her body trembled, shuddered, then she cried out and climaxed, the walls of her vagina spasming around his fingers, her mound pulsing against his mouth.

He wanted to thrust into her now, while she was still coming, but he wasn't wearing a condom. Besides, she'd said she wanted him in her mouth. He sure as hell wouldn't refuse that offer.

Gradually the tremors stilled, her muscles relaxed. He slid his fingers out, kissed her pussy gently. Then, his cock hard and aching with need, he climbed off the bed to pull down his jeans and kick them off.

Blood thrumming with anticipation, he turned to her.

And found her lying with her eyes closed, chest rising and falling slowly.

"Ann?"

She murmured softly, wordlessly but didn't open her eyes. Damn, she'd fallen asleep.

Another murmur, then she shifted position, curling up on her side, pillowing her head on her hands. Looking sweet and innocent.

Adonis stared down at his cock, so full and hard it pointed straight up.

Well, shit.

Ann woke to the excruciating bang-bang-bang of a jackhammer directly in her ear. "What the freaking hell?"

She bolted upright, then clapped both hands to her head so it wouldn't split open. The jackhammer must be pounding on her skull.

Morning light came in the window, piercing through sore eyes into her aching head. She'd forgotten to pull the blinds. Stupid. And wait a minute, light? What time was it? She squinted at the alarm clock. Five-thirty. Ah. No jackhammer, just her alarm. She slammed her hand on the off button.

Oh, crap, did her head ever hurt.

Eyes narrowed against that god-awful light, she spotted a glass of water and a bottle of painkillers on the bedside table. Gratefully she grabbed them and swallowed two pills. She must have gone to bed with a headache. But what was up with the pain in her back, shoulders, arms? This wasn't the usual ache from too many hours at her desk. Was she coming down with the flu?

By the time she'd finished the entire glass of water, she was starting to remember.

Adonis. Kayaking. That's why the sore muscles. Dinner at his family's. Too much wine. Surely she hadn't driven home?

No, he did. And . . . "Oh, crap." Bit by bit, it came back. Her going down on him in the car, him stopping her. She'd felt rejected, begged him to tell her she was pretty.

No pride. I had absolutely no pride. She buried her head in her hands.

And then they'd come back to her apartment and . . . A pitiful whimper escaped.

I told him he gave great orgasms. Admitted I'd never had multiples with anyone else. She moaned, horrified at her own behavior. "No, no, I couldn't have." *Did I really order him to eat my pussy? Then fall asleep like a selfish bitch, before he got his own orgasm?*

The last thing she remembered was an earthshaking climax,

then a wonderful sense of satisfaction and then ... the jack-hammer. Alarm. Whatever.

Adonis must have covered her and put out the water and pills before he left.

Why does he have to be so damned nice? I don't deserve it.

She owed him. There were no two ways about it. First, an abject apology for being a drunken, selfish idiot. And then, an extra-special orgasm. However he wanted it.

No question, the next time would be his turn and she'd do anything—absolutely anything—he wanted.

Assuming she could get up the nerve to actually face him again.

The more immediate problem was how to get herself pulled together and into the office looking and behaving like her normal competent self. Moaning with self-pity, she gingerly eased off the bed and dragged herself to the bathroom.

A shower helped, and the painkillers began to take effect. Concealer assisted with the purple bags under her eyes and the flush of sunburn across her nose and cheeks. A tailored suit gave her at least the illusion of professionalism. She made it into the office before seven, as usual.

Noise still hurt her head, so when her phone rang at seven-thirty she glared at it before answering.

"It's David."

"Oh!" A confused mess of emotions made her head pound even harder.

"I just got out of a meeting. Ann, I'll be in Toronto all week, there's no two ways about it. Our expert witness has been discredited, and we're scrambling to find others and do damage control before our case falls apart. You're going to have to take over the Healthy Life Clinic file. How are you coming with that memo I left on Thursday?"

"I'm fine, and how are you?" she muttered under her breath. Then, more loudly, "Joanne and I divided up the work and it's coming along well. Anything more we should look into?"

"Sorry, my brain's so involved with the problems here. Carry on, I trust your judgment." Then, his voice muffled, he said, "Yeah, I'll be right there. Give them coffee, okay?" To Ann, he said, "I have to go. Another meeting. Look, I'm really sorry, this is horrible timing. I'll call you later if I get a chance."

"I'm sorry you've run into problems. Concentrate on what you need to do, David."

His voice lowered to a murmur. "I'd rather be concentrating on you." In the background, she heard someone call him.

"Go on, you're needed." She hung up and flopped back in her chair.

Well, crap. Just, freaking crap.

Rubbing her temples, she reflected on what he'd said. Horrible timing. Hmm. Or maybe there was a bright side. He had time, away from her, to decide what he truly wanted.

If he came to her and they did get together, she wanted him to do it with a clear conscience and an open heart.

Clear conscience? Look who's talking!

13

Thinking of her guilty conscience, of course, brought Ann right back to Adonis. No way could she concentrate on work until she apologized. Her watch told her it was going on eight. Surely even Mr. Laid Back would be up by now.

She closed her office door, then hunted in her purse for the Pure Indulgence card he'd given her. He'd written his cell number on it, saying that's all he used. No point in getting a home phone with a different number each year when he returned to town.

The phone rang several times, then his voice gasped, "Hey."

"Sorry, did I get you up?" She winced at her own choice of words. *Get him up? Yeah, I got him up last night, and left him there.*

"No, I just came in from a six-mile run." Now he sounded only slightly out of breath. "Didn't have my cell with me, heard it ringing as I unlocked the door."

Lost me back at six-mile run. Her whole body shuddered at the idea.

"Nice morning, eh?" he commented.

Even through the smoked-glass window, the sun was bright enough to hurt. "Nice isn't the word I'd use," she said grimly, turning her back to the window.

"Uh-oh. Hangover?"

"Killer. Thanks for putting out the water and pills."

"Eaten anything?"

Her stomach did a slow, queasy roll. "God, no." When she'd stopped at the coffee shop she'd bought a bagel, then stuffed the bag in a bottom drawer so she didn't have to look at it.

"Bland food might help."

"Thanks, I'll bear that in mind." *When my stomach stops playing roller-coaster.* "Look, I called to apologize. I'm so embarrassed about last night."

"Hey, don't worry. You were cute."

She shuddered again. "I don't *do* cute."

Ann, a woman must never *use "feminine wiles" like playing cute, acting weak, using tears, to get her way. It's demeaning to womankind. You shouldn't even wear colors like pink, because people won't take you seriously.*

God, Mother, I need to get you and Jenny together.

"Did last night," Adonis said.

Did what? Oh. Act cute. Rubbing her aching temples, she asked, "Did I make a total fool of myself at your family's? I don't trust my own memories."

He chuckled. "Nah, just let loose a little."

"Oh, God."

"No, really, you were great. Warm and funny."

Her lips twitched for the first time that morning. "Ah. So, I'm normally cold and deadly serious? What the heck do you see in me?"

The chuckle turned into a laugh. "Can't win this one, can I? Come on, you know what I mean. You loosened up a bit."

"Enough that I fell asleep on you. I'm so sorry. It was so selfish."

"Selfish? Hey, you'd had lots of fresh air and exercise, plenty of good food and wine, topped it off with an orgasm. I can get why you'd fall asleep."

Topped it off with an orgasm I demanded *you give me.* "But I left you . . . you know. You didn't get yours."

"We keeping score?" Another laugh. "If so, I gotta point out, you're a few up on me."

She rolled her eyes. "I'm a woman, I can come twice in a row." *Oh, Jesus, did I really tell him he's the only man who's ever made me do that?* She cleared her throat. "But it's mean to get you turned on, take my own pleasure, then leave you, uh, hanging."

"Ann, it's not—"

"I owe you," she broke in. "I want to make it up to you."

Silence at his end. Too late, she realized he might have been going to say it wasn't a big deal. Now, she'd passed the advantage over to him. What would he dream up?

A sexual tingle zipped through her body, making her forget her assorted aches.

"You saying it's my turn on top?" he asked.

"Yes." She owed him, she really did. "You can have anything you want."

"Anything?"

She shivered in delighted anticipation. "Need some time to think about this?"

"No. Well, maybe the deeetails." He drew the word out in a tantalizing way. "But I know the basic thing. I want a day and a night. Next Saturday."

"Oh!" It was the last thing she'd expected. What on earth did he have in mind?

Hello, this is Nature Boy. I can make a wild guess. "Not camping. Anything but that."

Fingers snapped on the other end of the phone line. "Damn, never thought of that one. Keep going, you're giving me ideas."

She clamped her mouth shut. Then said, cautiously, "A day and a night is a long time."

"And I know you always have lots of work. So, work hard all week, then spend Saturday playing. With me."

Sex play with Adonis? Now there was motivation. She could be extremely efficient when she had a deadline or goal in mind.

"You said I could have *anything*," he said in a husky, sexy voice.

That sensual shiver hit her again. "Okay."

"Great. Hey, you feeling any better?"

"Headache, dry mouth, achy shoulders. I feel pretty much like crap."

"Poor Ann. You're dehydrated from the booze. Drink a ton of water, then try a little food. And do those stretches I gave you. They'll help you loosen up."

"I thought loosening up was what got me into this state in the first place."

He was chuckling as they hung up.

Stretches. She had got in the habit of doing them, and they'd helped with her stiff neck and headaches. Ann stood with her legs shoulder-width apart, knees soft, and stretched her head and neck slowly to the left, then to the right. She no longer needed the printed instructions; her body knew the routine.

Five minutes later, feeling a little better, she buzzed Joanne. "David's stuck in Toronto this week, so it's the two of us. Can you come in and we'll work out a game plan?"

"Hi, Ann. Happy Monday. Sure, I'll come right in. Can I get you a coffee on the way?"

"Sorry, Joanne. Happy Monday to you, too. And yes, coffee would be wonderful, thanks. Oh, and a bottle of water as well."

She opened the bottom drawer, took out the bag holding the bagel, and opened it gingerly. Her stomach didn't flip-flop this time, so she pinched off a piece and nibbled it.

Shoving aside a couple of stacks of accordion files, she put the Healthy Life Clinic material front and center on her desk. The file David had put her in charge of. Sitting beside the bagel Adonis had suggested she eat.

What was I thinking? Wanting a man in my life! I was way *better off when all I had to worry about was work.*

A knock sounded on her door. "Come in," she called, and Joanne entered with a bright smile. The perky redhead's hair was pulled back in a ponytail and she wore a calf-length skirt and a short sweater that tied at the front, both in shades of blue that complemented her eyes.

Joanne somehow untangled the coffees, waters, files, and legal pad she'd been carrying and sank into a chair. "Okay," she said in a teasing tone, "let's prove to the Toronto hotshot that we Vancouver girls can do just fine without him."

Ann grinned back. "Sounds like a plan." Thank heavens there was so much work to do. She could—had to—shove aside her personal life until tonight. Foursome night, thank heavens. She'd never needed her friends more than now.

She and Joanne spent the morning on the file—researching, brainstorming, making notes. Finally, Joanne said, "Enough. I need food and a stretch."

"What?"

"It's quarter past one. My brain's worn out, I can't concentrate any longer."

"Your brain's worn out? Come on, it's only midday."

"I'm not the Energizer Bunny," Joanne said with a grin. "I can't keep going and going like you. Come on, let's walk down to that new sandwich shop and check it out."

Maybe fresh air would banish the last remnants of her headache. Ann let herself be persuaded. She also gave in when Joanne suggested they sit at an outside table and eat lunch rather than carry their sandwiches back to the office and keep working.

"Lunch *break*?" Joanne said. "As in, I need a break from work, to refresh my brain. Let me tell you about this cool chick-lit mystery I'm reading. The heroine's a lawyer."

"What's chick lit?"

"You need to get out more. You ever watch *Sex And The City*? *Bridget Jones's Diary*?"

"I've seen *Sex And The City*. But I don't have much time for TV or movies."

"Or a life," she thought she heard Joanne mutter as the other woman lifted her soda can.

Jenny had suggested Presto Panini on Hornby for dinner, saying she craved their tiramisu. Besides, the prices were reasonable and it was in the two-for-one coupon book.

The restaurant was only three blocks from Ann's office, so she walked over. The air was fresh and crisp, and the maple trees on Hornby were taking on the first blush of fall color. Adonis was right, it *was* a beautiful day.

Her body had recovered from last night's overindulgence, but her back was still stiff and it felt good to get moving after a day at her desk. *Muscles. Who knew I had muscles?* It was a pleasant change to hurt from physical rather than mental exertion.

When Ann entered the cozy, bistro-style restaurant, Jenny was already there. She looked striking, her shiny black hair cascading over the front of a rose-colored sweater, as she talked to a waiter about wine options, Ann found out, as she took a seat across from Jen.

Wine. Did she even want to go there? But the girls always had a drink together; it was part of their ritual. "Could we get white?" Ann begged, figuring she'd sip very slowly. "I had enough red last night to last me a while."

Jenny's brows rose. She said, "Orvieto," to the waiter, then leaned toward Ann. "Drinking on Sunday night? Did David come back?"

Ann shook her head. "I'll tell you when we're all here." She gestured toward the door. "Here's Suzanne now."

If Jenny's trademark color was pink, Suzanne's was green—all shades of it, either matching or contrasting with her emerald eyes. Today she wore a denim jacket and a lime-green shirt and jeans, and was lugging a backpack that thudded heavily when she dropped it.

"Car broke down," she said. "It's in the shop so I'm bussing it. The last thing I need is another expense. What with all the travel, social stuff with Jaxon, long-distance calls." She sighed. "I love this relationship, but I can't afford it."

Rina hurried to join them, flushed and pretty in a loose scarlet top. They exchanged quick greetings, the waiter poured wine for all of them, then Ann turned back to Suzanne. "Let me help out with these dinners."

"You already do."

"I'm happy to contribute more." She glanced at the others. Suzanne, a vet student with a part-time job; Rina, making her living playing and teaching music; Jen, a freelance journalist. "Look, I make outrageous money. Let me spend it on my best friends."

Suzanne sighed. "Oh, Ann, I don't know what to say. Jaxon's offered to help, too, but I like to pull my own weight."

"Seems to me it's more fair if we all contribute according to our income," Ann argued. "If my take-home is four times as much as yours, I should pay four times as much. I'd bet Jaxon thinks the same."

"I have another solution for Jaxon," Jenny said. "Get him to move here."

"I like that one," Rina put in, smiling.

"Me, too," Suzanne said, then shook her head. "But it's too soon. We haven't known each other long enough. He has a new job, his mom's there, and his friends. I can't ask him to put all that aside and try a new life here. What if we don't make it as a couple?"

"Oh, come on, *Leave it to Beaver* girl," Jen said. "He's your Mr. Cleaver. You belong together."

They'd always teased Suzanne that she was looking for a modern-day version of Ward Cleaver, and she'd admitted it.

"Jen, we haven't met him," Ann pointed out, "so we can't judge. And I agree, Suze, you need more time together before making major decisions. Besides, he's an American citizen. He can't just move up here and work. He'd need some kind of visa or permit. It'd be even harder if he wanted to stay permanently."

"Unless they got married." Jen raised her wineglass in a toast.

Rina turned to Suzanne. "You love him, don't you? And he loves you?"

Suzanne's eyes took on an inward focus and her face softened. "Yes."

"Do you think that's going to change?"

Slowly Suzanne shook her head.

"Okay, don't rush into anything huge," Ann said, "but let him help you with finances. I bet he doesn't want you stressed out over whether you can afford to get your van fixed. He'd feel good if you let him help." She narrowed her eyes. "Just like I would."

Suzanne began to smile. "Okay, I'll . . . how do you lawyers say it? Take it under advisement? Now, can we look at the menus? It's been a long day and I need food before I seriously get into the wine."

They perused, discussed, and decided quickly. Ann, Jenny, and Suzanne all chose different pastas and sauces, and Rina went for a dinner salad with roasted chicken. "No dressing," she told the waiter as he collected the menus.

Ann took her first tiny sip of wine and studied Rina. The flush still tinted her cheeks, and her eyes were sparkling. "You look especially vibrant tonight."

"Thanks." Rina beamed, then turned to Jenny. "And by the way, the answer to your question is yes."

"Which question? Did I ask you a question?"

"A month or so ago." Rina looked like she was just barely hanging onto a huge, wonderful secret. "You wanted to know if Al was circumcised. Yes."

"You had sex with Al? Oh, my God!"

"Jesus, Jenny, keep it down," Ann scolded. "This is a tiny restaurant."

Rina grinned. "I kind of feel like screeching the news myself. It's been so long since I had an intimate relationship, this is just so cool."

"Girl, I'm hoping the word you want is *hot*." Jen winked.

"So, was it?" Suzanne said. "Was it hot? Is Al great?"

"Yes, and yes." Rina looked smug. "Okay, it's like Ann said about Adonis, it's maybe not the best sex of my entire life-time—" She broke off, shot a glance at Ann. "Is that still true? I'd really like to know."

Ann felt her sunburned cheeks flush brighter. "Multiple orgasms. Adonis is the best."

And I was drunk enough to actually tell him that.

"Woo-hoo," Jenny said.

"That's nice to know," Rina said. "Because with Al, it was really good. And this was our first time, so it'll only get better. Like with Adonis."

Jen snapped her fingers. "Give us the deets. Where? When? And most importantly, how? What did he do? Anything especially fun? Kinky?"

Rina laughed. "No fire poles were involved. I'll leave that to you and Suzanne. No, it was just perfectly, uh, normal. Dinner and talk, we went back to my place, fooled around, and one thing led to the next. I've known him long enough, I felt comfortable going to bed with him."

"Bed?" Jen probed. "You did it in that gorgeous brass bed?"

"Yeah, it was pretty conventional. Just plain old boy-on-girl action. But, wow, it felt wonderful. A man-induced orgasm is definitely different than a vibrator-induced one."

"Oh, yeah!" Ann said.

"I'll drink to that," Suzanne agreed, and they all clicked their glasses together.

"This is so awesome," Jenny said. "All four of us are getting laid!" Then she focused on Rina again. "Does he have a good bod?"

"He's in pretty good shape." Rina wrinkled her nose. "God, I'd feel too intimidated with a super-buff guy."

"But he looks good with his clothes off?" Suzanne asked.

"Well, with his shirt off. The rest I didn't see, just felt."

Ann shook her head. Her brain must be more tired than she'd thought. "Come again?"

Rina flushed. "When we got to, you know, that stage, I took him into the bedroom and turned the lights off."

"No lights?" Suzanne looked confused. "Candles?"

Rina shook her head. "Yeah, I'd like to see him. But if I do, then he sees me, too. And when I think about a man seeing my body, I get so inhibited I can't enjoy myself."

"Argh." Jenny grabbed her head in both hands and shook it. *God, no, we don't need the "is Rina too fat?" discussion now.* Ann stepped in. "I know what you mean. Inhibitions get in the way."

"You have inhibitions?" Jenny gazed at her curiously. "I didn't know that. What are they?" Then she waved a hand. "Okay, pushy, pushy. But inquiring minds want to know."

These were her best friends. Why hold back? Maybe they could help. "Performance."

They all looked puzzled, then Suzanne said, "Sure, you

want the guy to perform. But where do the inhibitions come in?"

Ann felt her cheeks glow brighter. "My performance."

Jen snapped her fingers. "Oh, yeah, you're Ms. Perfectionist. But Suze is right, Annie. Didn't anyone ever tell you it's the *guy* who's supposed to worry about performance?"

Ann shook her head. "That's not fair. A woman's in charge of her body. She's responsible for her own pleasure."

"Okay," Suzanne said. "So she lets her man know what she needs, and he gives it."

"Did you hear me say 'inhibitions'?" Ann asked. "That's not so easy to do. Though I admit, I've been getting into it with Adonis." *God, could I get any redder?* "Anyhow, I figure it's up to me to make sure I come, and of course the man should come, too. If he doesn't, I feel like there's something wrong with me."

"Well, orgasm isn't usually a huge problem for a guy," Suzanne said drily.

"Not unless he's really old." Jenny winked at Ann. "See, I told you you shouldn't date those old guys."

Rina put her wineglass down. "Has it happened, Ann? Your partner not climaxing?"

Great. Now it looks like I'm hopelessly incompetent in bed. "Two or three times," she admitted. "Once, the guy said he always had trouble relaxing at first. And it was okay after that, but man, I felt so much pressure to make sure he came. And one guy said his ex was a ball-breaker, and he hadn't been able to get it up since. Him I sent to counseling."

"Ann?" Suzanne tapped her arm. "You say it's the woman's responsibility to make sure she comes. So why isn't it the man's responsibility to look after himself?"

"Uh . . ." *Damn, she has a good point.* She gave a sheepish grin. "Because I'm a perfectionist and take responsibility for pretty much everything?"

"Aha," Jenny said. "She sees the error of her ways. If the guy doesn't O, that's his problem. Not your fault."

It was *on Sunday night.* Ann wrinkled up her nose. "Unless I fall asleep on him."

"Fall asleep?" Rina echoed, as Suzanne said, "You didn't?" Jenny came in with, "Way to go, hot stuff."

"What man was so boring a lover you fell asleep?" Suzanne asked.

"It wasn't that." She shivered, remembering the way Adonis had made her come. "It was Adonis, but—"

"Adonis?" they all squealed.

"Yeah, but it wasn't his fault. I was tired, drunk, he gave me this stunning climax, and the next thing I knew, I was waking up with a hangover."

"Oh, God, that's priceless," Suzanne chuckled as Jen hooted.

"It was selfish and unfair," Ann muttered.

"But kind of funny, you have to admit." Even kindhearted Rina was grinning.

"And it's not like the guy wouldn't know what to do with a boner," Jenny added.

Ann felt tension lift from her shoulders. Her lips curved. "So you're saying I'm taking this way too seriously?"

They were all laughing as their meals arrived.

After some taste-sharing, Jenny said, "Good food, but not as great as last night."

"Where did you eat?" Rina sliced a chunk of roasted chicken into half a dozen pieces.

Jenny grinned mischievously. "Had dinner with Scott's family."

"Really?" Ann said. "I had dinner with Adonis's."

"You what?" Everyone turned to stare at her.

"Later," she said. "Go on, Jen."

"Yes, do," Suzanne said. "Was it really awkward, with his

folks being German and having problems about you being Chinese?"

"Crap, I don't think I've ever been so conscious of my race as when I walked into that house and they all gaped at me."

As compared to Adonis's family, who took me in like I was one of them.

"They're all big and fair and sturdy, even his sister Lizzie, this gorgeous, statuesque blonde. She was really sweet and friendly, I liked her a lot. His mom was hospitable but I could see in her eyes she didn't want me there. His dad was gruff, the grandparents were quiet. I felt like I was under a microscope."

"That's rough," Ann said sympathetically. "How did Scott handle it?"

Jenny gave a bemused smile. "He's a sweetie, but honestly, he's such a *guy*. He missed most of the subtle stuff—either that, or pretended it wasn't happening. He kept hugging me, acting like it was perfectly natural for me to be there."

"Well, it is," Rina said. "You're his girlfriend. It *should* be natural."

"It should," Ann agreed. "But parents have their own idea what's best for you."

Jenny and Rina both nodded. Everyone ate in silence for a few minutes.

Then Suzanne asked, "What actually happened, aside from the icky vibes?"

"We had a long, drawn-out dinner." Jenny poked at her pasta then put down her fork. "In fact, I'm still full."

"I've never heard you say you're full," Ann said.

"Have to save room for tiramisu. Anyhow, there were pickled pig's feet—"

"Yuck!" Suzanne broke in.

Jenny waved a hand. "They were good. Then rollmops, which are basically pickled herring. Not my favorite food but okay. Then a delicious pot roast thing called sauerbraten, served with dumplings and red cabbage. And a rich poppy-seed cake for dessert. Even for me, it was a lot of food." She grinned. "I think I've met my match with Scott's family. They're the only people I know who can put away as much food as me."

Ann pushed her pasta away. "I'm full just listening to you. So, did they talk, too?"

"About farm stuff. I tried to ask intelligent questions. Lizzie and I talked about my job, and how important it is for women to be equal in the workforce. I don't think that went over too well with the older generations."

"It sounds so uncomfortable," Rina said.

Jenny nodded. "They kept looking at me like I was an alien who'd landed at their dinner table. Though I did overhear one compliment."

"Really? What?" Suzanne asked.

"After dinner, the other women had gone to the kitchen to clean up. Scott showed me his room—and no, no fooling around, not with his folks downstairs. He needed to gather up some things to bring back into town, so I went down to the kitchen to see if I could help. I was just outside the doorway when I realized they were talking about me." She wrinkled up her nose.

"Scott's mom said at least I seemed to like the food. I peeked around the door to see his grandma, who they all call Oma, say, 'She may not have much here'—and she kind of motioned to her boobs, which are definitely *much*—'but she has *gut* appetite. And isn't birdbrain.'"

The others chuckled. "Scott's been bringing big-breasted bimbos home?" Ann asked.

"I guess. Blond, no doubt. The good news is, the family didn't seem to approve of them any more than they do me."

"You'll win them over," Rina said. "Give it time."

"Lizzie and I are going to do lunch. She said she'd give me some pointers."

"How's it going with your own family?" Ann asked.

Jenny's eyes twinkled. "They still don't approve, but now the Jackmans have one-upped them by having me over for dinner. The Chinese way is, try to be first with the hospitality, and if you fail in that, then do it bigger and better."

"So they're inviting him over?" Ann asked.

"My sister Cat and Auntie Fang-Yin are pushing for it. They keep raving about his muscles and Auntie says he's a 'real man.' Not that I disagree." Jenny rubbed her forehead. "Thing is, Mom won't leave it at just Scott, she'll invite his whole family. I can see it now. Granny will top pickled pig's feet with chicken feet. And, oh, yeah, Scott's dad hates rice."

She shook her head briskly and turned to Ann. "So, what's this about dinner with Adonis's family? I thought he was your booty call?"

"So did I. But we did the kayaking thing and—"

"You did?" Rina looked shocked. "I was sure you'd cancel out."

"I had to go. It was his turn, and that's what he chose. Oh, my God, I didn't tell you! We have sex rules."

"You do?" Rina said, as Suzanne asked, "What are they?" and Jenny said, "I wondered when you'd get around to that."

"Taking turns on top," Ann said.

Jenny shook her head. "I hate to tell you, girlfriend, but there are lots of other ways of having sex than boy on top or girl on top."

"Believe me, I know that. No, it's more in the symbolic sense. On top means in control. If it's my turn on top, I get to decide what we do, how we have sex."

"Which Ms. Control Freak would definitely get off on." Suzanne grinned. "But what about when it's his turn? Doesn't it bug you to give up control?"

"Kind of," Ann admitted. "But it's not so bad. You see, I

made the rules and I choose to let him have a turn, so in a sense I'm still in control."

"If you say so," Jen said drily. "Whatever works for you."

"Anyhow," Ann went on, "I'm coming to trust Adonis. Sunday, it was his turn and he wanted to go kayaking, so I had to. I thought it was a pretty weird use of his turn, but it turned out to be a great afternoon."

She paused while the waiter cleared away their plates and offered dessert. Jenny ordered tiramisu but the others stuck with tea or coffee. Ann pushed aside her half-finished wine.

Then she filled them in on the afternoon and evening, finishing with, "It was a bunch of firsts. Stuff that's probably normal for you, like walking hand in hand along the seawall, having a guy buy you a thoughtful gift, enjoying the sunshine on a nice afternoon." She winked. "Hot sex up against a tree in the park."

"Oh yeah, do that every day," Jenny joked.

"But for me it was all new. And I liked it." She stretched, realizing her back muscles had tightened up again. "Mostly. And sex with him just keeps getting better. God, I have to tell you about Saturday night, and the feather and the chocolate cherries."

"Now you're talking," Suzanne said.

"Yeah, but . . . I'm feeling mixed-up," Ann admitted softly. "Like, maybe I wouldn't mind more R&R time in my life. And I think about how cute his baby nephew is, and what it would be like to have one of my own."

Three faces stared blankly at her. Then Jenny said, "You've done the impossible. Rendered us speechless."

Rina poked Jenny. "Yes, but in a good way, so shut up." She turned to Ann. "Of course you're entitled to fun, kids, everything you want."

Ann sighed. "I don't see how. Not with the career I'm working so hard for."

After the waiter had deposited drinks and Jenny's dessert, Suzanne said, "I have a career and I want everything else, too. Husband, kids, close relationships with family and friends. Not to mention a dozen pets."

Yes, Suze wanted a career and was working for it. But being a vet at a clinic was way different from being a top-notch litigator. "You'll have regular, reasonable hours," Ann said.

"So can lawyers," Suzanne said tartly. "Isn't that what Jaxon's finally figured out?"

"Yeah," Jenny pitched in. "Not all lawyers work insane hours."

"No. But that's what it takes to rise to the top." For Suzanne's sake, Ann was glad Jaxon had changed his lifestyle. But she had to admit, the lawyer in her figured he'd opted for a second-rate career.

Jenny shoved the plate of tiramisu into the center of the table and said, "Taste now, or forever hold your peace."

Suzanne dug her teaspoon into the dessert. "Ann, you are *so* in the same frame of mind that Jaxon was. He was so determined to be the first African American partner, he'd lost sight of everything else he wanted. Now he's less ambitious about his career. And he's got me, sees his mom and friends more, coaches those kids—and you know what? He's enjoying work more, too. He's helping real people, his neighbors, not big soulless corporations."

"That's great," Ann said, "but I don't see having a general practice like he does. I love the work I'm doing." Which reminded her . . . Softly she said, "What if David *does* leave his wife?"

"What do you think you'll do?" Rina asked, looking up from her chamomile tea. "You could have a career and a relationship. Does your heart tell you he's right for you?"

"You know how attracted I've been since I met him." She sighed. "Okay, confession time. Mother always told me to go it on my own, and I've done that. But I've secretly dreamed of meeting a man like David. Career-oriented like me."

"How does David feel about children?" Suzanne asked.

Ann drew in a breath, reflected, let it out. "We haven't talked about it. He's almost forty, has never had kids. Would he want to start now? How would we ever find time for them?" She shook her head. "If people have children, the kids should come first. Not be an accessory to an already busy life. Work should fit around the kids, not the other way around."

"Well said," Suzanne commented, and both Rina and Jenny nodded.

"So, anyhow, I don't see the kids thing working for David and me." Ann picked up her coffee cup then put it down again. *Damn. I'd never even thought—allowed myself to think— about kids until I held little Matt.* "Lots of couples have great lives without having kids."

"Of course they do." Rina's tone was supportive, but her eyes showed concern. "As long as that's what you want. But that's not how it sounded earlier."

"The truth is," Ann said, "I'd probably be a terrible parent. Look at my mother. I know she tried hard, I know she loves me, but—" She broke off, not wanting to be disloyal.

"You were a miniature adult, forced to grow up too soon," Suzanne said.

"The woman tried to clone herself, in you," Jenny put in.

"She has an amazing career and wants the same for me. What's wrong with that?"

"It's one-sided," Rina said. "She didn't teach you there are other options. And you didn't have a father to give you another perspective."

You have absolutely no need to know about that man, Ann.

"I can't believe she won't even talk about him." Jenny scowled. "Not fair."

"Adonis said I have a right to know. Even if it hurts her to think about him."

"He's right," Rina said. "And look at all the hurt *you've* suffered, when she refused to tell you. And by the way, you're so caring and generous, I think you'd make a great mom."

Ann closed her eyes, remembering Matt's warm weight. "Adonis said I was a natural."

"I *like* that guy," Jenny said. "That is one smart man. I vote for him. Dump David. The jerk can't make up his mind, he doesn't deserve you."

"If you want children, you should find a man who wants them, too," Rina put in gently.

As Ann toyed with her water glass, she glanced around the table. Jenny, in an interracial relationship with two sets of families opposing the match. Suzanne, in love with a man who lived in another country. Rina, starting a new relationship but afraid to let her lover see her naked body. And herself, with David. Adonis. Her mother. Her career.

"Life was a hell of a lot simpler a few months ago," she said ruefully.

Jenny's mouth tilted up. "But not half as interesting. So, get back to Adonis. The two of you got another date lined up? Whose turn on top?"

"His." She gave a shiver. "And he wants an entire day and night, next Saturday."

"Wow!" They all stared at her. "What's the plan?" Suzanne asked.

"If he has one, he's not sharing it. I admit I'm nervous." She lowered her voice. "He's mentioned tantric sex a couple of times. Talked about making love for hours." If she had performance anxiety over quick sex, how would she survive for hours on end?

"Oh my God, he can do that?" Rina asked. "I thought that

was a myth. Something that stars like Sting made up so they'd seem sexy."

"He says it's real. Jen, it ties into the Kama Sutra. Those pictures may come in handy."

"I think it also involves Eastern spiritualism," Jenny said.

Suzanne turned to Ann. "You must have researched this. You're such a stickler for facts."

"I'm afraid I'll scare myself out of having sex with him. The whole thing sounds weird."

"Weird?" Jenny wiggled her eyebrows. "Hey, if Scott could do me for hours, I wouldn't be calling him weird."

"And you said Adonis is only twenty-four?" Rina's eyes were wide. "Imagine what he'll be like when he's older and has even more control over his body."

"Crap, she's right." Jenny narrowed her eyes at Ann. "You lucky bitch!" Then she grinned that cheeky grin of hers. "If that's what happens Saturday, take notes, okay?"

"Researching another article?" Ann asked. Jenny was always looking for the latest trends for her human-interest articles.

"God, no, this one's purely personal."

"Make an extra copy of those notes," Suzanne said.

14

During the week, Ann and Joanne had a couple of brief conference calls with David, but Ann avoided talking to him privately. She didn't want to until he made his decision.

It was a strange week. She was working fewer hours yet getting more done—thanks to Adonis's and Joanne's advice. Stretches, regular meals, plus a break and a short walk at lunchtime. She found she didn't need caffeine to stay focused, and she was sleeping better and waking refreshed.

The noontime walking was good for her health but tough on the charge card. One day, she saw a painting of two loons in the window of a Native art store and had to have it for her living room. The serene, outdoorsy feel reminded her of kayaking with Adonis. On Thursday she bought a blouse she'd never wear to the office. Cream-colored, sheer, and floaty, it was embroidered in peach-colored flowers and green vines, and would look wonderful over her flowered teddy. And of course she had to get the dangly earrings that matched so well.

Thursday around six she loaded up her briefcase and headed

home to put on the amazingly comfortable kayak pants—her new favorite at-home wear—and her pretty new blouse. She was trying something new, taking a cue from the lunch-break idea. Rather than working at the office until eight or later, she'd go home earlier, microwave a frozen dinner, pour a glass of wine, and actually relax for half an hour. Tonight, curled up in a corner of her couch, she stretched it to an hour because she got hooked on the novel Joanne had loaned her.

After that, feeling relaxed and raring to go, she settled at her desk with her computer, a cup of chai, and a pile of work. Her mind caught on something Adonis had said when they'd been discussing the Healthy Life Clinic file. He'd commented on how he decided on treatments for patients, and asked how lawyers advised their clients—and what happened when the clients didn't want to take the advice.

She started to type notes and was so engrossed that the phone's ring made her jump. It was almost eight o'clock and probably someone doing market research or soliciting for a charity, so she let it go to the answering machine. Then, hearing David, she grabbed the phone. "Sorry, I was screening. I'm working on Healthy Life Clinic." Her mind still on the train of thought she'd been puzzling out, she said, "Can I run something by you?"

"Go ahead."

"Okay, leaving aside all the legislation, regulations, case law, legal argument, how about we focus on other professions? For example, it's a fundamental principle of our legal system that every person accused of a crime is entitled to a lawyer."

"Right."

"But you or I have no obligation to provide their defense," she went on. "There'll always be another lawyer who will take the case, and if the client's poor there's legal aid."

"Uh-huh."

"Okay, so why should it be each doctor's obligation to provide any treatment the patient wants? If we give a client our best legal advice and they instruct us to go against that advice, we have the right to fire them."

"Unless we're in the middle of their trial," he said. "Or it would otherwise seriously jeopardize their case. But yes, I see your point."

For the next ten minutes they tossed ideas back and forth, and she scribbled madly. Then he said, "Good start. Run with it, take a look at other professions, see what you come up with." He paused. "Good work, the way you're thinking outside the box. I got caught up in legalities."

She flushed with pleasure. "Thanks."

"Damn, Ann, you're great to work with."

"You, too. Even on the phone." Without seeing him, she knew when he'd raked his hand through his hair, she could envision the sparkle in his eyes as tiredness was replaced with enthusiasm. "You have a brilliant mind." And he looked damned sexy when he was exercising it.

"Ann, you make me feel . . ."

It had become personal. She shouldn't ask. "Yes?"

A small laugh. "And now the brilliant barrister's stuck for words. Young. Fresh, alive, stimulated. I've been in a rut, and you've woken me up. Intellectually—and sexually."

"I, uh, wow." She was flattered. And nervous about the sexual reference. It didn't feel right to be talking about sex with him if he was still with his wife. She took a deep breath. "Have you talked to your wife yet?"

"Started to. I'm staying at the house—in a separate bedroom—but I'm at the office so much, I rarely see her. We did cross paths yesterday before work, and I said I wanted to talk to her about our relationship. Clarice said, 'Relationship? You call this a relationship?' "

Ann's heart skittered. "And then what?"

"We both had appointments. We agreed we'd make time to talk later this week."

"What does she do?"

"C.F.O. of a big importer. Her hours are as bad as mine."

"Is that what went wrong with your marriage?"

"Partly, I guess. And we've grown apart."

"It would be hard to grow *together* if you're both always working."

"True. I guess our marriage wasn't important enough to either of us. Not compared to our careers." He sighed. "You know, we were crazy in love back when we were both in university."

"And you don't, uh, love each other any more?"

"We barely know each other."

How sad, that love could turn to . . . nothing.

Or is that a line he's feeding me? Maybe his wife does still love him.

"It wouldn't be like that for you and me, though." His tone was assertive.

"How do you know?"

"Our careers are top priority for each of us, as with Clarice and me, but in our case we'd work together. As a team. We'd put in long hours at the office, but we'd be there together and we'd go home together."

Could he say "together" any more times?

But isn't that my dream? A partner on the road to success? A partner who's intellectually stimulating—and hopefully great in bed, too, when we finally do make it home from the office?

"I'm just tired," she murmured.

"Pardon?"

"Sorry. Talking to myself."

She thought about his vision of their relationship. "David, if—and this is a big if—something did work out between the two of us, what do you think about having children?"

"Children?" The disbelief in his voice told her his answer. Then he said, warily, "I got the impression you didn't want any. You always talk about career aspirations, but this is the first time you've mentioned kids. They don't really go together."

"That's what I've always thought."

"Exactly. Not unless there's a live-in nanny. But then what's the point of having kids?"

"None." She shook her head. "Not if someone else is going to raise them."

"No, it'll be just the two of us, Ann. Partners in all aspects of work, of life. We make a great team." She could hear the conviction in his voice.

"We do." Everything he'd said was true. If he was divorced, he could offer the kind of life Ann had dreamed of. A fast track to a brilliant career, and a man by her side to share it all.

And she'd never have a baby like Matt to cuddle and love.

Adonis's sister Zoë had a career and aspirations. A man who loved her and was her partner in life. And a precious little child. So did Phil, with two children. And Suzanne, Jenny, and Rina planned to do the same.

None of them will make it to the top, the way I am, and you will, her mother said.

But I'm not you, Mother. Nor your clone, to use Jen's term.

Damn, it's all too freaking confusing. I'm not ready to decide anything. And it almost feels like David's pressuring me—and, damn it, he's still married.

"David," she said firmly, "I was wrong to start talking about this. First, you and your wife need to decide what to do. Focus on your marriage, not what might or might not happen between you and me a long way down the road."

"I will find time to talk to Clarice, I promise. Trust me."

She hung up, feeling unsettled.

Do I trust him?

Trust him to do what? Break up? But maybe that wasn't the

right thing. He needed to examine his feelings, talk to his wife, and find out how she felt.

Maybe what Ann didn't trust was that he'd actually shove work aside and put his marriage first in his mind. For once.

If he didn't do that with his wife, would he ever do it with Ann? Yes, their careers were important, but did she want to always come second to his?

If she loved a man, which would she put first: relationship or career?

How could I love someone and not put him first?

She groaned and went to pour herself another glass of wine.

Her mother popped back into her head. *Never, Ann, never let a man control your life. And never accept anything less than equal treatment.*

She was tackling the first issue—not giving in to pressure. How about the second? She sipped her wine. Yes, David treated her as an equal; it was one of the things that had attracted her. Although he was by far the senior lawyer, he asked for and respected her opinion.

But did *she* think of him as an equal? She looked up to him, hung on his words, basked in his praise. Was Jenny right? Was she looking for a father figure, because she'd never had a dad?

God, I hope not! That'd be sick.

But it was pretty strange, to know absolutely nothing about her own father. There had always been a shadow of uncertainty and pain lurking in Ann's heart. How could it not have affected her relationships with men?

Never let a man control my life? Sound advice, Mother. But nor should I let you always have control.

She slugged back the rest of her wine and dialed her mother's number. After the usual greetings, she went straight to the point. "Mother, tell me about my father."

When Meredith started the familiar protest about her not needing to know, Ann cut her off. "I have a different opinion.

There's been a hole inside me for twenty-eight years. It's my right to know who he was and what happened between you."

"I'm only trying to protect you."

Shit, maybe he really was a serial killer.

Ann took a deep breath. "It's time to stop. I'm a grown-up, I can handle the truth."

"Fine," her mother said flatly. "He ran out on us when he found out I was pregnant."

"I'd guessed it was either that, or he was some kind of criminal. So, who was the guy?"

Ann heard a very long sigh. Then, "Fine. If you insist. Let me pour a drink." She listened to clinks and rattles, knowing her mother was fixing a Bombay Sapphire gin and tonic, then her mother spoke again. "His name was Dylan Hanlon. I was in law school and had a summer job in Ottawa, working for the Department of Justice. I shared a flat with another student, in a ramshackle house that had been converted into apartments. Dylan and a friend were in one of the others."

"What did he do? Was he a law student, too?"

"Hardly. He waited tables and sang at a smoky nightclub."

"Wow. That's not the type of guy I pictured you going for."

"Nor I," her mother said drily. "It was the one time in my life when I . . . went crazy. Dylan and Jim were Americans. They'd burned their draft cards and come to Canada in the early seventies. Ever since, they'd been bumming around the country, doing whatever, scraping by."

"Vietnam draft dodgers." Of course she knew about that war, but it was so long ago.

"I grew up in those times, Ann. The sixties and seventies. A time of revolution, with young people protesting so many institutions. Male chauvinism, racism, the war in Vietnam. Of course the war was over by the time I met him, but I'd lived through the protests. I opposed the war, and he seemed glamorous to me: a man who'd chosen exile from his own country over being involved in an immoral war. Damn it, I was an idiot. He even played the guitar."

Meredith gave a choky laugh. "A side of your mother you've never seen, thank God. But I was caught up in the kind of experience I'd never allowed myself before."

"It was romantic," Ann said softly, touched by this image of a young woman who was so different from the Meredith who had raised her.

"It was stupid," her mother said vehemently. Then she gave another small, wry laugh. "But, yes, at the time it seemed romantic. I'd go to the club and hear him play and sing. He sang love songs, straight to me. School had kept me so busy I'd hardly had time to date, and the man swept me off my feet. I can't believe what an idiot I was."

"It's not so stupid to get caught up in a romance," Ann said, even though her mother had always told her it was. *Romance, lust, hormones—they all interfere with your ability to think clearly, to achieve your long-term goals.*

Now Meredith said, "Yes, it is. And particularly if the man's your opposite."

"But he wasn't. You both had ideals, believed in causes."

"He'd *had* ideals, maybe. Or perhaps those professed ideals were an excuse for running away from danger. The man had a habit of running from problems," she said bitterly. "He was a shiftless drifter. But at the time I didn't see it. I was naïve enough to believe we had something special. He led me on with pretty words of love. I should have realized he'd said the same words to other women all over the country. How many times have I told you? Never trust a man."

And now I know why you say that. "But you did, and you fell for him."

"I fell in love with him and he told me he loved me, too. We weren't big on condoms in those days; it was before AIDS. I got an IUD, but they're not infallible and I got pregnant."

"You must have been shocked."

"It was August, I'd had three crazy, romantic months, wasn't even positive about going back to law school in the fall. I had some idiotic notion of traveling with Dylan. Then I found out I was pregnant. So I told him."

When her mother didn't go on, Ann prompted, "And?"

"He told me to get an abortion." Meredith's voice was flat. "Then I made a fool of myself. Wailed about loving him, him loving me, and he said, 'Get real, it was a summer fling. You knew that from the start. Come September, you'll be back at school, and I'll head out west where the winters are warmer.'"

Wow, an eerie echo of Adonis. Though, with us, we have *both known from the start we'll be going separate ways. And, as for David, the last thing he'll ever be is shiftless.*

Her heart turned over for her mother. "I'm sorry, Mother. That must have hurt terribly."

"Mostly, it made me furious. At him, for leading me on. At myself, for being so stupid as to believe what a man said."

"Maybe he meant it. Maybe he did love you, in his own way, for the time you had together. Maybe he really did think you meant all along for it just to be a summer thing. I mean, you were in law school, focused on your career."

"Don't make excuses for him."

I'm only trying to ease your pain, make you feel less betrayed. "So this whole 'don't trust a man' thing comes back to Dylan Hanlon?"

"Of course not," her mother said quickly.

"What about Granddad?" Another touchy issue, though Ann didn't understand the source of the conflict between Meredith and her parents.

Her mother snorted. "A typical oppressive male. Didn't want my mother to work. She was no better, she was content to be a housewife. He didn't want me going to university. Said women shouldn't have careers and I should marry a local man. He even picked one out. When I defied him, he was furious. Then, when I got pregnant, he said that was proof I couldn't look after myself. It was the final straw."

But it couldn't have been. Ann remembered visits to her grandparents when she was a little girl. Still, she'd pushed Meredith enough for now. And it was late. Almost midnight in Toronto.

"Mother? Thanks for talking about this. It means a lot to me."

"Don't you go getting romantic notions about your father. He was a bum and you're better off without him. You're not thinking of trying to trace him?"

"The idea hadn't entered my head," she said slowly, wondering if she should. But why? What good could possibly come of it? Her life was complicated enough already.

"Remember, you don't need a man in your life. You're complete in yourself."

"I know." And she didn't need her father, just the information her mother had given her. She didn't need David, either. Nor Adonis.

But what if I want a man in my life? That's different, as I've learned from Irene Reeves.

"Good night, Mother." Softly she added words she'd almost never said aloud. "I love you."

There was a pause, then a flustered, "I love you, too, Ann."

Adonis went kayaking Thursday evening with Jag and Mike. They rented kayaks at Granville Island and paddled all the way up to Lighthouse Park, which meant crossing Burrard Inlet and dealing with choppy water. Mostly, they were working too hard to talk.

When they got back, they were starving for beer and pizza,

so they piled into Jag's SUV and went over to Simpatico's on Fourth Avenue. Though it was a Greek taverna, it served some of the best pizza around.

As usual, they argued over the choice, with Adonis voting for vegetarian and Mike wanting tons of salami. They compromised on a Hawaiian, with ham and pineapple. "Girlie pizza," Mike said disparagingly.

"And on the subject of girls," Jag said to Mike, "Don has a new one. I met her at Sunday dinner."

"Oh, yeah? What's she like?"

Adonis opened his mouth to reply, but Jag spoke first. "Name's Ann, she's a lawyer and very smart. Pretty, too. Way too classy for Don. Older, as well. A real woman. Someone to be taken seriously."

Mike's brows went up. "That right, Don? You taking this one seriously?"

"I take them all seriously." He winked. "While I'm with them." But the truth was, he did feel different about Ann. And it pissed him off, her being interested in that other guy. Weird, to find out at twenty-four that he had a jealous, possessive streak. But damn, Ann was special.

The pizza arrived and they pulled pieces free and began to eat. Adonis thought of how much time he'd spent with these guys, since they were just kids. And of the things they'd talked about, once they got over that macho "guys don't do that" notion.

Ann had talked with such affection about her Awesome Foursome. Well, he had his own Terrific Trio. Why not ask his best buds for advice?

"Okay," he said slowly, "I like Ann. Thing is, there's this other guy in her life. Sounds like he's more her type."

"Competition?" Jag grinned. "That's a new one. Usually girls fall all over you."

"The ones that aren't falling all over you." He turned to Mike. "Or you." The truth was, all three of them were chick magnets. Jag had dark, exotic looks and that killer smile. Mike, a cop, was strong and rugged-looking, a natural leader. As for Adonis, he'd been hearing that Greek-god thing since fifth grade. He took a long pull of beer. "So, what do I do?"

"Depends how important the girl is," Mike said.

"Ann's important," Jag said positively.

Adonis shot him a look. "Isn't that for me to say?"

Jag rolled his eyes. "Gimme a break, man. If she wasn't, you wouldn't put up with this 'other guy' shit. You'd have dumped her and we wouldn't be having this conversation. Besides, I saw the way you looked at her. Saw her with your family, holding the baby. You going to tell me Irene hasn't been on your case about Ann?"

Mike gave a snort of laughter and Adonis chuckled. "Yeah, Mom called. And all my sisters. They all approve, want to know when I'll bring her over again." He blew out a long breath. "And yeah, Ann's important to me."

"What d'you know about this other guy?" Mike asked.

"Lawyer." He pulled another slice of pizza free and bit into the tip.

"Crap," Jag said. "They'll have stuff in common." He glanced at Mike. "Sunday night, she was telling me and Andie about a case of hers. Don never said a word."

"I talk to her about her work. Just wasn't into it Sunday." Because he'd been pissed about the other man.

"If this guy's a lawyer," Mike said, "he makes more money than you. Works hard, has status. You don't buy into all that, but how about Ann?"

"Money and status?" He chugged another mouthful of beer. "She loves her work. I don't think she's doing it for status. But she is ambitious . . ."

"And you're not," Mike said, taking another slice of pizza.

"You sound like his dad," Jag said darkly. "Sunday night, he was pulling that same old crap. You've been there, you know."

Mike, who'd attended a number of Stefanakis family dinners, scowled. "Yeah. So, how's Ann feel about your work? She respect it?"

"When Dad did his usual attack, she stepped in and said I'm a healer." Remembering, he felt a warm glow. Still, maybe she'd prefer a man who was more successful. "But she's got a car, a condo, ritzy furniture. She's into nice stuff."

Jag took a long swallow of beer and said reflectively, "With girls, there's all sorts of things they want, but what's the biggest? Commitment. Right?"

"Oh, yeah," Mike said. "Don, no offense, but have you ever committed to anyone or anything for longer than a couple months?"

His family, but that wasn't what Mike was talking about. His work—yet he only did it part-time, and he was always moving around. A woman? "Nope," he said. "Never wanted to." Then, because his buds really were trying to help, he added, "Before."

Jag and Mike exchanged meaningful glances. "Going down for the count," Jag said.

"Yup, he's a goner." Mike took the last piece of pizza. "Okay, Don, here's what I figure. You can't play some role to win this girl. Be yourself." He glanced at Adonis's sticky fingers. "Well, maybe eat with a fork, but you know what I mean. If she doesn't like who you are, she's not all that great after all."

Jag nodded his agreement. "Better to find out now."

Simple advice, but sound. Ann had promised him a day and a night. A perfect opportunity to really get to know each other. If, at the end of that time, she chose the lawyer, there wasn't a damned thing he could do about it. Except call up his buddies and go get hammered.

* * *

Adonis arrived at Ann's at eight on Saturday morning and she buzzed him up. Her smile was warm, if a little nervous.

He caught her up in his arms for a quick kiss.

When she started to deepen it, he broke away. "We have lots of time. Let's take it slow." He had a plan for the day. Sexy, but slow and easy rather than rushed. It was his turn on top; they were going to make love his way, for once.

"You and *slow*," she complained, but there was a twinkle in her eye. "If I hadn't met your parents, I'd say one of them must be a turtle."

He studied her appreciatively. "Man, you look good."

He'd said to dress comfortably, and she'd combined the black kayak pants with a long, flowing top that was super-feminine. The fabric was light and kind of see-through, and what he saw beneath was that figure-hugging flowered teddy she'd worn Sunday night. The only earrings he'd ever seen her wear before were plain gold studs or hoops, but today she had pretty dangly ones with colored beads that matched her top.

She was as lovely as always, but this was a new look. Softer.

In fact, everything about her looked less edgy and tight. "How are you feeling?" he asked.

She smiled widely. "I've had a great week. Got all my work done, plus I've had more sleep, exercise, regular meals. I've been doing my stretches, and I've had almost no headaches."

He returned her smile. "That's great."

Her eyes gleamed. "You might also like to know my jaw's healed, too. Just in case I want to open wide for a, mmm, let me see. Hot dog, or anything else that relative size and shape."

The woman left him no choice, he had to hug her again. Which he did, lifting her off her feet and swinging her around. Her laugh rang out and he thought what a contrast she was to the uptight lawyer in the black suit who'd first walked into Pure Indulgence.

Her living room looked different, too, in small ways. A paperback lay open, facedown on the coffee table. A couple of pillows were scrunched into a corner of the couch as if she'd been reading or watching TV. And she had a new painting: stylized Native art of two loons.

"I like this." He moved closer to study it.

"Me, too." She glanced around the room, gave a proprietary smile. "My place is coming together." Then she turned back to him. "Okay, what's the plan? We're coming back here tonight, right? You promised, no camping."

He turned back to her. "I hoped we'd stay at my place." It was a gamble, taking her to his modest apartment, but today was about being himself. He needed to find out how Ann felt about the real Adonis, before his emotions got any more ensnared by this complex woman.

Her eyes narrowed. "I don't make a practice of staying at men's places."

Good to know. And he'd already learned she didn't make a practice of having guys stay over at hers. "How about you bring an overnight bag, just in case. Then you can decide later."

"I guess that's fair. Give me a minute."

"Bring a sweater, too. Fall's coming."

She went into the bedroom and came back five minutes later wearing a long olive-colored sweater and carrying her pink backpack. At the door, she slipped into sandals. "All set." The face she turned to him showed both anticipation and nervousness.

He touched her cheek. "We won't do anything you don't want to. I promise. All I ask is, give things a fair shot. Okay?"

She studied him, her tawny eyes looking deep inside for once, rather than darting away. Then she nodded. "Okay."

"Breakfast first, at Granville Island. Want me to carry your pack?"

The eye-twinkle was back. "Did you notice it's pink?"

"Hey, when Caitlin was a kid she made me carry a pink bag with Barbies all over it. I'm a tough dude, I can handle it."

She handed it to him and he slung it over one shoulder. Why should he be bugged about toting a girlie pink pack, when he had a lovely woman at his side?

They walked along the seawall, chatting comfortably about what they'd done during the week, pointing out flowers on a balcony, rowers passing by on the water. Sometimes he held her hand, sometimes he put an arm around her. Although the touching wasn't overtly sexual, the feel of skin brushing skin, the warmth of a hand through clothing, was sensual. He knew she was as aware of him as he was of her.

A couple of teenage girls walked toward them, with a beagle puppy on a leash.

"Oh, he's adorable," Ann said, letting go of his hand and bending to pet the dog, which squirmed in delight.

Adonis squatted too, to stroke the little guy. "Nothing like a puppy, is there?"

One of the girls said, "His name's Snoopy Too, that's T-O-O. He's only ten weeks."

"He's so cute." Ann's expression showed she was enjoying this as much as the pup.

When the girls finally pulled the dog away, Ann sighed. "I wish I could take him home."

Adonis claimed her hand and they started walking again. "So, Lawyer-girl likes animals."

"Yes. I've never had a pet, though. Except for Tyger, whom you've met."

He smiled, remembering the stuffed cat her friend had given her. "We always had a dog when I was a kid. Mom and Dad still do. They keep him outside on Sunday nights, or he goes nuts with all the people and food."

"Makes sense. What kind of dog?"

"Basset hound named Lenny. Mom named him after Leonard

Cohen because she says they both have soulful expressions." He shook his head. "I miss having a pet. But no way can I do it when I'm away four or five months of the year."

She nodded. "And I'm at work so much. Mind you, I'm trying something new—getting home earlier, taking a break, then working at home. Maybe I could get a pet, I'd like the company. Probably a cat, because they're more self-sufficient."

He hooked his arm around her neck, pulled her close against him. "Like you."

They discussed the merits of various breeds of cats and dogs until they reached the Island, where they switched to debating breakfast options. Adonis chose orange juice and a breakfast burrito with eggs, cheese, and veggies, and Ann went for a chocolate croissant and a bowl of caffe latte. They snagged a table in the Blue Parrot, with sunshine streaming through the window. Before sitting, she peeled off her sweater and Adonis had a fine view of her curves as the sun cut through the sheer fabric of her blouse.

His. For an entire day. He smiled, and so did she as she settled into a wooden chair.

"This is a whole new world," she said, glancing around at the normal Saturday-morning crowd. People having a snack, chatting, or reading the paper before doing the day's grocery shopping. "You know what I'm realizing? My mom and I are different."

"From each other, or from the rest of the world?"

"From each other."

He managed not to say, "Well, duh."

Ann gestured around, and those dangly earrings danced. "She'd consider this a waste of time. And pets are unnecessary. For her, everything's about career. She lives in her mind. Even food is just fuel, not something to be savored." She took a bite of the flaky croissant and gave a moan of pleasure that sent his pulse racing.

He reached over to flick a crumb away, letting his thumb caress her sexy mouth. "Life is to be savored. Work's important, but life's made up of so much else as well. Family, friends, nature, animals. Food, music." He grinned. "Sex."

She grinned back, and he went on. "I'm not religious, but it seems to me, however the world got created, we're here and all this wonderful stuff is here. It's a sin to not appreciate it."

Ann took a sip of coffee, then her pink tongue came out, like a cat's, and licked foam off her lips. "I worked hard this week to take this time off. You bet I'm appreciating every moment."

"Me, too." Mostly, he was appreciating everything about her.

"Every moment," she repeated. "Every detail. This scrumptious croissant, a perfect latte, the sunshine on my back, happy people around me. And you, Adonis." Across the table, her gaze was warm, intense. "Looking at you, in that black T-shirt that shows off your great build. Touching you." She ran a fingertip down his arm, making every hair stand on end. "Thinking about how I want to touch you later, when we're alone."

Man, the woman was two steps ahead of him. This was stuff he'd hoped to teach her about enjoying the moment, heightening sensation, building arousal. Seems like she'd figured it out already.

Would she have, with that lawyer?

No way. He, Adonis Stefanakis, was the first man who'd made her look beyond work and really explore her sensual side. Damn it, he was going to win this woman.

As she ripped bits off the croissant, her fingers were getting covered in chocolate. No, this wasn't the tailored, tooth-grinding lawyer who'd come to Pure Indulgence. His heart flipped over. He had to clear his throat before he could ask, "Good croissant?"

"Mm-hmm. Want a taste?"

"Yeah." Before she could tear off another bit, he reached for her hand and brought it to his lips. He popped a chocolaty finger in his mouth and used his tongue to clean it thoroughly, feeling his cock pulse with every lick.

She tugged her hand away. "Adonis! Not here." Her cheeks were flushed, and he guessed she was doing some pulsing of her own, in secret places.

He settled for bumping his knee against hers, and she didn't move away.

After breakfast, they picked up fresh bread, fruit, and a couple of interesting-looking cheeses for lunch, and salmon to barbecue for dinner. Then they strolled to the house in Kits where he rented an apartment.

As they went up the walk, Ann said, "Someone loves gardening. I have no idea what those pink and purple-blue flowers are, but they're beautiful."

He broke off a small pink blossom and stroked her cheek with it, then tucked it behind her ear. "Hydrangeas. My landlady Thea is the gardener. I help her out, since her husband Frank's arthritis doesn't let him do much in the garden."

"Nice house. Reminds me a bit of your parents'."

"Yeah. Family homes. Thea and Frank raised their kids here. They're retired now, and converted the upstairs into two apartments."

When he led her around the side of the house, she stopped dead. "Oh, this is wonderful."

More flowers, a flagstone patio with outdoor furniture and a barbecue, a birdbath, a sundial—and the wooden swing. Thea called it a loveseat swing. Under a canopy, two double-seater benches faced each other, with a floor between them. But the benches and floor were really a gliding swing that the occupants could make go back and forth.

He'd fallen for that swing the moment he saw it, and it seemed Ann had, too.

She almost skipped over to it, stroked the wooden frame, then turned a glowing face to Adonis. "There were a couple of these in the park down the street from my grandparents'. Grandma used to take me, and we'd spend hours swinging back and forth. I love it."

"Then sit. Let's swing a while."

"Your landlords won't mind?"

He shook his head. "They'd be flattered. Thea wanted one of these and Frank built it, before his arthritis got so bad."

"They sound great." She glanced at the house. "Are they home? Will I meet them?"

"They're away, visiting their youngest daughter. She and her husband just had a baby, so the grandparents are helping out."

"Everyone has family," she said, sounding wistful.

15

"Well, you have your mom," Adonis said. "And grandparents, too." He put the groceries down in the shade and held out his hand. "Come sit."

Ann stepped up and sat on one side, and he took the opposite side so he was facing her. She leaned forward, trying to get the swing moving. He lent his weight to the effort until they were gliding gently back and forth. A sexy motion. Too bad this garden had so many neighbors—but on the other hand, this morning was for building a slow burn, not leaping into hot sex.

"You haven't mentioned your grandparents before," he commented.

"They're not part of my life. We exchange cards at Christmas and on birthdays but that's it. They and Mother are barely civil." She sighed. "Her father was opposed to her going to university and having a career. When she got pregnant—oh my gosh, I forgot to tell you I talked to her about that—he said it proved she couldn't handle herself."

"Harsh."

She nodded. "When I was little, they looked after me when Mother was at work. Granddad owned a hardware store. Grandma did housework, sewed, cooked. I still remember her cookies: peanut butter, chocolate chip, oatmeal raisin."

"Nice."

"There were never homemade cookies in Mother's apartment," she said softly. "How could there be? She worked all the time." She'd stopped pumping the swing, leaving it to him to sustain the motion.

"What happened, that you stopped seeing your grandparents?"

"I guess Mother made more money. She left me at a day care that had extra-long hours, for professional parents. Visits to her folks fell off, then stopped entirely. Maybe they fought. I don't know."

"Too bad. Grandparents are great. They grew up in different times, have an interesting perspective." He grinned. "Spoil the hell out of the grandkids. At least Mom's parents do."

"And your dad's parents? They're still in Greece?"

"Yeah. I barely know them. They're the same age as Mom's parents, but they seem two decades older." He bent down, removed Ann's sandals, then pulled her legs up so her calves and feet rested on his thighs. "They're nice, just foreign. Old-fashioned. I was in Greece maybe three years ago. Traveled around, spent a week with them. They're not so good with English and my Greek is poor, but we made out okay."

Gently he stroked Ann's bare feet, then began to massage one of them. "Tell me what else you remember about your grandparents."

As she reminisced, he kept the swing gliding and watched the expressions cross her face. He eased up her pant leg and massaged her calf, thinking he could spend hours like this.

When he started to work on her other foot, she moaned. "That feels great. You have amazing hands."

"Thanks." After a moment he said, "It's too bad your grandparents and your mom don't get along. But that's them. It sounds like, at least as a kid, you had a good time with them."

"I did. But they probably disapprove of me just as much as they did my mother. A woman who's so into her career."

"Maybe. But the world has changed since our moms went to university. Not all old folks are set in their ways, some actually grow." He smiled. "My Greek Pappou and Yiayia are rigid; my Canadian Gramps and Nana are liberal and open-minded. Mom brought all her feminist ideas home and got them listening. She can be persuasive."

"I saw that. I wonder if my mother tried, with her folks. Or whether she just lectured? That would have got Granddad's back up."

"It's hard, when a parent doesn't want to listen. You get frustrated, give up." He well knew that, from personal experience.

"Yeah, tell me about it." Her head tilted. "Is that what happened with your dad? About having a 'real man's job'?"

He nodded, began massaging up her leg. Changed the subject back to her. "Have you tried to get closer to your grandparents?"

She closed her eyes for a moment, then opened them and sighed. "No. I accepted that Mother didn't want them to be a part of our lives."

He frowned. "As a kid you didn't have much choice, but now you're an adult. She has a right not to see them, but you have just as much right to have them in your life. If you want to." He let his fingers work deep into her calf muscles. "You know what they say, parent and child is a relationship where conflict's built in. Grandparent and grandchild is a whole different thing."

Her lips twitched. "You're not so dumb, are you?"

He shrugged.

Her smile faded. "It would hurt Mother if I started up a relationship with them."

"Why?"

"I'd be choosing sides."

He chuckled. "Jeez, Lawyer-girl, not everything has to be adversarial."

"You telling me your family doesn't set up situations where they force you to take sides? So it's a no-win, and someone gets mad?"

"Oh, yeah. But then we yell at each other and it blows over. We don't hold grudges, but it seems your mom does." Except for his dad, about Adonis not following in his footsteps.

"Seems to me—" She broke off.

"What?"

She shook her head. "Keep doing what you're doing with my leg. God, if I could have you there when I came home from work at night, I'd be—" Again, she stopped dead. "Sorry, I didn't mean . . . Honestly, I wasn't suggesting . . ."

"It's okay. I didn't think you were asking me to move in." Though the idea of being there when she came home was appealing. Especially if she did it at a reasonable hour, like she'd started to. Giving her a massage, sharing a meal, talking about their days. If she had to work after dinner, he'd go for a run, have a drink with a friend, visit family, read a book. Same stuff he did now. Except, when the evening was done, he'd be climbing into bed with a sweet, sexy woman.

His cock stirred. All morning, touching her, talking, watching her pretty face, he'd been super-aware of Ann. That awareness shifted between sexual and simply appreciative. He hoped she felt it too, because this is what he wanted for the day. To teach her that lovemaking was about so much more than a goal-oriented drive toward orgasm.

The swing glider had been in shade, but now the angle of the sun changed and sunlight slanted through to lay across Ann's upper body. After a moment she pulled off her loose sweater and stretched lazily. "I love the sun. And being outside. This week, I learned it reenergizes me to take a walk at lunchtime." The hydrangea blossom had fallen to the seat beside her and she picked it up, twirled it between her fingers, held it to her nose.

"Stop and smell the roses. Or hydrangeas as the case may be," he said. "Fresh air and exercise, you're taking breaks, eating more regularly. That's great, but how come?" Would it be too egotistical to think he'd had something to do with the changes in her life?

She tucked the flower behind her ear again. "You and the Foursome helped, and a paralegal I work with. She can't keep working without food and a break. She said—" Ann gave a soft giggle. "She said she wasn't the Energizer Bunny."

He chuckled too. "Couldn't keep going and going and going? Who can?"

"Not me. Or, if I do, my effectiveness decreases. Mother never seems to wear down but I've learned that for me it's better to take a break. So the net result this week has been, I put in fewer hours of work and accomplished more." Her face was bright with pleasure.

"That's great. And you're less tired, and not so achy."

She nodded. "Not that I don't thoroughly appreciate the massage."

"Any excuse to touch you," he joked.

"I've never known a man who was so into touching."

"I'm a touchy-feely guy." Her words reminded him of one of his dad's put-downs, and he couldn't keep the edge of bitterness out of his voice.

"Mmm. I'm not my mother, and you're not your dad either."

"Picked up on that, did you? Yeah, I know. You think he'll ever figure it out?"

"You're the only son. He's a Greek male from a traditional family. He had three daughters and I'd bet he really wanted a son."

"Yeah. Just his luck, after daughters he's proud of he got a son who disappoints him."

She was quiet a moment, then said, "You can't be a tile-layer, just to make him happy."

He shook his head. "And you can't be an Energizer Bunny even if your mom might like it."

His comment lightened the mood, as he'd hoped, and she smiled at him. "We're not doing so badly as we are."

"Not at all." She moved the leg he wasn't massaging and eased her bare foot into his lap, using her toes to caress his package through his jeans. "We're doing great. Especially now."

His cock grew and he pressed his free hand over her foot, holding it against him.

"You've surprised me," she said.

"How so?"

"When you said you wanted a whole day, I thought ... Well, you've mentioned tantric sex, and about making love for hours."

"Mm-hmm?" Good, she was getting curious.

"The breakfast, walk, swing, everything's been nice. Now you're touching me, I'm touching you." She cleared her throat. "And you're not dragging me into your apartment. I never know if you're really attracted to me."

"Are you crazy? God, Ann, of course I am."

"But, then, don't you want to have sex?" She was frowning.

He lifted her legs down, then leaned forward and smoothed the frown line from her forehead. Gazing into those green-flecked eyes, he said, "Haven't we been making love since the moment we met this morning?"

"I ... Oh." She leaned forward, into his hand, as he slid it down the side of her face, then through her hair. "You mean, every little touch—like this—is a kind of foreplay?"

"Isn't it? And talk? Sharing things." Using his index finger, he stroked along the outline of her lush lips. "Aren't you more aware of yourself, your sensuality, me, than if we'd just climbed into bed at your place?"

"Yes." She parted her lips, darted out her tongue, and licked his finger, sending a shiver of desire coursing through him. "I hadn't thought of it that way. I'm used to foreplay being really, uh, targeted." A flush moved across her cheeks. "To breasts, genitals."

"Believe me," he said fervently, "I have nothing against breasts and genitals. But the rest of your body's beautiful, too. Every part of you deserves to be touched. Cherished."

"Cherished? An odd word for a man to use."

He shrugged. "I'm not your typical guy. Thought you'd have figured that out by now."

She nodded slowly. "It's true. You're more masculine than the lawyers I know, yet more sensitive, too. You don't put on a blustery, macho facade. Won't follow in your dad's footsteps. You're your own person, aren't you?"

He gave a deep sigh of relief and pleasure. He'd wanted to show her who he really was, and he was succeeding. Best of all, she seemed to approve. "Trying to be," he said. "It's a journey, finding out what's really me, out of all the ideas offered—or thrust down my throat—by family, friends, people I've met along the way. Like Harmony, who opened my eyes to a whole different notion of sex." He caressed the lobe of Ann's delicate ear, set her earring to dancing, stroked down the elegant line of her neck. "One that involves cherishing."

"You're younger than I am, but farther ahead on that journey. I always accepted the 'me' my mother wanted me to be. I feel stupid. Teenagers are supposed to separate from their parents, and I'm only now starting to do it."

"Age is a meaningless concept." His fingers rested against her collarbone, feeling it lift with her breathing.

"What do you mean?" She raised a hand to caress the back of his.

"No matter what our age, we're each on our own journey."

Her hand lifted and stroked through his hair. "Adonis, you know who you are as a person. And yet—please don't take this as a criticism—I saw how your family was with you. Your sisters think of you as their baby brother and your dad wants you to 'grow up,' as he calls it. Meaning, settle down and join him in his business."

"Uh-huh. What are you saying?"

"I understand that you're doing work you love. And you don't like regular hours, you want freedom and flexibility. But I'm used to people who are ambitious."

Okay, now she was getting down to brass tacks. Judging him, the way his dad did. Comparing him to her lawyer friend. Finding him wanting. Pissed, he moved away from her to sit back on the swing seat. "What more could I want than what I have now?"

That frown line was back in her forehead. "I'd say material possessions, but I know how shallow that is. And maybe I put too much weight on my condo, my car. But don't you envision ever wanting some kind of stability? Security? A family of your own?"

Then she shook her head vigorously. "No, I'm being silly. This is where age *does* count. You're twenty-four; why would you be thinking about those things yet? Despite what Mother says, it's not normal to have a career plan in place at the age of ten."

She leaned toward him, captured one of his hands between hers. "But how about when you're thirty? Or forty?"

So, maybe he wasn't pissed, after all. She wasn't judging, just trying to understand. "Not sure I'll ever be a career-plan kind

of guy. I admit, I live more in the moment than for the future."
Curling his hand to link fingers with her, he said, "As for a family, yeah, I want a partner, kids. But I'm not sure that's tied to a particular age. It'll happen when the time's right on my journey. Could be next year, could be in ten years." Could be soon, with the woman across from him.

"And when that time comes?" she prompted.

"Jesus, Ann." But he had to smile. He'd wanted to move their relationship past the superficial, so he could hardly complain. "Yeah, of course I'd want to support my kids. My partner and I would have to figure out what kind of life we wanted."

"Go on." Her eyes were bright with interest.

"Look at my role models. Mom and Dad—and you can't find a stronger feminist than my mom. Zoë and Mario, Phil and George. All couples who have kids and believe in being good parents. They've each found a way that works for them."

"None of them go away for months each winter."

"Could take the kids," he said halfheartedly. Then, "No, you're right." He'd never thought that far ahead. But seriously, if he compared the merits of winter sunshine to the smiles of a kid like Caitlin, Colin, or Matt—well, there was no choice. "Might have to stop doing that—what did you call it?—snowbird thing. Buy a sunlamp instead and," he grinned, "take up nude sunbathing with my woman."

Deciding to turn it back on her, he said, "How about you? You like children but said you didn't see how you could manage a kid along with your career. Don't you think you could find a creative solution?"

She sighed. "I'd have to let go of some of my ambition." She stared into his eyes. "I wouldn't do it the way my mother did. I know she did her best, but a child should have play and laughter and cuddling."

Then she sighed again, a deeper, almost wrenching one. "Why would I think I could be a good mother? I'm Meredith

Montgomery's daughter. I'd probably drive my kid obsessively."

He gripped her shoulders. "No way. You're smarter than that. Smarter than your mother."

Her eyes widened. "No one who's met Mother has ever said that."

"Then they have the wrong definition of 'smart'." He remembered back to Sunday night. "Did you hear what Mom said, about a person with more life experience making a better lawyer? She's right. And my mom's damned smart."

Ann's lips twitched. "My mother against yours? Okay, everyone says mine's brilliant. But you know what I think? Your mom's wise, and that's even better."

God, but this woman was irresistible. He pulled her closer and touched his lips to hers.

The first time he'd kissed her, she'd wanted to rush things along, but now she responded the way she had on Sunday afternoon. Lazily, sensually, as if she'd be happy to kiss for hours.

He'd be thrilled to oblige, but any of a dozen neighbors might be watching. He broke the kiss and said, "Let's take this inside."

As he led her up the outside staircase, his nervousness returned. The yard and swing were great, but what would she think of his place?

He opened the door to the small kitchen with the sunny yellow paint he'd applied himself, then led her through to the living room. The furniture was old stuff that had migrated upstairs whenever Thea and Frank bought something new.

Ann glanced around. "Homey." She walked over to the bookcase and picked up a carved wooden elephant from India, then rang a temple bell from Thailand. "Souvenirs?"

He nodded as she lifted the picture of Pappou and Yiayia, in front of their house on Crete. Around the frame hung a medal on a ribbon.

"Your grandparents?" She touched the medal. "And this?"

"Pappou gave it to me. It's from World War II. He fought in the resistance, alongside a British liaison officer, and they became close friends. The man died and his widow sent this medal of his to Pappou. It's one of his most prized possessions."

"And he gave it to you." She put the picture back gently. "I really need to get in touch with my grandparents."

"Ann." He drew her into his arms, where she felt so natural and good.

"Ann what?" she murmured against his throat, her breath warm.

"Just Ann. I'm glad you're here."

"Me, too." She lifted her head and he expected her to kiss him, but instead she trailed her tongue along the line of his jaw, making his cock throb. "Foreplay," she murmured.

"Fast learner. Want some lunch while we're playing?"

She cocked her head. "Chocolate-covered cherries?"

"For dessert. How about we start with bread and cheese?"

"Seems to call for wine."

"There's a bottle of dad's white in the fridge." He threaded his fingers through hers and tugged her toward the kitchen.

Together they laid out a simple meal and he put the tray on the coffee table. Ann curled into a corner of the couch and he sat beside her. "Close your eyes and let me feed you some cheese," he said. "Tell me what you think."

She obeyed and together they sampled the cheeses, tore chunks off the loaf of fresh bread, sipped wine. In between nibbles and sips, they touched and tasted each other. Little nips, licks, caresses in unexpected places like the back of a knee, an elbow. Everything sensitizing them to their own bodies, and each others'.

"Take off your pants," he suggested.

"If you do."

He pulled off his jeans, glad to release the pressure against his erection. Underneath, he wore a pair of blue boxers. She stripped off her kayak pants, so now she was clad in just the gauzy blouse over a teddy.

Adonis pulled his T-shirt over his head. "Pretty blouse, but how about taking it off?"

She obeyed, then he said, "Want to go lie down on the bed? I'll put some music on. Anything special you'd like?"

"I don't know much about music. Pick whatever you think fits the mood. But, uh, would you do something else for me?" Damn, she was sounding nervous again.

"Sure. What is it?"

Cheeks flushed, she rummaged in her pack and handed him a small bag. "Put these on."

He pulled out a pair of boxers. In black silk. "Ann?"

Her cheeks went brighter. "I like them. Don't you think they're sexy? Not for every day, but special occasions."

His fingers drifted over the silk. He could imagine the fabric caressing his skin—and Ann's fingers touching him through the silk. As his groin tightened, he said, "Definitely."

After trading his plain blue cotton for her black silk, he selected music to intrigue her ears. Instrumental, Eastern in theme, not foreign enough she'd find it discordant, but with different sounds than she'd be used to. Then he took the wine bottle into the bedroom where Ann had pulled back the covers and lay on a fresh white sheet.

He stopped and smiled in appreciation. "There's a beautiful sight."

She rubbed a hand across her forehead. "Adonis, I remember the stuff I said when I was drunk. I asked you to lie, to say I was pretty. I'm sorry, that was dumb. I don't really want you to. It's enough you're attracted to me. I want us to be honest with each other."

"My God, Ann." He sat on the bed beside her, shook his head. "Why don't you see the same woman I do? Beautiful, smart, sensual, playful, loving."

Her lips moved, like maybe she was repeating the words to herself. "No one's ever told me those things," she said, so softly he could barely hear. "Mother's compliments were always qualified, like, 'Ann, you're intelligent but not brilliant, so you need to work twice as hard.' " Her voice rose, took on a tone that was patronizing and dictatorial.

"Good God, is that what your mother sounds like?"

She flushed. "Yeah. I hear her in my head, so it's easy to imitate her."

"Tell her to go away. There's no place for her here."

"Believe me, she wouldn't want to be here."

"Look, I've never lied to you. I never will. When I say you're beautiful, I mean it. In my mind, my heart." He glanced down. "My swollen cock."

She closed her eyes and smiled, like she was gathering his words and holding them close. Then she opened her eyes and reached up her arms. "Thank you. Now, are you going to come down here and kiss me? Snuggle up so I can feel you through the silk of those boxers?"

"Nope. I'm going to . . ." He lifted the wine bottle and poured a few drops on her chest.

Her body jerked in surprise.

He leaned down and let his tongue follow the trail of the wine, down into the valley between her breasts.

Holding his finger to the neck of the bottle, he tipped again, then used his moist finger to circle her nipple through the teddy. When it budded, he went back for more wine, and this time followed it with his mouth, sucking that tight bud through the fabric.

"Oh," she panted, "that feels good. I can't believe how sensitive I am."

"The benefit of all that stuff you didn't think was foreplay. Just wait, it'll get better."

"Promises, promises."

"And I told you I won't lie. Gotta learn to trust me, pretty lady."

He went to work on her other nipple, then poured a little wine into his palm and let it trickle down her mons to disappear between her legs. He went after it with his tongue.

"Oh, my God!" Her lower body lifted off the bed. She reached down and fisted her hands in his hair. "Oh, yes. More, please."

It would be so easy to make her come, easy to give in to the throbbing in his cock and plunge inside her, but today was about a different way of making love. Finally she seemed ready to open herself to his message.

He eased back. "Take off your teddy."

Fingers clumsy with need, she obeyed. As she did, he got off the bed. Turning his back, he took a few deep breaths, moving sexual energy from his genitals and dispersing it through his body. His erection subsided a little as he went to the dresser, where he'd set out a couple of bottles of massage oil he'd prepared last night. A "his" and a "hers." He picked up the "his" bottle, came back to the bed and stared down at her. "I haven't seen you naked since that first day. God, you look good."

Then he lay down beside her, not touching.

She glanced over. "Adonis?"

He passed her the bottle and closed his eyes. "Massage me. Start at my feet and work up."

"But..."

"You're turned on. I know. Me, too. But we're going to wait, because it'll get better."

"Control freak." But there was a twinkle in her eye.

"Try taking deep breaths. Imagine you're taking all that tight, ready-to-burst energy from that sweet pussy of yours and moving it through your body. Think of a warm, healing kind of energy spreading through you."

"Yeah, right." The bed shifted. "You know you're crazy."

He looked up to see her kneeling over him, eyes narrowed in bewilderment.

"My turn on top," he reminded her.

"You could make better use of it," she grumbled. "Like by actually being *on top*."

"Let's see what you say in an hour or two. For now, try the breathing."

"Fine, I'll *breathe*." She began to huff air in and out in exaggerated fashion, then her breathing became deeper, slower.

He closed his eyes. Listened to the music, to the small sounds of her moving around, felt the bed move. Smelled the fresh, woodsy scent of the oil as she opened the bottle.

"This is different than the ones you gave me to smell before," she said.

"Cedar, lemon, and sandalwood. A combination of the West and the East."

"Nice." Her hands, lightly oiled, began to stroke the tops of his feet. At first she moved tentatively, then, perhaps remembering how he'd massaged her feet earlier, she became more confident. "How long do I do this?"

"However long you want. We have all afternoon. But don't massage too hard or you'll get tired. You're not used to this the way I am."

"I know it felt good when you did this to me, but wouldn't you like it better if I massaged higher up?" She'd tried to put a seductive note in her voice, but mostly she sounded unsure.

"It's not about arousal. So steer clear of genitals, okay? This isn't a sexual massage, it's a relaxing, sensual one. It's about you enjoying touching and getting to know my body, and me enjoying the feel of it and the connection between us."

He settled in to doing just that, concentrating on the way his skin warmed under her touch, how each cell seemed to spring to life. She began to work her way up the fronts of his legs, reaching around to do the backs as well.

After a few minutes she said, "Can we talk, or is that breaking the rules?"

Ann's way of connecting. Words, more than touch. "Sure. What's on your mind?"

Her hands worked his thighs then skimmed teasingly across the front of the boxers and landed on his rib cage. "I didn't tell you, I asked Mother about my father."

"Great. How did it go?"

"The good news is, she actually talked to me about it. And he's not a serial killer." She massaged his pecs, beginning to dig in hard enough it felt really good.

"You thought he might be?"

She skipped up to his shoulders, rubbing absentmindedly as she told him what her mom had said. One day, he'd get her to relax enough to do a proper massage, to focus on touch rather than speech. For today, he was happy she'd chosen to share something important.

When she'd skimmed down his arms and showed no sign of massaging his hands, he said, "Okay, your turn. Lie on your back."

They switched positions and he warmed scented jasmine-rose-neroli oil in his hands, then took her left hand in both of his and began to work it gently. "I understand why your mom felt betrayed, but it could have been a misunderstanding. Like, Dylan thinks she knows it's a summer thing, but she takes it more seriously. That would be easy to do, for a woman who wasn't experienced about relationships." He spoke slowly, trying to ease her tension not only with his fingers but his voice.

As he massaged his way up her arm, she said, "I know. So here's this guy thinking he's got a great summer thing going, then she announces she's pregnant. The last thing he'd want would be a child." Her eyes were shut, she was trying to sound matter-of-fact, but he heard the hurt in her voice.

"He didn't reject *you*, Ann," he said softly. "He rejected a situation. He doesn't sound like the kind of man who'd ever settle down with a woman and kid." Ann's mom was right about one thing; neither of them needed a loser like that in their lives.

"A drifter. That's what she called him."

"If she knew that from the beginning—" He broke off, thought about it as he warmed more oil, started on her other hand. "Okay, maybe she should have had the sense not to fall in love, but I guess she couldn't have prevented getting pregnant. After all, they used birth control."

"I wonder if she thought it was some kind of sign?" Her eyes opened and narrowed as she stared at him.

"Sign?"

"If you're on birth control and still get pregnant, then maybe your love is meant to be. You're supposed to be together and create a child."

"You've never made your mom sound like a romantic."

She laughed softly, closed her eyes again. "That's true."

"But maybe she used to be." He used both hands to work her left shoulder. "She told him she was pregnant, she probably hoped they'd work things out."

"Yeah, I suppose so." Her voice had gone serious. "I guess that was her summer to be romantic. When it backfired, she never let herself feel that way again. In fact, she's never even let herself get close to anyone."

"Except you." His hands massaged down the tight muscles of her left pectoral to her breast, which was soft under his touch. No beaded nipple.

"Even with me, she's guarded about showing emotion. She's not into hugs, hardly ever tells me she loves me."

He glanced at her face, saw her eyes were shut but her eyelids fluttered. "That's sad."

"Yes, it is." Under his hands, she tensed. "And you know what? I'm pissed about it."

One of the things Harmony had taught him was that you couldn't be a fully sensual, sexual being until you healed your wounds. Massage, healing touch, could help a person do that. Was it a coincidence his hands were only inches from Ann's heart as she processed her feelings toward her mom?

"You have a right to be mad," he told her. "She cheated you of things a kid should have."

Her body stiffened again. "I'm being unfair. She tried her best."

"Maybe so." Touch firm but gentle, he stroked her chest, breasts, rib cage, trying to give her the warmth her mother seemed incapable of. "Doesn't mean you don't have a right to be pissed. Children should be nourished with hugs and kisses, praise and love."

"I wish . . ." She sighed and her muscles loosened. "I was going to say, I wish I had a different mother. But that's not true, I love her. I just wish she'd been different."

"Is it too late? Could she change?"

Her eyes were squeezed shut. "I w-wish. But she's set in her ways." She sniffed. "D-damn, I never cry. Tears are a waste of time."

But they were welling from under her closed lids. "That last voice sounded like your mom's," he said gently.

She sniffed again. "It was." A tear spilled over.

"I don't agree with her." He caught the tear with his finger and brought it to his mouth. "Tears help you let pain out, where it doesn't have so much power."

She opened tear-glazed eyes. "That your mom talking?"

"Yeah." Definitely not his macho dad.

As tears tracked down her temples into her hair, he said, "Your mom may not be super-affectionate, but you know she wanted you. She could have had an abortion or given you up for adoption, but she kept you. Loved you."

"I guess. But it puts so much pressure on me, being the only person she's got. Pressure to live up to her expectations."

She was still meeting his gaze and he looked deeply into her damp hazel eyes, feeling the hurt inside her. He took her by the shoulders. "Those expectations are hers; she owns them. She's the one who let rejection hurt her so badly she never lets anyone into her life. Focuses on her career, rather than risking her heart. You can be braver, you don't have be the same as her. Figure out what *you* want, and tell her."

"What if she says I'm wrong?" The tears were sliding freely now.

"Then tell her again." He lay down beside her and gathered her into his arms, felt the dampness of her cheek against his shoulder. For a while, he just hugged her close as she cried.

Then, when the tears eased, he said, "Tell her you love her, you respect her, but you have to find your own path. And if she loves you, she should try to understand and respect you back."

She sniffed. "Is that what you told your father?"

Crap. "Uh, maybe not quite like that. More like, I didn't want to be a tile-layer so I wasn't going to do it."

"Which he'd taken as rejection of everything he's worked for."

"Shit." He'd never thought of it that way, but once she'd said it, it was obvious. "I guess you're right."

"I know if I'd ever said I didn't want to be a lawyer, that's how Mother would have felt. But it was okay, she made it so fascinating, there was never anything else I wanted anyhow."

"And now?"

She eased away, wiped her cheeks with the backs of her hands, sat up. "I want friends, too. A life away from the office, maybe one day a family of my own." A little smile. "Perhaps a puppy or kitten."

He sat up, too, caught and held her gaze. "Those are all good things. Normal things. She's the one with the warped life, Ann. That's sad, and you don't have to be like her."

She nodded slowly. "Adonis, what's the thing you've most wanted from your dad?"

Even Harmony had never got to the bottom of his own hurts. He squeezed his eyes shut against the pain, then opened them again so she could see into his heart. "For him to say he's proud of me, like he does with my sisters."

"Me, too, with Mother. Every time she compliments me, there's some damn qualification. Or, what I've done is good but she wants more from me." She sighed. "And *I've* been trying. Now you, you deliberately chose another path. Neither way has worked out for us."

"Nope."

"So, what's the worst-case scenario?" she said thoughtfully. "They never say those magic words. But we know they love us. Right?"

"Yeah." He managed a small smile. "That's not such a bad thing to settle for."

"Some wise man once told me, conflict's inherent in the parent-child relationship."

The smile grew. "That was pretty smart. So, I should tell Dad I respect him and what he's accomplished, but his way isn't mine, and I wish he'd respect me, too."

"And if he's still on your case, remember conflict's normal, and he loves you."

God, she was beautiful, even all swollen and tear-stained. Beautiful and smart and brave. And sexy. Opening up the way they'd both done was even better than sexual foreplay. He felt so close to her, and he wanted to get closer. Until they merged. Body and soul.

It was so cool she'd finally got into the gazing-into-each-other's-eyes thing. He could see the moment she read his thoughts. The green flecks in her eyes sparkled. Her lips curved. "You haven't finished my massage."

"Later." He leaned in for a kiss.

She avoided his mouth, her smile widening. "Hey, aren't we doing hours of foreplay, before sex?"

"We've done hours. Now it's time for sex." He stripped off the silk boxers and leaned in again.

She evaded him once more, laughing. "Hey, mister, I thought you were the one who wanted *slow*."

Man, he loved seeing her happy. He clamped his hands on either side of her head and held her steady, them moved purposefully toward her. "What I want is you. Now. I want to be inside you."

Her expression softened. "I could go for that." And she touched her lips to his.

He took them, in a hard, fast kiss. It was maybe a whole second before she caught up. Then she fisted her hands in his hair and angled his head exactly how she wanted it, trying to take control of the kiss. He let her, but just for a moment, then his tongue was thrusting into her mouth as his cock pulsed to the same rhythm.

She wrapped her arms around his shoulders and fell back on the bed, taking him with her. His body covered hers; his penis nudged between her legs and found her sex. Hot, swollen, soaking wet. She lifted her hips, spread her legs. He plunged into her silky, fiery sheath.

"Yes!" she cried, clutching him with her arms, her legs, her pussy. "Oh God, I am *so* ready for this."

"Me, too." After all those hours of anticipation, he was right on the edge. Thank God she was, too. He reached between them to caress her swollen clit and she gasped, "Yes, more, just like that," so he gave her what she wanted as he thrust deep inside her.

"Oh, God, yes, keep going, I'm going to come." She let out a cry and began to spasm around him, deep wrenching shudders that stimulated his cock so he had to come, too.

Except—crap, he'd forgotten the condom. Adonis gritted his teeth, exercised every ounce of self control, and pulled out.

16

"Adonis? Don't stop. What's wrong?"

"Condom," he gasped, fighting his body's need to come.

"Oh, shit! No, I can't believe we forgot." She scrambled up to a sitting position, eyes wide with shock.

"Sorry, I got carried away. I'm clean, I swear. But . . . you're not on the Pill?"

She shook her head, looking dazed. "I hadn't been sexually active enough to bother."

"I didn't come." And wasn't going to now, thanks to his own stupidity. But that was the least of his problems. Ann could be pregnant. Crap!

"It only takes one sperm." She closed her eyes.

"I know. Jesus, Ann, I'm sorry." Pregnant. Not what he wanted right now in his life.

But yet, when he'd seen her with Matt, he'd felt in his gut that the baby should be theirs.

She sighed. "I didn't think, either."

Way to kill a woody.

She glanced down, sighed again, then took his wilting penis in her hand and it twitched hopefully. "Look, the odds are really slim and what's done is done. Let's not *obsess* over it."

Thank God. More than orgasm, what he really wanted was to reconnect with her.

"If anything happened, you know I'd be there." Whatever she decided. Though in his heart, he'd likely be voting that they have the baby.

Her gaze lifted and she stared at him, then she nodded. "Yes, I do know that. You're not like him. My father."

"Never," he said vehemently. How could a man desert his own child? How could he do anything but love and support the baby, and the child's mom? Especially if it was Ann, whom he already had such strong feelings for.

Gently she touched his face, tracing his eyebrows, nose, cheeks, then finally mouth. "I trust you. And that's huge for me." She gave a shy smile. "So's telling you that I do."

His heart warmed. "Thank you."

He put on protection and this time when they lay back down together and embraced, it was slow and gentle. Loving. As if their whole bodies were kissing. He didn't register the moment he slipped inside her because it was so gradual a transition. Her body felt soft, receptive, fluid beneath his. She wasn't tensing, trying to force an orgasm the way she usually did.

Instead she made small movements, little sounds of pleasure. She touched his back with featherlight fingers, explored from his shoulders down to his butt, teased her way down his crack, and made him squirm inside her. She gave a soft giggle. "Feels good. Do it again, Adonis."

"Seductress."

"I'm just feeling. Responding. Enjoying. Isn't that how you like it?"

"Oh, yeah." And that enjoyment was building a major case

of arousal. His cock was ready to burst. He could control the need if he tried hard enough. But why? The essence of lovemaking wasn't control, but mutual pleasure.

He changed angle, reached between them to stroke her as he thrust into her, picking up the pace. Her hand joined his, circling him at the base, providing even more stimulation.

His breath came fast and he realized her breathing matched it. They were perfectly in sync. His lips found hers and they clung, not kissing so much as just breathing together.

His finger caressed her engorged clit. She caught his bottom lip between hers and sucked on it, and that pressure went straight to his cock.

Then she let go his lip, gasped and cried out. He groaned and exploded inside her as she climaxed around him.

After, bodies glued together by sweat, they lay in each other's arms as their breathing gradually slowed.

"Wow," she eventually said. "You win. Your kind of foreplay definitely works for me."

"We both win." Though his body felt as limp as overcooked pasta, he managed to get up so he could deal with the condom.

Was it already too late? Were a couple of sperm swimming inside her body, looking for an egg to fertilize? A baby. His and Ann's. Yeah, he could handle that idea. But could she? Was he making any headway in convincing her he was the guy she wanted to be with?

She'd curled up on her side. When he slid in behind her, she yawned. "I feel so relaxed, I could go to sleep."

"Then do."

"But . . ." She twisted her head back, trying to look at him. "I promised you the day."

"You can use some of it napping. So long as I can spoon you." He snuggled even closer, curling his body around hers.

"Mmm. Just for a few min . . ." Her voice trailed off and he smiled.

Best guess, she didn't make a habit of falling asleep with a man. He might even be the first. And he very much liked the idea of sharing firsts with Ann.

If she was pregnant . . . No, he wasn't going to go there; he wasn't a planner. If she was, they'd talk, decide what to do. Together. But he couldn't help wondering—if she was, might that rule the other man out of the picture?

It was about an hour before she woke, stretching and poking her curvy backside into him in a way that worked pretty much like an alarm clock for his penis.

"Mmm," she purred lazily.

"I never did finish that massage."

She wriggled her butt into him suggestively. "From the inside out would work."

"I want to touch you. All over."

He found the massage oil and, starting with her feet this time, set out on his mission: to caress every square inch of her body.

Whenever he got too aroused, he used breathing and energy diffusion to calm himself. When her breathing quickened and she began to squirm, he taught her to do the same things. "For now, this is about physically connecting, my hands to your body. Enjoy it, give yourself up to the sensations. Let me get to know you this way. We can make love later."

"We'd better. You can't turn me on like this, and not finish the job."

Afternoon sunlight slanted through the window and he lost all track of time. After a while, he began to talk. But not the way she'd done earlier, about real life and problems. Instead, he used his voice as a caress, telling her how beautiful she was. Hoping she'd learn to appreciate her body the way he did.

When he finally finished, he said, "Want to try something else?"

"What do you have in mind?" Her voice was lower, more relaxed than he'd ever heard it.

"Sit with me."

"Sit?" She opened her eyes.

He shifted, so he was sitting cross-legged on the bed. "Sit like this, in front of me, knees touching."

She gazed at him skeptically. Then she shook her head like she was letting go her skepticism and shot him an amused glance. "Whatever you say."

When they were sitting, naked and cross-legged, touching only at the knees, he said, "Now we look into each other's eyes and breathe. You'll find, over time, our breathing will synchronize."

She held his gaze. "Is this tantric stuff?"

"Yeah."

"So what's it all about? My friend Jenny said it involves spiritualism? I don't want you trying to convert me to some religion."

"I won't. For tantric purists, it's about a spiritual union between woman and man. It's also about chakras. But I don't know much about that."

"Then, what does it mean for you? Why are you so keen on it?"

"It's about immediacy. Experiencing the moment fully, with all your senses. Knowing, respecting, loving your body. Sharing it intimately with another person. So intimately that, whether you're actually having sex or you're just breathing together, you can lose track of where you end and they begin."

"That sounds amazing," she said softly.

He nodded. "Tantric practitioners believe orgasm is a whole different thing than what we usually think of. It's a whole-body experience, and for a man it doesn't necessarily involve ejaculation."

She cocked her head. "Orgasm without ejaculation? That's your idea of fun?"

He chuckled. "Okay, I admit, I kind of like the ejaculation part. But not too quickly. See what's happened today? We touched and became closer, delayed the act of sex. And when we finally came, the orgasms were so powerful."

"True, but you can't do this every day. Spend hours building up to orgasm." She grinned. "Not even you, with your flexible schedule."

"You're right. But you can always take a little time first. Let your bodies and hearts connect rather than leap into sex. Like, slow kissing, the way we did in Stanley Park."

"Mmm, that was nice. Okay, you may be converting me." Then she fell silent and they sat and breathed together, the odors of the two massage oils mingling with the scent of sex.

He let his mind drift, and didn't veil his eyes to conceal anything from her. He thought how complex and incredible she was. Inside that womanly body was a brilliant legal mind, an ambitious professional, a caring but troubled daughter, a loyal friend. A person who was learning to open her eyes to the world around her, and take pleasure in it. A woman who was a wonderful lover, and would be an incredible mother.

Couldn't she see, looking into his eyes, that this was where she belonged? With him?

Well, damn. He really was falling in love with her.

"Adonis? What are you thinking? You look surprised."

He'd promised not to lie to her, yet he was sure she wasn't ready to hear the whole truth. He compromised on, "I care about you, Ann. You're special."

Her breathing, which had been slow and regular, stuttered. "I . . ." She flushed. "I care about you, too. But we're so different. I mean, the gypsy who heads for the sun and the lawyer who's building her career."

"Sure, we're different in some ways. But that's not bad. How do you grow, if you're with someone who thinks exactly the same as you?"

She nodded slowly. "Like me and my mother. She trained me to think the way she does. I never moved outside that. Not until I listened to my girlfriends, you, even the paralegal in the office. You think differently and make me question."

"Questioning is good. Lawyers do it all the time, right?"

"Y-yes. In our work." Her body shook with a silent chuckle. "I have such terrific analytical skills, yet I've never turned them onto my own life. Until now."

"We do things when the time's right."

"You honestly believe that? It sounds like leaving things to chance. Fate."

"And you believe in setting a goal and working toward it. That's fine. But you may not have—or see—all the information until you're ready for it. And goals can change."

"I suppose they can. And sometimes should." Her expression was reflective, then she frowned. "Sorry to break the mood, but my knees are sore. I'm not used to this position."

"Then we'll move. And how about food? The sun's going down, it feels like time for dinner." He climbed off the bed and she joined him, stretching her legs.

"I almost hate to get dressed and go out."

"Even for salmon on the barbecue downstairs?"

"Okay, maybe for that. But Adonis, you don't have to cook for me."

"We'll do it together."

"I don't know how to cook."

"You can make Greek salad. You helped last Sunday. It's easy."

"I'm a klutz. I'll chop off a finger."

"Ann." He took her by the shoulders. "You're not a klutz. Bet that's your mom talking."

Her shoulders shrugged under his hands. "I bump into things, knock things over."

"That's because you've been living in your mind, ignoring your body until it sends out urgent signals. Look at how different you are when you pay attention to that wonderful body. Like, with lovemaking today. Kayaking last week."

Her eyes had widened as he spoke. "Thanks." Then she flashed a grin. "All the same, be warned. If I do chop off a finger I'm going to be really mad at you."

They put their clothes on and worked companionably in his kitchen, with him putting baby potatoes on to boil, chopping parsley, making a fruit salsa for the fish while she assembled the salad. Then she put on her sweater and they went outside.

After he barbecued the fish, they ate on Thea and Frank's patio, with a couple of old-fashioned carriage lamps for illumination. Conversation drifted here and there, sometimes stopped completely, but even the silences were easy.

After dinner and the dishes, he said, "Feel like a bath together?"

"In that wonderful old claw-footed tub?"

"It's big enough for two." He drifted his fingers down her cheek. "So long as the two are friendly."

"I can be friendly."

He poured a few drops of lemongrass-scented oil into the bath and they settled in, facing each other. Touching gently, stimulating each other, but not too much. Then they changed position, so he was behind her. His penis pressed against her soft bottom, and grew in response. After lathering his hands with sandalwood soap, he smoothed them over her shoulders, arms, breasts. Lingering there and circling, teasing. Then he moved lower, caressed her sex, felt her own arousal.

"I want you inside me," she murmured.

"Me too. Let's dry off and go to bed." If they really became a couple, he was going to talk to her about going on the Pill and throwing out the condoms.

In the bedroom, he put one on his cock, securing it with a stretchy ring at the base. He intended to be inside her for a while, teaching her how to let arousal ebb and flow.

"What's that?" she asked. "Is it uh, a cock ring?" There was a quiver in her voice, partly humor, he thought.

"Something funny?"

"Just, the Foursome has a joke. Calamari rings and, uh, cock rings. But I've never actually seen one."

"Some go around the cock and balls. They can be used to sustain a hard-on, make it bigger, enhance sensation for the guy and the woman. This is just a basic one, to keep the condom on."

"They don't usually fall off?"

"You've never made love for hours. I'm not going to be this hard for all that time." He lit a couple of sandalwood candles then took a comfortable cross-legged position on the bed. "Come sit on my lap, facing me."

He helped her ease into the yab-yom position, so she was sitting across his lap. Her sex pressed gently against his. Then he began touching her with featherlight caresses. Her face, arms, shoulders, chest. After a few minutes she reciprocated. By the time they got to genitals, both were fully aroused.

"Now I really want you inside," she murmured, holding him in one hand.

"Then put me there."

She raised up, positioned him at her entrance, then slowly eased down, encompassing him with soft, wet heat.

He took her hands in his and held them down at their sides so they could concentrate on the way their bodies joined. Then he began to rock against her with small, slow movements and she said, "Nice." She rocked back, their bodies setting up a gentle rhythm, kind of like the glider swing that morning.

"It feels different, with the ring," she said, breathing faster. "More stimulation. It's kind of like when you use your finger." Her hips thrust harder now, and her cheeks were flushed.

"Slow down," he said. "Back off a little, breathe the way you did earlier."

"*I* can have multiple orgasms," she said through gritted teeth. "Why should I back off?"

"Because I think you'll have a stronger one if you do."

Her eyes narrowed. "I know my body better than you do."

"Yeah, but you've never tried anything like this before. Call it an experiment. And any time you really, really want to come, tell me and I'll make it happen."

Now her eyes went wide. "That easily?"

"Sure. You're a sexy, responsive woman."

She might not have done it consciously, but as they'd been talking her movements had slowed. She'd eased away from the edge of orgasm. "Adonis, it's often a struggle for me to climax. That's why I can be, uh, driven about it. I can get put off so easily."

"There's nothing wrong with letting it slide away. I'll make sure it comes back."

"If a guy tries too hard, that's a thing that can put me off." Her cheeks were pink. "Sorry, I know it's silly, but I figured I should warn you."

"It's okay, I don't try. Not the way you're talking about. All I do is listen to your body, help it go where it wants to. Lovemaking isn't about trying, it's about letting it happen."

"My friends call me a control freak. It's hard for me to let go."

"Trust me. Trust yourself." He lifted their clasped hands so their arms stretched out from their shoulders. That brought their chests and heads close, so he kissed her. Slowly, fully, using his tongue to stroke the inside of her cheeks, to mate with hers.

He eased away from the kiss and leaned backward, taking her with him, straightening his legs as she did the same. Now they lay on the bed, him flat on his back, her body matching his. Arms spread out at the shoulders, hands still joined. Her head tucked into his shoulder. Chest to chest, pelvis to pelvis, thigh to thigh. Him still inside her.

If she'd been sitting on top of him, she could have controlled the movement, rode him fast and hard if she wanted. This way, bodies plastered together, it was hard to make anything but the smallest of movements.

Still kissing, he started up that rocking motion again and she answered, sighing softly against his throat.

For the next two or three hours they stayed on his bed, changing position every now and then. Her on top, him on top, spooning her from behind, both kneeling, her on all fours with that sexy ass in the air. Varying the rhythm, so sometimes it was gentle and sometimes he thrust deep and hard into her. A couple of times he slid out, to let them both cool off.

She asked him to touch himself, and he did, while she watched. He sensed she wanted to do the same but was waiting for him to suggest it, and so he did. He loved watching her touch her own body, at first shyly but then with more abandon as she explored her own sexuality.

He put his lips and tongue to her pussy, tasting her juices, thrusting his tongue inside, suckling her labia and clit with soft lips. Then they joined again, tried another position.

A couple of times she cried, "Adonis, I can't stand it any longer," so he brought her to climax, sometimes with his cock, sometimes his fingers and tongue. After, he held her. Then they'd start up again.

Once she stripped off the condom, crying, "I need *you* in my mouth."

His cock was supersensitive by then, so he said, "Gentle,

okay?" Then he gave himself up to the incredible sensations of her wet tongue, those sexy lips. When he was on the verge of coming, he took her fingers, circled them around the base of his cock, and held their hands together there, tight, holding back ejaculation.

"You can come," she said. "I've had more than my fair share."

"Later. Inside you."

It had to be past midnight when, bodies slippery with sweat, muscles limp from tiredness, every inch of both their bodies kissed and well-loved, he knew it was time. His body gathered itself, hers answered, and he let everything he felt for Ann surge through him and pour into her as she cried out his name and gripped him, held him, took all he had to offer.

And returned it. He'd swear she returned it.

When Ann woke Sunday morning, nestled against Adonis's chest, she felt utterly contented. That lasted for less than a minute, before panic set in.

What am I doing? This was supposed to be about sex. His turn on top. Not about . . . whatever yesterday and last night were. How did he suck me into this?

Suck me into, for the first time in my life, being truly intimate with a man. Exploring my own sexuality in a way I hadn't even imagined. Trusting him totally.

Cautiously she inched back, trying not to wake him.

Ann, you know better than that. Never trust anyone other than yourself—but especially, never trust a man. And what were you thinking? Sex without protection? That's insanity.

Okay, Mother, forgetting the condom was dumb. But you're wrong about the rest. Adonis isn't Dylan.

He'd never run out on her if she got pregnant—though the chance was so slim, she wasn't even going to think about it.

He'd never knowingly hurt her. He cared for her, she'd seen it in his eyes, felt it in every movement of his body. And damned if she didn't care for him, too.

Don't be a fool. He's a drifter like your father. In two months he'll be gone. He won't look back, won't care about you despite the pretty words he's spoken. He'll find someone else.

She couldn't let herself in for being hurt that way.

And besides, what about David? He was no drifter, and she'd really had no chance to figure out what she might feel for him. God, how could she be feeling so conflicted about Adonis when she hadn't sorted out what was happening with David?

Get rid of both of them. It was Meredith again. *You see, I'm right. You don't need either one, and men only bring trouble into your life.*

She groaned, and beside her Adonis stirred.

"Hey, there." He rolled onto his side and smiled at her, all sleepy-eyed and tousle-haired and sexy. Looking better than anyone had a right to look first thing in the morning.

"Good morning." She began to scoot over to the side of the bed.

His hand caught her arm. "What's your hurry?"

Keeping her back to him—the better to resist temptation and conceal her utter confusion—she said, "Look, I had a great time, but I have to work today."

The hand tightened momentarily, then loosened again. "No time to fool around first? I promise I can do quickies, if that's what you want."

She sighed, then glanced over her shoulder. He looked puzzled, almost hurt. "I'm sorry, Adonis. I need time to think."

"Think?" There was an edge to his voice and he dropped his hand. "As in, analyze and obsess?" Before, he'd teased her about obsessing but this morning's tone said he wasn't joking.

She straightened her shoulders. "Yeah, I guess so. That's what I do."

Their gazes locked in a mutual challenge. Then she said, "Yesterday and last night were great but I . . . This is all so new and I don't know what to think."

"You could just feel." Then he gave a jerky shrug. "Or maybe you can't. You have to analyze before you know how to feel."

She didn't want to hurt him, but what did he want her to say? The truth was, her thoughts and feelings were such a muddle, she had to get away and clear her head. "I don't know. Maybe. Please try to understand."

He gave a slow nod. "Okay."

When she slid toward the side of the bed once more, he said, "Ann?"

Again she turned back. "Yes?"

"When you're analyzing, remember how good we are together."

"I kn-know." But wait a minute. He was hurt she was leaving and said he wanted her to just *feel*—and yet he hadn't told her his own feelings. Not in words, anyhow, and she needed facts, not impressions formed under the influence of bone melting orgasms.

She lifted her chin. "What do you want from me?"

He gestured to her, the bed. "This. Being together. Making love, caring for each other. Seeing where it may go."

Caring. Okay, he gave me a word, and it confirms everything I felt last night. And right now her heart was racing, her insides melting and . . . *Hey, wait a minute!* "But where can it go, when you leave for whatever sunny place you're going to this winter?"

He frowned a little, like that question hadn't even occurred to him.

Men. Maybe Mother's right. He's talking a bunch of pretty words he's never bothered to think through.

His brow cleared. "Come with me."

"Yeah, sure." *Is that the best he can come up with on the spur of the moment?*

"I'm serious. Come, spend months in the sun. I'll work part-time, you can do whatever you want. Walk on the beach, read. Relax. When I'm not working we'll explore, eat, make love for hours and hours."

She imagined it, for all of a moment. "Any woman in her right mind would be tempted, but that's not me. I can't—don't want to—abandon everything I've worked for."

"No." He sighed. "You're right, I wasn't thinking. I know how important your work is. So, you stay here, work like crazy and we'll keep in touch. E-mail and phone."

Suzanne and Jaxon had a long-distance relationship, though they did get together every two or three weeks. Ann had told Suze it was a test, to make sure they cared enough about each other.

"You want to concentrate on work anyhow," he said.

Can't argue with that, can I?

"Any time you felt like you needed a dose of family, my mom would take you in. My dad likes you better than me already," he teased.

"I don't know. I barely know you, and you're suggesting we carry on a long-distance relationship for months." *I wonder what the girls would say. I need advice; I've lost all perspective.*

"Anticipation?" he wheedled. "Absence makes the heart grow fonder?"

David's been absent for the last week. Has my heart grown fonder of him? No, but maybe that's because everything about our relationship is up in the air. If we were actually a couple . . .

Adonis's face darkened. "I don't want to lose you to him."

"What? Who?"

"That lawyer you told me about. You're thinking of him. After a day and a night with me, you're wondering how it'll be with him."

She closed her eyes against the hurt in his, but couldn't shut out his voice as he went on. "Do you really think it could be this good?"

Do I? David's older, more mature, intellectual, successful. Ambitious. Our ambitions match up. As lovers, who knows? We've felt that tug, the spark, since the beginning.

"Then go find out," Adonis said, thrusting himself out of the other side of the bed. Across its width, he stared at her, his normally warm brown eyes cold and harsh. "If you're going to be with me, I want you *with* me. Not thinking about him." He picked up the boxers she'd given him, tossed them aside, then stepped into his jeans. "Go figure it out. And let me know when you have."

A spark of anger flamed in her. *Where does he get off? All he's offering me is a month or two, then maybe we'll pick up again when he gets back. If he hasn't hooked up with some nature-girl, tantric sex expert who's more his type.* "Fine," she said coolly. "I'll do that."

Muscles stiff from all the unaccustomed positions she'd forced her body into, self-conscious under his gaze, she awkwardly gathered her clothes and pulled them on. Yuck. She hated to go home without a shower, but she needed to get away.

"I'll call you a cab," he said coolly.

"No, thanks." She ran her fingers through her hair, glad of her short, practical cut. "I'll walk. I need fresh air."

She got as far as the bedroom door, then had to stop and turn. They couldn't leave things like this. Across the room they stared at each other, then he said, "Oh, fuck, I'm being a dickhead." He came over and stood in front of her, bare-chested and tousled. "I just can't stand the thought of you with another guy. I hate that you might care more for him than me."

Biting her lip, she stroked his cheek. "I understand. But let's not snipe at each other."

"You're right." He reached out and she went into his arms for a hug.

"Adonis, I'm not saying I want to stop seeing you. I just need time to think."

"Yeah," he said gruffly. "Do what you need to do." He eased her away. "Want me to walk you home?"

She shook her head, smiling to ease the rejection. "I need to be alone."

Not that all the thinking did her any good, nor did the long shower once she got home. She was as confused as ever by the time she'd put on her old jeans and settled at her desk with the Healthy Life Clinic file.

Time for a dose of real life. Things I know how to handle.

Forcing herself to concentrate, she began reading some judgments Joanne had printed out. After an hour or so, she turned on her computer to check another case name that had come up.

When her e-mail program opened automatically, she realized she'd never been off-line for so long. Oops. There was a message from David, sent late last night. She clicked it open.

Ann, we have things under control. I'm coming back Sunday. If the flight's on time, I'll be downtown by late afternoon. Can you meet me for dinner?

Damn.

Now she realized she hadn't checked phone messages either. David had called, saying the same thing as his e-mail and asking her to call.

How can I see him today, after just being with Adonis?

But I have to know what's happening with David. Have to sort out my feelings, or I'll go freaking nuts.

She was staring at her phone when it rang. The call display

showed David's name. Heart thumping nervously, she answered.

"Ann, I'm glad I caught you. I'm at the airport in Toronto and my flight's about to leave. Thought I'd try you, since I hadn't heard back."

"Sorry, I forgot to check messages. I only got yours a minute ago."

"Anyone ever tell you you work too hard?" he said affectionately.

If he only knew. She swallowed, feeling guilty as hell. "Takes one to know one."

"So, what about dinner?" he asked.

Maybe she should pick him up at the airport—but then they'd be alone in her car. She'd prefer a public place; it felt safer. "Dinner's fine. What time?"

"I'll need a shower." She heard a yawn. "I'm beat, it's been a hell of a week."

"Maybe you should—"

"I want to see you. You'll give me a second wind." Already his voice had picked up energy. "Seven o'clock? How about at the hotel? The lounge is nice. I eat there often."

She wanted to insist on someplace other than his hotel, but he'd had a long week; he'd want what was easiest. Besides, even if he had split up with his wife, there was no way she'd be leaping into his bed tonight. Waking up with one guy and going to bed with another was definitely not her style. "All right, I'll meet you there."

"I can't wait to see you." His voice was husky, intimate.

"M-me too." Mostly because she had to find answers soon.

She worked hard until it was time to change for dinner. Then she stared into her closet for long minutes. What message did she want to convey? Not sexy; that was inappropriate. She didn't own anything sexy, anyway, except the teddies she wore under her regular attire.

Her wardrobe was mostly business clothes. Damn, she needed some variety.

Sighing, she chose an elegantly styled white silk shirt to wear over slim black pants. She rolled up the sleeves and left a few buttons undone to reveal the lacy neckline of a white teddy.

She was going for classy yet feminine, but when she studied her reflection she wasn't sure it worked. *I'll probably be mistaken for a waitress, but it's the best I've got.*

She was just leaving when her cell rang.

Damn, is that David calling to cancel again?

No, the call display showed her mother's name. She answered as she picked up her purse and keys. "Hi, how are you?"

"Am I interrupting anything?"

Thank God she didn't call yesterday! "No. I've been working all day. I'm just heading out for a quick dinner." She locked her door and headed for the elevator to the underground parking. "How are things with you?"

"Good. I've been invited to speak at a symposium in Amsterdam next year and I've just acquired a sizable Hong Kong firm as a new client."

"Terrific."

"Listen, Ann, I've made a couple of phone calls about your plan of doing Charter work. Checking out firms you might go to."

My plan? Did I say I had a plan? Much less, to leave my firm? Yikes! "You didn't say I was thinking of leaving Smythe Levinson?"

"This was utterly confidential. I've done some checking and I'm not sure Smythe Levinson is the best place for you. David Wilkins is excellent, but there's a small firm in Ottawa that's a better fit. Brett, Noble and Payton."

"I've definitely heard of them."

"Check them out on the Internet. They specialize in Charter law and have three very experienced lawyers."

Wow, how ideal. "Can you hang on a minute? Just let me get out of the parking lot." It was impossible to handle a stick shift, back out of a parking spot, and also talk on a cell phone. She dumped her phone in her lap. When she was on the road, she retrieved it. "Sorry. Go on."

"I was told in confidence that Charlie Noble is retiring in two years. If you juniored him, you could step into his position. The firm could be Brett, Payton and Montgomery."

Holy freaking wow! A partner in a prestigious law firm, doing work that challenged and fascinated her. "That sounds amazing." *Everything I've been working for, and earlier in my career than I could ever have hoped. God, I really could succeed as brilliantly as Meredith.*

"I can get you an interview, and I believe your record and personality will stand you in good stead."

In other words, Mother's reputation would get me the job. Then I'd have to measure up. But I could do it. I'm bright, motivated; I'd work even harder.

"This is a rare opportunity, Ann," her mother went on. "Research it and consider it thoroughly, but don't take long. Some other ambitious lawyer will hear about it and get in there."

"I will." She already knew the biggest downside: the firm was in Ottawa. Her girlfriends were here. And Adonis. On the other hand, her mother and David lived in Toronto; she'd be closer to them. But what did it matter? She'd be working so hard she'd have no time for any kind of relationship.

I'd be the kind of lawyer Adonis's mom thinks is narrow, out of touch with real life.

"Thanks so much, Mother. I really appreciate this." She was on the Cambie Street Bridge now, clear sailing to the hotel. If only the rest of her life were so straightforward.

But, thinking about relationships had reminded her of something. "On a different topic, I was considering getting in touch with Grandma and Granddad. Would you mind if I did?"

There was a pause, then, "Why would I mind? But why do you want to?"

"I'd like to get to know them again. After all, they're family."

There was a pause, long enough for her Miata to glide through two green lights. Then her mother said, "Is something wrong? The last two or three times we've spoken, you've sounded different. Unsettled."

"I guess I am, a little. Thinking about where I want to go with my career, my life."

"This is no time to doubt yourself. You've always been so sure, so focused."

And how much of that was your doing, Mother?

"I'm twenty-eight. It's a good time to take stock."

"I can tell you what you'll see. You've spent years laying a solid groundwork, and now is the perfect time to capitalize on it. Don't let anything sidetrack you from your priorities."

"No, I won't," Ann said softly. *Once I figure out what they are.* "I have to hang up now. I have traffic lights to deal with."

"If you move to Ottawa, you'll have to get a sensible car. That toy of yours won't handle the snowy winters."

"Good night, Mother."

Ann patted the dashboard of her car affectionately. Another part of her Vancouver life she'd miss if she moved back east. *But, oh my God, I could be partner in one of the leading firms in the whole freaking country!*

As she pulled into a parking spot, she realized that her mother's call had distracted her from worrying about seeing David. But now her nerves were back, full force.

Five minutes early, she reached the Sutton Place lounge before him and secured a relatively private corner table. The place, called Gerard, had a clubby English feel, with leather chairs, tapestries, a fireplace. She sank back into leather, reluctantly gave the martini menu a pass, and settled on a glass of California Pinot Noir.

She was studying the food menu—not that she'd likely be able to eat, she was so nervous—when she heard David's voice as he greeted the host.

As she lifted her head, the other man said, "Good evening, Mr. Wilkins. We've missed you this week."

David hadn't seen her. She was glad because it gave her a moment to react, unobserved.

Chatting easily with the host, he was dressed in tailored casual pants and a golf-style shirt, both in soft, expensive fabrics. Clothing that clung to his lanky frame in just the right way. His dark hair gleamed damply; he was fresh out of the shower.

Yes, she still found him attractive. He was mature, casually sophisticated. So different from Adonis's Greek-god beauty and natural style. How could she be attracted to two men who were opposites?

Her stomach flip-flopped and she felt sick with anticipation. What was David going to tell her? And how would she respond?

The host said to David, "You're dining alone, as usual?

"No, I'm joining a colleague. She—" He glanced around, then broke off, smiling at Ann and making her heart skip nervously. "Ah, she's already here."

"I'll bring you your usual," the host said and David replied with an over-the-shoulder "Thanks" as he strode toward her.

17

If she stood up, David might hug her, try to kiss her. Ann wasn't ready to handle that, so she stayed seated and tried to smile. "Hello."

"It's so good to see you." He touched her shoulder, then took the chair across from her.

A waiter appeared with a tumbler of amber liquid and a glass. "Macallan twenty five years old and spring water," he murmured. "Are you ready to order, Mr. Wilkins? The rack of lamb is particularly good tonight."

"No rush, let's have a drink before we order. Ann, is that all right?"

"Of course," she said with relief, knowing her nervous tummy couldn't deal with food.

David added water to his Scotch, tasted it, and sighed with pleasure. "Excellent."

The waiter left and Ann sipped wine, her hand trembling. When she put the glass down, David caught her hand in his.

She tugged it away. "David, that's not appropriate."

He sighed again, less happily. "Ann, I talked to Clarice. We agreed. Our marriage is over. We're filing for divorce."

OH, MY GOD. She gulped. *I don't think I really believed he was serious. Holy shit, he's getting a divorce.* "Uh, that's . . . I mean . . ." She swallowed and tried again. "You both agreed? She didn't mind?" In the background, her brain was saying, *What now? What happens now? What does he want? What's he proposing? What do I want?*

"She said it made perfect sense," David said. "And she's right."

Sense? "But, are you okay? How do you feel about it? You can't just end something that's lasted over ten years without some . . . something. Can you?" Ann tried to figure out what she felt. Confusion, anxiety. The truth hadn't sunk in yet. *And what happens next?*

David shrugged, rubbed a hand over his jaw. "Honestly, our marriage ended a while ago. We were both too busy to notice, much less try to save it. I think she was relieved I'd raised the subject. Now we can both move on."

To what? David, what in freaking hell happens next?

His face lightened, softened. "Damn, I wish I could touch you. Let's go to my room, I'll have our drinks and dinner sent up."

Nerves screaming, she shook her head. "I'm afraid of what might happen. David, I don't want to rush anything. Up to now, you were married. I've tried not to think about us having a relationship. Now, you say you're getting a divorce. So," she cleared her throat, tried not to scream out the words, "what happens next?"

He leaned forward. "Like I said on the phone, we make a good team. In work and, I think, in life. Come to Toronto with me."

Oh, Jesus. He really means it.

"We'll do Charter work together," he said. "If there are two of us, we can take on more, build that into one of the firm's specialties. Compete better with some of the top names."

"Like Brett, Noble and Payton." The name slipped out.

"Yeah, and Aaronson, Mellors. They're the two top firms."

That's the work side. First, as always. What about the rest? "What else, besides work?"

"Live together. Get a nice apartment close to the office. See how things go, get married if everything works out."

Get married? He's just decided to get a divorce, we've never even kissed properly, and he's talking marriage? This can't be real. She tried to focus, to figure out exactly what he had in mind. "No kids, no pets? A career-focused couple?"

"Right. Maybe we'll even set up our own firm. Wilkins and Montgomery." He grinned. "Doesn't that sound great?"

"Oh my God," she murmured. They could make it one of the best in the country, if they worked hard enough. Side by side.

"Exactly," he said smugly.

No, this is crazy, I have to put on the brakes. "You're— we're—getting way ahead of ourselves."

"You have to know where you're heading, in order to get there."

She shook her head, confused for a moment. Was that her mother's voice, or David's? Right. His. "You and my mother would *so* get along," she muttered.

"I hope so. I've met Meredith a time or two at Bar events. She's brilliant. I admire her immensely. She must have been a great role model to grow up with."

"In many ways."

Ann had grown up in a tight twosome unit with her mother in charge and no room for friends or play. What David was proposing sounded very similar. Not to mention, he was trying to arrange her life just the way her mother always had.

No, he means we'd be equals. Doesn't he? Or would I always be the junior partner, at work and at home?

She stared into his handsome face. Yes, she was attracted to him. But why? She had to get over her juvenile case of hero-worship and truly believe she was his equal. The question was, without the hero-worship, would she still be as attracted?

"It's driving me crazy I can't touch you," he said, taking another swallow of Scotch. "Look, I know I'm saying this wrong. But Ann, I'm not some naïve romantic kid, to get down on one knee and swear undying devotion. I'm a man heading into middle age, who's building a very good career. I'm attracted to you, I like how you make me feel, and I like to think I make you feel good, too."

"You do."

"When I met Clarice, we were both young and we had that head-over-heels-in-love thing. But it burned out. I don't want to do that again. You and I make sense, in so many ways. Similar goals, respect, physical spark. If we give ourselves a chance, we can build all that into the kind of solid partnership that will get stronger with time."

"Not the most romantic offer," she said drily.

"Yeah, but that's not us. We're too practical."

Maybe he's right. I've never been romantic, so why start now? Being practical and focused has got me a long way, and if I team up with David my career will move even faster. Plus I'll have regular sex and some guy companionship.

But damn, shouldn't there be a little romance, when we're talking about a future together?

Or, she could build her career even faster by following up on the opportunity her mother had offered. Go back to being all work, no play. Having a man—men—in her life was too damned complicated, anyway.

I'd hurt David. He wouldn't be shattered, though. Like he

said, he's practical, not romantic. That's reassuring, if not exactly flattering.

Adonis was hurt, thinking of me with another man. His feelings for me are stronger.

But it's my feelings that count.

The waiter returned. "Ready to order now?"

"I think so," David said, glancing her way. "Ann?"

No, I can't do this any longer. There's something I need, and I'm going for it whether it's wrong or not. I have to find out how much chemistry we really have. "Could you give us ten minutes?" she asked the waiter. "I have to talk to Mr. Wilkins outside, but we'll be back."

"Of course." He nodded and departed.

She turned to David, who was staring at her in astonishment. "Come with me," she said, getting to her feet. "We're going to your room. I want a kiss. One kiss, that's all."

His face lit up. "Now you're talking." He rose quickly and hurried her over to the other wing of the hotel and up in the elevator.

As soon as they were inside his room, she forced words past the nervous lump in her throat. "Now. Kiss me now."

"God, you don't know how long I've been waiting for—"

"Now." She stretched up, grabbed onto his head, and pulled it toward her.

He responded eagerly, circling her with his arms and hauling her body up against his, slanting his lips across hers then hungrily sliding his tongue into her mouth.

She'd wanted this moment ever since the first day they met. Ann ran her hands down his back, feeling his lean strength. Against her belly his cock was rising, pressing against her and her sex responded with a throb of need.

His kisses were demanding, and she tried to keep up but her mouth was just learning the shape, the taste of his. She wanted to explore, savor. There was passion in David's kiss, no question, but she didn't truly feel connected to him.

Well, damn. Adonis has me hooked on his thing about slow kissing.

Adonis. Here she was, kissing David, rubbing against his erection, and she was thinking about Adonis. *When Adonis and I make love, I forget all about David.*

David's hand was between them, undoing a couple more shirt buttons, thrusting inside her teddy to cup her breast. Her nipple budded at his touch.

Wait, this isn't what I want. She pulled her mouth from his and pushed away from his body so he had to remove his hand from her shirt. "David, I said a kiss."

He groaned. "Ann, I'm so turned on. We can't stop here."

She was getting aroused, too. But he was rushing her, and she truly didn't want more than a kiss. "We have to stop," she told him. "I'm not having sex with a married man." *Even if it might help me sort out what I feel.*

"I'm getting a divorce, damn it!"

"Yeah, and you and your wife decided that when?" She stepped away farther, buttoning her shirt. "A whole day or two ago? David, this is too quick."

"Not for me. Come on, you know this is right. Why waste time?"

"Because I'm not sure it *is* right! Didn't you hear what I've been saying the last couple of weeks? I told you I don't want you to rush from one relationship to another. I said you need time to sort out what you want."

"I know what I want." He thrust his hands into his pockets, looking like a sullen child.

"Well, I know what I *don't* want. To rush into a rebound relationship. Weren't you listening when I said all this?"

"I figured you'd change your mind when I was free."

No, he didn't listen. Or, if he did, he didn't respect what I was saying. "Let's go back downstairs."

"I can't go like this." He gestured to his erection.

"Then you know what? Why don't you order room service? For yourself. I'm not hungry anyway, and I think we both need some time on our own. To think."

"Crap." He ran his hands through his hair. "I fucked this up, didn't I?"

He looked so rueful she couldn't help but smile a little. "Yeah. Pretty much."

"Just because I want it so badly. Will you forgive me? Give me another chance?"

One day, two men, two spats, two apologies. She said the same thing she'd said to Adonis. "I need time on my own to think."

"I understand. I'm sorry I rushed you." He sighed. "I'll try to behave myself."

"At the office, it's all work," she warned. "Agreed?"

"Yeah. Of course. We're both professionals."

He came closer as she watched warily. Raising both hands, he placed them gently on her shoulders, then leaned forward to kiss her forehead. He stepped back. "If you think about this— us—you'll see the sense in it."

Sense again. So far he's given me a sensible argument, and lust. No romance. He hasn't even said he cares for me.

And I haven't figured out if I care for him. We could probably have good sex once we found our rhythm as a couple, but would we ever spend hours making love? Ever gaze deeply, lovingly into each other's eyes the way Adonis and I did?

Wait a minute? Lovingly?

If it hadn't been Foursome dinner night, Ann would have had to schedule an emergency lunch. As it was, she skipped out of the office early, avoiding David, and went home to work. She changed into her kayak pants with the flowered teddy and new blouse, and got so caught up in a case that she didn't notice the passage of time. When she checked her watch, she realized she was going to be late, so she didn't change, just popped the dangly earrings into her ears.

Jenny'd picked the dinner spot, one they hadn't been to before. She'd heard about it from a *Georgia Straight* restaurant reviewer. It was a tiny place called Henry's on MacDonald, with an Asian chef, an eclectic menu, and reasonable prices.

Sure enough, Ann was the last to arrive. She barely noticed the decor or the other customers, just rushed straight over to her friends. "I'm so glad to be here."

"Hey, look at you," Suzanne said.

"I love the blouse and teddy," Rina said. "And what great earrings."

"You didn't come from the office," Jenny said. "How come?" Her expression was concerned. "You're not sick, are you?"

"I was working at home. No, I'm not sick, just overwhelmed and confused."

"Take a breath, have some wine, and tell us," Suzanne said, filling the only empty glass with red wine.

Ann sipped appreciatively, then took a few deep breaths, the way Adonis had taught her, and tried to relax. "It'll take a while. How about everyone else? Do you have big stuff too, or little stuff? I don't mind going last, as long as we have lots of time to talk." God, just being with the Foursome made her feel like things would work out okay.

"Good stuff, but nothing major," Rina said. "Al came to an operatic society concert last week, which was totally sweet of him, and we had dinner on Saturday." She beamed. "We had sex both nights and it was really nice."

A friendly young waiter came over to discuss the specials and take their orders. Rina went with orange roughy, the night's fish special. Suzanne chose seafood pasta, Ann ordered a pork and apple dish, and Jenny picked osso buco.

Rina said, "So, that's it for me. Jen, how's it going with your and Scott's families?"

"We all had Sunday dinner at my house." Jenny shook her head so vigorously her lovely hair fanned out in a circle. "There was Mom and Dad, Granny and Auntie, Cat, and a couple of aunts and uncles thrown in for good measure. So the Yuens would outnumber the Jackmans. On Scott's side there was his sister, his parents, and his grandparents."

She paused to glug back some wine. "The older generation females prepared a huge feast, picking the weirdest stuff they could. Then they set the table with only chopsticks—but Cat and I put out knives and forks when they weren't looking. Then, we ate." She shrugged.

"How did everyone get along?" Ann asked. "Come on, Jen, give us the specifics."

"Man, you sound like a lawyer sometimes." Jenny flicked back her hair. "Okay, as it turned out, food was the big unifying force. They all love to eat. And once Scott's father realized he wasn't stuck with rice, that he could eat noodles, he dug in. In my family, eating well and asking for seconds is the way to the cook's heart. And they all did that." She gave a snort of laughter. "Scott's dad even kept forcing more food on me, like he'd done at their house. The Jackmans are trying to fatten me up."

"That's so not going to happen," Rina said.

"How about conversation?" Ann asked. "Did they talk about anything other than food?"

"Both sides probed about Scott and me. Our jobs, health, work habits. And the oddest thing happened." Jenny's eyes widened. "Dad asked Mr. and Mrs. Jackman why they let Scott take such a dangerous job."

"As if they had a choice," Ann said. "Didn't they try to turn him into a farmer? With no luck?"

"Totally. But here's the weird thing. Mr. Jackman said, 'A man isn't afraid of a little danger. Firefighters are heroes. They save lives.' Then Mrs. Jackman chipped in, saying they're proud of Scott." Jen gave a burble of laughter. "You should've seen Scott's and Lizzie's faces, and the grandparents'. They all gaped at Mr. and Mrs. Jackman like they'd turned into aliens."

"Nothing like a little attack to put a parent on the defensive," Suzanne said.

Note to self: Try that with Adonis's dad and see if he springs to his son's defense.

Quickly she added a footnote. *That is, if I keep seeing Adonis. Oh man, I hope it's my turn soon! I really need my friends' advice.*

"Anyhow," Jenny went on, "after they were gone, the postmortem began. It started out disparaging. But then Mom said she was pleased they'd liked the food. Auntie said it's good Scott has a big family and they're so close. Granny said they're obviously hard workers."

"How did it go at Scott's end?" Ann asked. "Have you talked to him since?"

"Yeah. They think we're all so tiny and fragile, they can't imagine how we can actually do a hard day's work. But they're impressed my family owns the travel agency and the apartment building. Oh, and the grandparents said it was good how we all respect Granny and Auntie."

Ann put an arm around Jenny's shoulders and hugged her. "That's so great. It's a wonderful start. You and Scott must be thrilled."

Jenny's lips curved. "Yeah. We are. It's way better than we'd expected."

Their waiter brought their dinners and refilled their glasses, then Jenny said, "Okay, that's me. Suzie Q, what's new with you?"

"I'm going down to San Francisco this weekend." She grinned at Ann. "And, yes, I'm letting Jaxon pay my way."

"That's great," Ann said.

"Next week, I'll have lots to report," Suze said. "But that's it for now. Your turn, Ann."

"Where to start?" Ann took a bite of pork and chewed slowly, reflecting. "I suppose a chronology of events is the most straightforward."

"Lawyer again," Jenny commented. "Okay, give us the *specifics* in *chronological* order."

Another note to self: Stop talking like a lawyer when I'm out with friends.

"Tantric sex," she said.

Three jaws dropped. Then, "What?" "No, really?" "What's it like?" "How long can he last?" Questions flew so fast she couldn't keep track of who was asking.

"Okay, now I've whetted your appetites . . ." She took them step-by-step through Saturday, and as she did, her body came alive, remembering.

"I never knew I could experience so many sensations," she said. "Not just sexual, but sensual, to use Adonis's word. All my senses were on the alert." She grinned. "Red alert."

As they were now. Especially her sex, thinking how he'd felt inside her. "I have a whole different concept of orgasm," she said, keeping her voice low so diners at neighboring tables couldn't overhear. "Before, it was like there were distinct stages. Buildup, then climax."

The other three nodded. "And now?" Suzanne asked.

"When you've been making love for hours, the whole thing becomes a process. Sometimes there's virtually no buildup, a really big orgasm is just suddenly there. And sometimes the orgasm is kind of gentle but it seems to go on and on, in pleasurable waves that keep coming, and it's through my whole body, not just my—" she lowered her voice again; these tables really were too close together—"not just my vagina and clit. It was like my breasts were climaxing, my stomach, my mind."

"Heart," Suzanne murmured.

Ann's heart fluttered in response. "Dangerous word. I'm so confused. He wants us to get more serious, and I'm tempted. I've never felt so good with a man before, and it's not just the sex. We talk about work, family, he makes me think and question. He's good for me and I . . . I really care for him and he does for me, too."

"Then go for it!" Jenny said, loudly enough to make heads turn.

"He's leaving in less than two months and he'll be away until spring. And he does this every winter." She glanced at Suzanne. "It's different with you and Jaxon. You can get together every two or three weeks."

"You told me it would be a test of the strength of our relationship," Suzanne pointed out. "But, yes, across the world is a tougher test."

"Why does Adonis do this?" Rina asked. "Go every winter?"

Ann sighed. "He has a whole different lifestyle than me. I don't think he has an ambitious bone in his body. He doesn't want to own anything, works part-time, spends lots of time doing outdoor stuff. He hates cold winters, so he heads for the sun. He does what feels right for him."

"If he really cared about you, wouldn't staying with you feel right?"

And there it is. The elephant in the living room that I've been avoiding. "Yeah. Wouldn't you think? If sunny winters are more important than being with me . . ." She shrugged.

Jenny chewed on her bottom lip. "Is your work more important to you than Adonis?"

"Uh . . ."

"You're thinking, after years of concentrating on work, that maybe you do want a significant relationship. But what kind?"

"How do you mean?"

"Just the kind that's a pleasant diversion," Jenny said, "when you can fit it in around your big focus on work? If so, that's kind of compatible with Adonis."

And David, though in a different way. Work would always come first.

Ann shook her head, even more confused. "I'm not sure. But let me tell you what else has been going on. First, there's my mother."

"There's always your mother," Jenny muttered.

And you don't even know about the voice in my head, Jen! "She knows of a top firm where I could probably get in, do the work I want, and be a partner in a couple of years. No time for relationships, but a real career fast track." Ann didn't mention that the firm was in Ottawa.

She went on. "And then there's David."

"He was out of town last week, right?" Suzanne asked.

"Came back last night. Having split up with his wife."

"Holy crap!" Jenny said. "I didn't think he'd really do it."

"Me, either. I was playing with a hypothetical, and now it's become real."

"What does that mean for the two of you?" Rina asked.

"He has it all figured out. A career and life partnership, with the emphasis on career. Not a passionate, head-over-heels love affair, but if things worked out we'd get married. No kids, no pets, an apartment." She swallowed. "In Toronto."

"No," Jenny said. "You're not allowed to move away."

"Jen," Suzanne chided.

Jenny sighed dramatically. "Okay, selfish bitch here. What I mean is, I don't want you to move. Damn it, Annie, I need you."

"*You* need *me?*" She'd always thought of it the other way around. "Jen, you're always so breezy and confident, and you have lots of other friends, too."

"You three are the people I trust the most. The ones I can really talk to. I need you to help sort me out. All of you. We're a team, the Awesome Foursome. Rina's the heart, Suze is the soul, I'm the wit, and you're the brains. We shouldn't be separated."

"I feel the same way," Ann said softly. "But it could happen. Suzanne might move to California, I could move to Ontario. Life brings change."

"I only like the good ones," Rina said. "I'm with Jenny. I don't want us to split up. Not for a man, not for work."

"The firm my mother suggested is in Ottawa."

"Fuck," Jenny said. Then, with a sly expression, "Okay, so you have to choose Adonis, it's the only option that works. Adonis and us. Right, Annie?"

They all chuckled. Jenny could be counted on to lighten the mood.

Rina reached for Ann's hand. "You've told us your choices, and of course the other one is to keep doing what you've been doing. Not move, not get together with Adonis *or* David. But how do you feel about each option?"

Feel. Rina wants me to feel. So does Adonis. Can I do this?

Ann closed her eyes, felt the warmth of Rina's hand and the support flowing from her friends. She focused on the Charter firm her mother was promoting. "I'd be too lonely in Ottawa. Yes, the career opportunity is amazing and my mother'd be happy, but I'd be alone."

"You'd make friends," Jenny said gruffly. "Not as good as us, of course. But you don't have to be alone. You could meet a great guy, too."

"Thanks, Jen, but I wouldn't have time. There'd be more pressure than here."

Keeping her eyes closed, Ann took a breath. "Okay, the David option. I could have the career I've dreamed of, and a man in my life. That's more than I'd ever counted on." She sighed. "But, without you guys. Or kids, pets, time to walk outside in the sun."

"But how do you feel about David?" Rina prompted.

Ann opened her eyes and glanced at her friend. "I kissed him and I'm still not sure. It was . . . okay. First-time awkwardness. We'd get over that. But I don't think we'd ever have . . ."

"Romantic love? A grand passion?" Rina asked gently.

Ann shook her head. "No. But maybe I'm not the type."

"Every woman's the type," Suzanne said. "Which brings us to the Adonis option. What would that be like?"

"My career wouldn't move as fast," Ann said promptly.

"Why?" Jenny asked.

"I'd take more time away from the office. Up until now, it's just been these Monday nights, but there'd be visits with his family, time for just the two of us. Kayaking, picnics. He wouldn't want the same thing David does. I'd have to cut back on work." She paused. "No, I said that wrong. I'd want to, because those other things are so much fun."

"But you could still do this Charter stuff that gets you all excited?" Jenny asked.

"Yes. It's not a big focus at the firm here, but now I'd be the expert. I'd get those files."

"What about children?" Suzanne asked. "I mean, you did tell us about the condom thing. You could—" She broke off.

"Be pregnant. It's really unlikely, but possible. I'm trying to avoid thinking about it. But I know he'd be there to support me. We'd decide what to do together."

"How does he feel about kids?" Suzanne asked.

"His family's really into them and Adonis is great with them." She told them about his sisters and their husbands, and how they managed kids, work, and marriage. "He's mature in some ways but he isn't ready to settle down yet. God, he's twenty-four." She laughed softly. "I'm not ready for kids, either, and yet I'm starting to think they're kind of appealing. Down the road."

"The boy'll settle down as he gets older," Jenny said. "He'll stop this winter gypsy thing."

"If he really cared about her, wouldn't he do it now?" Suzanne asked.

Back to the elephant.

"There's no longer such a thing as a normal relationship," Jenny said slowly. "Every one is odd in its own way."

"What matters is, if you love each other," Rina added. "Ann, you haven't said how you really feel about Adonis."

Three concerned faces stared at her.

Her heart throbbed painfully. "I could. Too easily."

"Romantic and passionate love?" Rina asked.

Slowly she nodded.

"But not with David," Rina said.

Ann gripped her head with both hands. "I'm not even positive I'm attracted to David for the right reasons."

"Older man," Jenny said.

"Damn. Yes, I've thought about that."

"So you have two men who are pretty serious about you," Suzanne said. "You're going to have to decide soon. You can only commit to one."

"I know," she said grimly. "That's what you're supposed to be helping me with."

"Annie?" It was Jenny. "Which Ann are you?"

"Pardon?"

"You're a different version of yourself with each guy, right? With David, you're the intellectual career woman, the side-by-side partner, and the two of you might end up having an affectionate relationship. He'd probably get along with your mother, if she could ever forgive you for hooking up with a guy. Fair statement?"

Ann nodded slowly.

"Okay, with Adonis, you're still an intellectual career woman, you're a partner in a relationship that's emotional and passionate and is likely to get more so. You'll go kayaking, barbecue outside, shop at Granville Island. You'll get adopted into his family, you'll be babysitting, you'll likely have kids of your own one day. And God knows what your mother will say, but it's your life, not hers. Right?"

Every word Jenny'd said sounded right. Ann nodded again, and realized Rina and Suzanne were doing the same.

"So, which Ann are you, at heart?"

"I don't know, it's too early to tell. The person I am with Adonis is so new to me."

"Her cheeks glow, she doesn't take painkillers, she wears feminine, sexy clothes," Suzanne said. "She makes love for hours on end, the most fulfilling sex she's ever had."

"Close your eyes again," Rina said, and Ann obeyed as her friend said, "Think about that Ann. She may be new to you, but I think she's been inside all along. Just waiting to get out."

A memory popped into Ann's mind. When she'd told Adonis that driving her car with the top down made her feel like a different person, he'd said, "Or the real you."

"She's the best of you," Rina went on. "Everything you can possibly be."

Everything I can possibly be. Not a clone of my mother, but a woman in my own right. A woman who can have it all.

"It just took the right prince's kiss to awaken her," Rina finished softly.

"You're such a crazy romantic." But Ann was smiling. Then she laughed. "And maybe, so is the real Ann."

* * *

The next morning, Ann knew exactly what she had to say to everyone.

First, she phoned Meredith. "Mother, I can't tell you how much I appreciate your checking out the opportunity in Ottawa, but I'm not going to pursue it."

"Why not? You won't find anything better."

"I hope I will. A life that includes more than just work. I've decided that's important to me. And I'm going to stay here. My life's in Vancouver now."

"I . . . I'm dumbfounded. After all you've worked for . . . All I can say is, I'm very disappointed in you."

Big surprise. "You know what Granddad said when you wanted to go to university? How he told you what you wanted to do was wrong? Please don't do that to me. I'm different than you are. I respect your goals and I hope you can respect mine. And, even if you don't, I know you'll still love me."

"Love you?" Then Meredith's voice softened. "You're my daughter. Ann, of course I'll always love you."

"I know. And I'll always love you."

Next, she buzzed David and asked him to have lunch with her, then she called Adonis to see if he could get together that evening.

"I was going to call you," Adonis said. "I need to talk to you."

That was a little ominous. Even so, it didn't change what she intended to say to David.

When they were seated at Griffin's restaurant in the Hotel Vancouver, she got to the point before nerves got the better of her. She told David, "I like you and respect you, but I want a different kind of life. A career, yes, but a home life, too. I'm sorry I didn't know sooner. I feel so bad for letting you believe we might, uh . . ."

As she'd talked, his face had aged before her eyes and her heart ached for him.

He sighed heavily. "You never made any promises. And you did get me to examine my life, which was sorely overdue." He leaned toward her. "Damn, Ann. You're sure? I thought we were so well suited. Such a great team."

The old Ann would have been tempted, but the new one just said, "So did I. But I've done some serious thinking about my life, too. I discovered some things that surprise me. I'm so sorry I didn't know sooner."

He nodded. "So am I."

They gazed at each other for a long moment, then he said. "Well, I suppose that leaves work. Can we still work together?"

"I hope so. What do you think?"

He smiled without humor. "Of course. We're both professionals, above all." Another long pause. "Well. Shall we check out that buffet, get some lunch?"

"I'm not very hungry." In fact, even though she knew she'd done the right thing, she felt like crying.

"Me, either. But let's get a salad, and we'll talk Charter law."

He was right. It was a good place to start again. She smiled gratefully. "Let's do that."

She and Adonis had arranged that he'd come to her place at seven. At five o'clock, one of the senior partners dropped into her office and asked her to do a quick opinion for him, to be ready by first thing in the morning. The way he framed it, she didn't feel she could refuse.

Pissed off, she called Adonis. "I'm sorry, some work just landed on me and I have to do it tonight. I guess we should postpone." *Damn. I want to talk to him* now. *And what kind of foot is this to get off on, if I'm going to tell him I'm serious about him?*

"How much work?" he asked.

"About three hours. We could still get together, but I'd have to do the work afterward. It's for a senior partner and he's relying on me."

"We can do that. Or you could finish it up then come over to my place, and I'll feed you and pamper you."

Wow. Looked like that "need to talk to you" thing he'd said that morning hadn't had negative undertones after all. "I could go for that. If you don't mind."

"No problem. I'll go for a run, pick up some groceries, whip up something that's not time sensitive."

Looking forward to seeing him gave her extra motivation, and she finished the job in less time than she'd thought it would take.

When she climbed his steps, wearing a business suit and plain pumps, she wished she'd taken time to go home and change. But when he opened his door to her, wearing a T-shirt and the black silk boxers, gave her a big smile and said, "Hey, Lawyer-girl, you're home early," she was glad she'd come straight to him.

And when he gathered her into his arms, she went eagerly, meeting his gentle kiss with one of her own. Then she snuggled closer, burying her face against his shoulder. Soft fabric, warm, hard man underneath. Mmm, nice.

Hardening man. Right now she was too tired to feel truly sexy, but she knew Adonis wouldn't mind waiting. "Long, tough day," she murmured, "and this feels so good."

"I'm glad you're here." He kissed her forehead. "What do you feel like? Massage, glass of wine?" He pushed her back so she could see his wicked grin when he said, "Hot monkey sex?"

She laughed. "Later. Right now I'd love some wine. Then food. I'm starving."

His cock was pushing against the boxers and her sex throbbed in response, but he'd taught her that waiting could be even better than rushing into things. They'd talk, and if the conversation went the way she hoped, she'd relax and unwind.

Over the course of the evening the energy between the two of them would build, and later he'd make sure she got an orgasm or two. How amazing, to feel so confident of a man.

"You like dolmas?" he asked. "They're my Yiayia's—grandmother's—recipe, updated a bit by my mom."

"Mm, home cooking. Your mom made them?"

"Sexist. No, I did."

"You *made* dolmas? For me?"

He touched her shoulder, nudged her through the kitchen to the living room. "I figured I'd eat a few myself."

When she sat on the couch, he bent down, took off her shoes and said. "Pull off your panty hose. Unless you'd rather I did it."

She wriggled out of them and stretched her feet gratefully while Adonis went to the kitchen. He came back and handed her a glass of wine. "Dad's red. Hope that's okay."

"I don't know." She grinned. "It's dangerous stuff. Makes me dump my inhibitions."

"Good." He sat on the coffee table, lifted her feet to his lap, and began to massage. "Dinner needs another twenty minutes. Relax, then I'll feed you."

But she couldn't relax, with so much on her mind. "Adonis, you said you wanted to talk."

"Yeah." His face went serious. "I've been doing a lot of thinking. Some of the stuff I said to you, it was crazy."

Her heart sank. After all her angst, he didn't want a serious relationship. And yet, he was being so nice. To soften the impact, when he told her? "Yes?" She braced herself.

"About this winter thing I do, going someplace sunny—"

"I know. It would be hard to be involved with me, when you were off in Thailand or wherever. You'd want to be free to see other women."

He stopped massaging for a moment, then started up again. "No, I wouldn't. You're the one I want to be with. And I figure, if you have a decision to make, me versus this lawyer guy, you should have all the information."

"I decided."

His hands tightened, then released her feet. "You did?" He swallowed loudly and she could see the tension in his face. "That's why you wanted to see me tonight?"

"I told him I couldn't—didn't want to—get involved with him."

His face brightened, then turned wary. "And what about me?"

"I have strong feelings for you, Adonis. I want to see where they go."

He was beginning to smile.

She continued. "If you still want to, let's spend time together until you go, and if it works out, I'll wait for you and—"

"I'm not going."

"What?"

"That's what I meant, when I said I was talking crazy. I don't want to leave you, Ann. You're different than any other woman I've been with. Yeah, I hate the cold, love the sun, but you're more important than the weather, for Christ's sake."

She began to chuckle. "Glad to hear that. I kind of thought so myself."

He caught her hands in his. "I'm falling in love with you. I want to be with you."

"F-falling in love?"

His eyes were warm as he reached out to caress her cheek. "Don't be scared. It doesn't hurt. You can do it, too."

"I think I can," she said, feeling warmth flood through her and her eyes grow moist. "I think I have been."

He kissed her, and, as their lips met, they held each other's gaze and she felt closer to him than she'd ever been to anyone else.

His eyes twinkled gently when he eased away from her.

"While I've got you softened up, and I'm withholding food from a starving woman, I have a favor to beg. And it's a big one."

"Those dolmas had better be good," she teased. "What is it?"

"In the depths of winter, how about a two-week holiday someplace hot?"

A holiday with Adonis. Ocean, beach, palm trees, tropical drinks. Long, lazy nights of love under a swirling wooden ceiling fan. No work, no responsibilities, just hour after hour, day after day, of doing whatever they wanted to. Together.

"It's an awfully big sacrifice." She tried to hold back her grin, but she'd never felt happier in her life.

"I'll make it worth your while." He smiled, that dimple flashing at her.

"You damn well better."

"Hold that thought." He took her glass of red wine from the coffee table and started for the kitchen.

"Hey, where are you going with my wine? Doesn't this call for a toast?"

"Yeah," he shouted from the kitchen. "Don't tell my dad or he'll be insulted, but I figure it calls for better than Stefanakis house red."

He returned, carrying two glasses and a bottle. Of champagne.

"Adonis!"

"What can I say, I'm an optimist. And a romantic."

Tears of joy slid down her cheeks and she brushed at them impatiently. "Well, damn, I think I am, too."

"And after we toast ourselves," he said softly, seductively, "I have plans for some of the champagne."

"Plans?"

"Mmm. I've never tried doing a massage with champagne. Think your erogenous zones might like that?"

She grinned at him. "Erogenous zones? Remind me what they were. Wasn't it ears? Throat, back of the knees?"

He began to unbutton her shirt, revealing the sheer black teddy underneath. "I had in mind something a little more immediate." He ran a finger around one of her nipples and it tightened under his touch.

Sensation flooded through her, and surged hotter when she saw his erection pressing against the front of the black boxers. "That's so good," she murmured. "But could you head further south?"

"It would be my pleasure."

She reached out to cup him, through silk. "And mine."

1

_____

The Isle of Mists, in the Eastern Archipelago,
Principalities of Arcus

Meg saw the seals from her window, their silvery coats rippling as they thrashed out of the sea and collected along the shore. She'd seen them sunning themselves on the rocks by day and had watched them frolic in the dusky darkness from that dingy salt-streaked window in her loft chamber many times since her exile to the island, but not like tonight, with their slick coats gleaming in the moonlight. Full and round, the summer moon left a silvery trail in the dark water that pointed like an arrow toward the creatures frolicking along the strand, lighting them as bright as day. Meg's breath caught in her throat. Behind, the high-curling combers crashing on the shore took on the ghostly shape of prancing white horses, pure illusion that disappeared the instant their churning hooves touched sand. In the foaming surf left behind, the seals began to shed their skins, revealing their perfect male and female nakedness. Meg gasped. It was magical.

Her heartbeat began to quicken. She inched nearer to the window until her hot breath fogged the glass. The nights were still cool beside the sea—too cool for cavorting naked in the moonlight. And where had the seals gone? These were humans, dark-haired, graceful men and women with skin like alabaster, moving with the undulant motion of the sea they'd sprung from in all their unabashed glory. They seemed to be gathering the skins they'd shed, bringing them higher toward the berm and out of the backwash.

Mesmerized, Meg stared as the mating began.

One among the men was clearly their leader. His dark wet hair, crimped like tangled strands of seaweed, waved nearly to his broad shoulders. Meg's eyes followed the moonbeam that illuminated him, followed the shadows that collected along the knife-straight indentation of his spine defined the dimples above his buttocks and the crease that separated those firm round cheeks. The woman in his arms had twined herself around him like a climbing vine, her head bent back beneath his gaze, her long dark hair spread about her like a living veil.

All around them others had paired off, coupling, engaging in a ritualistic orgy of the senses beneath the rising moon, but Meg's eyes were riveted to their leader. Who could they be? Certainly not locals. No one on the island looked like these, like *him*, much less behaved in such a fashion. She would have noticed.

Meg wiped the condensation away from the windowpane with a trembling hand. What she was seeing sent white-hot fingers of liquid fire racing through her belly and thighs, and riveting chills loose along her spine. It was well past midnight, and the peat fire in the kitchen hearth below had dwindled to embers. Oddly, it wasn't the physical cold that griped her then, hardening her nipples beneath the thin lawn night smock and undermining her balance so severely she gripped the window ledge. Her skin was on fire beneath the gown. It was her finest.

She'd worked the delicate blackwork embroidery on it herself. It would have seen her to the marriage bed if circumstances had been different—if she hadn't been openly accused of being a witch on the mainland and been banished to the Isle of Mists for protection, for honing her inherent skills, and for mentoring by the shamans. But none of that mattered now while the raging heat was building at the epicenter of her sex—calling her hand there to soothe and calm engorged flesh through the butter-soft lawn . . . at least that is how it started.

She inched the gown up along her leg and thigh and walked her fingertips through the silky golden hair curling between them, gliding her fingers along the barrier of her virgin skin, slick and wet with arousal. She glanced below. But for her termagant aunt, who had long since retired, she was alone in the thatched roof cottage. It would be a sennight before her uncle returned from the mainland, where he'd gone to buy new nets and eel pots, and to collect the herbs her aunt needed for her simples and tisanes. Nothing but beach grass grew on the Isle of Mists.

Meg glanced about. Who was there to see? No one, and she loosened the drawstring that closed the smock and freed her aching breasts to the cool dampness that clung stubbornly to the upper regions of the dreary little cottage, foul weather and fair.

Eyes riveted to the strand, Meg watched the leader of the strange congregation roll his woman's nipples between his fingers. They were turned sideways, and she could see his thick, curved sex reaching toward her middle. Still wet from the sea they'd come from, their skin shone in the moonlight, gleaming as the skins they'd shed had gleamed. They were standing ankle deep in the crashing surf that spun yards of gossamer spindrift into the night. Meg stifled a moan as she watched the woman's hand grip the leader's sex, gliding back and forth along the rigid shaft from thick base to hooded tip. Something pinged deep inside her watching him respond . . . something urgent and un-stoppable.

Her breath had fogged the pane again, and she wiped it away in a wider swath this time. Her breasts were nearly touching it. Only the narrow windowsill kept them from pressing up against the glass, but who could see her in the darkened loft? No one, and she began rolling one tall hardened nipple between her thumb and forefinger, then sweeping the pebbled areola in slow concentric circles, teasing but not touching the aching bud, just as the creature on the beach had done to the woman in his arms.

Excruciating ecstasy.

While the others were mating fiercely all along the strand, the leader had driven his woman to her knees in the lacy surf. The tide was rising, and the water surged around him at mid-calf, breaking over the woman, creaming over her naked skin, over the seaweed and sand she knelt on as she took his turgid member into her mouth to the root.

Meg licked her lips expectantly in anticipation of such mag-nificence entering her mouth, responding to the caress of her tongue. She closed her eyes, imagining the feel and smell and taste of him, like sea salt bursting over her palate. This was one of the gifts that had branded her a witch.

When Meg opened her eyes again, her posture clenched. Had he turned? Yes! He seemed to be looking straight at her. It was almost as if he'd read her thoughts, as if he knew she was there all the while and had staged the torrid exhibition for her eyes alone to view. She couldn't see his face—it was steeped in shadow—but yes, there was triumph in his stance and victory in the posturing that took back his sex from the woman's mouth. His eyes were riveting as he dropped to his knees, spread the woman's legs wide to the rushing surf, and entered her in one slow, tantalizing thrust, like a sword being sheathed to the hilt, as the waves surged and crashed and swirled around them.

Still his shadowy gaze relentlessly held Meg's. For all her extraordinary powers of perception, she could not plumb the depths of that look as he took the woman to the rhythm of the waves lapping at them, laving them to the meter of his thrusts, like some giant beast with a thousand tongues. She watched the mystical surf horses trample them, watched the woman beneath him shudder to a rigid climax as the rising tide washed over her—watched the sand ebb away beneath the beautiful creature's buttocks as the sea sucked it back from the shore. All the while he watched her. It was as if she were the woman beneath him, writhing with pleasure in the frothy sea.

Captivated, Meg met the leader's silver-eyed gaze. She could almost feel the undulations as he hammered his thick, hard shaft into the woman, reaching his own climax. Meg groaned in spite of herself as he threw back his head and cried out when he came.

She should move away from the window . . . But why? He couldn't see what she was doing to herself in the deep darkness of the cottage loft . . . Could he? All at once it didn't matter. A hot lava flow of sweet sensation riddled her sex with pinpricks of exquisite agony. It was almost as if *he* were stroking her nipples and palpating the swollen nub at the top of her weeping vulva as she rubbed herself, slowly at first, then fiercely, until the thickening bud hardened like stone. She probed herself deeper. She could almost stretch the barrier skin and slip her finger inside, riding the silk of her wetness—as wet as the surging combers lapping relentlessly at the lovers on the beach. A firestorm of spasmodic contractions took her then, freeing the moan in her throat. It felt as if her bones were melting. Shutting her eyes, she shed the last remnants of modest restraint and leaned into her release.

The voyeuristic element of the experience heightened the orgasm, and it was some time before her hands gripped the windowsill again instead of tender flesh, and her gaze fell upon the strand below once more. But the silvery expanse of rock-bound shoreline edged in seaweed stretching north and south as far as the eye could see was vacant. The strange revelers were gone!

Meg tugged the night shift back over her flushed breasts, though they ached for more stroking, and let the hem of the gown slide down her legs, hiding the palpitating flesh of her sex. Her whole body throbbed like a pulse beat, and she seized the thrumming mound between her thighs savagely through the gown in a vain attempt to quiet its tremors and made a clean sweep through the condensation on the window again. Nothing moved outside but the combers crashing on the strand. But for the echo of the surf sighing into the night, reverberating through her sex to the rhythm of fresh longing, all else was still.

No. She hadn't imagined it. The naked revelers mating on the beach had been real—as real as the seals that frequented the coast. Selkies? Could the shape-shifter legends be true? She'd heard little else since she came to the island.

Meg didn't stop to collect her mantle. Maybe the cool night air would cure the fever in her flesh. Hoisting up the hem of her night smock, she climbed down the loft ladder, tiptoed through the kitchen without making a sound, and stepped out onto the damp drifted sand that always seemed to collect about the door-sill. Nothing moved but the prancing white horses in the surf that drove it landward. Waterhorses? She'd heard that legend, too: innocent looking creatures that lured any who would mount them to a watery death. Real or imaginary, it didn't matter. The people she'd just seen there having sex were real enough, and she meant to prove it.

The hard, damp sand was cold beneath her bare feet as she padded over the shallow dune toward the shoreline. The phantom horses had disappeared from the waves crashing on the strand, as had every trace that anyone had walked that way recently. There wasn't a footprint in sight, and the sealskins Meg had watched them drag to higher ground were nowhere to be seen, either.

Having reached the ragged edge of the surf, Meg turned and looked back at the cottage beyond, paying particular attention to her loft window. Yes, it was close, but there was no way anyone could have seen her watching from her darkened chamber. Then why was she so uneasy? It wasn't the first time she'd touched herself in the dark, and it wouldn't be the last, but it had been the best, and there was something very intimate about it. The man who had aroused her seemed somehow familiar, and yet she knew they'd never met. Still, he had turned toward that window and flaunted himself as if he knew she had been watching, exhibiting his magnificent erection in what appeared to be a sex act staged solely for her benefit. Moist heat rushed at her loins, ripping through her belly and thighs with the memory.

Meg scooped up some of the icy water and bathed the aching flesh between her thighs. She plowed through the lacy surf where the lovers had performed—to the very spot where the mysterious selkie leader had spent his seed—and tried to order the mixed emotions riddling her. Absorbed in thought, she failed to feel the vibration beneath her feet until the horse was nearly upon her. It reared back on its hind legs, forefeet pawing the air, its long tail sweeping the sand—a *real* horse this time, no illusion. Meg cried out as recognition struck. There was a rider on its back. He was naked and aroused. It was *him*, with neither bridle nor reins to control the beast, and nothing but a silvery sealskin underneath him.

He seemed quite comfortable in the altogether, as if it was the most natural thing in the world to sit a horse bareback, naked in the moonlight. She gasped and gasped again. The horse had become quite docile, attempting to nuzzle her with its sleek white nose as it pranced to a standstill. She didn't want to look at the man on its back, but she couldn't help herself. He was a beguiling presence. As mesmerizing as he was from a distance, he was a hundred times more so at close range. Now she could see what the shadows had denied her earlier. His eyes, the color of mercury, were dark and penetrating, and slightly slanted. Somehow, she knew they would be. And his hair, while waving at a length to tease his shoulders in front, was longer in back and worn in a queue, tied with what appeared to be a piece of beach grass. How had she not noticed that before? But how could she have when he'd made such a display of himself face forward? Besides, her focus was hardly upon his hair.

Her attention shifted to the horse. At first she'd thought its mane and tail were black, but upon close inspection, she saw that they were white as snow, so tangled with seaweed they appeared black at first glance. But wait . . . what had she heard about white horses whose mane and tail collected seaweed? A waterhorse! The phantom creature of legend that seduced its victims to mount and be carried off to drown in the sea . . . But that was preposterous. Nevertheless, when its master reached out his hand toward her, she spun on her heels and raced back toward the cottage.

His laughter followed her, throaty and deep. Like an echo from the depths of the sea itself, it crashed over her just as the waves crashed over the shore. The sound pierced through her like a lightning bolt. The prancing waterhorse beneath him whinnied and clamped ferocious-looking teeth into the hem of her night shift, giving a tug that brought her to ground. She landed hard on her bottom, and the selkie laughed again as she cried out. Plucking her up as easily as if she were a broom straw, he settled her in front of him astride.

"You cannot escape me, Megaleen," he crooned in her ear. "You have summoned me, and I have come. You have no idea what it is that you have conjured—what delicious agonies you have unleashed by invoking me." His breath was moist and warm; it smelled of salt and the mysteries of the Otherworldly sea that had spawned him. "Hold on!" he charged, turning the horse toward the strand.

"Hold onto what?" Meg shrilled. "He has no bridle—no reins!"

Again his sultry voice resonating in her ear sent shivers of pleasure thrumming through her body. "Take hold of his mane," he whispered.

His voice alone was a seduction. He was holding her about the middle. Her shift had been hiked up around her waist when he settled her astride, and she could feel the thick bulk of his shaft throbbing against her buttocks, riding up and down along the cleft between the cheeks of her ass. The damp sealskin that stretched over the animal's back like a saddle blanket underneath her felt cool against Meg's naked thighs, but it could not quench the fever in her skin or douse the flames gnawing at the very core of her sex. The friction the water horse's motion created forced the wet sealskin fur deeper into her fissure, triggered another orgasm. Her breath caught as it riddled her body with waves of achy heat. She rubbed against the seal pelt, undulating to the rhythm of the horse's gait until every last wave had ebbed away, like ripples in a stream when a pebble breaks the water's surface.

In one motion, the selkie raised the night shift over her head and tossed it into the water. Reaching for it as he tore it away, Meg lost her balance. His strong hands spanning her waist prevented her from falling. Their touch seared her like firebrands, raising the fine hairs at the nape of her neck. The horse had plunged into the surf. It was heading toward the open sea, parting the unreal phantom horses galloping toward shore.

Salt spray pelted her skin, hardening her nipples. Spindrift dressed her hair with tiny spangles. The horse had plunged in past the breakers to the withers. Terrified, Meg screamed as the animal broke through the waves and sank to its muscular neck.

"Hold on!" he commanded.

"I cannot," Meg cried. "His mane . . . It is slippery with seaweed."

All at once, he lifted her into the air and set her down facing him, gathering her against his hard muscular body, his engorged sex heaving against her belly. How strong he was! "Then hold onto me," he said.

"W-who are you?" Meg murmured.

"I am called Simeon . . . amongst other things," he replied. "But that hardly signifies. . . ." Heat crackled in his voice. Something pinged in her sex at the sound of it.

He swooped down, looming over her. For a split second, she thought he was going to kiss her. She could almost taste the salt on his lips, in his mouth, on the tongue she glimpsed parting his teeth . . . But no. Fisting his hand in the back of her waist-length sun-painted hair, he blew his steamy breath into her nostrils as the horse's head disappeared beneath the surface of the sea.

Meg's last conscious thought before sinking beneath the waves in the selkie's arms was that she was being seduced to her death; another orgasm testified to that. Weren't you supposed to come before you died? Wasn't it supposed to be an orgasm like no other, like the orgasm riddling her now?

The scent that ghosted through her nostrils as she drew her last breath of air was his scent, salty, laced with the mysteries of the deep, threaded through with the sweet musky aroma of ambergris.